"Your memory goes back too far." Broken Echo's voice was low and sad, as he settled, cross-legged, at Andrew's side. "I think you might be a good man after all, but your memory goes back too far. Stay away from me when the moon is new. Or I will take all of you."

Andrew was hoarse. "I've had enough of you, Broken Echo. You and your damned elusive games. Everyone has seasons, but no one mimics the moon." He tried to sit up, but found that he could not. His back, raw and stiff, refused to support him.

"When I'm young and angry, I've been stealing your memory. Soon you will have nothing left but the visions of this house. Then you will have no choice."

"No choice, but what?" asked Andrew. From somewhere chains rattled hollowly, but Broken Echo was gone. . . .

Please be sure to ask your bookseller for the Bantam Spectra Books you have missed:

Black Trillium by Marion Zimmer Bradley, Julian May and Andre Norton
The Chaos Gate Trilogy by Louise Cooper
  The Deceiver
  The Pretender
  The Avenger (coming in November, 1991)
Chronicles of the King's Tramp by Tom DeHaven
  Walker of Worlds
Cromm by Kenneth C. Flint
The Deathgate Cycle by Margaret Weis and Tracy Hickman
  Dragon Wing
  Elven Star
  Fire Sea
The Dragon Revenant by Katharine Kerr
Full Spectrum 3 edited by Lou Aronica, Amy Stout and Betsy Mitchell
The Songkiller Saga by Elizabeth Scarborough
  Phantom Banjo
Universe 1 edited by Robert Silverberg and Karen Haber
When the Music's Over edited by Lewis Shiner

SPIRIT CROSSINGS

Claudia A. Peck

BANTAM BOOKS
NEW YORK · TORONTO · LONDON · SYDNEY · AUCKLAND

SPIRIT CROSSINGS
A Bantam Spectra Book / May 1991

SPECTRA and the portrayal of a boxed "s" are trademarks of Bantam Books, a division of Bantam Doubleday Dell Publishing Group, Inc.

Grateful acknowledgment is made for use of lyrics from "Christmas in the Trenches," words and music by John McCutcheon. Copyright © 1984. Used by permission.

ISBN 0-553-27641-7

Published simultaneously in the United States and Canada

Bantam Books are published by Bantam Books, a division of Bantam Doubleday Dell Publishing Group, Inc. Its trademark, consisting of the words "Bantam Books" and the portrayal of a rooster, is Registered in U.S. Patent and Trademark Office and in other countries. Marca Registrada. Bantam Books, 666 Fifth Avenue, New York, New York 10103.

PRINTED IN THE UNITED STATES OF AMERICA

RAD   0 9 8 7 6 5 4 3 2 1

DEDICATION

To "Doc" Alec, Kathy Mavournin, John McCutcheon, Sharon Webb, Kate Wilhelm, Rufus W. Beamer, III, Craig Strete, Pat LoBrutto, Bruce Kawin (the patience of the angels), G. B. Kinneavy, Ed Nolan, Joy Harjo and Suzanne Benally, all of whom know what for; to my father, who should have been here for this; and to those for whom the word cryptozoic has special meaning. To my family, who has eagerly awaited the advent of they knew not what. Most of all to the lovely town of Greenback, which, though I have borrowed its name for the sake of geography, bears no resemblance to the small Southern towns synthesized into the one in this novel, save in the kindness, warmth, and generosity of its people.

CHAPTER 1

Andrew walked down the sloping yard to the lake's edge and examined the shoring that kept back the waters. Broken pieces of marble were scattered among water-smoothed bricks. He bent down to examine them. All the pieces had some sort of engraving. BEHOL one of them said. And another, BE-HOLD AND SEE. The largest piece read PREPARE FOR DEATH AND FOLLOW ME. He smiled. Where had they come from? Whoever shored up the land with these had probably hauled in a load of marble from the local cemetery. Not a bad idea actually. Marble probably held up well against the water. Still, Kate wouldn't be particularly pleased with them, and it wouldn't be that difficult to change them for more standard shoring. Another job to add to his growing list.

After all, he and Kate wanted to get a boat for the next summer. He could see the four of them, he, Kate, and the two boys pulling up in a spray of water, laughing, the remains of picnic on Billy's chubby face. As they docked the boat, they would look down through the clear water to a shore lined by bits of tombstone. PREPARE FOR DEATH AND FOLLOW ME. What is it, he thought, about even homogenized funeral verse that slips beyond the cynic and back to the kid at the local graveyard after midnight? In an habitual gesture he pressed a thumb to a spot at the bridge of his nose.

A fish leaped from the muddy water, just missing an old, flat-bottom fishing boat that rocked and sputtered to a halt. Andrew laughed to see its cocky flip of a tail. He could hear a small man at the back of the boat cursing softly and methodically as he tried to crank the engine. The fisherman raised his head and glared up at Andrew as though Andrew were someone who had never had anything go wrong in his life.

Wiping his face with a grimy handkerchief, Andrew nodded at the fisherman, then looked out across the lake and smiled faintly. The setting caught him as it had the first time he'd seen it. Back toward the end of the cove, the water narrowed to what would have been a swamp in Georgia. Instead this small area was the thumb to a glove of a lake, full of twisty coves branching off to the side. The peninsula of land he had bought was the area that served as the space between the thumb and the forefinger, and, in any direction, across the lake from the nearest neighbors.

When he and Kate had come to look at the place, they'd both felt comfortable with it immediately, but more, they'd loved the part of the lake it fronted. Most of the houses on this end had been built in the 1800's or earlier, and so the area had a well-lived-in grace like the soft shine of a worn piece of wood. Since this was their first real home, he and Kate had wanted a place that had elegance and yet still had the echoes of an earlier time. This house fit the neighborhood as well as it fit their own needs.

To Andrew's left, just a short distance into the mouth of one of the coves, was a neatly painted brown house with a sweeping lawn that jutted down to a long roofed boatdock with two fishing boats rocking in the mooring. Behind the boats, tied to the bank, was a luxury pontoon. A large-shouldered man with a fishing cap strolled the dock with his hands in his pocket. The man shaded his eyes and stopped to stare at a cat clambering down from the roof over the dock. He waved to Andrew, who waved back, and then glanced across to his right where a warning beacon flashed like a gleam of cellophane at the end of a small spit of land.

A woman wearing a large-brimmed straw hat came down the slope from the brown house and called to the man on the dock, who by this time stood looking out over the water, the sleek, black cat on his shoulder. He turned, the cat doing a balancing act, and started up the lawn toward her. She tilted back her straw hat, put her hands on her hips, and waited for him.

Her movement stirred Andrew from his daydreaming. He returned to the van, lifted the last box, and carried it across the porch and into the house, putting it down with an involuntary whuff. Pushing up the sleeves he had been continually rolling all morning, he wiped his face with his handkerchief again and sat down on one of the Queen Anne chairs by the door. He looked around the living room at the unmatched set of mixed era antiques.

It was a good thing that the house came completely furnished or he'd have never been able to move by himself all the furniture required for a place this size. He'd been relieved when Kate had immediately approved of what was already in the house. It had not been difficult to get Waterman, the real estate agent, to throw in the furniture. The morning they signed, Andrew remembered, he had been uneasy because Waterman seemed almost too eager to close the deal.

"What's the matter, Andy?" Kate had asked him, as she raised her arms and pinned her hair in a smooth French twist. He admired again, as he had so many times before, the fine line of her waist and her small, firm breasts.

"Why don't we go out and look the place over once more before we sign, Kate? Better yet, let's wait awhile and look around some more." He paced around the room, dressed only in his socks and underwear. As he paced, he absent-mindedly slapped his left fist into the palm of his right hand.

"It's signing fright you've got, Andy; you know we looked at every house for sale in the area, and some of them were pretty rotten," she reminded him, as he watched her slip on his current favorite, the navy silk blouse he'd given her for Christmas.

"I think it's more than that."

"What is it then?" Her green eyes were very still, and he could see that she was holding back her reaction, just the way she always did when something meant a good deal to her. She had found this house and fallen in love with it from the beginning. Even though he had initially liked the house as well, it had been Andrew who insisted that they be practical and explore all their options.

"I have this feeling we've overlooked something."

"What? We've checked the wiring, the plumbing, the roof, the insulation, the well, the property value, and the quality of the land for farming." She tapped the back of her brush against her hand.

"The water line then."

"Andy, the water hasn't risen past the watermark we saw in the fifty some-odd years since the Hiwassee's been dammed." Her voice held just-in-check irritation, then she softened. "I know you're worried because we haven't sold the condo in Marietta; but I've got a showing on the fifteenth with a family who've been to see it twice already. And if we don't sell it," she shrugged on her navy pinstripe jacket and walked over to him, putting her arms around his waist, "we'll just tough it out until we do. Property goes fast in Marietta, you know that."

"Maybe I am worried about the prospect of owning two places. I'm not so sure it's a bad idea to worry."

"Or could it be that you don't like Waterman much?" she asked shrewdly.

He stared at her for a moment, then said in a quiet tone, "We couldn't ask for a better place, I don't suppose." He hugged her. "You're the only real estate agent I could ever stand to be around." It would be silly, he thought, to turn down the old Praeter home just because he didn't like Waterman. It had plenty of room for the four of them, and more; he and Kate would have the luxury of rooms of their own. Her weaving room and his office. The boys would have their own bedrooms. And even though small Southern towns were notorious for closing ranks against newcomers, they were far enough from town to live their own lives.

"I'm going to show the nearby town of Maryville what real estate is all about," she said lightly. "So we can grab up the horse deal of a lifetime for the boys. Got to make good on our moving bribe."

"As if we had to bribe them." He laughed. "They started packing two weeks ago. They were set on the move sooner than either you or I."

"Don't go gettin' cold feet on me, Andrew J. You know that Marietta doesn't give out tenure. It saves the suckers money to hire all you greenhorns on for three years and then cut your throats and move on to fresh blood. Small towns have job security. Isn't that what we said?" She punched him lightly on the stomach and backed away to straighten her clothes. "And you love this place, Andy."

He winked.

"Admit it, Andy, you love it more than I do. If I hadn't been so set on getting it, you would have bought it anyway." She laughed at his mock look of surprise.

"All right, Katie, just for a moment, we'll agree that I'm at least fond of the house."

"That you love it," she corrected, whirling into his arms.

"That I love it," he said, bending down to kiss her. "That it feels like home. That I've memorized every inch of the place, just as I've memorized every inch of you."

"You are a corny sap with a bad memory, and you probably wouldn't remember one square inch of either of us."

"That's why you're here, no doubt, to keep me in line." She pulled him into the closet and kissed him until his ears rang.

Andy smiled as he remembered that moment. They had been quite late to meet the agent.

By dusk Andrew had set up his office in the library and unpacked several of the boxes of kitchenware as well. At that point he decided to quit for a while and look around his property before dark.

Somewhere around the side of the house lay the Praeter family graveyard, though they'd not found it when they'd looked around with the agent. Some old fellow, squatting to his heels on the rattleboard porch in front of the Greenback Drugstore and spitting tobacco juice between words, had mentioned the graveyard as though it were a county landmark.

The graveyard turned out to be through the tangled thicket just beyond the backyard and off to the right of the house, a thicket that Kate and he had decided not to penetrate the day they had been shown the property. They already planned to clear the underbrush and put up a volleyball net. Andrew could already imagine the ground cleared, fall in the air, and two small towheads bounding awkwardly after a ball. He entered the thicket, branches brushing against his coat like stubby fingers.

The graveyard itself really wasn't much: four or five tumble-down markers and one large, pink marble tombstone on which was carved the name of Joseph Praeter in gothic letters. The inscription on the stone had been split down the middle, but it read:

BEHOLD AND SEE AS YE PASS BY,
AS YE ARE NOW SO THEN WAS I;
AS I AM NOW SO YE MUST BE,
PREPARE FOR DEATH AND FOLLOW ME.

Andrew rubbed the back of his neck. Then he frowned. Maybe the shoring hadn't been hauled in from the local cemetery at all, maybe those broken stones were Praeter's rejects. Even though the inscription made Andrew uneasy, it amused him to think of some tombstone carver, trying to please an exacting customer, carving stone after stone.

"Heard you were moving in here," came a laconic young voice from behind him.

He jumped.

Leaning against the fence was a stocky-figured teenager cleaning his fingernails with a large Buck pocketknife. His cloudy-blue eyes looked Andrew up and down. He folded and shut the knife carefully and put it away. "My name's Larry Bryge. I'll be in your history class, I reckon." The teenager moved around through the gate and held out his hand, shaking Andrew's with a firm, slightly damp, grip.

"I'm An—Mr. Jackson," Andrew said, as Larry released his hand. He smiled wryly. "I would gather that news gets around fairly quickly here."

"You might say that."

He wondered why Larry had come by. To see the new teacher for himself, to report back to the other kids in town, to let him know there might be a bit of resistance with a newcomer? Maybe a bit of all three. He smiled. "Yes, I've come up ahead. My family's going to join me tomorrow. I drove in just last night."

"Heard your truck." Larry wiped his hands on his jeans. They were straight legged and looked as though he'd had them for a while. Nothing like the kids in Marietta with their seventy dollar stiff, designer versions. "Do you think you'll like it here?"

"Seems like a nice place. Good buy, anyway." If he kept on like this, he'd be talking like the boy. He cleared his throat.

"Must be the history teacher in you then, that makes you like this place, I reckon."

"What do you mean?"

"Old Praeter was a slaverunner, you know, one of two in East Tennessee. Nobody much liked him around here for that. He went crazy when he got older. Family had to chain him up in the basement."

"God, that's horrible."

"Served him right, I expect. My grandfather said that because he used to chain them up down there, he went twisted to the grave."

"In the cellar?"

Larry nodded.

"His family?" Andrew asked, the beginnings of a smile coming to his face. Must be one of those country storytellers trying to catch me out, he thought.

"No, the slaves," Larry said, and pulled his knife back out of his pocket, opening it slowly, and then carving a fine line into the top rail of the driftwood fence.

Andrew lifted an eyebrow, thinking, there must be more to this boy than I thought. "Would you like a Coke?" he asked abruptly.

Larry smiled a slow smile and nodded. "Might be nice."

Two-hundred-year-old bones, Andrew thought, and followed Larry from the small family plot. He felt the same sort of thrill he'd always felt when he discovered some little-known fact. No homogenized pap here, he thought. As they left, the bushes and low hanging tree branches trailed along his arms. The sensation was similar to the touch of Spanish moss. He pushed the underbrush back with irritation, but the feel of it remained with him all the way to the house.

Larry stayed for an hour. He leaned back on the kitchen chair, the legs of which creaked as though they might split at any moment, and told Andrew story after story about Greenback and about Loudon County. He said nothing further about the Praeters. Andrew kept his curiosity in check, certain that the teenager would say something else before he left.

Larry drained his soft drink. Finally, as he stood up, Andrew asked him, even though conscious he was giving Larry a psychological advantage, "Do you know any more about the Praeters than what you told me earlier?"

"Now you're the history teacher, aren't you?" Larry said

with a sly smile. "Seems to me like it should be easy for a city fellow like you to run that to the ground."

Andrew smiled slightly and he nodded. Larry had given him a dare. "We'll see," he said.

"There is something to keep in mind, though," the boy said slowly and somewhat insolently. "I grew up beside this place. It's been here a long time, and it's kind of like the trees. It'll be here after you're gone. To a place like this we're all just a breath of wind passing in the night."

Strange way to give me the neighbor you're crowding me speech, Andrew thought. "We'll be here for a longer breath than you might think. We're settling here." He was pleased that his voice was quiet and firm. Just the sort of tone to set with a student who'd been pushing his territory. The teenager didn't back off, however. He simply nodded as though Andrew had confirmed some assessment he had made. Somehow Andrew was left with the feeling that he hadn't answered anything that Larry had said. He watched Larry leave, a bravado in the way he swung his arms as he walked across the lawn and around the edge of the house.

The kitchen seemed strangely silent afterwards. Andrew looked across the table and tried to imagine Andy and Billy sitting there together. No doubt Billy would have tipped over his plate; he never wanted to eat much, so dinner was a nightly battle with him. Kate and he always hoped that Billy would grow out of it, but he had shown no signs of it so far. Andy would be happily eating whatever was available while quivering on his upper lip would be the remains. He wouldn't tell them about Joseph Praeter, he decided. They were small boys, five and seven, and they tended to swagger and boast a lot, but they still pulled the covers up to their chins and imagined monsters in the closet. No need to stir them up.

Sooner or later they'd hear about Praeter, but by that time the story would have less force. Remembering the gentle innocence of their faces at breakfast the morning he had left, Andrew shivered. It never took much to shatter that in a child. He hoped they retained theirs for a while. That was probably too much to hope for, but at least he hoped they wouldn't become as cocky as young Bryge. Sighing, he walked over to the light switch, turning it off with a definitive click.

It was quite late by the time Andrew assembled Kate's loom in the downstairs alcove with adjoined their bedroom. He was so tired that connecting each piece of wood felt like the completion of an intricate puzzle. Each tongue-and-groove piece had to be put together just the way he built it originally, in careful steps. He wished he'd never made his wife such an awkward loom. Most of them were much easier to assemble, but he had thought she would be pleased with something handcrafted. And it hadn't helped his temper any to have forgotten the order of assembly, so the procedure had been filled with the same sort of steady cursing that Andrew had heard not much earlier from the would-be fisherman. However, he persisted because he knew Kate would be happy to avoid the job herself.

When he put the last part into place, a settled sort of feeling came to him, as though his family had begun to ease into the house the way a cat would into a well-worn cushion. Too bad, he thought, that Kate and the boys weren't with him to enjoy it; yet he puttered happily because they weren't. In a couple of days he'd have to attend a staff orientation meeting, and next week he would be teaching history to a bunch of lanky-legged, work-booted teenagers like Larry. In the meantime, today was his, his to fall into a new pattern of life. And, though he was sorry that they weren't here to do the same, he still enjoyed the time alone with the secret guilty joy of a boy playing hooky. Any more time and he'd have been lonely, but a day or two of solitude was just fine.

He went to bed still filled with that same feeling of stolen pleasure. As he lay there, looking out through the large, small paned open window, he could hear small waves lap against the shoreline rock. He fancied that if there were no stones to hold it back, the water would lick up the ground at the tip of the peninsula and on up to the house.

He wiggled his toes and slid a little deeper under the covers. The sound of the waves, and a light breeze which swept through the weeping willow tree just outside the window, dropped him quickly into sleep. His last, drowsy thought was that it made a kind of sense, blood and kin sense, for one of Andrew Jackson's descendants to come back to Tennessee. Old Hickory back from Georgia. In a way it felt like coming home.

Andrew woke to a bright, curtainless sunshine and a scratching beside him. Thinking he must have fallen asleep in the middle of reading the boys a story, he reached out a hand to pat Billy on the head. And then he remembered where he was. Half asleep, he thought, oh damn, must be rats, have to clean the cellar out before the kids get here. Opening his eyes, he looked up to find a gray squirrel not an inch from his nose waving its claws and chattering angrily.

Still not really awake, Andrew leaned backward and tumbled off the side of the bed. He heard the squirrel clawing around above him, and he wondered if it was tearing the sheets to ribbons. When he got up, he found the squirrel seated in the middle of his pillow, head cocked, glaring at him as though he had taken its home. Around the squirrel on the bed was a maze of tiny dirt tracks. He swept back his arm to knock the animal from his bed.

Then he heard a quiet chuckle behind him. The muscles in his back tensed. How had someone gotten in? He had locked all the doors and windows the night before, and latched the screen on his bedroom as well. His body had already launched itself in a whirl in the direction of the sound, while he was still trying to remember where he'd packed his shotgun. He checked himself at the moment he completed his turn.

In the corner, seated cross-legged, was an old, dark-skinned, "peach-wrinkled" man, as they called them in Georgia. Wrapped around his head and covering most of his black and gray-streaked hair was a faded blue cotton cloth folded in a turban, and he wore leather-fringed clothing and a pair of flat-heeled shoes. Traditional Cherokee garb, the history teacher in Andrew gauged automatically, nineteenth century. Meanwhile, Andrew's other, more primitive part suddenly lost his breath with a whoosh. The old man stared at Andrew calmly, his eyes like black moonstones.

"What the hell?" Andrew blustered. "Who are you?" He wanted to throw that old man out of his house, but he couldn't seem to move. He felt as though he still hovered on one foot, the other in mid-air, as though he were still in the act of moving toward that old man.

The Indian played silently with the beads that hung from his fringed shirt, the habit of doing so obviously as well worn as the beads.

He heard the squirrel scrabbling around behind him. Afraid to turn around, he stared at the old man. But, though Andrew had not taken his eyes away for a moment, he realized that the stranger was no longer there.

"What the hell—" he said half under his breath. He turned to pitch the squirrel from the room. And it seemed inevitable, all of a piece with the beginning of his morning. No squirrel. No tracks covered the bed. Flipping the covers up, Andrew looked under them, knowing he would find nothing. He searched every inch of the bed and could not find a sign that there had ever been anything on it except a restless sleeper wrapped in a twisted cover.

The wind rustled the water outside until it slapped the shore like wet sheets against tombstones, and Andrew stared out the window at the choppy water.

Finally, shaking his head, he moved into the bathroom where he doused himself in a sink of cold water, and then dried off briskly.

Later, walking out of the room, he tried to ignore a sound that could have been a quiet sort of laugh, a sound which followed him like a whisper from the room. The faint noise didn't disappear until he reached the kitchen, lit the gas, and placed a very full teakettle of water on the eye of the stove, silently vowing to have a fierce cup of coffee. He'd always dreamed in a way fast and furious in a new place, but this dream had been the most confused, yet real, dream he'd ever had.

While he sipped his bitter coffee, Andrew remembered the moment of his baptism, age six. The wild-eyed minister placing his hand on Andrew's head with a grip like the feet of a hawk, the shove which sent him into an ice-cold river, the gasp for air. He had come up with a mouthful of water and the minister had shouted, "He's resisting the spirit, oh yes God," and shoved him back under the water. The long moment under water, the magic of light-filled bubbles of air trailing to the surface, the buoyancy of the liquid holding him, the tingling of his skin like a sudden realization, the dim, muddy surface of the lake, and as he rose to the top he could see the procession of faces like a string of distorted Christmas lights framing the one clear face of the minister, with his hawk-shaped nose. The nose, Andrew suddenly realized, was the same as that of the Indian in his dream. He hadn't thought of his Southern Baptist background in years. What would Jung make of that? Andrew shook his head and set the cup down on the counter.

Midafternoon, and they still haven't gotten here. Almost without realizing it Andrew had begun to pace the small tip of the peninsula and to stare at the road which wound itself through the small, rolling hills behind the house. Who knew when the phone company would get around to pushing the button that turned on their line? Probably Monday. At any rate, he was certain Kate wouldn't think to call, because she wouldn't expect the phone to work yet. Still, he had begun to worry.

Their green Volvo was a bit old, and he could visualize his family stuck on some section of the interstate. He shouldn't have let the Triple A expire before the move. And he should have switched the left rear tire. Kate had promised to buy a new one before she left, but he thought about her driving down the interstate, dark red hair blowing in the wind, the back seat of the car full of kids, dog, and plants like a living jumble, and smiled. She probably hadn't.

When the swing on the porch creaked a slow and steady back and forth, Andrew looked up, realizing the wind had freshened.

He remembered that he had meant to clear out the cellar before his family arrived. Kate had examined the cellar on her first trip to the house and said that it was sound, but contained nothing much of interest. When the two of them toured the house, the agent opened the door, gestured vaguely into the darkness. "Light's burned out."

He wondered what he'd find in the cellar. Maybe some glass to add to his collection, or some old blue mason jars. He had always been especially fond of those. Andrew screwed a new light bulb into the socket at the top of the stairs and pulled the kinked chain, which bounced in the air and cast a shadow across the wall. As he went down the stairs, the musty smell of the cellar rose to meet him. When he reached the floor, he set down his cleaning supplies and looked around. There were no rusted tools hidden away in the corners, no jars perched on small shelves or ledges. Nothing at all, he thought in disappointment, except a little mold and mildew on the walls. Andrew bent his head to keep from hitting the sloped ceiling.

In the corner, underneath the stairs, he found a padlocked, half-size door. Near the door he picked up a rag of faded red cotton resting beside a large loop embedded in the wall and one link of rusted chain, the sort which at one time had been used to bolt down wagons or large machinery. Joseph's chains, he thought, and laughed a bit uneasily. Around the edges of the room, he could see the remains of a whole series of these links bolted to rings sunk in the base of the stones which made up the wall of the cellar.

Slaves bred or held in the basement. When he'd listened to Larry Bryge and his stories, it had all sounded like one more titillating bit of over-the-grave conversation, a history teacher's stimulus. It was not until that moment, as he stood on the earthen floor, that he fully realized what Joseph Praeter had done with his slaves, and what his family had done to Praeter in turn, if Larry was to be believed. The old guy must have kept the slaves chained in this basement, a part of the original house, until he had them ready for sale to the market in Atlanta. Andrew could almost imagine them in the basement, mothers, fathers, children, all resting in the darkness after a day's work on the Praeter farm, cursing those chains and waiting for market day. He must have grown them like a crop, Andrew thought, or had he? He couldn't have kept them in the cellar for any length of time. Surely he must have brought them in during the night and kept them here just long enough for a quick resale.

No one could have lived in this cellar for long. Had Praeter truly been chained down here just before he died, or had it just made a good tale, something for the locals to tell their grandchildren? No wonder Waterman had skipped the cellar. It had probably scared away a few superstitious prospective buyers. The agent had probably been afraid of losing another sale. Andrew frowned. He didn't like the idea of the boys being down here actually, he decided. They could keep the cellar off limits. He trailed his fingers along the coarse cinder block wall.

In a moment he scuffed back around to the stairs and started up them. A shadow fell across the stairs. At the top stood the Indian Andrew had seen that morning. A black bird, like a war hawk, had been painted on either side of his face. This morning the old fellow had seemed merely mischievous and, like the squirrel, irritated because he had been disturbed. But now, as Andrew stared at him, he looked angry. The old man's hand rested on the light bulb. And it wasn't until man and light were gone, the door shutting firmly at the top of the stairs, that Andrew reacted in an out-of-sync dance, a step behind. He reached the top of the stairs and turned the knob. The handle turned and clicked to a halt. Andrew pounded on the door, but nothing happened. He shook the knob angrily.

At last, sinking to his heels at the top of the stairs, he wondered how long it would be before Kate and the boys arrived. What would he do about them? Nothing really threatening had happened to him yet, but he couldn't risk his family in a place like this until he'd—until he'd what? he asked himself grimly; done something about the ghosts? And just how was he supposed to do that? Faulty plumbing, leaky roofs, he'd been prepared for that, but ghosts? He'd have to think of something fast, because if he suggested moving to another house Kate was not going to be easy to deal with. But he'd be damned, Andrew shivered violently, if he'd risk his family here.

They could move into a hotel for a couple of days until they figured out what was going on. He and Kate could—

He scratched his nose. It made no sense. A prankster Indian ghost in an old Southern mansion? And if it was only a dream it had to have been a fairly solid one to lock the door. If a place like this was going to have ghosts, it should have been some of those slaves or Joseph Praeter, not a nineteenth century Cherokee Indian. Ironic that it was a Cherokee. What would old Andrew Jackson have thought about that? His name had been a Cherokee curse for a couple of centuries. He hadn't been too well liked by the blacks for that matter.

He could make decisions about the place later. Now he had to find a way to pry open the cellar window, and get out to meet his family before something else happened. Before something else happened. He stretched out his hand for the railing and found it after fumbling a few moments. Standing up, he felt his way carefully down the stairs. Except for the muffled clump of Andrew's footsteps, there was not a sound in the cellar, and he couldn't hear any noises from outside. He was in what seemed to be a soundproof room.

As he reached the bottom of the stairs, he stumbled over the pile of cleaning supplies. The metal pail rolled around on the ground and the mop and broom fell on top of it, ringing the metal. His heart gave a quick syncopated beat, and he began to breathe more quickly. While he hesitated a moment, he thought he heard the faint chink of chain against stone, but he heard nothing more, so he took a step forward, intent on searching the walls for a small window or a vent. His toes rested against something solid.

Standing there, frozen with one foot forward and one resting back a step, he began to think that the Indian had perhaps something more in mind than locking him in the cellar. He listened for some indication of what he had been locked in with, and heard nothing at all. The pressure at the edge of his shoe increased, and Andrew drew it back hastily.

Perhaps five minutes passed in silence. Andrew took a step to the left and met with the same unyielding pressure. To the right, the same. Hemmed in, he thought. And behind him on the stairs, he felt a hot breath on his neck. Oh my God, he thought.

He began to be so sensitive to the presence of whatever circled him that the skin on his arms tingled, the back of his neck felt raw. Though the cellar was quiet, he heard a beat which he belatedly realized came from the pounding of blood in his ears. The beat grew louder and louder until he swayed dizzily.

the ebb and the flow, the rhythm and the blood, the moving of a great, white surge which came through the soles of his feet and the top of his head, meeting together in the center of him like some whirlpool of sensation, until he could scarcely feel himself at all. No, not at all. A moving, and a roaring, until he moved with it, swayed with it, picked up the mop handle and broke it over his knee like a stick. Throwing himself to the ground, he reached for the pail, rolled over to a cross-legged seat and began to pound on the metal surface with his two pieces of broom, and the rhythm grew louder and louder, and the sense of it was strong and clear, ay, like the syncopated beat of a skinhead drum, with a tone which was loud and demanding. Something familiar to him about the sound, but that was the last vagrant thought of his because the rhythm and the beat took him like so much driftwood to the shores of the white sound, and he played, and he played, and he played. At first the feeling was heady and light, he enjoyed the rise and the fall of the stick against metal; but after a while it became wearisome and his arms grew heavy and numb. A hand on his arm, there rested a small hand on his arm which gripped him until he played to a slow halt.

When he opened his eyes, he felt disoriented. The cellar flickered until he could not see whose hand gripped his arm. But he saw the cellar door was open by the light which glared its way down the stairs. He closed and opened his eyes until he could find the blur of a form beside him.

A woman's low voice spoke, "Mr. Jackson?"

"Who are you?" he asked softly, as though his voice were an echo.

"Jess McSpadden, one of your neighbors."

He nodded a slow, exaggerated nod.

She stared at him for a moment, and Andrew expected her to ask him what he was doing locked up in his cellar in the dark, pounding with two pieces of a mop handle on a pail which, he saw as he looked down, was as dented in as though someone had pounded the bottom of it with a large hammer. But she said nothing of the sort.

Instead she placed her hand on his arm again and asked him in a quiet tone, "Why don't you come upstairs and I'll fix you some tea?"

Why didn't she ask him what the hell he was doing, Andrew thought as he stood unsteadily. Then he followed her up the stairs, closing the door behind him as though he were closing it against a storm. He had the sensation, when he leaned his back against the door and rested for a moment, that he rested against a solid, oak door and that, in every other direction, lay the wind.

CHAPTER 2

The house returned to him bit by bit until at last he no longer felt as if there were nothing solid but the door behind him. He felt light and hollow, but his mind seemed possessed of an unusual amount of wordless clarity. No definitions. He had no definitions for what had happened, and yet already he had an eager addiction, the pull of something sensual and unseen. He knew that if he could just think about the rhythm of the drum beat, a rhythm he had heard somewhere before though he couldn't remember where, that he might know what had been happening to him. What was in the cellar was not Cherokee, not even Indian, he knew that. It had the feel of something richer and wilder.

He had always been a skeptic; still, if there were ghosts, they frightened the people who had seen them. He had felt no fear, except for that moment in the cellar when he had been hemmed in, *crowded to stillness*. Be honest, Andrew J., his inner voice mocked, you've been seduced.

Andrew could have stayed as he was for quite some time, leaning against the door. Still, even though the last thing he wanted to do was make small talk, he realized that this encounter was only his second contact with his new neighbors and that he really should go in and attempt some sort of normal conversation. Though what you said to someone who'd just seen you doing what he'd been doing in the cellar, he had no idea. In fact, he wondered why she hadn't simply walked quietly back out the door and left him to his cellar frenzy. Then once home again she would, of course, have called the high school principal to question his choice of a history teacher. "Rather far gone, I think," she would say to him. And the principal would lean back into his well-worn swivel chair, stick his boots up on the desk, and nod thoughtfully. "Perhaps I should reconsider," he would say.

Maybe *he* should reconsider. Maybe the loss of his first teaching position had knocked him off the rails. In that case what he needed to protect his family from was him, he thought wryly.

"Mr. Jackson." He heard her low voice coming from just across the hall, "Your tea is ready."

As he walked into the living room, he wondered if he could get rid of the neighbor *and* the Indian before Kate and the boys came. The cellar, he thought, I'll lock the door to the cellar. Private showings, a mocking voice said to him from within. And just how long do you think those will last?

The living room, the bland rose cushions on the Queen Anne chairs, the smooth mahogany furniture, all seemed foreign to him. The only piece of furniture he liked in the whole room was the small half grandfather clock hanging on the wall. The woman looked more familiar than the room, and he'd seen her only the one time across the lake.

She reminded him in a way of the old Indian, though he couldn't have said why. Her face was one of contrasts, hard, angular jaw, soft mouth, thick, black eyebrows. And he felt an immediate sense of ease in her presence. He nodded to her as he sat down. He noticed that her hands were trembling as she picked up the teacup in front of her. Odd that he felt comfortable around her when she was obviously ill at ease.

"Where'd you find the teapot?" he asked and heard his stilted tone with an inward wince.

"What? Oh. I brought my own along, because I was sure you wouldn't have yours unpacked yet." She glanced nervously around the room.

Brought her own along? Andrew frowned. Was that a

custom, visiting new neighbors with teapot in hand? She did not say anything else, so, after a moment, he tried again. "It's nice of you to drop in to visit a new neighbor so soon."

"Yes, I know you weren't expecting company." She stopped and looked at him. In the abrupt tone and the still face, he sensed a sudden, momentary helplessness.

Oh, this is going to be a terribly awkward conversation, he thought to himself resignedly. I hope she leaves soon.

"You're the second neighbor I've met already. Yesterday Larry Bryge came by, though I must say he was far from bringing his own teapot."

"Yes, well, this house has been vacant for a while. I imagine he spent some time here. The Bryges are as territorial as wolves." She lifted her hand to her head and took a deep breath. "Look, Mr. Jackson. It's just not the time for small talk. I came here to tell you something. Now that I'm here I just can't seem to start. I don't know you. I don't know you at all or how you'll take things, especially after seeing you," she waved vaguely, "down there. But it can't wait."

I've lost my job, he thought. The school's burned. The neighbors don't want me here. What? Andrew forced himself to say nothing. Instead he simply waited for her to go on with the silence of one who has no choice.

"It's your family. There's been an accident."

He froze, staring at his cup, and then he set the cup down quite deliberately. "Now look here, Mrs. . . ."

"McSpadden, Jess McSpadden."

"Look here, Mrs. McSpadden, what kind of game are you trying to play?" His voice rose. And even though he could see by the stricken look on her face that what she was saying had to be so, that, incredible as it seemed, she was the one delegated to tell him about his family, he couldn't seem to stop.

"It's true. They were injured in Maryville."

"The police would be here to tell me about that sort of accident. No way would a neighbor be given that kind of news, especially since I—we've just moved here," he corrected himself doggedly, and then his voice trailed off. Too cruel, he thought, it was too cruel a thing for someone to be doing to a new neighbor. The police would have come to tell me, wouldn't they? And then he realized that he must have been saying that last sentence aloud, for she answered him.

"The police are all out of town." Her voice was husky. "One

of them's at the University of Tennessee's summer graduation; another is taking a pregnant woman to the hospital. It's a small town, you know," she said apologetically. "I'm the bank president," she added as though that explained everything. She sat back, took a deep breath as though to start again. "We go by the heart, not by the book."

"Where is my wife?" Andrew asked, a small, numb fear starting in him.

"Your wife and your children were killed, Mr. Jackson—Andrew," she spoke gently, her anxious eyes on him.

What now? What now? he thought over and over as she continued to speak. He stared at her, the rims of his eyes already sore as though he'd been grieving for days, as though he'd known before he could possibly have known. And while he watched her mouth move without really understanding what she was saying, he imagined himself calmly walking through the door of the house, down the sloping yard to the water's edge, balancing his toes upon the smoothness of the tombstones and their rough broken edges, and then stepping off into the water. Had it only been a few hours ago that he had imagined their motorboat pulling happily into shore? He could nearly see Billy's one dead tooth (where he'd smashed it on a tree stump) grin. He could nearly feel the movement of his fingers as he tugged the bill of Andy's cap down over his eyes. And Kate with the thick red strands of hair blowing across her face. But he couldn't see her eyes. It troubled him that he couldn't see her eyes.

"It happened quickly. They can't have felt much pain."

Andrew looked down at the coffee table.

How the hell do you know that, old woman? He opened his mouth, to say that. Instead what came out was, "Where—"

"They're at the Blount County Morgue in Maryville. They hadn't gotten to the Loudon County line yet—" her voice broke. He heard her rise. She came over to him and put her hand on his shoulder. "Is there anything I can do, Andrew?"

Why hadn't he waited a day, so they could have all come up to Tennessee together? Because, his thoughts jabbed at him, you wanted one day alone. Andrew realized she was still waiting patiently for his answer. He took a ragged breath and stared at her wordlessly.

"I'll stay for a while if you'd like me to."

He shook his head.

"Is there any call that you'd like me to make, any arrangements that I can settle for you until you have a phone?"

He started to shake his head again and then he realized that he needed to know how to get to them, to make sure that—besides, something would need to be done. And there were Kate's parents to think of. No, he could call them tomorrow when the phone was switched on. What could he have been thinking of? He couldn't let a stranger tell them about—Why was he so damned logical? She stood there waiting, damn it. For what? For me to say it's all right now. You've told me, and I've taken it well, so now you can go.

He cleared his throat. Everything is moving in slow motion, he thought desperately, when will it speed up? "Will you call the Maryville police?" Maryville, they were so close. He took a deep breath. "Call the Maryville police, and tell them I'm coming right over to—" he looked up at her, "I don't want them there any longer than they have to be."

"I brought a sketch with directions to the station." Her hands met him as she handed him the map. The coldness of her skin surprised him. How hard this must be for her, he thought suddenly, relieved that he could think of someone else, even for a moment.

"Is there a funeral home in Greenback?"

His question came as a surprise, he could see that. She looked as if she wanted to ask him if he was sure, but she spoke with composure. "I would have thought you would take them home."

"I'm—I'm not sure. I might want them buried here. There's a burial grounds on the property."

The surprise on her face was evident. As though she were asking: in the *Praeter cemetery*? However, when she spoke, she said "There's no funeral home in Greenback. Maryville has two. I can't think—" She ran her fingers through her hair. "I can't remember their names, but they're in the yellow pages. Would you like me to—"

"No, I'll call them." Andrew turned his coffee cup around and around. His inner voice grated, No trespassing.

She paused. After a moment she said, "I imagine that, being new in town and not having any of the—of your other relatives here, you'd much prefer to be left alone for a while. When you're ready, your neighbors will be here; but you'll have to make the first move. There's not a person on this cove will intrude on you until you are." She gave a nod as if to say, I'll see to that. Then she added, "I've left you my number on the kitchen table. Call anytime." She patted him on the shoulder.

He locked the door behind him and followed her out to the driveway. She hesitated for a moment and leaned up against her car. Then she said, "Take this house in small doses, Mr. Jackson. Make your way to the fields where the land is at peace."

Patting him on the shoulder one last time, she got into her car. Though grateful for the touch, Andrew found it difficult to look at her again. But as she drove away he looked after her, wondering what Jess McSpadden knew about this place. Tears sprang to his eyes. It was a bitter irony that he had nothing left but to distract himself with speculation about empty mysteries.

From the cove to the Maryville city limits was twenty-five miles. Andrew drove them on automatic pilot. The road wound around. He turned the curves with a quick, smooth skill, thinking she didn't take care of herself, so I must be careful.

It took him about fifteen minutes, once he'd reached Maryville, to find the hospital and another ten to locate the morgue. He made the drive with an increasing urgency, and it wasn't until he pulled into the hospital parking lot that he realized why he felt such a sense of haste. He had been hoping, all the long drive, that if he just arrived quickly enough by some miracle his family would still be alive.

He walked the long echoing corridors until he found a nurse to direct him to the morgue.

The county coroner met Andrew at the door. He was a short, dark, practical-looking man with a weariness in the set of his shoulders and a look of sympathy in his eyes.

"We'll try to make this as easy for you as we can," he said quietly.

Walking through the door ahead of Andrew, he moved to the left side of a covered table. Andrew followed him, though he hesitated a moment as he saw the coroner gently lift a white sheet and fold it back to reveal Kate. Her body rested on a steel cart like a flimsy cafeteria table. Two other men stood nearby, one of them in a police uniform and looking as though he would rather be anywhere than in this particular room.

The Kate that lay on the table had been bruised, but not much touched by the accident, or so Andrew thought until the attendants turned her over and he saw her left side. It was as if half of her had been left in peace and the other half had not. She had plucked her eyebrows. She never plucked her eyebrows. And then he realized that they must have begun the embalming process. Her hair had been brushed until it clung with static electricity to her face and neck. Through the hair, on her left side, he could see glimpses of a massive bruise running from her temple down to the collar of her turquoise shirt.

"That's my wife," he said hoarsely, and he touched one cold hand.

After a few moments, one of the officers nodded to him awkwardly.

They walked over to the wall. The coroner rested his hand on the front of the drawer. "Are you sure you want to see?" he asked quietly. "They were rather..."

Andrew looked at the man with his hand on the drawer that held his son. "Yes," he said.

The drawer came out with a faint clunk, and then extended further. From somewhere came the faint scent of formaldehyde. Again the coroner folded back a sheet. Andrew looked down at the mangled body of one of his sons. The legs were twisted around each other. The face had been completely crushed. He wouldn't have known it was Billy, if not for the fact that his left hand, the one he'd had a fish-shaped mole on since he was a baby, was intact.

He nodded. His breath had a catch in it. "That's Billy."

The coroner gently closed the drawer and slid back the one just below it. He looked for a long while at the bruised mass of a body, in worse shape even than Billy's, and then he said, "That's Andy." He turned away for a moment. All of them. I've lost all of them, he thought dazedly, and his hands reached up to take huge handfuls of his hair. He pulled until he could feel a searing pain in his scalp. And, as he did, he rocked back and forth from his heels to his toes, listening to the slow click of the hard soles on the floor, like the ticking of a clock. It seemed to be the only sound in the room.

The county coroner came over and placed a hand on Andrew's shoulder. After a moment he said, "You can leave as soon as you've signed the identification papers, Mr. Jackson. Would you like us to take any further steps to verify the boys?"

Andrew looked at the coroner as though he had spoken in tongues. "There's no need." His voice came out muffled, and he cleared his throat and tried again. "I'm sure." He reluctantly dropped his hands and straightened his jacket.

After signing the papers with a large scrawl, Andrew said without looking at the coroner, "I'm going to get in touch with the funeral home now. Do you think I can call them from here?"

"Certainly. You can use the phone in the outer office." The coroner took the papers from Andrew and leaned back as if he would like to say something else, though he was obviously uncertain what. At last he said gently, "I'm sorry." Such gentleness from a stranger made him feel far too vulnerable. He shrugged his shoulders and turned away to leaf through the phone book. The coroner walked into the other room.

There were two funeral homes in Maryville, Fowler and Howe. He called Howe, explained what had happened and told the director that he would like to come on Monday and make further arrangements. Then he called South Central Bell to request immediate phone service. He would need to call all the relatives. That done, he turned the slow, shadowed way toward home.

Two or three miles outside of Maryville he began to wonder where the accident had happened. He looked for signs, for skidmarks, broken glass, their old green Volvo. He knew that thinking he would see the car was foolish, because the police officer had already showed him the junkyard where they had stored the vehicle until he officially released it. But he looked for it anyway.

The further he drove, the more anxious he became, certain that he had missed it, equally certain that around the next curve he would somehow, magically, see the spot and know it. Soon he would be outside that radius, that circle in which, just a few short hours before, they had travelled. His hands tightened on the steering wheel. He began to peer ahead and to look frantically from side to side. Didn't they leave crosses on the side of the road where there were accidents? And then, as he came up to a large, sweeping curve he saw three crosses, one large and two small. He pulled into a sideroad and stared at the crosses numbly.

For several moments he sat in the car, and then his hand raised to the door handle and dropped away. Raised to the window, as though to roll it down, and dropped away. He blinked his eyes, willing himself to cry, willing himself to say that here. Here his family died. There were the swerving marks across the road. There the bits of glass that had once been solid windows. And yet nothing. Nothing seemed different about this stretch of road. There was nothing beyond those small things to note the fact that they had passed, or that they had not. That they had lived and laughed and felt the wind against their faces, and made jokes about how many miles before they could stop for Billy's eternal bathroom breaks. "Eternal," he whispered.

And suddenly he found himself, without knowing quite how, driving madly down the road, and though he didn't know how long he'd been driving or where he was, he did know that he had passed the turnoff to Greenback and that he was on his way to Atlanta. The tires whipped faster and faster underneath him, and somehow he was driving on some sort of endless highway without being sure where it would take him, or what the hell he'd do if he got there. The wheels seemed to whisper "coward, coward," but he brushed away the sound irritably and drove still faster.

He had no more idea when or how long he'd been on the road, then he understood how or why, sometime around three o'clock in the morning, he found himself pulling into the driveway of the Old Praeter Home. Bewildered, he listened to the sound of the Bryge's dogs barking in the distance as though the noise of his return were the noise of some ancient wolf circling angrily around a den it couldn't bear to leave.

When he walked inside, he wasn't sure what to do with himself. Kate, he found himself repeating under his breath.

It was by a sort of blind weariness that he found himself on the couch where he sat for a long while, before he rose. Then he wandered in and out of the rooms, up and down the stairs, walking as though sitting down were too much of an agony, and movement too much of a shell shock. And, as he walked, he seemed to sense small bodies, Billy under one arm, Andy under the other, tousled heads turning to look up at him, and he thought he heard the echo of Kate's footsteps, a small-boned woman, moving with a firm energy to match him step for step.

At last Andrew entered her room and sank to the floor wearily, resting his head against the loom he had so painstakingly reconstructed just the day before. The loom, he thought, would be his only shrine to her since nothing else bore so many memories. He had first met her in a craft hall where she had been weaving, the sunlight glancing across the strands of her hair as she bent over the yarn. He had made this loom for her as a gift and as a reminder of that bond. Every piece of wood had been smoothed with her in mind. He would never touch it.

Eventually the night came, and a full moon shone through the window. It glanced across his hands like a searchlight, as they slowly oiled, over and over as if it would never be enough, the surface of the wood.

Andrew woke to the sound of a cleared throat. The air in the room felt stale, and the sunlight came in through the window like heat. Opening his eyes, he saw again the Chero-kee. The man had no paint on his face, but a robin perched on his left shoulder, pecking at the faded blue turban.

Again he was in motion before he realized it, leaping from the floor to rush at the old man with hands outstretched. He moved toward the old man who stared at him, and in his eyes were neither kindness, nor sympathy, nor dislike. It was the Indian's expression that stopped him as he came closer, the rage in him subsiding as quickly as it had come. He slowed to a halt about five feet away and let his clenched fists drop slowly to his side. For one crazy moment Andrew had blamed him for their deaths. And yet who knew what this old man and the house could do?

The silence stretched into something so long it seemed to Andrew like noise; the Cherokee shrugged his shoulders and turned away, the robin looking back over his shoulder like a second pair of eyes. And then the old man was gone. Andrew glared at the empty hallway for a moment, and then turned to the window and looked out across the lawn to the lake. He felt a sudden indifference. So what if an Indian ghost lived on

the premises? What did that have to do with him? I'll ignore
you too, old man, he thought.

He looked out the window, out there where nothing seemed
to match the way he felt. The sun was blazing across the
blue-green water; the waves moved caressingly across the
water-path of the barges. Skiers drifted into the lake like
slowly diving fish, and he watched the scene as if what he saw
were a garish sort of carnival.

All day long he tried to make himself do something while
he waited for the funeral home to call and tell him they were
ready for him. He knew he should call his family, but he
didn't have the energy to go out. He waited for the phone to
be switched on. He couldn't decide to unpack, and he
couldn't decide to pack. He couldn't make up his mind to
stick to anything.

Whatever he did, it really didn't matter. After a while he
would find himself retracing his path from the night before.
As he paced the halls, he tried to catch the Indian out;
though he altered his patterns again and again, he didn't find
the old man. Instead, he found that his movement took on
the hypnotic quality of a dance. Once he came through the
doorway and stared at Kate's empty loom. Then he moved,
rustling through one of the boxes in the room until he found
her thread. He grimly dressed the loom, his movement fierce
and rapid, as though he covered up the picture of a shattered
car that stared at him from inside the frame. What did it
matter, he thought to himself bitterly, when he had finally
finished and was panting for air, that it was all in a knot which
no self-respecting weaver would ever have had? It would
never be used again.

The phone rang like the voice of a stranger. Andrew
thought it would be the funeral parlor at last. Instead the
voice which breathed into his ear was his sister's. "Andy, we
heard about Kate and the boys on the news last night. I
called you as soon as your phone worked. I'm sorry—" She
paused for a moment and took a deep breath. "We're going to
help you," she hesitated, "with everything. Where would
you—"

"Here," he said softly, "here. I want the three of them to

be buried here on our land in the Praeter family graveyard. I want the funeral to be here."

There was a silence on the other end of the line. At last, when he thought she might have hung up, she asked doubtfully, "There?"

"That's right," his tone was final.

"Have you phoned the funeral home yet?" He could tell by the tone of her voice she hadn't given up the thought of dissuading him. She would bring it up again when she arrived.

"Yes. I'm waiting for them to contact me now."

"I've called all of our family. Would you like me to tell the rest of the relatives and her family?" she asked carefully.

"Call the relatives. I can't deal with Aunt Hattie. I'll tell Kate's mother and father. I need to be the one to tell them."

"Is there anything you need?"

He paused for a long while thinking, Kate, I need Kate. "Andy?"

"No. When are you coming up?"

"Tomorrow. We'll be there tomorrow. I don't think Greg can get there until Wednesday though."

He sighed. "That's all right. We won't have the funeral until Wednesday or Thursday anyway."

She waited for a moment and then said, "Andy I—well, I'll see you tomorrow. Get some sleep."

He replied with difficulty, "I'll try." Then he added, "and Margaret, I—sis, thanks."

Andrew could almost hear the relief in her voice. "Whatever I can do, Andy," she said softly.

When she hung up, he stood holding the phone, thinking that he wished Kate were here so he could tell her about all of this. She would have known how to tell her parents. He called Kate's parents and informed them as gently and as quickly as he could. It seemed to him that the call went on for a long while before they could bear to let him go.

Even after the phone clicked, he held the receiver to his ear as though waiting for something. After a while he lowered it with a sigh, still cradling it in one hand. When would the funeral home call, he wondered, when would they call? He set the receiver gently down on the phone, feeling the slow give of the plastic buttons on the body of the telephone. Everything seemed somehow alive to him at that moment, even the phone itself, and he could hear a silent humming in the plastic, like a swarm of waiting bees, and that humming was a promise of calls to come. They would release themselves into a loud interruption soon. He could hear the ringing long before it would begin.

The funeral director did not at all want Andrew to bury his family on the Praeter land. He told Andrew that he would have to have a special permit, that a crew would have to go out and determine proper distance from the house to the burial site, that it would be a much more expensive funeral. And as he talked, he ran thin, nervous fingers through a black head of hair that looked as though it had been combed that way all afternoon. His voice rose in a nervous quaver.

"I don't care about the legalities," Andrew said finally. "I simply want it done. Please make the necessary arrangements." His voice was cold and final. After that he stayed no longer than was necessary to select the coffins. When he left he closed the door behind him softly, though he'd liked to have slammed it. As he walked to the car, he kept envisioning the director in one of his own bronzed specialties, a thought which gave Andrew an ironic sort of pleasure.

That night, though it was a fine summer's evening, Andrew felt cold, so he built a fire in the library fireplace. He had the lights on at first, but after he stared at the floor-to-ceiling bookcases for a while and thought about how full of people's lives they were, he turned the lights off. He stared at the flicker of the fire as it ate its way into the small chunks of hickory and pine.

There came a moment, when the fire died down to a glow, that Andrew noticed the Cherokee seated at the hearth with his knees bent up to his chest and his arms wrapped around his knees. As the Indian watched the flames, he crooned a chant so softly Andrew couldn't understand the words, a chant that gave Andrew a sense of covering over his exhaustion, an exhaustion like the aftermath of a storm. He sat there in the darkening room, watching the fire, listening to the old man, and thinking.

It was funny, really. He knew nothing about this old fellow

who had never spoken a word. And yet it didn't matter at all.
How many people, even people who thought they were
communicating, understood each other? Probably fewer than
a half dozen, and those probably fewer than a half dozen
times in their lives. What did people have to go on, really,
but a certain sense of presence? Presence and a way of
looking at the world that couldn't be put into words. *That* is
understanding, Andrew thought, only it comes more with
strangers than with friends or family. Too many things get in
the way and tangle up the lines. And then there were all the
things that were never resolved, which seemed like nothing
while you were with them, all the things he'd never resolved
with Kate. Maybe that was the problem people had. They
talked too damn much. And talk was true and not true.

It felt good to sit in silence. Not to have to say anything.
Yet even with the quiet, Andrew couldn't feel settled. He
rested still, because he couldn't do anything else; but stillness
was an illusion, for he could feel an inner hum that vibrated
through his muscles though it could not move them. And it
seemed to him as he stared into the center of the logs and
their nest of fire, that there were faces in the center of the
coals, burning like tiny human torches, and that all the faces
were his.

CHAPTER 3

They came in like a flock of plump Georgia pigeons and, as Andrew listened to them, he could hardly believe they were his family. They brought hams and roasts and sandwiches, potato salad, pinto beans; in short, they brought enough food to provide for all ten of them for a month. It amazed him that most of that had vanished down their throats before the night was over, a night in which they talked until nearly dawn.

There was no sign of the old Indian, though Andrew wondered briefly what sort of appearance he would make, and whether the aunts would run screaming through the house. It was easy, now that his family was here, to think that he had imagined the whole thing as a part of the romance of moving into what he regarded as an historic house. If he had been imagining anything in particular surely it would have been something like Southern belles on the porch sipping mint juleps. Andrew couldn't understand himself. He'd always been a skeptic, yet here he was accepting the whole thing so easily and at a time when he certainly should have been thinking of other things. Anyway, if there was a ghost, and the whole thing had not been his imagination, then surely the old man had made a quick disappearance at the sight of Aunt Hattie.

Andrew watched his relatives. They wandered about the house and exclaimed over the furnishings. They asked him questions about what he was going to do with the house, and whether he'd remain in Greenback, and Aunt Hattie, as usual when there was a death in the family, advised him, nodding her little straw hat with the huge pink plastic rose on it, to remarry immediately.

"And I don't know, dear, why you aren't burying your dear family in Marietta where they ought to be," she said emphatically, nodding her head again until the rose bobbed.

"Aunt Hattie," he said slowly through clenched teeth, "I intend to bury my family here on our own land, the land of our first home. And I don't want to hear any more about it. The arrangements are made."

The conversations in both the living room and the kitchen stopped abruptly. Andrew's sister, Margaret, sizing up the situation, promptly rescued him. Margaret took a very bewildered Aunt Hattie by the shoulders and gently turned her around enough so that Andrew could get out of the corner. She did this all so smoothly that Aunt Hattie wasn't quite sure what had happened. Aunt Hattie shook her head. Margaret stared at Andrew as if to say, Why are you so set on this? We'll talk later. Andrew grimaced and walked stiffly away.

"Now, I was just telling dear, sad Andrew—"

"I believe that dear, sad Andrew needs a little bit to eat, Aunt Hattie," said Margaret as she drew the aunt into the living room, "and I wanted to ask your advice about the music for the funeral."

"Well, I think that 'There's a Church in the Valley by the Wildwood' would be rather nice." Aunt Hattie's voice trailed off into the living room.

Greg looked across the room at Andrew and rolled his eyes. Andrew forced a smile. Greg winked. Aunt Hattie had been a joke between them for years. As a small child, Greg had done imitations of Aunt Hattie that had reduced the family to helpless laughter, but he had never felt about her the way Andrew did.

Andrew watched Greg settle back into his chair and listen as one of the cousins gushed, "My, how distinguished you look, Greg, with that premature streak of gray in your hair. I declare, you're the spitting image of your father when he was in his prime, with those big brown eyes and that curly brown hair. It's good to see you, even though we're all here on such a sad occasion." Andrew winced. Southern womanhood at its worst. Sugarcoat the grief and flirt with the relatives. He could never imagine someone like Jess, for example, talking to anyone this way, much less her relatives. It sounded like something straight out of *Gone With the Wind*. Thank God she was a distant relation and he didn't see her more than every few years or so.

Aunt Hattie always got to him, even though she meant well. She had been the instigator of many of the encounters a child dreads most from an adult, the "my how you've grown" syndrome. And of his ritual drowning in the river. It was Aunt Hattie who had been responsible for his parents' late conversion to the Southern Baptists. He had suffered through most of it, taking into account his parents' feelings. The last time he'd lost his temper with her had been at their funeral, nearly the last time he and she had spoken. She had wanted Andrew to meet her sister's cousins' girl so that he could begin right away with a new family to make up for the one he'd lost. He had gripped her by the shoulders and shaken her until her face whitened.

Marriage and geographic distance had relieved him of most of Aunt Hattie's solicitude. His family's death, it seemed, had revived their connection again. He tried to remind himself that Aunt Hattie meant well. She loved him, had loved him ever since he was a little boy. But he didn't believe that. That was his parents speaking. She didn't love him. She couldn't, because she had never taken the opportunity to get to know him.

Several of his cousins looked as though they'd like to talk, but none of them seemed to know quite how to approach him. Andrew didn't want to give them any encouragement, so he looked down at the plate onto which he had shoveled a huge pile of mashed potatoes.

Andrew was still at the table when Kate's parents came in. He watched Bart Josephs weave his way through the other relatives. He clasped Andrew to him and said gruffly, "You're all we got left, boy."

For the first time since he'd been told of the wreck, Andrew felt free to let tears spring to his eyes. He looked over Bart's broad shoulder to see Mary, Kate's mother, hovering behind him. She patted Andrew's head as if he were a small boy. He hugged Bart and then her, feeling as though she were much more fragile than the last time he had seen her. Since his mother and father had died, the two of them had become like parents to him.

"Andy," she said softly, "oh, we'll miss them, won't we?"

"More than I want to think about," he said to her, and felt a tear he couldn't seem to blink back slide down his face.

"Go ahead and cry, Andy boy," she said. "You haven't been, have you?" She patted him on the shoulder.

"No, seems like my eyes have been bone dry."

"You've had a lot to mourn in the last couple of years." She gestured to her husband, who reached into his pocket and pulled out a newly folded handkerchief. She handed it to Andrew who looked at it as his sudden signal for release.

He could hear Aunt Hattie in the other room, her quavering voice singing, "Swing low, sweet chariot, coming for to carry me home," and he smiled. The tears brimmed over and slid slowly down his face. From the stairs came the sound of his two young cousins swishing down the banister railings and landing with a thump at the end of the stairs.

"But life goes on, doesn't it, Andy?"

He listened as his cousins' voices joined Aunt Hattie's. "Somehow," he sighed, and patted her on the shoulder. "But it seldom waits for you to figure out how."

Andrew walked slowly from the car to the funeral home door. He'd asked the director to let him come ahead so that he would have a few minutes with Kate and the boys before the funeral. A funeral attendant ushered him into the small room where they lay in the caskets. Andrew walked to the front of the room and stood for a long time staring down at Kate. He said silently to her, Why didn't you give me time to say goodbye? Why didn't you buy a new tire? Why the fuck aren't you here? How do you think I can make it without you and the boys?

"Kate," he said in a low voice, and reached down to touch her face. For a moment he thought her skin was warm, but it was a momentary illusion. He brushed his fingers across her forehead, and it radiated that same stiff coldness as his parents' skin at their funeral.

The casket lids were closed on his two sons, as he had

requested, and he didn't feel any need to open them. He'd rather remember how they'd been. Even knowing that behind the lids were two, shapeless masses made it painfully clear, clear to the bone, that they were gone. Still, he slid his hand over the two caskets, and his fingers lingered, speaking to them, tracing the grooves around the edges.

I tossed you the ball. You were only three, but you threw it ten feet, the next time twelve, your arm rising in slow motion as you squinted at the ball coming toward me. It sank solidly into my glove and you raised your elbow and pointed to it, "Look, dad, muscles," you yelled, and then ran around to the driveway of the condo to wave at Kate where she stood watching from the window. Billy, just a chubby one year old with curly hair, ran after you. You could never get bones and muscles straight when you were young, Andy, and now they never will be.

From the bustle just outside the door he knew his relatives had arrived. An attendant came into the room and touched him on the arm. "Mr. Jackson, would you like to talk to the minister a moment before the funeral?"

He shook his head. He'd never been much of one for organized religion, and, though the ceremony might have an easing behind it, he had no idea what to say to the minister or what the minister could say to him. The only thing he'd ever appreciated about those long-ago enforced Sundays had been the music, and the opportunity the sermons gave his mind to wander.

And today he resented the hell out of the ceremonies, the fake rituals that people would make from what had happened. The people who would come by and wish him artificial or, at the very least, awkward and meaningless condolences. He had always hated the way that people created ceremonies for the things that were already gone, the empty shells that remained, as though they could hold onto what was gone by circling around it. They seemed to think they could somehow force themselves to remember the reality of the past. No, that wasn't it. He frowned. It was as if they tried to create a memory of what they thought had happened. Time wouldn't have remained still and their memories would have been altered if those who died were still alive; why the hell did

they think they could freeze-frame things just because a
person had died? He hated funerals because nothing real
ever seemed to happen at them.

The organist came in and settled herself with a rustle of her
sheet music. Wondering what Aunt Hattie and Margaret had
come up with, Andrew moved to a seat at the upper left, and
sat quietly as his relatives filed into the pews around and
behind him. Kate's mother and father were seated just at the
end of his row. His sister, Margaret, sat to one side of him,
though he'd not seen her come in. And his brother, Greg,
slid in on the other side. He nudged Andrew sympathetically.

Andrew turned around for a moment and saw that the high
school principal was there, and Jess McSpadden and her husband, as well as some others he didn't recognize. They must be
Greenback people, he thought dully. Margaret squeezed his arm
and he looked at her. Her long, brown hair was brushed and
shining, and her eyes, always changeable, were muted in color.
He took her hand in his and held it even when his grew cold.

His only coherence during the sermon was an image. He
closed his eyes and saw a thick, white fog, and through the
center came two glowing, black moths. Is that it? he wondered
blankly.

Somehow he got through the funeral. He heard the minister's words as though through glass. After the service, everyone in the room, even those he didn't know, came up to say
something to him. He watched their mouths move, their
heads bob, and he tried to nod where he thought it was
appropriate. He said things, but he had no idea what he said.

Soon the funeral director came and ushered Andrew to the
hearse. Andrew walked slowly behind the pallbearers and
thought about the Praeter family burial plot. He hadn't even
decided what he would do with the house now that they were
gone, yet he seemed to have made a decision already. He had
tied himself to this place so firmly by that one decision. Why?
Maybe he had hoped—Hoped what? He shook his head and
looked out the window uneasily. Fields sailed by the windows,
fields with weeds and fields with cattle grazing drowsily.
It seemed to him that it should be raining, that no one
should be going about their daily lives while a hearse drove
quietly down the country lanes. He wanted to yell out the
window, "Mourn, damn you, or at least stop for a minute,"

but he was somehow comforted by those slow, calm parades of snapshots which flashed by the window.

The hearse pulled into the driveway behind the old Praeter home, and the other cars came one by one to a slow halt behind it. Andrew stepped into the yard and waited for a moment, then followed the minister and the pallbearers to the small, overgrown set of family plots. As he walked, he could hear the quiet steps of his family behind him. The gravediggers had been there before the procession, and there were three freshly dug rectangular holes in the ground. Above each of them was a metal framework onto which the pallbearers set the caskets.

Andrew felt dizzy. He closed his eyes for a moment, and when he opened them it seemed as if two of the caskets opened as well. Almost in a trance he walked up to one of the caskets and saw Andy, resting there without a mark on him, and then he saw the boy get up and quietly leave. Andrew swayed. It might not have been Andy, he thought. I couldn't tell anything from looking at that body. He might still be somewhere. Alive.

"Are you all right, Andrew?" He heard his sister's voice. She caught hold of his right arm.

When he opened his eyes, he hadn't moved at all and the caskets were closed.

To Andrew's left he suddenly felt another cool and insubstantial hand. He looked over in surprise, and there was the Cherokee tugging at him, trying to say something. The old man's mouth moved in a slow and exaggerated way, but there was no sound. Andrew swayed again. The Cherokee was gone. Margaret looked at Andrew for a moment and then helped him to a seat.

As everyone settled in their seats and the minister stood and began to speak, Andrew thought wildly, Do you, Andrew Jackson take this woman, Kate Josephs, to be your lawfully wedded wife?—until death do you part? Somehow it hadn't seemed real, even though he'd felt sure, as sure as anyone could on their marriage day, that this was what he meant. And that sort of vow wasn't one you ever made aloud for your children, but surely it was there, implicit.

He looked up, wiping his eyes with his handkerchief, to find that the service was nearly over, and the minister was intoning the words of a muffled prayer. Just behind the minister in the shadow of the trees, had he seen the old

Cherokee beckoning to him? When Andrew squinted, he thought he could see the whipping of the bushes. Whether he had or not, it comforted him to think of the Indian. Andrew shook his head and stood, bracing himself to take the onslaught of familial hugs and the heavy kindness which felt almost more difficult to bear than cruelty.

Aunt Hattie's small, rattling Chevrolet pulled out of the driveway, and Andrew heaved a sigh of relief. Margaret stood beside him with her hand on his arm.

"I knew Aunt Hattie would go last," he said, and turned to Margaret.

"Nothing changes," she said and laughed a weak laugh.

"Everything," he said bleakly, "changes."

"We haven't been much help to you have we?" She hugged him and then pulled back. A tear gleamed in the crease of her nose.

"You did what you could. Nothing much would have—"

"Andy, why did you bury them here?" She looked away from him, across the lawn, as if to give him a moment to compose himself.

"I don't know, sis." He shrugged and made a restless movement away from her. When she let him go, he turned his back on her for a moment and then turned around again. He shrugged his shoulders once more. "I honestly don't know. It was important."

"I could tell that," she said softly. "You were much too set on it for it not to be but—"

"Right now I don't feel very connected with any place, I—one place should have been as good as another but—" he shrugged again. "Maybe it was that I wanted them buried in somebody's family plot." He looked at her.

"We have a family plot," she reminded him, her eyes darkening.

He was silent, sure that he had hurt her.

"Well, it's done now." She sighed. "I suppose if you ever regret it, you can have them moved."

"Yes," he said doubtfully.

"Will you do something for me, Andy, though? Will you tell me when you know?"

"You mean *if* I know, don't you?" He smiled crookedly and

patted her on the shoulder. Her hair slipped under his fingers like silk.

"You'll know," she said firmly, a little worried pucker at her eyebrows.

"I'll miss you, Margaret." He kissed her on the cheek.

"Then come see us. We're only two hours away."

To Andrew that seemed like two years, but he smiled and said, "Of course, soon."

"No, I mean it, Andy," and he knew that, as usual, she had read his state of mind.

"When I can," he said softly, and he could see that she was relieved.

He held that relief to him as he went back inside to join Greg. It had been kind of his brother, Andrew thought as he climbed the stairs, to the front porch to leave them alone to say goodbye.

"You've got to pull yourself together." Andrew's brother, Greg, stood quietly in the doorway, a suitcase in hand.

"I'll be all right, Greg. Not to worry."

"Not to worry! It's been two days since the rest of the family left. You scarcely talked with most of them. And even though the principal excused you from the school's training sessions, you're going to be teaching day after tomorrow. Look at you, man; you look like hell!"

Andy looked up from the eggs he was scrambling. He had not taken a bath in two or three days, much less shaved. He knew he looked disreputable. "I am a bit of a mess," he admitted ruefully, as he glanced down at the wornout terry cloth robe, the mismatched socks, and caught that strong smell of the unbathed which he'd been ignoring ever since the funeral.

"Take care of your appearance, Andy; you'll feel better." His face had that look which only a family member wears, half concern, half exasperation. "I'd like to stay longer, but I've got a contract due out for the museum. I can't push it back any longer."

"That's understandable. Life goes on," said Andrew, and he swigged an imaginary bottle of liquor.

"But before I go—" Greg hesitated. "I've got to ask you

something. Why the hell did you have them bring that car back here?"

"The car?" Andrew turned back to the stove and stared at the spatula as he tossed the eggs around the skillet.

"You know what I'm talking about. Having the police bring you the car your family wrecked in! And why did you put it up on blocks out in the side yard. It makes no sense. It's just bad for you."

"It shows less that way. Nosy neighbors."

Andrew began to whistle a slightly off-key tune.

Greg shifted his suitcase to the other hand.

He said quietly, "I don't have much money, Greg, not after buying this house. And now I won't have Kate's salary to supplement mine. I need to fix that car up and sell it for what I can get for it." Andrew shook his hair away from his eyes. He had told Greg that to pacify him, but he was well aware he had deeper, less conscious reasons for having them haul the car over, especially as smashed as the frame had been.

"Find another way to make money or I'll loan you some, give you some. Bringing that car back here is a damn morbid thing to do. In fact," he leaned both hands against the doorframe like Samson testing his strength, "I don't know why you're staying here, Andrew. There's no reason. In among a bunch of strangers. Your family is gone. None of us knows why you buried them here!"

That's it. The thing that Greg should least have said and most wanted to say was out. Andrew was silent for a moment. To Margaret he could say he didn't know, but for Greg there would have to be a reason.

"Greg," he said simply, "if I had taken them home, buried them in Georgia, gone back on my word to the school system here, I would have made their death worth nothing at all." It was true; it was the way he felt, but it wasn't enough.

However, it seemed to be enough for Greg, who nodded, a look of relief on his face, and then looked away. "Well, I've *got* to get back to Virginia, little brother, so I'd better get on the road."

"I'm glad you stayed later than the rest," Andrew said and came over to give Greg's hand a quick, firm shake. He clapped him on the shoulders. "I needed to have someone around, you know?"

Greg looked at him with concern, his large pale face

unusually intent. "You did better than this when Mom and Dad died. In fact, I often thought you seemed to get over them—" He broke off his sentence and looked away. Then he said quietly, "Don't say anything. That was out of line, I know." He paused for a moment, "Are you sure you'll be—"

"I'll be fine," Andrew said, averting his gaze in a brief flicker, and then looking Greg in the eyes. Even though he loved his brother, he was looking forward to a bit of peace, an end to the family probing. He had grieved. He had been as close to his parents as Greg or Margaret. What did Greg know about it anyway? Andrew suddenly wanted his brother gone so much that it was all he could do to keep from leaving the room. All of you grieved, he reminded himself. You don't have any more right to measure his grief than he had to measure yours. It was the echo of that grief, the vibrating waves which moved between them, that made it so hard for him to be with his family.

And there's another reason you want him gone, isn't there, Andy? His thoughts mocked him. You haven't seen the Indian since the funeral. And you locked up the cellar. He shook his head impatiently.

Greg stared at him for a moment, a worried look on his face. At last he said, "All right, then. You get rid of that car, hear! It'll do you no good to have it around."

"Right," said Andrew. He walked with Greg to the driveway. But he had no intention of selling the car. An odd shiver ran across the back of his neck. He felt something close to excitement.

Greg closed his door and started the engine. He nodded at Andrew as though he couldn't quite think of anything else to say. Then he backed noisily out of the gravel driveway and waved. He drove away in a cloud of dust.

Andrew walked quickly around to the side of the house. He stared for a moment at the smashed green Volvo which rested in the center of his yard. Then he walked over and very deliberately opened the door to the driver's side. He sat down in the seat and his fingers clutched the steering wheel.

He stared unseeingly before him, as his hands tightened around the uneven handgrips. The lumpy plastic pressed into his palms harder and harder until the numbness began to spread up his arms and into his chest. He welcomed its coming, a slow movement like the rising of lakewater. Raising his head, Andrew closed his eyes and began to hum tunelessly.

CHAPTER 4

Andrew lay in his bed, restless, the muscles in his back so tight that no position seemed comfortable. Sleep wouldn't come. When Greg had been still in the house, Andrew had slept as though drugged; but now the loneliness came seeping in. And with it the realization of the extent of his loss, a realization which brought pain when it didn't bring numbness. It seemed to him that he could believe their deaths, but he could not rid himself of the expectation that when he turned around Kate would be facing him, her body curled in sleep, her auburn hair spread out across the pillow, that his children would still be padding down the hall saying sleepily, "I don't want to stay in my room. There's a monster in the closet. It has hair with eyes." And even though he knew they were gone, like a reflex not yet in check, he thought of things to say to them, remembered the ways they moved, the shapes of their heads, their laughter, and he still had the need and the expectation for those things, those familiar expressions of who his family had been.

He even missed that damn fur rug of a dog, and he had always hated that dog. He'd wanted to get the boys a proper dog, a husky or a malamute. They had picked up a cringing stray that had been abandoned on the streets and that snapped as often as it fawned, though it never actually hurt anyone. "It has arthritis," they used to say in solemn voices as they passed their hands over the top of the dog's back so that it hardly stirred a hair.

He closed his eyes. The room floated around him. A sound came from below. It drifted up the stairs like the ghost of a crazed laugh. Then a ripple of notes in dissonance, fingers run across the keys of an out-of-tune piano.

Andrew slowed his breathing until it sounded shallow and even. The ripple of keys came once again, and with them a quick frisson of anger. He hadn't seen the Indian in days, but who else could it be down in the lower room, keeping him awake? And it only made him angrier to think that there was not a piano in the house and therefore nothing for the old man to play.

Rising lightly from the bed, shivering as he felt the covers slip from him, he stood for a moment listening. A louder flurry of notes sounded like the bounce of a cat upon the keys. Andrew pulled on his shorts and walked quietly down the carpeted stairs. The music grew louder but no less dissonant, as he came nearer, until at last he stood in the living room. In the right-hand corner, just beside the boarded up fireplace, was a white baby grand piano. Just this afternoon in that area had stood a curio cabinet and a planter. In fact, Andrew had dusted the cabinet. As he watched, the piano faded, then slowly wavered into the more familiar cabinet, then piano again, then cabinet. The piano, he noted, was painted with cheap latex, and the painter had not been a very good one, because there were thick globs of hardened paint on the sides, dripping down like hot candle wax. The room was quiet. Turning to go, he heard one flat bass note bounce, yet when he looked around the curio cabinet, and the large begonia-filled planter at its side confronted him.

Like he had so many times before, he began to wonder if he was going crazy. I saw that Indian before Kate and the boys died, he told himself. Seeing the ghosts can't have anything to do with their death. But what about this? Maybe I'm just building some sort of pattern that reinforces what I have seen, some illusion brought on by grief. Pattern. He laughed bitterly. What sort of pattern do you think you've built with a mad old Cherokee and a badly painted piano?

Still, he had been under a lot of strain, what with finding a new job, moving to a new area, regaining his old confidence in his teaching. Maybe he was easier to crack than he thought.

The room was quiet and still as he left it. He climbed the stairs as though he were carrying a heavy load on his back. When he was in bed once more, covers up and tucked in around his shoulders, he heard the music again, a very out-of-tune rendition of the first movement of Beethoven's Fifth Symphony, but without the final note. The sound belled in the air as though it had been softly pedalled. Andrew longed to go down and play the resolving chord; this time he couldn't seem to move, and, in spite of his efforts to stay awake, he still heard the muted horn-like call when his eyes closed, until finally the music faded like a summons to sleep.

In the morning he woke feeling as though he had slept with a hot wind blowing around him. His throat was parched, and his tongue was dry. In the kitchen he drank some water and put the kettle on for tea. It was at that point he remembered his dream, and only then because he found himself whistling, under his breath, the theme to Beethoven's Fifth.

For some reason he felt much more cheerful this morning. It even seemed possible to him that what he'd seen the night before had been no more than a dream. Ghostly pianos. It would take more than an out-of-tune piano to scare him off the place.

Andrew pulled up a chair at the table, waiting for Kate to come down so that he could tell her, and he leaned his elbows on the table before it occurred to him that she would not be coming. This was one tale he would not be telling her.

Staring at the plastic tablecloth on the table, his fingers plucking at the one burned hole in the center as though they were picking at a scab, he set his teeth against the emptiness, which he had forgotten for a moment. Then he shook his head firmly. He had to do something to keep himself busy, otherwise he'd never be able to teach tomorrow. Staying alone around such a large house was bound to give him the willies. He'd go into town and do some grocery shopping, maybe stop at the bank and arrange a checking account. It would do him good to see some people.

After a shower and a shave, Andrew put on some neatly pressed navy cotton slacks and a white V-necked shirt. As he drove into town, the curves in the road slid by under the tires, and he concentrated on that sensation, trying to let himself live in the moment, because moments like these created tiny islands of peace.

When he pulled into the parking lot in front of the small brick bank, he saw a series of long tables and a cluster of neatly dressed women behind them. Several young children were standing around in front of the tables trying to finger pieces of baked goods or digging change out of tight jean pockets. One of the women behind the table was Jess McSpadden.

She waved, and then said hello in a low, pleasant voice when he walked her way.

"What are you selling?" he asked her, feeling like a miner coming out of a dark tunnel.

"Baked goods for the community center," she said, her eyes kind. "Would you like to buy some?"

He started to say no, and then he realized that though the last thing he wanted was something sweet, he could at least contribute to the community center. Reaching into his pocket, he pulled out a five-dollar bill and said, "Make some kid happy."

"Sick, more like," she smiled. "I think I'll divide your gift out a little. Is that all right?"

Andrew nodded and felt his eyes prickle. He blinked until the sensation disappeared. Looking at the cluster of kids who had noticed the whole transaction and were rapidly squirming toward his end of the table, he turned on his heel abruptly and decided to forego the bank account for today. He didn't think he could bear to walk past them.

Instead he decided that he would do some research on the Praeter place. He turned and called, "Jess, does Greenback have a library?"

"Yes." She waved. "Right around the corner and up the stairs."

Climbing the narrow wooden stairs to the top floor, he was

surprised to find the library larger than he expected. There were neatly labeled shelves, and he could smell the old books.

The librarian, an attractive woman in her thirties, came out from behind the desk. "You must be Andrew Jackson," she said with a smile and a firm handshake. He glanced down and saw the wedding band on her hand. Her smile faded slightly, but she said, "The new history teacher."

"Yes, I am," he said, sorry for his involuntary, flirtatious glance, a reflex from happier days. "But how did you know—"

"This is a town of five hundred, Mr. Jackson." She paused. "Appropriate, don't you think?"

"Pardon me?"

"Andrew Jackson."

"Right," he said, giving her his first genuine smile since the funeral.

"Well, what can I help you with Mr. Jackson?" Her green eyes twinkled at him. "I imagine you've come to see what sort of books are available for your students."

"Not today, although it's good to see that you've got a reasonable library."

"Why thank you," she smiled. "The library supports the school here, you know. But the books will be for your students primarily. For your purposes you'll find it more useful to go to the Loudon County library."

"I don't suppose," he tried to keep his tone of voice from sounding abrupt though he didn't quite succeed, "you have any information on Joseph Praeter or on the house which used to belong to the Praeters?"

She frowned briefly, a light wrinkle creased her forehead, and then she shook her head slowly. "No, as I said, you'll find more adult historical information at the Loudon library. I can order materials for you, if you like, but I don't think that sort of thing is available on loan. I believe you'll have to go over there. Oh, and you could check the county courthouse while you're there, too, for former owners and that kind of thing. Sorry I couldn't be of more help."

She smiled at him again.

"No problem. Thank you for your time."

She nodded pleasantly to him and then sat down again at her desk. He could feel her eyes on him as he walked back down the steps, and he wondered what sort of expression they held: surprise, puzzlement? Something had flickered in them when he'd asked for information on Praeter, but perhaps it had been no more than surprise that he'd been asking for that sort of thing just a few days after his wife's death. Or had she known? Well, he had no time to wonder about what other people were thinking; he was probably just reacting like a raw nerve anyway. Andrew shrugged and put it out of his mind.

When he got to the bottom of the stairs, he reached toward the doorknob, and it receded from his grasp. The door opened to the outside, and he found himself facing Larry Bryge. Larry's eyes widened for a moment, and then he gave Andrew a shrewd grin.

The librarian called down the stairs. "Oh, Mr. Jackson, you might try talking to Dorothy McKinney. The McKinneys used to live in the house, and she's a big history buff. Besides, I think she's a Praeter descendant."

"Thank you," he called without looking back up the stairs. Larry's grin widened. Andrew looked at him for a moment, and then walked past him without comment.

As he opened the exterior door, he heard the librarian say, "Yes, Larry, we've got the books you ordered on voodoo and the loa, but they really look like a load of junk to me."

"You're speaking to the junk man," said the laconic young voice, and then the door closed on whatever else he had to say.

Andrew got into his car and waved at Jess McSpadden as he backed up. She waved back and then handed a boy with an armload of books her last cupcake. Andrew pulled away, staring straight into Larry Bryge's cupcake smeared face. Though he waved, the boy merely looked at him. Now why was Larry beginning to get on his nerves?

As the car rolled smoothly down the first straight country road he'd seen since he arrived, he let his thoughts drift, feeling the haze that had been with him for several days temporarily lift. The atmosphere of the house had settled down around him like perfumed silk, and it wasn't until he was away from it and into the fresh summer air that he realized he'd been inside day and night for almost a week. Relieved to be out again and feeling almost cheerful, Andrew rolled down the window and let the wind whip his hair. He whistled the theme from Beethoven's Fifth all the way to Loudon.

Loudon was a town not much larger than Greenback, though it did have three or four gas stations to Greenback's two, and a main street with a few department stores, not to mention a store entitled Bogus Auto Parts. Andrew found the courthouse on the main street with no trouble at all. As he walked up the steps he saw a sign that said Library and pointed to the side entrance. Since he knew he'd find some information about the house with the county records, he decided to visit the library last.

His feet thumped along the worn wooden boards of the courthouse porch and down the long wooden hall until he came to a door with a sign marked County Deeds and Records. Although the clerk was talking on the phone and gesturing with a stub of a pencil to illustrate his point, he stopped for a moment, asked Andrew what he wanted, and told him he'd be with him in a moment. When he got off the phone, he disappeared back into another room and returned with a thick, dusty book, bound with metal pins in the corners, and put it down in front of Andrew.

"You can look at it over there," he pointed with a tilt of his head to a table along the wall with a couple of hardback chairs at either end.

Andrew saw at a glance, once he found the listing for the house, that the place had been sold several times. In fact, he realized, tracing down the listings which ran for a couple of large pages, it had not been kept by any owner for more than five years, and that included Joseph Praeter. Praeter's son had sold out quickly a couple of years after Praeter's death.

The house had been built in 1798 and had been assessed on a regular basis since that time. He smiled to see the queer old figures. Looking over the names again, Andrew's eyes widened. The house had once belonged to an Indian named John Broken Echo by a Cherokee land grant, rescinded shortly after Broken Echo's death. He stopped for a moment.

Did this account for the Indian? A leftover from the 1800's? There was a short period of time, say about ten years, Andrew knew, in the early 1800's, when the Cherokees received land grants in Tennessee. Not long before the Trail of Tears, something he had little cause to feel pride in his ancestor for. But it must have been unusual, no, one would think well nigh impossible, for a Cherokee to receive such a large grant of land. The Praeter land had been a twenty-five acre parcel then, though the property had been sold off over the years, until what was left of the original land amounted to a little over five acres. At any rate, how had Broken Echo gotten such a substantial land grant so far from the Smoky Mountains? Some sort of mystery there, Andrew frowned.

"What's the matter, sir?" came a rusty voice from the counter.

Andrew looked up, his expression abstracted. "I've just been looking up the records to a piece of property I bought, and there are a few things which puzzle me."

"Why don't you try me? I've been around here quite a few years."

Looking up, Andrew realized that the clerk who waited on him was gone, and an older man, thin and white-headed, had replaced him. Andrew glanced at his watch and saw that more than an hour had passed.

"I've moved into the Old Praeter Place, or so everybody calls it, over on the lake between Greenback and Lenoir City."

The man's eyes flickered.

"Do you happen to know anything about the property?" Andrew asked nervously.

"What would you like to know?"

"Well, for one thing, it says in the records that the property was, at one time, given as a part of the Cherokee land grant, back in the early 1800's. I wondered if you knew—I'm a history teacher, you see—" Andrew hesitated.

The man nodded as though to encourage him.

"Well, I wondered why such a large piece of prime riverfront, what would have been riverfront then, got to be part of a land grant. Especially twenty-five acres."

"Seems to me like I remember once somebody saying," the man leaned on the counter and looked at Andrew with interest, "that a Cherokee married one of Praeter's daughters after the old man took crazy and couldn't do much with her. It angered her brothers to death, but they wanted to see her taken care of, so they had something to do with that grant by selling the land to the state with some sort of provision. There's lots of stories about that place, you know. It's pretty well known around Loudon County."

"What do you mean?"

"Well, it sure must have been a scandal at the time, what

with Praeter running slaves, getting scalped by a Cherokee, and then his daughter marrying the son of the one that scalped him. There aren't so many good stories around about a quiet area of the country like this, though you might be surprised by some of the history we have even so."

The old man straightened up, and smiled, tugging at a thick moustache which hung over his lip like a cavalry captain's epaulet. He looked as though he would tell Andrew more, but the door swung open and in walked a man in an immaculate black pinstripe business suit.

"What say, Judge," he said, and looked as though he'd completely forgotten Andrew. The judge approached the counter, and Andrew heard the two of them conferring quietly.

Andrew stood indecisively for a moment and then shrugged his shoulders. He'd go around to the library and then maybe come back to see the clerk. It sounded as though he knew a good bit about the house, and Andrew would like to ask him some more questions.

Something straight out of one of those old Southern romance novels, he thought as he made his way around to the side of the courthouse. He could imagine the whole thing as a series of newspaper headlines, an activity he sometimes did with his history students. *Colonial Scalped by Band of Cherokees, Driven Mad*. And then, *Family Chains a Scalped Praeter in Basement*, or perhaps, *Daughter Marries Broken Echo, Family Protests*. They still must have been glad to leave the house behind them, even if they gave it over as a land grant to a man they didn't approve of. It might have been that guilt colored their decision, guilt at the idea of living where they'd kept their father like an animal. But the daughter's motivations were a mystery to Andrew.

Kate would have loved this sort of thing. Her real love of history had been part of what had drawn her to being a realtor, the opportunity to pore over old deeds and sell historical properties. Though they'd bought a condo in Marietta, he'd always known what she really wanted was an old house with a history. She'd wanted the boys to grow up with some sense of roots. After losing his family, he knew that roots were merely an illusion. Still, he could pursue an illusion with the best of them.

He reached the entrance to the library, a glass door with

the hours painted on it and a closed sign hanging on the inside where it could be clearly seen through the glass. Andrew looked at the hours. Closed on Friday at one. He had missed it by about an hour. If he'd known that, he'd have gone here first, he thought in disgust. But it figured that such a small town would not keep the sort of hours the Atlanta libraries did. When he reentered the records office, the small, black-haired man he'd seen the first time was back behind the counter, and there was no sign of the old clerk.

"Can I help you?"

"What happened to the old guy who was here for a while?"

"Oh, you must mean my father. He comes in while I go to lunch, likes to think he's not retired yet." The man gave a small, nervous smile.

"I was just talking to him, and there were some things I'd like to ask him."

"Well, you'll have to catch him another time. He's gone up to Knoxville with Judge Olson. Don't guess he'll be back before dark."

Andrew frowned.

"You can find him here every Friday at lunchtime though." Andrew lifted a questioning eyebrow. "Fridays I don't have as much help," the man explained. "Is there something I can answer maybe?"

"He was telling me a story about the Old Praeter House."

The clerk laughed. "Well, he's the one for that then. I never did pay much attention to the tales he collects. Why don't you come back by next week?"

"Maybe I will," said Andrew, but he knew he'd be teaching school by then. Still he could probably call the old guy. "What's your father's name? I might give him a call."

"Oh, he doesn't have a phone. The old man doesn't believe in them."

"Well then, just his name. I'll try to catch him here."

"Everybody just calls him Turkey Haines."

Andrew smiled. "Thanks a lot then, Mr. Haines. Is that your name too?"

"Right, Johnny Haines."

Andrew shook the hand the clerk extended over the counter and then left, still thinking about what he'd learned. When he settled into the front seat of his car, a peace settled in around him as well, like a faint trace of sunshine.

It wasn't until the tires crunched the gravel driveway and came to a halt that Andrew realized he had forgotten to go shopping. He decided that he'd have dinner and then go back for groceries, but as he came around the porch he saw a neat row of plastic containers and casserole dishes lined up across his front porch. Each of them had a masking tape label on the front with a name on it. Obviously the ladies of the neighborhood had come calling and had left him some food to remember them by.

One of them, he noticed, had a note sticking out from it. He bent down and unfolded it slowly, and looking at the bold handwriting he knew it was Jess McSpadden before he saw the sweeping "JS" at the bottom of the page.

Mr. Jackson,

I brought these by for several of the women in town who wanted to make sure you weren't starving. We were all sure you probably weren't in the mood for cooking. Hope you enjoy them. If you give me a call when they're empty, I can return them for you with your thanks.

Nice of her, he thought as he folded the note. Wonder if she'd realized that he'd been driving out of town and wouldn't be home for a while. Probably so, she didn't miss much, and she seemed to be making good her promise that he'd be left alone until he was ready. He smiled wryly. Whatever ready meant.

The look of those neatly stacked containers gave him a warm feeling. They certainly knew how to make somebody welcome around Greenback, and to leave them to heal in peace.

Picking up several of the containers and stacking them double under one arm, he carried them into the kitchen. And it wasn't until he'd set them down that he realized he heard a sound like the piping of a wooden flute coming from the cellar, and he looked across the kitchen to the open door, a door which beckoned like a very clean-cut sort of shadow, and drew him without a murmur into its depths.

Drifting about in white cotton dresses like so many shadows of grace were dark black figures which swirled and danced, turned and danced, and their faces were men's and women's, but pulled tight like formal masks. Their bodies flowed like water around a small, open-sided platform with a roof on which twined flowers, and hung skin-covered long drums. He found himself in the circle of dancers, panting heavily, and raising his feet again and again.

They flowed like water and he moved like stone. The drums beat heavily, insistently. One, two, three, pause, one, two, three, pause, and after what seemed a very long time, when that sound had entered his blood like the rhythm of the heart, there came a series of rapid, syncopated drum notes which he recognized vaguely as those he had tried to sound with his broken broom and his miserable metal pail.

As they danced, they scuffed over a series of markings on the floor, while the lamps of flame flickered and sailed shadows across faces shiny with sweat. From somewhere across the room came a deep laugh and the sound of a guttural "huh." Women in the corner combed the ringlets of a bright blue ram.

Bodies slipped in around the circle and stood watching the dance, some of them no more than eyes to him as they swayed and swayed. The movement with which these figures joined the dance seemed to him a part of the rhythm of it. Someone ahead of him stumbled forward, precariously erect on one leg, and he grabbed her by reflex, supporting her against the push of the crowd. Another dancer across the circle went down as though felled. A great shout went up, "Legba!" and he felt a hand drawing him out of the circle, a hand he struggled against, but which held him like iron. He found himself stumbling up the steps and then coming out into the light like a man out of a cave.

It was, he saw blinking, the old Indian who had half dragged him up the stairs and was now closing the door behind him without saying a word.

"Why?" Andrew asked, but the Indian shook his head without answering.

Feeling as though he had come out of some depths like a diver, that slow, subtle slide of water past skin like the caress of trailing fingertips, Andrew merely looked at the other, until at last he said as though remembering, "You're John Broken Echo."

The other looked at him without surprise. The simple yes, his first word from the old man, seemed commonplace and strangely flat.

But even as Broken Echo replied, Andrew began to wonder. The man he had seen in the bedroom had been old, his back bent with age. This man, still not young, stood with an unbent back, though the face was the same.

The Indian turned around and walked away from Andrew without looking back, until Andrew called after him.

"Wait, wait, I have so many—Why are you here?"

The other stopped, but did not turn, and said, "Ask, yourself rather; why are you here?"

Andrew felt it then without knowing why, the other's great leashed anger. He cleared his throat, but could think of no response.

After a moment, without turning around, Broken Echo said slowly, "You should leave now. The cellar has more than you can carry, you who are not the horse of a loa. Soon the moon will change. I have given you a truce because of your family, but only until the moon is new."

CHAPTER 5

Andrew turned his hand over, still feeling the tingle on the palm where Broken Echo had touched him. *Touched me,* he marvelled as he ignored the phone which continued to ring with all the persistence of a toothache. Finally he walked over and picked it up. "Hello," he said.

"Andrew, this is Robert Boyles. I just wanted to call to let you know that you don't have to come to school tomorrow. In fact, you can take a week off. I insist upon it."

"I think," Andrew said, and then stopped. "I think I'd like to come to school tomorrow. I'd like to be able to give myself something to do."

"I want you to take some more time, Andrew. I know you think you'd be better off with a classroom full of teenagers to occupy your mind; but I'm sure that, like all of us, you need some time after a death, particularly when you've lost your whole family." He cleared his throat.

"I would really like to come tomorrow," he spoke carefully.

There was a silence on the other end of the line. At last the principal sighed and said, "I tell you what. Why don't you take tomorrow off? It's Friday anyway. It makes little sense to come in at the end of the week. Then I'll check with you again over the weekend and see how you're feeling, say on Sunday. And if you've still got a mind to come in on Monday then, I won't say any more. I guess you know yourself best."

"But I'd really—"

"Good," the principal said heartily, "then it's settled. I'll talk to you Sunday."

He put the phone down slowly. The house seemed close and dark around him. Even though it was daylight and the lights were on, he felt suddenly that he was in a closet, and that feeling made him angry. He walked around the house with determination, looking for Broken Echo, but, though he searched each room, he could not find the Indian. Finally, Andrew, with that same formless anger inside, left the house. He hesitated for a moment, thinking of sitting in the Volvo. It had become a ritual for him, and seemed almost calming. But he was too full of anger for that. Instead he walked across the driveway to the road.

He must have gone four or five miles before he realized that he had begun to run. He slowed his pace down to a jog, and only then did the exertion catch up with him. The slow huh of breath with each movement of his legs told him he had pushed himself too far, but he continued anyway.

By the time the road curved closer to the lake, it was dusk. He came to a stop at a broken down boatdock with a few small fishing boats and a couple of metal canoes tied out along the dock like so many tincans at the end of a dog's tail. Following the sound of his feet on the rattling planks, he walked up to the small half door of the dock office.

"How much is a canoe?"

The man behind the door, an old, grizzled fellow with a fishing hat so worn Andrew could scarcely tell that it had once been orange, tilted back his chair. "To rent or to buy?" came the low, practical voice.

"To rent."

"Seven dollars an hour or twenty dollars a day."

"An hour." Andrew placed seven dollars on the top of the half door and the old man stuffed the money into his front pocket. Then, pulling a bunch of keys from his pocket, he opened the door and padded along the dock in his bare feet. Andrew followed him.

When the lock which secured the chained canoe squeaked

open, the fellow didn't bother to unchain the canoe. He simply nodded and slouched back toward the office. Andrew pulled the rusty chain through the ring, left the padlock sitting on the dock, and dropped the chain into the front of the canoe. Glancing into the canoe he checked the paddles and the orange seat cushion, and stepped into the middle seat, his feet remembering the old balancing act.

He moved out of the dock area and into the cove in a few swift strokes. Then he flicked on the small clamped light at the front of the canoe.

To the rise and fall of the paddle, the dipping in the water and the slow mesmerizing glide, Andrew began to go over things in his mind. Everything's adrift, he thought, staring at the water. He had bought this house which Kate had set her heart on, a house she had not spent one night in.

And suddenly it seemed, with the buying of the house, that not one element of his life remained the same. It had all come into question.

The dark settled in around him, that twilight time when nothing could go wrong and the world was at peace, when children ran through fields and baseballs sailed just one more time across the plate, a safe time when he could allow himself to question.

Ghosts with solid hands. *Ghosts*, he thought incredulously and dipped the paddle with a long stroke that sent the canoe several feet across the water and into the current. And God knew what danced in the basement. Threats, new moons, Cherokee warriors, and the old man had said something about loa. Hadn't Larry been checking out a book about loa? What had the old man meant by "he who was not the horse of a loa." Was Larry a "horse"? The cellar was his wasn't it? Not the boy's. What the bloody hell was happening here? About time he asked that, wasn't it? he thought angrily.

With the anger he pushed back a sort of guilt, a sense that what he had decided to do was wrong. He had been using his fascination with the house to ward off sorrow, to keep from thinking about what he would do with his life. And, if that were so, then perhaps, he thought unwillingly, it worked the other way as well. He had been dwelling on the death of his family in a way almost theatrical, to ward off the fascination of the house, and to make their deaths unreal, to pretend that tomorrow they would come back to him and life would go on as they'd planned. What use did it do to be rational, he wondered bitterly. You lived your life in what you thought was a reasonable manner, and it only took one event to show you the illusion which made something solid out of shadows.

Still, it didn't matter, did it? he thought, the anger crystal-lizing as he paddled first on one side of the canoe and then the other, aiding a swift-moving current. He would stay. He'd buried his family here, and now, by damn, he wasn't leaving. No one, not even a Cherokee remnant, would drive him out of that house. And he wouldn't admit, even to himself, the extent to which he had become mesmerized by what lay in the basement, drawn to quick addiction. He had a need not to question, not to ask too much about what he could neither explain nor walk away from.

In that moment he relaxed and let the current take him where it would.

By the time he met the McSpaddens, quietly moving back toward their cove in their motored pontoon, Andrew realized that, like a homing pigeon, he had been making his way back toward his own area of the lake. From the center of silence he had reached, he waved at them as though they were old friends. They waved back, softly hailing him across the water. Andrew turned the canoe their way and came up alongside, holding lightly onto the outer bar of their pontoon. Giving each other a quick smile, they rode that way, and then, without saying a word, Jess's husband offered Andrew a hand up. Andrew took it, then hooked the chain of his canoe over the bar in a loose knot. He nodded to the two of them, and sat down on one of the cushioned rails.

They rode quietly for a few moments. Then Jess said, "This is James, my husband. James, this is Andrew." The two men shook hands, bending slightly across the expanse between one side of the pontoon and the other. She rested her hand on her husband's knee. James pulled a pipe and a pouch from his front pocket and tamped the tobacco.

"I see you're enjoying the lake," he said, after puffing his pipe alight.

"It's a nice area of the country." Andrew put a hand back to rub his shoulder, suddenly feeling, for the first time, the strain of muscles he hadn't used in that way for some time.

Probably eight or nine years since I've canoed, he thought wonderingly. His legs began to tremble. He set his feet squarely on the floor, and felt the muscles quiver.

Looking out across the lake, he watched the path of the light at the front of the slowly moving craft, and then the shimmer of the water which spread out behind them. Shortly he realized they were even with his house.

"Thanks for the lift," he said, stepping off to the sidebar of the pontoon.

"Why don't you come over for supper?" the two of them asked almost simultaneously.

"You can canoe back later," added James, "or we'll give you a ride."

"Take a raincheck," Andrew said, watching the shape of the two of them silhouetted against the lighter color of the cushioned rail. It brought back memories. Kate and he had been going to get a pontoon. He could see the slow pursing of her lips as she had said the word, pontoon. And he could hear the boys' gleeful echo, like a small boys' choir, pon-*toon*.

"Thank you," he added gruffly. Then he lowered himself into the canoe, casting off toward shore with a quick, hard thrust to pull himself out of the current. He found, as he went, that the current was stronger than he had thought. He had to really move to get himself to shore without drifting past the rounded tip of land that was his.

By the time he had gotten to shore, the pontoon was docking across the lake, and all he could see was the rise and fall of their large boat light. The switching off of that light seemed to him like a quiet good night. After beaching the canoe and promising himself he'd return it in the morning, he stood looking up at the moon for a few moments. The shape of it, a little over three quarters and very nearly full, seemed to wink at him. Go ahead, Broken Echo, he thought. Take me on. Andrew felt a surge of combativeness.

He waited for something, a sign, the Indian himself, he didn't know. When at last it seemed evident nothing was going to happen, Andrew walked slowly up to the dark, waiting house.

When he rose in the morning, padding down the stairs and into the kitchen, the house felt like an empty envelope, as if his decision to stay had leashed something. There was no sound that was not his sound in the house, no stirring in the back rooms as though something drifted forever out of sight. Though the cellar door stood open again, despite the fact he'd left it closed, nothing lured him down the steps. And if he had gone, the promise of the open door would have been an empty one.

His day lay sunny and dreamless before him, and Andrew filled it with hard work. Kate had planned a flower bed in the backyard. He prepared the soil, as though the crumbling earth had no connection with the pick of his hands or the movement of his arms.

Andrew circled the bed with stones from the back yard, and then heaped the remainder onto a rickety wheelbarrow he found beside the shed in the backyard. Then he carried them out to the shore. It took him the rest of the day to finish, section by section, the shoring at the edge of the water. Only when he finished, did he allow himself to carry the marble pieces around back and dump them in a series of large, battered trash cans. This was one job, he told himself fiercely, that he didn't have to do now that Kate and the boys would not be there to be disturbed by tombstones, but he refused to leave them. They reminded him of too much. He had a grim satisfaction in finishing this task, even though he knew the garbage men would not be around to pick up the trash until the following Tuesday. That is, if they didn't curse him under their breath and leave it for a week or two.

Saturday, he thought, tramping into the house to fix himself a sandwich, and feeling as though Monday would be slow to come. Temporarily he felt comfortable with the house for the first time, as if his run and his canoe ride had had an unlooked-for effect. Now that he felt at home with the house, he began to long for the routine of school. Perhaps by Monday he would wish he had taken the principal up on his offer, but he didn't think so. He had to structure some of his time and ward off enough grief to survive. He was the last one.

He opened a can of tuna fish and dumped it into a plastic bowl. No, when Monday came he would be out the door at least a half an hour earlier than he needed to be, and eager to begin his first day with his students. He would make a pact with himself. While he was at school he would think of his family as alive. The thought of a new town, a new school, and students who were bound to be different from those he found in a suburban area intrigued him. It occurred to him that the area between Knoxville and Greenback had a lot of history in it, and that he just might have the bait he needed to hook his students before they realized he had. Knoxville had been the center of a good deal of conflict during the Civil War. He thought about it as he munched his sandwich and decided to make another visit to the Loudon library. If it's open, he reminded himself.

As he drove into Loudon, he thought about the way things had been before when he'd taught. Kate had always been interested in the beginnings of things, his new classes. She had served as his sounding board for ideas until he found himself something that had all the punch of the opening paragraph in a good novel. He would miss that interplay with her, her talk about what it might take to convince a new client, and his about ways to hook his students. They had had something special, the two of them, a sense of partnership. And he wondered if he would be as good a teacher without her. How quickly would he burn out now? Andrew had always prided himself on the fact that he'd kept his excitement for teaching, but he'd never really realized how much of that came from Kate's support. *She was the core of me.*

He had difficulty putting that thought behind him when he pulled up to the courthouse. His old zest was gone, though he did feel faintly pleased when he found two books of local history just as the clock struck five and the librarian announced closing time. After she stamped them for him, she closed the covers and leaned on the books, as she said, "Now, Mr. Jackson, I want you to keep in mind the due date on these books."

He agreed, smiling in spite of himself, at the careful nodding of her head. Even a smile seemed, these days, like a moment of safety.

"Too many teachers think they can keep our books forever, and I want you to know you'll get a fine the same's all the rest." She handed them to him with all the firmness of a primary grade teacher handing a student his first pencil.

"I'll bring them back on time," he said, still smiling. She

watched him go down the stairs, and, as he opened the door, he heard her disbelieving sigh, the sigh of all those who became, for the moment, the guardians of order and deadlines.

The kindergarten teacher had laughed at Billy for days because he'd told her that he knew why she didn't have a "real job." She just couldn't get out of the parking lot in the mornings. "Do you think I live in the kindergarten room?" she had asked him. But Billy had gone through some convoluted logical chain to come at his knowledge, and he had shook her question off with a kind of abstract confusion, and returned to the original point. "I know why you don't have a real job," he'd said again and run away to find his friends to tell them his discovery. When had he realized that teachers had homes as well and that their lives weren't turned off as soon as the last student left the classroom?

When he reached the driveway to the house, he saw a dilapidated pickup truck parked squarely in the center of it. Leaning at its side was the old man from the dock.

"I'm sorry," he said to the man. "I forgot to get that canoe back to you last night." Andrew thought, I'm getting forgetful, foggy. He had felt that way since the funeral. Details, he concluded wearily, were continually escaping him.

The man grunted and shoved his hat back farther on his head. "You owe me twenty dollars," he said.

"Say," said Andrew, "how much would it cost to buy that canoe?"

"Fifty dollars cash."

"What do you say if I—"

"Have to pay for the night first." The old man chewed slowly on a wad of tobacco, and Andrew could barely make out his words.

"I'll tell you what. I'll pay you sixty and take the boat."

"Cash money."

"Cash money."

"You've got yourself a deal." The old man held out his hand, and Andrew solemnly counted the money into it, feeling happy to have gotten off with ten dollars. However, from the look on the old man's face, he probably could have talked him down to fifty total, Andrew judged. Still, not bad for a metal canoe that would have cost him, even used, a hundred in Atlanta.

The man shoved the money into his pocket. "Much obliged," was all he said as he turned away. He got into his pickup and backed out quickly. Andrew watched him go. And maybe forty, he thought. He'd always heard country folks were bargainers and now he believed it. He frowned. If Kate and the boys had still been alive, they would have bought a pontoon by now. The canoe seemed immeasurably lonelier.

Andrew walked into the house just in time to catch the phone ringing. He picked it up, recognizing at once Jess McSpadden's characteristic tones.

"Why don't you come over for supper tonight, and take us up on that raincheck?" she asked, and he realized that she must have taken the more-or-less silent ride last night as a sign he felt ready for company.

He heard himself answering yes, though the moment before she called he'd have sworn he wanted nothing more than to spend the evening quietly in front of the fire, perhaps prepare a bit for class. I've got the rest of the weekend for that, he told himself, and arranged to be at their house by six-thirty.

The car crunched down the long gravel lane past a small house, a trailer, and a larger place with a closed in porch on the left, and then came to a dead end at the back of the brown house he'd so often stared at across the lake. Three expensive looking beige cars were parked in the driveway. Just in front of them on the concrete lounged a large, solid black tomcat which stared at him with sleepy, yellow eyes.

Andrew walked past the cat and looked for a moment at the curved patio and the U-shaped front of the house. There were two doors in front, one a kitchen door and the other one a formal front door. He knocked on the door at the kitchen. He heard the swish of water, and then the silence which came after it shut off. In a moment, Jess opened the door.

"Come in," she said with a smile.

The kitchen was sunny and open with a round, Formica table through the center of which ran a pole connected to the ceiling and the floor. Andrew sat down on one of the wooden chairs which circled the table.

"Well." She laughed. "I must be getting hard of hearing or I'd have heard you drive up."

"Looks as if you were busy;" he pointed to the set of pots on the stove.

Jess laughed. "I know how you men like your food."

She looked at him intently. "Would you like a cup of coffee? James should be along any minute and then we can eat."

Jess poured him a cup of coffee to which he added cream. He turned the cup around in his hands for a moment as though unsure what to say. "Where is James?"

"You couldn't pull him off the lake before dusk. He's washing up down at the dock. Been fishing all day."

"I knew a man in Georgia," he said, and smiled, "who missed his daughter's graduation because he was out fishing."

"His wife must have given him a good one over that." Jess turned around to look at him and brushed her hair from her eyes.

"No. As a matter of fact, she just laughed. They had a real good understanding, those two. His daughter, though, that was another story."

She laughed, and said, "I bet."

Andrew leaned back in his chair and closed his eyes for a moment, feeling the steam from the coffee rise toward his face. I'll never see Andy and Billy graduate, he thought.

James opened the door and came into the kitchen closing it behind him. The screen door slammed shut like an echo.

Andrew examined him, surprised to see just how large-framed a man he really was. Weathered skin, lines around the eyes, but still quite young looking for a man who might just be in his seventies.

"How are you?" He nodded to Andrew and moved around to the other side of the table and sat down. Pouring himself a cup of coffee, he asked, "What's for dinner, honey? I'm hungry," he said, before she could answer. She smiled as though accustomed to what had obviously been a rhetorical question.

The dinner was more than Andrew normally ate: fluffy homemade biscuits, country ham, green beans and peas, topped off with a homemade apple cobbler. Eating was sprinkled with conversation like a slow spice: fishing lore, Greenback people, seasons on the lake. . . . As it continued,

Andrew began to relax. James finally pushed back his chair and stretched out his feet. He leaned back and looked Andrew in the eye. "Are you going to sell that house?"

Jess looked over at James and placed a hand on his arm. He smiled at her gently.

"What do you mean?" Andrew asked to gain time, the signals between the two of them reminding him of Kate and feeding his anger at the question.

James scratched his head. "Well, it's a mighty big place to be living in by yourself."

"I have no intention of selling the place." His tone, despite his attempt to keep it pleasant and firm, sounded harsh. The question had been a jolt to him, because he'd begun to feel comfortable in their presence, though he didn't know either of them very well.

Jess patted her husband's arm calmingly. "James didn't mean any harm," she said to Andrew. "I'd guess it'll be a while before he'll be thinking of that, James," she added softly.

James looked at her in surprise.

"That house has a lot of history in it."

Jess gave him a steady look.

"And my family's buried there."

"There's a lot of history around here period," she answered. It was plain from the look on her face that she would have liked to say more.

"Yes, I've been doing some research on that. I want to work with my history class some from that angle."

James leaned forward, a slight frown on his face. And with that they were off on a long discussion of the history of Greenback. It turned out that, before Jess had worked with the bank, she'd been a teacher during the Depression. She knew a fair amount about the history of the area. It wasn't until Andrew got up to leave that he realized James had become more and more silent. Andrew said good night to him, and then impulsively added, "You know, what would you think about taking me fishing some time?"

The older man's face brightened immediately. "Be glad to. Good to have you visit."

Jess walked Andrew to the car. "How are you doing?" she asked just as he opened the car door.

"Not too badly," he answered, staring out across the lawn toward the lake.

"James is right, you know." Her tone was abrupt. "You ought to think about selling that house."

"I won't sell," Andrew said, opening his car door with a jerk.

"You'll have to be a stubborn man, Andrew, to stick with that house." She laughed uneasily.

"What do you mean?" he asked, curious to see what she would say.

"Nobody's ever lived there for long. James, he's not from around here. He just asked you about selling because he's a practical man. But—" she hesitated, "it's an unsettling sort of a place."

"Do you believe in ghosts, Jess?"

She brushed her hand through her hair. "You've seen something?"

"Something. I'm not sure what."

"My sister lived there for a while, you know."

"Your sister?"

"Dorothy McKinney. She stayed longer than any of the others."

"Did you see," he asked, his tone carefully neutral, "anything?"

She shoved her hands in her apron pockets. "No, I didn't see anything. Oh, I heard a few noises: music, something rattling, that sort of thing, a couple of times when I was over to visit with her. But Dorothy, she said it was the ghost of an old Cherokee that made her leave."

"How?" he asked, wondering if Broken Echo intended the same for him.

"She woke up one morning, and found him in bed with her, snoring to beat the band." Jess laughed.

He climbed into the car, shutting the door firmly, and then leaning out the open window, he said, "I've passed that stage. I'm not too worried. Thanks for supper."

She cleared her throat. "I wouldn't go talking about it around town, though. There's not too many who are willing to say they believe in strangeness, you know." She stepped back from the car. "I'd board up that cellar, if I were you," she called after him as he backed the car up.

He stopped the car for a moment. "Oh no," he said, "I'm

going to make moonshine in that cellar." And laughed at the look of shock on her face.

"Listen," she said with a sudden nod of decision. "Don't joke about that house. Burying them there won't do any good."

"What do you mean by that, Jess?" His mouth came down tight after each word.

Her hand lingered at the top of the car door. He reached over as though to roll up the window.

"It won't bring them back, Andrew."

His anger was as swift as his reply. "I don't know what the hell you're talking about, Jess."

She stepped back, eyes thoughtful, without saying any more. The gravel spun out beneath his tires as he pulled away.

Andrew woke up listening. The house lay quiet around him. Yet for some reason he feared the quality of that silence more than any noise. He lay in a cold sweat, listening to the quick thumping of his heart. That was it, he thought. He'd been dreaming. And all of it came back with vividness then. He'd been dreaming of the time he and his father had been to a picnic down in Miami. He had gone to visit his father soon after his parents' divorce and found him a moody and sullen man. But finally, perhaps in desperation he thought now, his father had taken him to the picnic. Fake key lime pie, barbequed hog, fire baked onions, deviled eggs. He and his father had eaten silently, watching the chattering strangers around them. Then they'd leaned back for what had been billed as a Haitian dance. And Andrew, when he'd almost jumped awake, had been dreaming of that dance. Now why had—and then he knew. For the beat of the drums, the drums that played for those trumped up and artificial dancers, as fake as the dye in the key lime pie, had been pounding the rhythm he'd heard in the cellar. And with that memory, he stayed awake for a long while.

CHAPTER 6

Andrew wandered around his land until after dusk, sniffing the honeysuckle, and listening to the rasping buzz of the cicadas. The longer he walked, the less the thought of returning to the house appealed to him, even though he knew he ought to make an early night of it if he were going to be ready for school the next day. His first day in a new classroom, even if he did very little more than distribute textbooks and get acquainted, would be wearing. And to begin where he intended, with the history of those who settled Loudon County, would require some showmanship. He found, as he walked, that he had gone around his five acres, the parameters of his land. His land. The thought pleased him. A breeze ruffled his hair, as he stood looking out over the next hill where a wavering light like a candle shone through the window. In the dusk it looked as though the house, which he knew to be the Bryges', had the shape of one of the old log cabins. He squinted at it.

To the side of the Bryges' house he spotted a small and indistinct figure with its head bent to graze. After a moment he thought that it looked like a half-size white deer. Andrew stared at it uneasily. From overhead came the sound of wings beating the air. He looked up to catch a glimpse of birds, but the air had darkened so that he could not be sure. The hairs on Andrew's arms began to rise. He suddenly thought he had crossed some invisible boundary unawares and left himself open and unguarded. From off in the distance he heard a faint call. It sounded like a wolf.

The wind began to rise. It whipped the nearby lake with such force that the water moved like river rapids. On the surface of the lake he saw a large, dark boat which slipped quietly down the channel. He felt a sudden hatred and anger against the strangers in that boat.

He put his hand to his forehead and staggered. He fell sideways, landing against the rough bark of a tree. Someone grabbed Andrew by the hair from behind, jerking him backward. Whoever it was held him firmly by the hair. An arm snaked around and bound his arms. Andrew stepped on the other's feet and punched backward with his elbows, but to no avail. The stranger countered his moves as quickly as he made them.

There was the smell of something pungent. He heard a language he did not recognize. Other men came through the woods. He heard their voices and their bodies moving behind him. Four of them, he thought and pretended to relax for a moment. He stood quietly, trying to determine their positions.

One of the men began to chant.

> Anagali:sgi gigage:i iyu:sdi . . .
> U:ghvhada iyu:sdi . . .
> Dhiv:datsi iyu:sdi . . .
> Wahhya gigage:i iyu:sdi . . .

The words began to form like shadows on the walls of his mind:

> Like the Red Lightning . . .
> Like the Fog . . .
> Like the Panther . . .
> Like the Red Wolf . . .
> I make my appearance.
> I will be walking in the very middle of your soul.

He heard the shifting movements behind him. The men

were continuously moving. Who were they? What were they going to do to him?

Again a wolf howled in the distance. In front of Andrew stood the small, white deer. It snorted and looked at him with anger.

> Now! Now the Smoke of the White Tobacco
>   has just come to wing down upon you!
> Now! The Black Long-eared Owl
>   has just come to cling to you!
> Now! The Black Raven
>   has just come to cling to you!
> Now! The Black Eagle
>   has just come to cling to you!
> Now! Loneliness will be your fate!

Something sank to the ground in the underbrush on his left side.

> I will be walking in the very middle of your soul

Again, another thing thrown to his right.

> I will be walking in the very middle of your soul

And to each side he heard something thrown.

> I will be walking in the middle of your soul.
> I will be walking in the very middle of your soul

There was a pause, and then one of the men came around in front of him. This man leaned forward until his face was within an inch of Andrew's. The Indian, not the ghost from the Old Praeter Place but another, younger Indian, had a painted face covered with the sign of the hawk. He looked at Andrew with contempt and then spat in his face.

Andrew began to struggle again, but the other man kept his hold easily. Then one by one the others came around, all in the same paint, all with buckskins and carrying tomahawks and bows and arrows. These spat on him as well. There was a certain feeling of ritual even to the spitting, as though something had been completed.

He smelled the stink of his own fear. Desperation gave him strength. He began to elbow and kick the man's feet, to search for holds to throw his attacker, when suddenly there came a blow and a ripping pain at the edge of his hairline. It burned like a heated knife, as it ripped across the top of his head. He fell to his knees and then settled heavily to his side.

Two came and stood over him. "We should go to Heywasse," said one.

"No, to Natahali," said another, who came back to bend over Andrew, staring at him. He held his breath, though with his pain and fear, he found it hard to do so. In a moment, he thought wildly, he would sputter and the Indian would realize he was still alive. *Hovering above, watching the scene as though detached, he knew the sensations of his body, the longing for air, the sweat of fear, the closed eyes, as well as he saw the Indians indistinctly with that other, stranger part of him.*

Don't move, he said to himself over and over again like a chant repeated by one who had forgotten the reason for it. He lay quietly in the darkness and became slowly aware of his surroundings, but he did not open his eyes, and his breath came very shallowly. The top of his head felt as if it had been scrubbed by a harsh grade of steel wool. There was a scent in the air like that of freshly congealed blood, and he restrained the urge to wipe his forehead with the palm of his hand. His body felt as ungainly and as difficult to manage as a cornstalk figure. And he rested in that body, yet hovered above it, attached by a fragile cord, a tentative thread of light. Breathing. Andrew heard someone panting and saw a dark figure bending down to hang a limp scalp more securely to the end of a lance. Above him, from the four, came another brief and whispered chant.

He closed his eyes more tightly and no longer felt such a press of bodies standing around him. He spun dizzily from two parts into one and then into an inner darkness.

The night call of a screech owl brought him back to consciousness. Light and frail, heavy and tired, he was anchored to the ground. Moving a finger seemed as difficult as moving his body, and yet as easy. Moving, then, became a combination of slow, grotesque dance steps in a horizontal crawl. He crawled and moaned, crawled and fainted, scrabbled a few feet farther with his fingers, and called hoarsely for help.

Where did it come from that urge to continue, that feeble yearning for life? Then again, the second crawling movement like a dance. The night had grown pitch black before he came within a few feet of the yard and collapsed, and then light again by the time he made it to the steps that led to the porch of the old Praeter house. When Andrew lifted his head, he found his way to the door blocked by a large, wet pile of stones, heaped in no particular order. He gave a rasping sob as he recognized the marble he had pulled so laboriously from the lake. Though Andrew couldn't see in the dim light or with the wet stickiness which seemed to blur his vision, he knew, as though he had fingered each engraving and then taken those stones upon his back, what they said. He stopped, body sprawled halfway up the steps, and wept.

CHAPTER 7

He walked into a small, stuffy office and leaned on the wooden countertop. Seated at a desk behind the counter was a harried-looking woman leafing through a pile of papers. He cleared his throat.

She looked up, her large, brown eyes startled behind a pair of Calvin Klein glasses. "Oh, you must be Andrew Jackson," she said at once. "I'm Clara Brown." She got up and moved gracefully to the counter.

He nodded uncomfortably.

"Well, I'm sure you're eager to get started." Her face took on a sympathetic, motherly look. Obviously, he thought, she was taking the burden of the conversation from him.

"Here is your gradebook, your paddle—"

Andrew lifted an eyebrow.

"Seldom used, but physical punishment's not necessarily out-of-date around here." She smiled. "—and a stock of chalk. Use that carefully. We're always short on supplies. Your textbooks are in the classroom. I'll put the inservice materials you missed in your mailbox. After you've looked them over Mr. Boyles asked that you stop by later on today for a briefing. You're in room five, the first one on your left. Good luck."

She placed a cool hand over his briefly, and nodded.

"Thanks, Clara," he said, moving slowly toward the door. She nodded and returned to the stack of paperwork on her desk.

One moment he was opening the office door, and the next he entered the classroom. The next he was facing a group of students. He had no memory of the time between at all.

Thirty students seated in wooden desks stared at Andrew. He looked back at them. Three fourths of the class was composed of teenage boys sprawled into chairs that seemed to be too small for them. A couple of them eyed him challengingly: one boy with a burr haircut and a scar on the left side of his face, and another with lanky blond hair and sleepy eyes. Those two could be trouble. One rather pudgy boy in the back had already fallen asleep. The remainder were wary and attentive. Looking at his roll, he wondered if he was in the correct classroom. These students didn't have the look of honors students at all. He began to check the roll. Unlike the Marietta schools, which went strictly by alphabetical order, his roll was divided into separate lists for males and females. He sighed and called the first name on the female list.

"Leona Berry."

A tall, lanky girl raised her hand.

As he continued with the roll, he watched the group of girls whose names he was calling. Seated, for the most part, in the center of the room, they talked among themselves quietly. Two of them looked interesting.

"Cynthia Dunn." One of them, a girl with a wild bush of a haircut who looked as though she would have fit in well in Atlanta, raised her hand. She looked as though she'd have a quick comeback for anything.

He watched the other girl while he went through the small list of the females in the class. Though Cynthia Dunn had the mark of a quick thinker, this second girl was probably one of those slower on the start and quicker on the finish. She had an air of suppressed intellectual excitement at odds with her rather bland, khaki appearance. Beige hair, beige clothes. Washed out freckles. Limp, dishwater hair. Last on the list, had to be her.

"Sylvia Walker."

She raised her hand as if she were swinging at a volleyball.

The door closed behind a late student slipping into class. Larry Bryge. Andrew looked at Larry with a tinge of disapproval. Larry simply grinned and sat down in one of the seats near the back. Someone laughed and then turned the laugh into a cough.

Well, it is the right class, Andrew thought wryly. He wondered if the workload he'd arranged would be too difficult. While he worried about it, he called the rest of the roll, forgetting even to check the two potential troublemakers, an error he knew he'd be sorry for, probably before the class period was over. When he learned their names quickly, that always gave him a temporary upper hand. "Hey you," on the other hand, had very little effect. Though that sort of memory trick hardly solved his problem.

Had he planned for the wrong sort of class? Too late to alter the structure of the course. If he had to revamp his plans, it would have to be later. And he had made them open-ended enough that it might be all right.

"My name is Mr. Jackson. I'll be your history teacher for the year." He added dryly, "No doubt you are already acquainted with any other vital statistics."

Someone in the back laughed.

"This class is the honors history segment and is split up into two semesters. The first semester is American History. The second World History. A semester for either one is hardly enough to get through the dates, much less anything interesting." He grinned. "I don't know about you, but memorization is not my favorite activity. Since I assume it's not yours either, I've opted for supplementing the class with in-depth projects on the portions of history we'll be covering less thoroughly. That should see to it that both semesters are considerably more lively than they would be otherwise."

He paused and took a deep breath, watching the class. Some of them seemed interested, some of them bored, and Larry Bryge looked as though he were waiting for an opening for mischief. He glanced back, Andrew noted, toward the fellow with the scar. "Gunner," Andrew heard him call softly.

He began to pace at the front of the classroom. "We'll concentrate this fall for the first six weeks on the Civil War, the second six weeks on the Revolutionary War and the period just prior to it, and in the third six weeks on World War I and II from the American perspective. We will also briefly cover the more recent decades of American history in that last six weeks as well."

Larry Bryge lifted an eyebrow, ostentatiously yawned, and stretched out his legs until they reached under the seat in front of him. A girl beside him giggled.

"Your projects, then, will concentrate on those periods of particular concerns that are not covered in class. You will be responsible for one large project each six weeks in addition to a number of smaller assignments. These projects can be a mixture of written, oral, and media presentations." He paused. "Questions?"

"Uh, excuse me, Mr. Jackson;" Larry gave added emphasis to the name; "but all that we have in the way of media is one broken down slide projector and a couple of film projectors with screens."

"No tape recorders?"

"A couple of record players," chimed in a dark-haired girl in the front row.

"I have a tape recorder," he said, swinging around restlessly. "You're welcome to use it when the time comes for these projects. I also have a slide projector and screen."

Larry leaned over to the girl in the next row, and stage whispered, "Isn't he impressive?"

She looked at Andrew and shook her head.

Larry raised his hand. "Excuse me, Mr. Jackson, but aren't you going to say more about yourself? I mean you haven't really talked about your *ancestor*, have you? Or what he did to the Cherokee? I mean, making 'em march over thousands of miles from the South to the West and killing nearly three quarters of them is worth some mention, don't you think? Being so interested in history, you must know all about the Trail of Tears. I'm sure the class would be interested."

Larry looked back to Gary, the boy he'd called to before, and waved a casual hand. Score one for the troublemakers, Andrew thought grimly. Had he looked up Jackson's family history? Did he know any descendant of Jackson's had to be illegitimate? His tone was calm. "He was an interesting president and a complex man. Like most of the people of his day, particularly in Tennessee, he held contradictory views about the Indians and the blacks. But we'll be talking about

Jackson in due course, Larry," he said firmly. "For now it's more important to get a start on the way we'll be working together." He distributed stacks of textbooks to the front desk of each row, and then continued.

"Now, here are your books, and you know our emphasis. I suggest that you begin by reading the sections on the Civil War, and by thinking about what you might do in the way of projects for the first six weeks. At the end of this week, I'll expect a list of five suggested topics for special projects from each of you. By the following week you should have selected one which you will pursue on your own for the remainder of the six-week period."

He cleared his throat. "Five of you may do class presentations. The rest of you will have to content yourself with papers." He paused. "For this six weeks, that is. You'll all get in a project sometime during the year." He turned toward the blackboard. He could sense the students behind him busily figuring: five papers, one oral project. He heard a groan from somewhere toward the back of the room and turned around slowly.

Larry Bryge raised his hand. "I'd like to do a class presentation;" his arrogant young voice sounded as if he'd said something like, "I'd like to sit on your face."

"I'll select those after I've seen how many people are interested in oral presentations and what those people plan to cover," Andrew answered firmly. And I'll make damn sure yours won't be one of the first set, my friend, Andrew thought, his face heating up slightly as he looked Larry in the eye. After all, those have to be topnotch, he thought as he moved back to the board.

After quickly sketching the geographic layout of the nearby city of Knoxville, he perched on the front of his desk. "But that's enough of the business aspect for now. Tell me something. Why do you think we're beginning with the Civil War?"

Several of them began to look as though they'd prefer to dive under the desk. Larry and Sylvia had a "well if you don't know why ask us" look on their faces. Cynthia Dunn raised her hand slowly and thoughtfully. "Because most history classes never make it past the Civil War?"

Several of the students laughed. Andrew grinned and swung his leg. "Well, that's certainly one good reason. I suppose we all know the period from the Revolutionary War through the Civil War until we're bored to death with it, and that is one reason I was interested in beginning where we are. But a minor reason."

"Because we're in the South," drawled Larry, "and we have a lot of reason to remember the Civil War."

"Certainly that." Andrew paced up and down at the front of the classroom. "I'm not sure what history means to most of you, but I can guess. A dry subject. Something long gone. One of your requirements. Am I on the right track?"

Susan Haskell smiled in confirmation, her green eyes twinkling. The long, lanky blond nodded his head. Cynthia Dunn seemed faintly surprised.

"Beginning probably about now a lot of you are going to make decisions that will follow you around the rest of your lives—"

Larry's eyes rolled in the classic, "oh no, not another one of those" gestures.

He smiled inwardly, but continued without seeming to notice—"and those decisions have a lot of the same sort of following power that history has. What we study is often a string of those same sorts of decisions by groups or cultures, and, like many of us, groups or cultures never seem to learn." He made a wry face. "One of the reasons that people often say history repeats itself."

"So the Civil War will be around in a hundred years or so?" Sylvia Walker smiled.

"He said what repeats is very seldom exactly," said Cynthia.

"Think of the Revolutionary War here in the United States. What is another event that was similar, but had somewhat different results?"

"The French Revolution," called out Gary, sitting straight up in his seat.

"That wasn't the same thing at all," said Susan Haskell.

"Didn't have the same results," corrected Larry.

"Think it over." Andrew stopped in front of his desk. "So let's begin by tracing an event forward from the Civil War and seeing what kind of effect it might have had on us today. Nothing so obvious as the major issues. Can anyone think of something?"

"Women as spies," said Cynthia quietly.

Andrew raised an eyebrow. "Women as spies it is. Can any

of you think of how that might have affected the South during the Civil War?"

It was some time later when he paused from his animated mix of discussion, question and answer session to say, "That's right, Larry, during the Civil War Knoxville was split between the Union and the Rebel soldiers, much of that due to the efforts of female spies in the area. In fact, the whole of Tennessee was split, though not neatly by any means, and perhaps not for the same reasons. Can you tell me which forces were in control in Knoxville?"

A classroom of faces stared back at him blankly. Larry Bryge crossed his legs and eyed Andrew with a sneer. Just then came the sound of a rather shrill bell.

"Well, never mind. We'll begin there next time and try to trace forward our same topic to the present. For today and for some time to come we'll be looking at history as a root system of sorts. But think about the difference if you were to view it in another light, say as a river, or even a suspended solution. What would that do to our neat little construct of today?" He nodded pleasantly and watched them file out of the room in a somewhat puzzled fashion. Not too bad for the first day. He'd whip Bryge and those other two in to line in a few days. If he could do as well with his other classes, he would get through fine.

Larry stopped at Andrew's desk. "I'd really like to do a presentation, or at least a study, on the old Praeter house during the Civil War period."

"Why, Larry?" Andrew asked with a faint sense of unease. He reached up and fingered a small cut on his forehead with a puzzled frown. Larry doing a study on *his* house. Andrew's discomfort increased. Trouble, Andrew, this is trouble. He stared at Larry.

Larry's face was unreadable. "It was a prison camp for Union soldiers during the Civil War." He shrugged his shoulders. "Local topic."

"Let me think about it," he said, glancing down at the material on his desk and avoiding Larry's eyes.

"I can bring in some materials." Larry's voice was eager.

"All right, then;" Andrew gripped the textbook in front of him with unnecessary force. He forced a smile. "Bring them in and let me have a look. I'll decide after I've seen what you've got to start with."

Larry nodded and turned away.

What was it about that boy that got under his skin? He shook his head impatiently. Besides the fact that, at least part of the time, Larry was the picture of a knowledgeable country road tough; while the rest of the time, often just moments later, he was brashly pursuing an intrusive project. Andrew frowned. The door closed behind Larry with a click of finality. He bent wearily over his desk, the palm of his hand, by habit now, resting on his chest.

An hour until the next history class. He leaned his head on his desk. During that hour, which he was supposed to use as prep time, he probably should go around and meet some of the other teachers. However, he hadn't the heart for it. Or perhaps strength was a better word.

It had been a trial to get to work at all. His body felt detached at the joints. Even now he moved far too stiffly.

He identified with these young students with that look of endurance on their faces, like that blond haired boy with the scar, what was his name? Gary. That's the way Andrew had felt about school, except for the old history class. Something to be endured, to wait your way through. Something unavoidable like a long illness. He would not think about this now; he had made a pact with himself. Remember?

The door swung open and Mr. Boyles, the principal, walked into the classroom. "Well, Andrew." He took a draw on his pipe. "How did your first class go?"

"Fairly well, I think." He leaned back in his chair and looked up at the older man.

Mr. Boyles was a man in his fifties who looked as though he'd spent most of his life on the farm rather than as the principal of a school. He had the calloused hands, the see-forever peaceful eyes and the straight-backed walk of a farmer.

When Andrew had come for his job interview, he had liked the man immediately. And it was obvious that the students did as well. Something about a school atmosphere that reflected itself almost the moment one walked in the door. This school mirrored the man: relaxed, informal, yet disciplined. Since Andrew had missed the week's training sessions, he wasn't certain yet what Boyles expected, but he felt sure that they'd get along.

"You're surviving then?" Boyles took another draw on his

pipe, and then bent down to tap it on the side of his plain, well-worn western boots.

Andrew laughed self derisively, and then nodded. "I'll be fine," he said, with more confidence that he felt, but he was certain that Boyles was enough judge of human character to know that.

"Right." Boyles stood up and then leaned on Andrew's desk. His expression was suddenly purposeful. "Well then, here's some information you might find useful." He laid a neatly labelled packet down on the desk. "Check it over and come by my office this afternoon. Mrs. Brown did mention that to you, didn't she?"

Andrew nodded again.

"Good. Then we'll talk about what you can expect from Greenback High." He hesitated. "I'm sorry about your family, Jackson. That was a rough blow."

He nodded and looked away. Then he said with effort, "Thank you for mentioning it. People find it difficult to talk about, I think."

Boyles looked at him for a moment. "No use ignoring the hard times," he said gruffly. "Let me know if you need anything."

"Thank you, I will." Andrew watched Boyles walk out of the room, his shoulders slightly hunched.

He fingered the cut on his forehead again and sighed. Andy had had a cut on his forehead at about the same place. He'd been a climber from the time he was a baby. When he was three, he'd climbed up a neighbor's trellis and fallen on the metal edge of a rolled out window. The woman had brought Andy to him, blood streaming down the side of his face and pooling in his eye. At first it had seemed that he'd landed on his eye, but when they'd cleared the blood away, the cut had been superficial. He'd had a large, triangular scar much like Andrew's cut. Where had his own come from? For the life of him he couldn't remember. He leaned back in the swivel chair and whirled around and around slowly, as he waited for the next class.

Flipping through the pages of the in-service material Boyles had handed him, Andrew shifted in his seat restlessly. It was three o'clock and he was tired of waiting outside Boyles' office. The first day had been a long one, and he was more than ready to go home.

He glanced across the room toward Clara, the school secretary. She smiled at him warmly. He wondered whether she was married. She didn't wear a ring. He wondered if she was happily married, and hated himself for the disloyalty of that thought. It stung him with a pained awareness of his loss, but he couldn't stop himself. He imagined the warmth of her bed, the husband poised— He and Kate should have had one last time together. The door opened. Andrew lifted an eyebrow in surprise. Larry just nodded and grinned, as he sauntered by Andrew's chair. The grin widened. Too much for Andrew's liking. Like a Cheshire cat in heat, he thought.

"Come on in, Andrew," Mr. Boyles called.

"Did you get a chance to look over that material yet?"

"Yes, I glanced over it, though I'll read it more thoroughly tonight." He removed a pile of magazines from the seat fronting Boyles' desk. He sat down and nodded his head to Boyles in what he hoped was a pleasant manner. Why did that kid unnerve him so?

Boyles leaned back in his seat. Andrew noted enviously that Boyles looked as fresh and energetic as he had that morning. Though the man's dress was casual, his neatly trimmed sideburns and pepper-and-salt hair gave him a perpetually well groomed look.

"Just talked to Larry Bryge. He seemed quite intrigued by what you've assigned them. Something about a special project he said."

"Interesting."

"Hmm, got your back up already, have you? Larry's a good one for that."

"Let's just say he's a bit combative."

"More than a bit." Mr. Boyles leaned forward. "Larry will calm down after while. He's always been tough on new teachers. Has been ever since he's been in school."

Andrew relaxed and settled back in his chair.

"Now I wanted you to understand about your honors class. You may think they're an odd lot after your experience in the Marietta school system, which I understand is a suburb, a wealthy suburb at that, right?"

He nodded.

"Well, these kids—your class contains students of promise,

potential, let's say. This is a farm community, and many of the students in this school will stay in Greenback. They'll be farmers and damn good ones."

He leaned over the desk and looked at Andrew.

Andrew nodded again.

"Your students are those who are going on to college, for the most part. One or two of them show signs of very high potential. The rest of them have been ragged unmercifully for their interest in school. They're defensive. Quick to challenge authority. Nonverbally for the most part. Do you follow me?"

He smiled. "I've already begun to get the picture."

"You've got your work cut out for you, Mr. Jackson. They've made up their minds about their other teachers, pro or con. You've got the last shot at them before they graduate and hit the road. It's your job to knock that defensiveness out of them. Make them proud of themselves. And if you don't teach them a damn thing else, you'll have taught them plenty. But I'm definitely expecting you to do that. If you don't succeed, at least partially, you'll find that I have quite a lot to say about it."

He straightened up. He could see why the school had the atmosphere it did. The Boyles outside the office was an easy-going, caring sort of fellow. The Boyles inside the office took no time saying what he meant. He grinned in spite of himself. Far better to work for a man who said what he meant. His old principal had been a slick manipulator.

"I'll do my best, Mr. Boyles."

Mr. Boyles leaned back in his chair. He looked at Andrew contemplatively. "Now, about the community. This is a small town. News travels fast, particularly about newcomers. You can expect that everyone in town knows about you now. They're kind people. They'll be kind to you. They would have been kind at any rate, but they will be particularly so with your recent loss. But they'll be wondering about you too. What you're like and so forth. I know you don't feel much like it now, but as soon as you can, you'll need to get out and about soon and let them see you. Go to a social event. One thing about small towns such as this one is that the socializing is almost a part of your job. I expect it of you. I realize that expectations like that are seen in a different way by urban teachers; but it really will make a difference in your classroom." Boyles stopped and shot Andrew a questioning glance.

This part of the speech he'd heard before he interviewed for the job. So the request was no surprise. Going out into the community would be harder to bear now; he wasn't sure he liked the fact that Boyles felt a need to press it under the circumstances.

He cleared his throat. "I'm sorry to make a point of that. If it was me in your shoes—I'd crawl into a hole and come out about five years down the road. And I couldn't blame you if that's what you want to do. But—"

"I understand. I'll get out when I can."

"Good." Boyles' chair snapped abruptly upright. "One other thing. Remember that there is very little you do in a town this size that won't be known and talked about, including what goes on in your classroom. We're all related here, you know."

Mr. Boyles got up and paced around the room, his worn cowboy boots thumping the floor. "That'll be the biggest change for you, I expect. We're more informal here, but more noticing too." He stopped for a moment. Then a smile flared across his face. "That's about it, I reckon. Look over those papers now."

"I will."

"Any questions?"

"No, I think you've given me enough to think about."

Mr. Boyles came over and shook his hand with a quick firm grip. "Good. Welcome aboard then."

The quiet, shadowed road and the surrounding farmland with its rolling hills seemed a contrast to his rising sense of uneasiness as he drove, his hands gripped to the wheel of the car. The play of the light and the shadow on the blacktop ahead of him was a sensation as familiar as his childhood road trips, trips when he had absorbedly watched the illusion of water vanish time after time on the road ahead of his parents' car. He missed them. At least he had Kate's parents.

The tires veered off into the gravel and he jerked the wheel of the car until it squealed back onto the road. Just in time to pull back out of the way of a hay truck coming from the other direction. His fingers trembled on the steering wheel, vibrating with a nervous thrumming like a continuous sort of tick. His thumb jerked restlessly.

Three figures standing over him, one of them pulling his hair.

He pulled over to the side of the road, coming to a stop with a rising cloud of dust around the car. Since the funeral there were times his mind just blanked out, as if it didn't know how to function any longer. He felt a frantic need to know what it did in those moments. A quick wash of sweat dripped into his eyes.

The whole top of his head tingled.

Across a pasture he watched the blurry figure of a horse trot back and forth with a quick nervous pace. Suddenly the horse faced the car from across the pasture, running headlong toward the car and pulling up just short of the barbed wire fence. It snorted and shook its head. Andrew pulled out a handkerchief. He wiped his face. The handkerchief came away soaked.

Crawling along the ground with the feel of raw gravel underneath his fingers.

Again that disorienting sense of his mind in motion, and then a sudden, jerky stop. A blank wall of dizziness. Every sound was suddenly distinct. He rested his head on the steering wheel listening to the quick tick cough of a tractor sputtering to life, the sound of nearby cattle, a plane overhead. He could feel his chest heaving as though it were the beat of the tractor engine, faster, rougher, the jerk of a quick roar until all he could hear was the sound of someone panting. Himself.

With a blind physical longing, Andrew wanted to turn the car around and drive nonstop to Georgia. Why hadn't he kept going that night? He did not want to drive onto Praeter land, walk into that house, that empty house, and see—what? The moving form of an Indian in the hallway. He shivered; his teeth chattered. What was happening to him? A fear surrounded him like a second skin at the thought of looking into Broken Echo's eyes.

Closing his eyes, he banged his head gently against the steering wheel and then rested it quietly there for a moment. And now he was seeing things. For the first time he began to wonder if he had been too quick to go to work, but the thought of remaining in the house had been completely unpalatable. And now he was seeing things. He felt a tear tremble at the corner of his eye and brushed it away impatiently.

The horse neighed and paced back and forth quickly at the fence, just a few feet from the car. It shook its head as it ran and glared at Andrew, trumpeting at the car as though it were another horse. Breathing faster still, Andrew stared at the horse. The moment at which they looked at each other was endless. Finally Andrew broke eye contact. He sagged against the seat of the car and closed his eyes, forcing himself with effort to breathe deeply, slowly. He was aware of nothing else but that, until at some point he pulled himself forward, listening to the sound of his wet shirt pulling free from the upholstery.

It was another long while before he sighed and then pulled back onto the road. The horse, a bay he could see now, followed beside the car to the end of the fence row, left behind only when Andrew pulled past the end of the pasture.

At the moment he drew past the horse, his uneasiness and fear left him with the rapidity of the clearing of a river fog. He rolled down his windows and let the wind whip his hair, the speedometer sliding its way up to fifty as he swung smoothly left and then right along the curved road. With the rapid, competent movements of the wheel, he felt increasingly free, back, for a brief time, into the reckless confidence of the driving style of his teenage years, even though some dimly knowing part of him knew it was wrong, that it wasn't really the same at all.

It seemed only moments later that he pulled onto the road leading to his driveway.

The car teetered on the edge of the ditch, wheels hovering over the edge.

Again that unsettling sensation of blankness. Was he having attacks of aphasia? He had heard something about the disease, but he couldn't remember exactly what. Behind him a car gave an impatient honk. Without looking back to acknowledge the prompt, Andrew slowly rolled the car down the gravel, rocks crunching under the wheels, and pulled to a stop. Was it his imagination, or did a haze waver over the house, like the ripple of heat rising from a summer road? He looked at the house.

Then turning the car around, he drove out of the driveway

and along the road that led to the McSpadden's house. Maybe Jess's husband would like to go fishing.

The boat rocked against the water, fishing line bobbing against the side. James cleared his throat and shifted his weight. Andrew opened his eyes and looked at the older man.

A weathered cap rested on James' head, almost as though it had grown there. He had the look of a man about whom everything seemed of a piece. Bluff, outdoor confidence. As though he never had been anywhere else.

James reached into a paper bag. "Sandwich?" he asked, pulling out a Ziploc bag with two sandwiches in it. "Thought we might get hungry."

"I should have brought the food, especially since you're loaning me your equipment. I will next time." Andrew took the sandwich; then he leaned back to stare across the still waters of the large cove they had come some distance into. "What do you think it was like back then?" he asked abruptly.

"Back when?" James' voice sounded testy.

"Back when old Joseph Praeter built his house."

James shifted his weight in the boat again. Andrew could see his muscular forearms, light gold hairs glinting.

"River going through. No lake. Wild sort of land. Lots of animals, bird life."

"No, I mean the people."

"Rough land. Tough people. Why, I bet they had a lot more going on than most nowdays."

Andrew shook his head. That wasn't what he meant. He didn't know exactly what he had meant, but it had nothing to do with the idea of the old pioneering spirit. Maybe he was wondering something about the Praeter family—something about their personalities. How had Praeter's sons and daughter thought of him? The daughter obviously had some grudge against her father if she married the son of the man who'd for all purposes killed him. She'd even stayed on at the family home where her father had been scalped.

Andrew closed his eyes and leaned back further, feeling the gentle tug of the pole and the fishing line move with him.

"Family was always into some mischief. Way I heard it." James's line spun out quickly, and he began to reel it in with a quick, practiced sound. "Some folks said they were cursed." Andrew heard him net the fish. "Why do you want to live in that big old place anyway?"

Andrew sat up and looked out across the lake. "Little late to be thinking of that now."

"What do you mean?" James pulled on the brim of his fishing hat.

Andrew shrugged. "Just that I don't know how easy a large house like that would be to unload quickly. I'm stuck for a while."

"That why?" James stared at him with a hard to read expression.

"What do you mean?"

"Seems like if you sold it, you'd have to decide what you wanted to do."

"You may be right," Andrew admitted easily. "I need some time to let it rest."

James settled back against the side of the boat. "Makes sense, I suppose," he said grudgingly. And they said nothing more for some time.

Andrew stared out across the cove to a fringe of ferns waving lightly in a breeze Andrew couldn't feel. The ferns parted at the edge of the bank. A boy stepped out through the ferns and to the edge of the water. He looked across at Andrew.

Andrew blinked his eyes. The boy looked like his son Billy. He looked around for a moment, looked at Andrew again, and then stepped out across the water in a gliding motion. Andrew stood up, the boat rocking wildly, and prepared to dive in. The breeze tossed the boy's curls. He glided *across* the water. The boy took maybe three steps and then sank into the water with what seemed to be scarcely a ripple. Andrew looked at James, who was sitting forward in the boat, his hand shading his eyes, looking straight toward the place where the boy had disappeared.

"Did you see that?"

"Were you thinking about swimming? Looks like the wind is freshening. Maybe we'll get a bite or two now. The fish in this cove sure do seem to love the wind."

"No, I mean the boy."

"What boy?"

"The one who was on the bank."

James looked at Andrew oddly. He shook his head. "Well, there wasn't any boy there that I saw."

Andrew blinked. "Right across where that fern is."

"I've been fishing over on that bank with waders. Nothing around that fern but marsh area—that marsh'd come up over a boy's head pretty nearly."

"Must have seen him over a ways."

"Maybe so."

Neither one of them spoke for a while. James kept looking at him.

At last Andrew said, "It's getting on dusk. Don't you think we ought to be getting back?" He pulled his jacket more tightly around him.

"'Bout to say that myself." They reeled in their lines. They rode back in silence. Some thirty minutes later when they reached the dock, Andrew thanked James for the fishing trip.

"Sure you had a good time?" James asked. "Didn't catch a fish."

"I enjoyed it," Andrew said, trying to sound sincere, smiling at the older man. "I'd like to go again."

James nodded, the corners of his mouth tipping into a slight smile. "Could be arranged. Next time though," he looked as though he started to say something else for a moment; "you bring the sandwiches."

"You got it." Andrew shook a strong right hand. "Say hi to Jess for me."

"I'll do that."

Andrew watched James' muscular back as he walked up the slope. Then he slowly walked along the incline until he reached his car.

Andrew pushed the front door open slowly. The house was dark. The living room, eerier than usual in the quiet blackness, seemed an open invitation to the jitters. He stumbled across the room and flipped the light switch, thinking that any moment there would be the touch of a hand on his shoulder.

There was, of course, nothing unusual in sight when the light flared. That would be too easy, he decided. He listened to the empty house for a moment and then walked resolutely into the kitchen.

Lying, sprawled on the steps

He was growing used to these moments when his mind refused to function, he mused as he opened the kitchen cabinet. The kitchen was quiet, empty. He put some water on to boil and sat down. It wasn't until he was well into his cup of tea that he heard something, a kind of clacking from the upstairs. It had a familiar, almost comforting sound, but he couldn't think what it reminded him of. Then he remembered. He was on his feet and moving toward the stairs. The loom—that sound was the clanking of Kate's loom, and the rhythm was much the same as hers.

Up the stairs, two at a time, and into the workroom. The clanking slowed to a stop just as Andrew wrenched open the door and looked into a very still room with the loom at its center. All the tangled jumble that he had left the night of the accident was gone. Strung across the loom was a three-quarters finished weaving.

He walked slowly toward the center of the room. He stared down at the tapestry—a weaving of what seemed to be the eyelid and most of a very large eye. He bent forward, sniffing the wool, watching a slow, damp series of spots form on its surface.

The wind whispered. Andrew looked up. Broken Echo stood in front of the window, a slight breeze blowing the curtains to either side of him. He drew the curtains around him until he was covered with the thin, gauzy material, until only his eyes and the top of his head were uncovered.

Andrew's lips tightened. He stood for a moment, then he whirled and ran down the stairs and into the kitchen, yanking the pantry door open and pulling out a thick-headed hammer. In the next moment he was back in Kate's workroom and jerking the tapestry, thick thread by thread, from the frame. He pounded furiously until he had reduced the loom to a mass of jagged pieces and splintered wood. You can't have my history, old man.

His chest heaving, he turned to Broken Echo. The Indian covered his eyes with the gauze of the curtains. In a moment the drapes fell into straight, limp folds and he had gone. Gone too quickly. Andrew could feel the weight of the hammer like a stone in his hand. He threw it from him, and watched it smash through the window, the splinters flying from the center of the hole in an angry slow motion.

The slanted strip of moonlight glared across his face. Andrew became aware of the tears streaking his face, the taste of salt against his cracked lips, the wood beneath him, the stiffness of his limbs. He lay on his back against the floor of his wife's workroom, listening to the vague sound of his own moans as though they were the cries of some wounded animal in the underbrush outside. Raising a piece of what remained of the loom in a protective motion, he warded off what he saw. The mangled frame and scattered shards of wood, the jagged hole at the center of a small picture window.

The room held a coda of silence, as if it had been filled with echoes just the moment before.

He rose slowly, cupping the piece of wood to his chest. Slowly, still holding the piece of wood with one arm as if it were an infant, he moved to pick up the pieces scattered around the room, to place them in some kind of order within what remained of the framework of the loom. Carefully, he arranged the pieces until they satisfied him, then he picked up a skein of thread from the corner and began to stitch them together in the way one would stitch up an open and angry wound. As the stitches bound the framework tighter and tighter, he hummed under his breath, the song so familiar to him that he could not remember it, so tender that he cried as he stitched. It reminded him of all the unspoken, bittersweet memories of home.

CHAPTER 8

"If it is true that the Civil War was caused by a strong disagreement over the issue of slavery, then why do many of the transcripts of conversations with Southern soldiers show that many of them were against slavery?" Andrew paused and cleared his throat.

No one answered. The entire group of students, Larry included, looked at him blankly.

"Think about that one until tomorrow." As Andrew watched the class begin to file out the door, he smiled. Things seemed to be going well. He even had them running to their books to look up points to argue. Andrew yanked at a lock of his hair absentmindedly.

He looked up, startled, as Larry leaned over the desk. He had a bright, defiant look on his face, and his drawl, as he began to speak was even more pronounced than usual.

"I'd like to talk to you about the class presentations, Mr. Jackson," he said, his voice seeming to Andrew to linger mockingly.

"What is it, Larry?" Andrew leaned back in the chair and looked up at him.

"I turned in my suggestion for a presentation the second day of class, but it's been nearly a week and a half and you haven't said anything yet."

Andrew hesitated. Larry was the reason he had put off assigning presentations for the class. "All right, Larry, I'll let you do one this six weeks. Tomorrow I'll assign the class dates. You can sign up for a time then."

"Yeah, but you haven't approved my topic."

"What topic?"

"The old Praeter house."

"Why—"

"I brought you the material last week. Didn't you look it over?"

Andrew raised his hand to his head. "I guess that I'd forgotten about that, Larry."

"Do you have it here?"

Andrew shook his head, but he felt uncertain. "I believe I took that home."

"Would it be okay then if—"

"All right, all right. You can do the Praeter Home as a project," Andrew snapped. "I'll see that you get your material back tomorrow."

Larry leaned closer to the desk. "Would it be all right then if I came around one of these days to look the place over?"

Andrew started to shake his head.

"For my report, I mean," Larry added smoothly.

As he leaned back further in his chair, he said, "No, I don't think that'll be necessary. You have plenty to say as it is. I understand that the house has quite a history."

Larry looked at him in a way Andrew couldn't interpret. Then he said, "I could just play hooky one day."

Instead of flaring up, Andrew merely said firmly, "Trespassing is a serious offense. I wouldn't provoke me if I were you."

The boy glared at him.

"You just be sure that you stick to our topic—the Civil War. And leave the house itself to me."

"Don't you worry, Mr. Jackson. I'll do that." Larry straightened. His words were not at all convincing, but the boy obviously didn't intend them to be. There was something peculiar about Larry. Perhaps Andrew should go over and meet the boy's family sometime soon. They might shed some light on his behavior.

At first Andrew had assumed that Larry's resistance had come from that sort of independent stubbornness the mountain people had. Now it seemed to him that there was more to it. Why had the boy been looking at voodoo books? And why was he so set on the Praeter house? Though Andrew couldn't think of the place as his or as any sort of ordinary home, he felt as though the word territorial hovered in the air between them every time Larry challenged him. This was a house with a title, Broken Echo's home, a place where he never knew what or when something might happen. Perhaps that sort of thing had its own attraction for a boy of Larry's age. And why did he himself have such hostility for the boy? Andrew leaned his head on the desk. His head felt flushed, feverish, and a slight chill ran over his arms. He sighed and decided he had simply been thinking too much about a "monkey puzzle" student. It wasn't too late to transfer Larry. The boy might be smart, but he was also far too much of a wise ass for Andrew. He could do without a student like that his first year. Which was, of course, probably why he had one. Students were always down quickly, like ducks on a junebug, on uncertain teachers. By next year he'd have it under control.

Picking up his books, he left the classroom for the courtyard. Perhaps the sunlight and the faint tinge of fall colors would revive him. "Oh God, Kate," he murmured, pressing his hand to his chest, "I miss you."

Andrew drove along the quiet, sunlit roads toward home; he watched the occasional fall leaf drift from the trees ahead of him. Like the vanishing mirage that children watch so carefully on the road ahead of them in the summer, those leaves were disappearing as he arrived at each tree from which they came. His own memory seemed a summer mirage, as if he had made his way back to Locke's blank page. He felt suddenly puzzled. Had he thought this before?

And why, he thought abruptly, had he told Larry he hadn't read his material when he had some hazy memory of looking it over? One moment he remembered things, the next they were gone. The next moment he remembered them again. It was if he were slipping out of gear. "Ah, Kate," he said, "I'm fooling myself. I didn't do a very good job today, and I'm not up to handling an uneven and temperamental student like Larry. I'm irritable. It's not a good way to start." He hadn't taught like this since his first year in teaching.

It seemed only a moment before Andrew pulled into Jess's driveway, gravel almost speaking under his tires, and he couldn't quite understand how he had gotten there or why he had come. But she was already beside the car by that time, so he smiled at her and opened the door.

"Come on in and have a cup of coffee," she said. "Or would you like to sit outside and—"

He shivered suddenly. "No," he forced a smile; "let's go on inside."

"The first couple of weeks of a new job always make for long days, don't they?" she asked, and turned without waiting for an answer.

He had been carrying on a conversation for some time without really knowing what he was saying. Jess had been looking at him with an increasing sense of speculation and sadness. When James came in the door she jumped up in relief, and went over to him. "You know, James, I believe Andrew liked his fishing trip with you. He's just been saying that he'd like to go out again." She nudged her husband encouragingly. "Aren't you going this afternoon?"

Andrew stared at them both. He didn't think that was what he had been saying at all, but he couldn't be sure. Maybe he had.

"Want to come along?" James asked gruffly, but Andrew could see that he was pleased.

Humoring him. She was humoring him, Andrew thought, but he couldn't help but be pleased by her concern. Well, he'd go then. He nodded to James, and stood up slowly. "Good day for it," he said, feeling as though he could, for the moment, become James, become that quiet, gruffly confident man.

In moments he was watching the spray fly around him, and watching the boat pull into a cove and settle to quietness in the water. Drops of water still hovered in the air, glistening, falling in slow motion. He wondered at the dragging on his heart, the metabolic change.

James reached into a paper bag. "Sandwich?" he asked, pulling out a Ziploc bag with two sandwiches in it. Andrew ate the sandwich mechanically, while he leaned forward in an old man's hunch to stare into the still water.

The older man flipped his line into the lake's surface with a gesture that spoke of the stroke of fingers against water.

"Why do you always come to the same cove?" Andrew asked.

James looked at his fishing line. He cleared his throat. "I don't. I've fished every cove in Fort Loudoun and the Tellico." His voice was unsurprised.

"Last time we came here."

"Not the same cove." James still didn't turn. His body had the stiffness of a curious, waiting tension.

Andrew cast his line out slowly and settled back into his seat. He watched the circle of ferns at the shore wave in the breeze. He tugged lightly, from time to time, on his fishing line.

A boy stepped out through the ferns and to the edge of the water. He looked across at Andrew. Andrew stared at him. The boy had blond hair and thick, almost bushy eyebrows like an old man's. He had on a pair of ragged white shorts with bright blue clocks on them, and a faded red T-shirt. They looked very much like some clothes that Billy had loved and worn until they fell apart. Andrew had thrown them out before he left Marietta. Billy must have fished them out of the trash, Andrew thought, and then he blinked his eyes, startled. The boy looked around with a gesture so like Billy's and then stared without any expression straight across at Andrew again. He stepped out across the water with a gliding motion. Andrew watched the breeze blow the boy's hair, and saw the stubby foot reach out again. The boy took maybe three steps and then sank into the water with what seemed to be scarcely a ripple. In a moment a large fish leaped up from that exact spot.

James laughed. "Maybe we should be over there," he said, and took a draw on his pipe.

Andrew looked at James, who was sitting forward in the boat, his hand shading his eyes, looking straight toward the place where the boy had disappeared.

"Did you see that?"

"Good sized bass, looked like." James' hands turned the reel in a stiff, jerky movement.

He shook his head. It was as if he had lived through this

fishing trip so often that he knew it by heart: a large cove, two fishermen, a vision of a boy. He couldn't even seem to care that his mind was functioning like a detached retina, somehow out-of-focus. He observed things, both real and illusory, without drawing any conclusions. Perhaps that was a part of the shock of grief.

Now he made himself acknowledge what he had been afraid to think. His sons could be alive; those boys he identified could be someone else's, maybe, like the passengers in the other car. He wanted to believe that, though he knew better. Alive or dead, he told himself, they wouldn't be here in this cove, stepping out onto the water as though it were frozen. It's common, so people tell me, to think they're still alive. I need to just let these things float through my mind without catching hold. It's believing they're alive that catches you up in some sort of craziness it's hard to come back from. He flipped the fishing line further out into the lake.

"It's getting on close to dusk," James said after a while. "I suppose we'd better be getting back." His voice held the sound of relief.

Andrew blinked his eyes and nodded. "I think you're right," he said.

It wasn't long before he heard the man's laugh echoing, "Next time," he said, "you bring the sandwiches."

"I'll do that," said Andrew. He shivered as he walked to his car.

When Andrew reached the house, he found all the lights blazing, and the door standing wide open. His shoes thumped in an uneven rhythm; as he ran toward the porch and the ground sank spongily beneath him. Had it been raining? Just as he reached the steps, Larry stepped out the front door grinning a sly grin. He rocked on his heels back and forth in front of the doorway, his hands jammed in his back pockets.

"What are you doing here, Larry?" Andrew raised his hand.

"I came over to ask you a question about my project and I found your door wide open." His grin dared Andrew to find another explanation.

"And what did you do then?"

"I didn't think you were here. I saw you heading out on the boat, so I checked around to see if anything got disturbed." His tone of voice was smug. "Doesn't look like it." He paused. "'Course I only saw the inside of this place the time you invited me in, so I could be wrong." And that's another lie I dare you to call me on, his mocking grin said.

"You're not to come around here again, Larry." Andrew stepped forward and gripped the teenager's shoulder. "If you have questions, you can ask me at school like anyone else."

"You're going to eat your own tail if you're not careful," Larry said callously. "Like an old snake holed up in a hollow log."

"What I am in this house," Andrew said very carefully, "is on my own time. And I intend for it to stay that way. If you want to take on the Praeter House as a pet interest, there's nothing I can do about it, but you'll not be making regular visits."

"Not that's downright unneighborly," Larry drawled stepping aside from the doorway. He didn't seem in the least disconcerted. Instead he stood on the porch staring at Andrew and fiddling with the knife in his pocket.

Andrew stepped toward him. Larry tugged at the knife in his pocket, then, slowly looking into Andrew's eyes, drew his hand out without the weapon. Andrew stepped toward him again, and Larry clenched his fists, pressing them against Andrew's stomach, a pressure Andrew scarcely seemed to notice as he pushed the teenager slowly off the edge of the porch.

Larry spoke in a very tight voice, "You better watch all that burning you been doing, or you'll be having the fire department down on you." Then he hesitated, as though he hardly understood his own antagonism or his indecision in carrying it through. Finally, without saying any more, the boy turned and walked across the yard.

He watched Larry until he was a dimly moving figure, brushing his way past the shrubbery and then disappearing under the shadow of the trees. Perhaps he was too hard on the boy. Larry probably felt the same lure that he himself had for the house, and probably understood his attraction even less than Andrew did his own. Still, both of them seemed to become possessive and territorial where the house was concerned. In this context, logic or reason was alien.

The house seemed undisturbed. In the glaring light of the living room, he looked toward the fireplace quickly, searching to see if the tapestry was hanging above the mantel. He saw it, just as he had seen others like it for the past nine days. He ran across and lifted up the huge weaving of an eye, rolled it up, and shoved it into the fireplace as though the ritual were a familiar one. He set fire to it with one quick puff of the gas from underneath. Good that he had a gas fireplace, he thought, or the wool would never burn.

The smell of singed wool rose from the fireplace. Andrew sat down in one of the chairs by the door and watched it slowly catch fire. He opened the door to let some air into the room. He wanted nothing more than to make his way wearily upstairs, but he had learned that, if he left the room too soon, the weaving simply appeared, slightly singed, on the wall again. The smoke rose idly from the fireplace, the sound of tinkling piano keys drifted through the room, and chains rattled against the basement staircase. There were footsteps approaching; they moved slowly up the steps, dragging one foot behind. Again there was the rattle of chains, but it stopped. They never go past the third stair, Andrew thought dizzily.

A window rattled with the wind, and Andrew paused during his lecture, losing, for a moment, his train of thought. He cleared his throat.

Sylvia Walker raised her hand. "If the war wasn't about slavery, I mean, if some of the Southern soldiers didn't really want slavery, then what were they fighting for?"

"What do you think?" Andrew suddenly couldn't remember her name, but he looked at her encouragingly. None of them had been ready to discuss that at the beginning of the period. Perhaps they were now. She simply shook her head.

"What were some differences between the North and the South?" Cynthia crossed her legs and suddenly looked scornful. Andrew ignored her. He knew by now she had little patience with what she considered lazy thinking.

At last Jim, one of the boys who, at the beginning of the week, had not been the most talkative, rattled off a series of comparisons. Andrew nodded. The boy leaned back and smiled.

"That's one set of answers. Why don't we take a look at some of the soldiers' correspondence next time? Susan Haskell, see me after class and I'll give you a series of letters to look through. Pick a couple out that you think are interesting and bring them in to read next time. Okay?"

She nodded, looking faintly pleased.

"Now . . ."

The class stirred and began to gather their books. The bell rang, but Andrew ignored it.

"I've decided that Jim, Cynthia, Sylvia, Andrea"—that was it—"Andrea, and Larry, can do the projects this six weeks. You five seem to be the ones who are the most eager to explore the Civil War. If you'll stay after class, you can sign up for your presentation date.

"All right, that's a good start," said Andrew, winding up the discussion. "For next time, let's think about the ways in which straightforward answers to complex questions become myths that we carry on in history. For instance, why do all the history books tell us that Columbus discovered America when we know very well he wasn't the first to do so?

"By the way, speaking of myths. The rest of you have already at least begun to look around for information on your topic, I hope. George," he nodded to a tall, quiet looking boy in the back of the room; "I believe that you haven't turned in the title of your topic yet. You're the only one, you know."

"I have it now, Mr. Jackson."

"Fine." He nodded to the students as they left the room. George slipped Andrew a piece of paper. Andrew passed a sign-up sheet to the five students and listened as they argued amicably over dates. He stepped back from the desk. Larry signed quickly and moved over to Andrew.

"Did you bring my materials, Mr. Jackson?" Larry talked in a tight, compressed voice totally unlike his usual drawl. He avoided Andrew's eyes.

"Right, I have them here." Andrew spoke pleasantly, as he slid open the desk drawer. "I remembered that I hadn't taken them home after all."

"Does that mean you didn't look them over?" An incredulous look came over Larry's face.

"Glanced at them," Andrew said casually, "but I didn't really get the chance to read very much."

"I thought you were interested in that old place of yours."

Larry stared at Andrew as if he didn't know him. "You sure are a strange man—" he cleared his throat. "Don't you remember last night that you—"

"What about last night, Larry?" Andrew asked.

Larry didn't answer. He shook his head like a bull with a tick in his ear.

At last Andrew said, "I am, I mean I was going to look over your materials, but I—well—I really didn't have the time." He shrugged guiltily.

Larry moved away from the desk and looked back at Andrew as he went out the door. He had a very puzzled expression. Had the boy selected that topic because he thought Andrew would like it? Perhaps. If so, Andrew thought grimly, he was going to be disappointed.

Mr. Boyles stuck his head in the door. "Hi, Andrew, want to come to the lounge for a cup of coffee?"

"I would, but I have to get something run off on the ditto machine before my next class. Anything particular you had in mind?"

"No, just wanted to talk a bit. You haven't been around much to socialize with and I thought we could get together. Say, I understand you've started your history class with the Civil War."

"That's right." Andrew looked at him shrewdly.

"Some of the kids are complaining to their parents about that."

"Oh, why is that?"

"They think you're trying to rile them up about it."

"Just stir up their ideas a bit."

"Well, keep it up. Be good for this bunch, I'm thinking. Pretty soon they'll start to talk and you'll think the dam has burst."

"Common thing, then, their quietness?"

"That's right;" Boyles's voice was genuinely hearty; "takes them a while with all of us and particularly with a new teacher." Boyles waved and was out the door before Andrew could say thank you. Knows when to drop by. Maybe something's bubbling in this class after all.

Andrew walked down the hall to the office watching the students as he went. It was a small school. He knew most of the students' faces by now and many of their names. He nodded and spoke to them as he went along. He enjoyed seeing lively, attractive faces in the hall. They were never, even the best of them, quite so lively in the classrooms. Though they did more often say interesting things in class than when they were talking among themselves, since their conversations to each other seemed to be a sort of shorthand emotional code.

He entered the office and smiled at Clara Brown. What would she look like with her clothes off, he wondered idly. With those glasses gone? She should wear a deep red dress sometime. It would bring her alive.

She looked at him calmly, then went back to her work, stamping papers with a large, curved stamp and covering them with neat red ink parallelograms.

He looked at her for a moment, and then went into the inner office to use the ditto machine. Before he had finished the class handout, he had purple fingers and a series of crumpled copies which hadn't made it through the curving cylinder of the ditto machine. As he watched the last of the copies and the cylinder meet, he slowly wiped his hands on a paper towel.

Dipping the paddle into the water, Andrew moved the canoe slowly up the cove against the current. Although he knew that with this current it would probably take him hours to make it to the large cove, Andrew didn't really care. He watched the paddle lift up and down, the quiet slipping of the wood into the water, while he ignored the beginning of an ache in his upper shoulders.

The water slipped by. The shore moved as though it were crawling. The weeping willows dipped their mouths into the water, and he paddled until he felt as though he had huge knitting needles sticking from his shoulder blades. By the time he reached the large cove, the muscles in his wrists had begun to ache fiercely, and he had a pattern of splinters in the palms of his hands, a pattern like an eye.

The cove was the same as it had been the several times he had been fishing there, a quiet, large place with trees hanging over the edge on one side and a thick fringe of fern circling the opposite shore. Dusk was beginning, and he could see the looped lights of fireflies circling a nearby tree.

Andrew paddled slowly toward the ferns, his eyes intent

upon the waving, lacy plants. Nothing else moved. He heard no noise past the rise and fall of his paddle in the water, felt no movement except for the motion of the fireflies now behind him. When he reached the area where he had seen Billy, he steadied the boat with the paddle, tied the canoe to a branch, and gingerly put on his waders. There was a rising breath of wind in the air. He felt the chill of it. Soon it would be October, and there would be no more fishing.

The water lapped against his feet, then his legs, and further up to his waist as he stepped into it. He could feel the stir of what seemed to be a fish moving around close to his knees. Stumbling against a stone, he righted himself. Then he began to move slowly toward what seemed to be the shoreline.

CHAPTER 9

Andrew hadn't realized how many people lived in Greenback. There must have been at least eight hundred of them jammed into the small auditorium. The ushers had had to bring in extra folding chairs.

According to the flyer Sylvia Walker had handed to him at the beginning of his second school week, this event was known as Comedy Night. When he wanted to know what he was in for, she simply shrugged. But he persisted, and at last she winked and said, "Anything, you know. It's just a way to remind us all we belong together enough to be silly about it."

And she must have been right. As soon as the crowd settled down to a murmured roar, the first act walked onto the stage. A large-boned, angular woman in a calico dress and a hat with the price tag hanging down from the side called out in ringing tones, "Howdee, I'm just so proud to be here. Me and Brother—"

The crowd began to laugh and to clap so that she had to pause for a moment until they were more quiet.

"Who is that?" Andrew whispered to the person next to him.

A large, motherly looking woman with her hair drawn back in a bun looked at him and smiled. "Why that's Minnie Pearl; don't you know who that is?"

"No, I mean, who is she impersonating?"

"Why Minnie Pearl."

Andrew sank back into his seat and listened in bemusement to a monologue about Minnie and her imaginary brother, Brother, and their adventures with the Nashville railroad.

Next came two fellows in their forties. They wore overalls and western shirts and carried banjos in their hands. They had the look of straight-faced comics. Without a word to the crowd they began to strum a solo, then a slow duet, and finally launched into a tune Andrew recognized as "Dueling Banjos." In the back two or three women got up and started to clog, their heels clicking vigorously in time to the music. The crowd clapped time. The man on the other side of Andrew spilled Coke in Andrew's lap. With a quick apology, the man tossed over a handkerchief and then renewed his clapping.

Though Andrew wasn't very musically inclined, the music was lively and he soon found himself clapping along. He enjoyed the feeling of being part of a healthy crowd who didn't seem to care if he mistakenly clapped on the offbeat as often as he clapped on the beat. The people to either side of him laughed and cheered. Andrew called out, "Whowee!"

When the tune ended, they strummed the strings with a huge sweep upward, and two buckets of water dropped on their heads. It shouldn't have been funny, but their faces were expressionless and they didn't move at all from their cane-backed chairs. The crowd roared, and Andrew, with a slightly self-conscious look, roared along with them.

After they left the stage and someone mopped up the floor, out came a series of children's acts of the sort commonly seen at school talent shows, except that they all emphasized some sort of humor. The two most notable were a group act with a skit entitled "Is It Time Yet, Ma?" and a high school girl, who Andrew recognized with surprise as Sylvia, doing "Tiptoe Through the Tulips" in big-pocketed tramp's outfit complete with a huge yellow-and-purple-polka-dotted handkerchief into which she blew her nose at the end of each verse. The applause for each of these acts was enthusiastically polite.

Most of the people in the crowd had settled back as though they were patiently waiting for something.

Feet sloshing through the reeds, bending down to steady himself, moving doggedly through the ferns toward shore

Andrew, by this time, would just as soon have gone home. Though the beginning had drawn him into a community feeling, the middle of this show seemed like the middle of any other interminable school or community production. The community feeling had gone and he missed Kate and the boys achingly. He should have never come.

The empty shoreline, the deserted sweep of the land beyond the river's edge

For the first time an announcer, dressed in a shiny black tuxedo, walked out onto the stage. "Ladies and gentlemen, may I have your attention please for the grand finale of the evening, a lovely group for the swimsuit competition this year." He waved his hands gracefully at the small band seated in front, and they began to play "The Tennessee Waltz."

Onto the stage stepped a procession of large, hairy chested men in a variety of one piece women's swimsuits. Each man, regardless of the color of his suit, wore fire engine red high heels and lipstick to match.

Andrew stared at them. His sense of being a part of the crowd dropped from him the moment they appeared on stage. If this had been Atlanta, he might have assumed they were gay; here in Greenback, he was not quite sure what they were doing.

The woman on his left laughed and tapped someone on the shoulder in the row in front of her. "Would you look at that Chester Johnson! What a pair of legs that man has! He couldn't pass for a woman in the dark with a towsack on now could he?"

People began to laugh and call out to different ones. "Turn around a little there now, darling."

Andrew looked around him, trying to determine the mood of the crowd. Perhaps it would have been funnier if he had known who the men were. He leaned back in his seat and listened.

Suddenly he realized that Mr. Boyles was up on that stage, Boyles with a lowcut purple suit, Boyles in heels. Andrew shook his head in amazement. Well, Boyles certainly had taken his own advice. He was right in the thick of the community activity.

He was still thinking that one over as the last contestant paraded across the stage, and Boyles was picked as the hands down winner for "his self confidence and poise." As the swimsuit competition ended and the band packed up their instruments, Andrew made his way down the bumpy row of auditorium seats, and through the small groups of people talking while they drifted toward the parking lot.

Some man in a saggy pair of overalls and a worn flannel shirt, a man he didn't remember ever seeing, stopped him and started talking about his late fall pea crop.

"Look," Andrew finally said as politely as he could, "I don't think I know you."

"That's all right, isn't it? We're all neighbors." The man peered at him over the tapped rim of a pair of crooked glasses.

"That remains to be seen." Andrew made his way through the crowd, ignoring as best he could the occasional outstretched hand of someone bent on being neighborly. In this way he shattered what had been nothing more than a momentary belief in warmth. He collapsed against his car with a muttered curse. It hadn't all been torturous.

One thing he would have to admit: The evening had completely taken his mind off things. Kate would have loved this evening. And the boys would have been squirming to go home from the word "Howdee." He reached down to pull a splinter from his fingertip, worrying at it until it came loose. The feeling, Andrew thought, was clean and empty. He was lonely and yet, for the moment able to think, without pain, about how his family might have responded to Greenback. That was the sort of thing that kept his grief within manageable boundaries. It served as a counter for the plunge into the crowd and the sudden realization of what had only been an illusory contact with the people around him.

He didn't belong here yet, and perhaps he never would. The whole event tonight had seemed an inexplicable rite, something inbred and odd. But then that might be the way that any sort of ceremony looked to a cultural outsider. And that's the historian in you, Andrew, he told himself wryly, seeing trends in isolated events. Or isolated people, his thoughts echoed bleakly. And now that you're feeling sorry for yourself, Jackson, it's time to head for home. He opened the car door as if it were as heavy as cast iron.

Andrew sat up in bed. He had been dreaming of Broken Echo, running around and around the house, but then he wasn't running at all, he was rolling. He looked like the moon and he was rolling along the floor, a soft luminescence trailing behind him like the path of a firefly. One moment the arc of that trail was full-bodied and round, the next it sailed like the spiral of a new moon. Beside that rolling orb scrabbled the claws of a squirrel. Sporadically the squirrel paused to gnaw on the legs of the furniture. He woke to the sound of its teeth. Twice now he'd dreamed about the old Indian and the moon. Perhaps he'd dreamed more often. The dreams had the familiarity of repetition.

He looked out the window, watching the curtains billow in the night breeze. The darkness around him was soft. The moonlight suddenly seemed kindly, but he could tell by the thoroughness with which he had come awake that he would not get back to sleep for several hours. He rolled over and looked at his clock. It was two in the morning. And he had to get up at six-thirty. Sighing, he rolled back over and, for a few minutes, lay looking at the ceiling. Then he got up and shrugged on a bathrobe.

After padding down the stairs, he fumbled his way across the room and out onto the proch where he stood for a moment indecisively staring along his property line at the trees swaying with the wind. Though it was a cloudy night, here and there the moon shone through. At the water's edge, the moonlight shone on one small tree bent nearly double, its branches dipping down into the water. Beyond that, in the darkness at the center of the channel, came the sound of a quiet paddle and a clear, masculine voice calling, "Stroke, stroke."

What were they doing on the water this time of night? He listened intently, but, though he listened for several minutes, heard nothing further beyond the sound of the paddle striking the water.

He walked quickly down the steps. The moon broke through the clouds, so that it shone clearly upon the channel and outlined a boat in the water. The boat was larger than

Andrew expected: six people seated in the back three seats. At the prow, like a stiff figurehead, sat a man with his back to the water. He wore a great black overcoat, and he waved what looked to be a large, old-fashioned revolver in one hand. It was he who said at the moment the light revealed them, "Stroke, stroke."

The other three seats each contained two people whom he could scarcely see. As the foreman called stroke, the others responded by leaning as far forward as they could and stroking together rhythmically. As they moved he heard, clearly across the water, the sound of metal jangling. Andrew ran down the lawn toward the shore, his legs pounding rapidly, his breath becoming more and more abrupt. The shoreline seemed far away, much farther than usual. He crossed a rock outcropping which he didn't at all remember.

"Stroke, stroke." Now he could see them distinctly, gliding down the river. A white man in a huge, black coat, and six black men, the moonlight gleaming on their backs. The boat rapidly moved down the channel. The men made no sound. Andrew tried to keep up with them, but soon they were beyond his small point of land.

Sitting down beside the small, bowed tree, he watched the sluggish current of the water. Though he still had not determined what the other events connected with the house were all about, this he could be certain of. This thing he had seen had been a small, clear moment of the past: Joseph Praeter leaving with his slaves for the markets in Atlanta on one of those protectively cloudy nights more than a century ago.

There were many things that one could probably say about Praeter, but one thing Andrew knew for certain: Despite the surreptitious leavetaking, Praeter had had guts. One man on a boat alone with six slaves, even in chains. He had weapons, of course. Still, he couldn't have been sure they wouldn't hit him with an oar and heave him overboard. He must have made those journeys with very little sleep.

What made this house the way it was? A sort of time processional. He didn't know how it all connected, but he felt certain that, if he were observant enough, he could piece together the meaning of what he had become enmeshed in. If he didn't break, as he knew he was very close to doing, in the attempt. He had been granted, like the lifting of the clouds, one small moment of lucidity. It was in that moment he

realized how very far he had gone down the split path of
fragmentation, and how very divided he had become.

Worse, he was even aware of the glimmer of the moment's
departure, as he rose to move slowly up the hill, feet inexorably
climbing, despite any thought to the contrary, toward the
battered family car.

Andrew glanced, from behind the curtain, at an old man
with a vaguely familiar moustache banging on his front door.
"Anybody home?" he asked in a vigorous, cracked voice.

As he opened the door, Andrew said, "Yes?"

The older man shook his head, and said, "Have you
forgotten me then?"

"I—well, yes, I suppose I have. You're—"

"Turkey Haines."

Andrew opened the door a little wider.

"I'm the clerk at the Loudon County Courthouse."

"Oh yes, now I remember. I'd been meaning to get back to
you for quite some time."

"Meaning to get back to me! Why you invited me over for
dinner!" The old man was clearly taken aback. His adam's
apple jerked as he swallowed, and his eyebrows snapped.

"I what?" Andrew stepped out onto the porch.

"Well, I wouldn't drive all the way over here just on a
wild hunch that you might have dinner waiting." Turkey
Haines hunched his shoulders.

"I'm sorry, Mr. Haines. I just haven't been myself lately. I
don't recall inviting you to dinner." Andrew hesitated. "I
hope you'll forgive the fact that I forgot you were coming, just
lay it down to the fact that I—well, anyway, I hope you'll
forgive me." He cleared his throat. "Why don't you come in
and we'll sit down and talk? I've got supper on the stove
cooking and there's enough for both of us."

"I don't know as I want to—"

Andrew interrupted him eagerly. "Look, I'm really sorry
about all of this. If you leave now, it'll be a disaster all
around. Why don't you come on in?"

"I never did go to dinner where somebody forgot I was
coming," the old man grumbled, but he followed Andrew
inside. "Wouldn't have anyway, you know, if you hadn't said
you couldn't make it over to Loudon during the day."

"I think a good dinner will set things to rights. Do you like meatloaf, Mr. Haines?"

"Would have to say that a good meatloaf would go a long way towards setting things to rights." Turkey Haines grinned. "I brought something to contribute, you know." He waved a small Mason jar with a clear liquid inside. "Thought you might like some moonshine. Didn't figure you folks down Atlanta way had probably had the chance to taste some of that."

"Can't say as I have." Andrew forced a smile. Blindness, he thought. Staggering drunks. Well, it won't hurt to have a little.

"Yeah, you're in for a real treat."

"Nice thought, Mr. Haines."

"Now call me Turkey if we're going to be eating together. I never had any use for being formal."

"Have a seat, Turkey, and I'll go check on our supper." Settling gingerly on the Queen Anne sofa, Turkey Haines looked around at the living room. "Nice place you've got," he said to Andrew.

"Make yourself at home." He walked into the kitchen, checked the meatloaf and the potatoes. Though he had cooked a large meatloaf, he always cooked that way so that he could eat for several days, he had no idea why he had put on so many potatoes or why he'd made such a large corn casserole. How could he have forgotten that he'd called the clerk up at the courthouse to invite him to dinner? Leaning on the table, Andrew stared fixedly at the stove.

"Say, Andy, what do you say about some of that moonshine while we're waiting for dinner?"

He took a deep breath and straightened up. "I believe I would at that, Turkey. I'll bring some glasses." He put the glasses on the counter and stared at them for a moment. Then he picked them up, though he felt them shaking in his fingers. Taking another deep breath, he walked into the living room.

"Say, tell me something, Turkey." He handed the old man a glass.

"What's that?"

"What did I sound like on the phone?"

"You mean you think it was somebody else?" Turkey poured a full glass for Andrew.

"Maybe."

"No, it was your voice all right. Though you sounded more like a city man when you called than you do now. No, I'd swear for a fact that that was your voice."

Andrew looked at his glass for a moment, and then raised it for a drink.

"Watch that stuff. It has a kick like a mule."

But the taste of it was familiar on his tongue, and he took a gulp without sputtering.

"I'll be;" Turkey Haines raised his eyebrows. "Now, I thought you said you hadn't had moonshine before."

"I didn't say, but you're right. I've never had it." He leaned back in his chair, and moved around until the cushions were comfortable.

The older man poured his own drink without another comment, though he clearly was disappointed that the moonshine had had no more effect.

"Hold on a minute, Turkey; let me go check on dinner." Andrew got up and walked slowly into the kitchen.

The meatloaf seemed to wriggle in his hands like a large fish. Andrew lifted it to the table, took a large spoon from the drawer, and scooped two large piles of meatloaf onto the plate. Steam rose from the plates. Andrew noticed belatedly that the top of the meatloaf had gotten burned. He cut the top off of each pile and threw the two burned pieces toward the garbage can. Both of them landed with a plop just short of the can, and he grinned. Then he added casserole and boiled potatoes to the plate, and carried it out to the living room.

"What would like to drink, Turkey?"

"We're drinking it." The old man smacked his lips again.

"Why so we are." He handed Turkey a plate and then sat down.

After a while Turkey said, "Nice meal, Andy."

"Thanks."

When they started on their second helping, Andrew leaned forward and stared at the old man intently. "So tell me about this place."

"Well, what do you want to know?"

"Joseph Praeter's daughter, for one thing." Andrew leaned back in his chair. "She married a Cherokee, the son of the man who scalped her father, wasn't that what you said?"

"That's it on the nose." The old man took another swallow and smacked his lips in satisfaction.

"Well, why'd she go and do a thing like that for?"

"From what I hear, she hated that old man, hated him like poison. He kept them all on a tight string, even for back then. And the family didn't have many friends because of his business. The folks around here thought it was shameful, him running those slaves all up and down the river, when everybody knew Tennessee didn't have land for slaves. Greenback folks have always been kind of different. They didn't hold with slaving. Maybe because a lot of them are chock full of Cherokee blood anyway."

Turkey Haines waved his glass in Andrew's direction. "They didn't like your ancestor much either, you know."

"What do you mean?"

"I heard tell anyway that you're kin to Andrew Jackson himself, and named after him to boot."

"How'd you know that?" Andrew took another quick drink of moonshine. "There were quite a few children who were named Andrew Jackson in Marietta. There's one in Greenback. You couldn't be sure."

"Got it from the Loudon County librarian who got it from her sister over't the Greenback library. We don't miss much for stories around here." Turkey Haines saluted Andrew with his glass, and then gulped the rest of his whiskey down.

"I suppose they didn't like him much," Andrew said, following suit. "Old Hickory didn't hold much with Cherokees, even though a couple of them saved his life one time. I guess after the Trail of Tears they had it in for him big time."

"You just better reckon."

They both grinned and Turkey poured two more glasses of moonshine.

"Anyway, daughter, Clarissa, I think her name was, no kind of Christian name anyway, the daughter up and married that Indian to the scandalization of the community just after old Praeter went crazy from the scalping. I tell you it was the talk of the community, I reckon, what with she and her brothers chaining the old man downstairs, and her a-marryin' that Indian. Her brothers couldn't stomach it after a while. I hear tell they moved down the river towards Memphis. Her mother, Evaline, died of a broken heart of the anger between Joseph and Clarissa."

"Do you know any more then?"

"Not much more about that. That was a long time ago. Praeter died a couple of years later, and then the daughter followed him. Riding a horse over there on the other side of Greenback." Turkey gestured vaguely toward the door.

"Horse reared up and fell back on her." He took a bite of meatloaf. "The Indian, they say, died here just about the same time."

"Broken Echo."

"That's the one. Funny thing about it, though. They never did have any kids." Turkey took another swallow of whiskey.

Andrew looked up, his eyes widening. Broken Echo stood at the doorway to the kitchen, a plate of meatloaf and an empty glass in his hand.

He walked casually over to the couch and sat down next to Turkey Haines. Haines didn't seem to notice.

Broken Echo poured himself a glass of moonshine.

"What are you looking at?" Turkey Haines looked at Andrew.

"Nothing," said Andrew, spilling his food from the plate.

"Boy, you better learn how to eat." The old man finished up the last of his meal.

Andrew scooped the meatloaf back onto his plate and put it down on the table. "What happened to the sons?"

"Oh, I don't know. I think they made a fortune in Memphis at the lumber mills."

Broken Echo nodded at Andrew in confirmation.

"How did the Indian die?"

"Nobody knows exactly. Just up and died in the house. He's buried out there in the family graveyard, but they never could keep a tombstone on his grave, so the story goes. They keep disappearing."

Broken Echo patted Turkey Haines on the shoulder. "I don't believe in tombstones."

Turkey kept right on talking. "Then I guess you know this house was a Civil War prison camp for the Yankees, don't you? I guess you would, being a history teacher and all."

"I heard something about it."

"Yeah, I guess this old house has seen a lot of hard times." Broken Echo smiled at Andrew. He waved his hands expansively. Andrew tried not to look at him.

"What about the people who've lived here since then?"

"None of them stayed very long, 'cept the McKinneys.

Everyone who lived here would all talk about pianos playing at night, and none of them had pianos, and about the house changing around on 'em. I guess they either drank too much of this stuff;" Turkey poured himself the last bit of moonshine. Then he seemed to reconsider it, and he poured half of what he had in his glass into Andrew's. "Or this place is haunted."

"You believe in that kind of thing?"

Turkey looked through the empty glass in his hand. "Might say as I do, and might say as I don't."

Broken Echo winked at Andrew.

"I wonder who played the piano."

"Wasn't old Praeter. That was a bit after his time."

"Maybe someone from the prison camp," Andrew prompted.

"Maybe. When did they make pianos anyway?"

"No idea," said Andrew. "I think I'll look it up." Then he said softly, "Kate played the piano. She played Beethoven." Andrew squinted at Turkey. He seemed to be moving farther and farther away.

"Nothing else?"

"The only music she knew."

"That's really all I know about the place." Turkey leaned back. "You know, I came here because you wanted to pump me, and you've gotten what you wanted. But I want something too."

"What?" Andrew looked at him with some suspicion.

"No, it's nothing to do with this place. I'm an old man with a lot of hobbies, and one of them is collecting stories about this county; but I like history. I've read myself out with Southern history, and started tracing its roots backwards to the Indians and the blacks. Right now I'm steady on reading about where the slaves came from. A lot of slaves from this area came from Haiti; did you know that?"

Andrew woozily shook his head.

"There are all sorts of bad movies about the lives they brought with them, their beliefs and their customs. But I've been looking into voodoo, and it turns out to be a lot more complicated and interesting than people think. It's not all pins in dolls and black magic."

"So what are you saying?"

"Both the Haitians and the Africans, they believed that souls hung around after death."

"Along with ninety-seven other religions," Andrew managed to get out.

Turkey rolled his glass across the floor. Andrew watched the rim of it circle around slower and slower.

"They thought they kept them in these jugs and they could bring them out when they danced. After they'd been in jugs a long time, they got stronger, like good moonshine. Kind of added themselves together. When the people danced, these spirits took them over, mounted them, like horses. They sort of became the spirits for a while. The book I read called the spirits loa. They were stronger than ghosts."

That explains it, thought Andrew woozily. He read this stuff in a book. None of it sounded like Turkey.

He heard Turkey's feet moving away from him across the living room. "They were ghosts?" Andrew stretched and lay down on the couch.

"More than ghosts;" his voice came from the door. "I guess I'll ask you about this another time. Besides, it doesn't seem like you know much about it."

Was that what Broken Echo had meant about the cellar, that the ghosts had become loa? What had he said? "The cellar is more than you can carry; you who are not the horse of a loa."

And that was the last thing Andrew remembered until he woke up in the morning with a crashing headache. He still rested in the same chair, though his shoes had been removed.

After gazing blearily up at the wall by the stairwell at yet another weaving, the colors blurred and uneven, Andrew got to his feet. Fighting the feeling that the room was moving with him, he passed by the weaving with a salute. "Welcome home," he said, and stumbled against the stair railing.

"Today," Andrew said, pausing to take a drink of water from the quart-size glass on his desk, "We'll talk about the Battle of Bull Run."

He began to pace up and down the sides of the classroom. "What, as best you can tell from your reading, was the importance of the second Battle at Bull Run?"

"Was it," Cynthia Dunn shook back her bush of a haircut, "because the South lost a battle that later proved to be the breaking point of their morale?"

"A partial answer. Why do you say that the South *lost* the battle?"

"Well, because they—"

"They won the battle, but the victory cost them." Larry drawled.

Andrew grimaced. He could hardly bear the boy in the classroom these days. Larry could not seem to settle into the class, and sometimes Andrew imagined he had a wildcat hunched over a desk, rather than a feverish young student. He sighed.

"It was admittedly a bad battle, but there were many as bloody as Bull Run." Andrew paced down the left side of the classroom. The boards creaked under his feet. Pausing by the window, he looked across his classroom. Anyone walking in the door would hardly believe this was the same bunch of students. The individual projects were what had "lit their fire." The irrelevance of that tune went whistling through his mind. "Come on, baby, light my fire." He suddenly flashed a memory of Clara Brown's soft, finely veined arm.

"They were gallant in the face of butchery, weren't they?" asked Sylvia Walker.

Sylvia the romantic. Andrew smiled. Was this what Clara had been like as a girl? Probably.

"That's right," said Gary Parker, the thin, blond boy with the scar. He had not yet materialized into the classroom threat Andrew continued to expect. His voice was open, eager. "They were going up a hill against such a strong position they knew they'd never make it. And they watched the men around them die in piles. They'd won other battles, lost soldiers before, but never like that. It was hopeless. And that General, what's his name—he shouldn't have ever ordered them up there."

"And what were they supposed to do?" Larry turned around in his seat. "Just give it up? Turn their swords over?"

"I didn't say that," shot back Gary. "I was talking about military tactics."

There, across the room, was something which struck Andrew silent just as he was prepared to launch the discussion well.

At the edge of the classroom, by the door, stood a boy in a well-worn striped T-shirt, so faded that the colors were no longer distinguishable, and a pair of shorts almost too short for him. On the boy's head perched a red Atlanta Braves cap and written across the brim in large white block letters was the name ANDY.

Leaning aginst the window behind him, Andrew raised a hand to his head. The silence of a stopped discussion was the loudest silence of all, he decided. Blood pounded in his ears, like a tomtom of a voice, out-of-control, out-of-control.

"Son," he said softly. The boy walked slowly around the room, trailing his fingers across the tops of empty desks, across the unaware and unfeeling heads of Andrew's students. He moved toward Andrew as though nothing else in the room existed.

Andrew closed his eyes. A hand rested on his arm. He shivered. Sylvia Walker's voice came to him dimly.

"Mr. Jackson, Mr. Jackson."

Looking up, he saw Sylvia at his side, her hand on his arm. The classroom was strangely empty except for the unnaturally still bodies of his students. His body lurched to his desk. He managed to sit down. Resting his face on his hands, he took several deep breaths, trying to ignore the shocked murmuring of his class. His fingers were cold and lifeless against his eyes. He'd lost it. He was supposed to be all right, all right, damn it, in the classroom.

At last he looked at his students. "It's almost the end of the class period anyway. We'll resume here tomorrow."

The filed out with unusually solemn faces with none of their customary afterclass banter. All, that is, except for Larry Bryge, who stopped at his desk. Some students, Andrew thought wearily, are perennial desk stoppers. They can never leave a classroom without it.

"Mr. Jackson, do you think—"

He tried to make his voice even. "Can we talk about it tomorrow, Larry?"

"Yeah, sure. I hope you feel better, sir."

"Thanks, Larry." Andrew just barely kept the edge from his voice, an edge perilously close to breaking through.

"What about it, Clara?" Andrew asked, holding the small half door which led to the inner office open invitingly. "Would you like to go to dinner? We could drive to Maryville if you know a nice place to eat."

He watched the slow movement of her hand as it rose to tuck a loose strand of hair into place.

"I make it a point never to go out with recently widowed men;" her voice was merrily casual, but firm. "Try me again when you've gotten your feet on the ground. You're still looking shell-shocked to me." Pushing her chair back from the desk, she slipped her coat on and reached for her purse. "Feeling the quiet out there a bit, are you?" Her voice was suddenly warmer, more sympathetic.

Andrew nodded slowly, feeling a confused mixture of relief—what could he have been thinking about; desolation—another night of a weary kind of frenzy, he didn't want to think about what had happened to him in his classroom; and desire—he'd like to throw her across the desk and tear off those layers of clothes—what was it about death and grief that made sex a dangerous and perverse need? He needed to feel human warmth and that was natural. But the anger and the desperation. That was dangerous. By the time he had opened his mouth to speak again—he hardly knew what he intended to say—she had slipped by him and was at the door, her hand on the knob.

"I'm not ready for the violence of your loneliness, my dear," she said softly and was gone, while he was still thinking she could hardly know how right she was.

CHAPTER 10

Andrew shivered and turned over. The breeze from his bedroom window reached through the sheets. He wound them around him tighter and tighter, but the cold air still reached him. He rolled over and leaned over the side of the bed, wrapped like a mummy, one hand extended in search of the blankets he had cast off in the night. His back tingled with the physical awareness of another presence.

"Your memory goes back too far." Broken Echo's voice was low and sad, as he settled, cross-legged, at Andrew's side. "I think you might be a good man after all, but your memory goes back too far. Stay away from me when the moon is new. Or I will take all of you."

Andrew was hoarse. "I've had enough of you, Broken Echo. You and your damned elusive games. Everyone has seasons, but no one mimics the moon." He tried to sit up but found that he could not. His back, raw and stiff, refused to support him.

"When I'm young and angry, I've been stealing your memory. Soon you will have nothing left but the visions of this house. Then you will have no choice."

"No choice, but what?" asked Andrew. From somewhere chains rattled hollowly, but Broken Echo was gone. "No choice but what!" Andrew coughed again and again. Then he unwound the sheets and pulled on a pair of jeans and a T-shirt. His intention was to make himself a cup of tea; instead he found himself out on the lawn, walking toward the side of the house. "I won't let you steal my history, old man."

Fog blew in thick from the lake until Andrew could scarcely see the smashed car, but by now he knew the shape of the old Volvo by heart. The door opened stiffly, and he sat down on the clammy seat as though it were the only place he belonged, fingers automatically reaching for the keys, thumb closing against empty fingers. The fog, coming unchecked through the windows, settled in around him until he could scarcely see the dash. Ignoring the leaden weight at his wrists, he lifted his hands to the steering wheel. At the moment his fingers gripped the wheel there came a small, melodious piping from the seat beside him.

Andrew tried to lift his fingers and to turn his head to see who was in the seat beside him. Instead, he found himself staring straight ahead into the fog, while he hummed along to the music of a slow and breathy tune. What was his wife's name? Andrew gripped the steering wheel more tightly. How could he forget a name that he had known as well as his own for these ten years or more? A name he had whispered in her ear as he stroked the gentle curve of her waist. He knew his sons' names—Billy and Andy—but he couldn't even think where they'd met. It had suddenly become very important to remember.

A flourish of trills and then silence. "Her name was Kate," came Broken Echo's voice.

Andrew tried desperately to move his head, even one inch, but he could not.

"You met her at a folk music festival in Atlanta. She was weaving in the crafts room."

For a moment Andrew could remember; he could see her, see her with that inner floating sight like a bubble of clarity. He had stood at the door, one hand on the doorjamb, and watched her silently. She had bent forward, just so, her hair falling down over her face as she had pushed forward the shuttle on the large loom, the sunlight shooting in through the window and falling like a bright shadow over her red hair, almost gold in the sunlight. She had turned, just so, her eyes wide and questioning underneath eyebrows flaring like wings, her hand lifted to brush her hair back out of the way. And in the place where that wonderful grave face should have been, there were blank features like those of a doll.

"Is this what you meant," he asked angrily, "when you said that you were stealing my memories?"

"Those were what seemed most important to you. I wanted you to leave. If what tied you here drove you to leave, it seemed a fair bargain."

"How do you know what tied me here?" Each word sounded as if it belonged by itself. "And what makes you think that you have the right to steal what is mine?"

"Why bother to speak of what we both know?" Broken Echo's voice was casually contemptuous. "Have you forgotten whose descendant you are?"

Andrew yanked his head around. Now he could see the old Indian. There was a sudden sense of pain, a blurring of his vision.

"I was a man of sanity too. Once," said a cultured, Southern voice, Praeter's voice. Andrew identified the voice, but he no more knew how he did that than how he heard it in the first place. It came from nowhere. Or perhaps it came from Andrew's own mouth.

"Once," came the whispered echoes of trailing voices. A small pottery flute dangled from Broken Echo's fingers. The vinyl on the car seat crackled as the old Indian shifted in his seat.

"What else have you done to me?" Andrew whispered. "And why the sudden change of heart?"

The noise of the pipe, which rested seemingly silent between Broken Echo's fingers: "I can't stop what has begun." Broken Echo rolled down the car window on his side.

"You said that before."

"You must live it. The trail of the lonely, the tunnel of the lost. And come out the other side." He shrugged. "Or not. I really don't think you'll make it, particularly with the way you're handling things at school." His voice was playful and indifferent.

Andrew looked out the window. The trees hung dark and thick against the fog. On the hood of the car curled a miniature white deer. The deer looked back at him. Broken

Echo leaned out the side of the car and began to play a tune, the fingers of one hand extended carefully toward the deer.

"I don't know the way!" Andrew pounded against the dash.

Broken Echo wiggled his fingers. The deer lifted its head. "I come from a long line of those who guide."

"Until the moon is new. Then your younger self tries to chop me up into little pieces." Andrew's voice was bitter.

"A point. Still, that makes it easy to know when to trust me. Not everyone is so accommodating."

"You call ambiguity accommodating."

"In its own way."

The eyes of the deer grew large and luminous. Andrew watched them swell until there was no more than a pinpoint of light in their center. From that pinpoint came a hand swooping like a hawk.

He lay on the floor.

"Was it so necessary for you to drive me from the house?" He looked up at the large hand reaching down toward him. No response.

"And now?" Andrew coughed until he could no longer see.

"I said I'd guide you. Isn't that enough?" The old man's hand lifted Andrew to his feet.

"If you're trustworthy."

"A thought left up to the deer."

"Where are we going?"

"If you expect to return to your classroom, we have much to do." Broken Echo lifted Andrew like a child. "It will be a temporary solution, as temporary as the one you've arrived at, but less damaging. You understand that."

"I *hear* you."

"It will do." Broken Echo chuckled. "How you could have thought that making yourself believe they were alive part of the day would work for very long, I don't know."

They were in the cellar, Andrew belatedly realized. There was a lifting and a sighing of shadows all around the cellar, a movement of tossing light, and the sound of bare feet against the earth. Skin brushed against his. The drumbeats stirred into a slow, thick rhythm. From behind Andrew came laughter, and a cloth against his back. At the other end of the cellar swayed a black man in a large, black frock coat and sunglasses. Someone waving a cane like a baton. The others whispered and giggled. There was a rustling of cloth.

Leading a procession of small, dark men in white, men who carried large gourds with gaping mouths as holes, Broken Echo circled Andrew. He was chanting softly. The men dipped and bobbed at the end of each phrase. The movement of the cane circled with the dancers. The man in the frocked coat began to turn in a grotesque slow motion, as the edges of his coat trailed the ground.

"And this," Andrew whispered, watching the man slowly revolve, "is supposed to make it possible for me to keep teaching?" What had Turkey said? Something about the ghosts being kept in gourds and their spirits coming out when people danced. But different than ghosts. They came out to take people over. He shivered.

Rising up from the center of the dancers, hovering and floating above them, a small blue eye regarded Andrew. It sailed slowly in his direction and then stopped just in front of him, the eyelid lowering in a prolonged wink. "Possession is nine tenths of the law," a small, mocking voice said.

He couldn't understand it. Which place was he? One moment he danced in the cellar, and the next moment he lay sprawled on the hood of the car. He had weeks ago lost track of time, but now even places seemed as insubstantial.

The metal of the hood was warm. He felt that first and marvelled that the old mangled engine could make so much heat. Broken Echo sat in the front seat, staring out at him. The car hummed with life. Around Andrew went the shifting bobbing shapes of small, quick bodies, of large, shambling men in chains, the movements of dancers in the fog. He lifted his fingers to his eyes. They were large and luminous as the deer's; they were pinpoints of light in a crowd of circling strangers. They were the cry of something lost and forgotten. His body was insubstantial. All that held him there were the tips of his fingers, sensitive and aware. The feel of metal against his hands, the glance of the light across his eyes, the echo of bodies moving closer, the deer, dancing light, light as the touch of nettles, across his back. "How long," Andrew breathed quietly, his voice as soft as the deer, "will it last?" The only answer was the slowly dying hiss of his final word.

"Today," said Andrew, perching confidently on the front of his desk. "We'll talk about the part the raiders played in the

Civil War, particulary a man some of you have been researching eagerly;" Andrew paused to smile at Jim; "John S. Mosby."

Jim looked upset.

"Don't worry, Jim. There'll still be a good deal for you to discuss. We're only going to talk about strategic policy and pivotal points in the war affected by the raiders." He paused again and looked out over the classroom.

"The raiders," Leona Berry said eagerly, her eyes flashing, "were the ones who were the most active in the war, weren't they? My great grandfather was in Mosby's raiders."

"What do you mean the most active, Leona?" asked Cynthia Dunn. "Nobody was exactly sleeping on the job."

"Everybody was sleeping." Larry laughed. "They were all dead on their feet."

"Except for the calvary." Jim sat up, the desk almost bouncing into the aisle.

"That's cavalry, Jim." Andrew corrected.

"Well," said Leona, "the raiders were like guerrilla troops. They attacked somewhere, and then they were gone before the Yankees could do something to them."

"What strategic advantage did that give them?" Andrew asked quietly.

"They lost very few men," said Susan.

"They could be off somewhere to rest before they struck again," said Cynthia.

"And they stole a lot of their weapons that way," said Larry, picking his fingernail with his Buck pocketknife.

Andrew stared at him until he put it away.

"Why are we talking about Mosby?" Sylvia asked. "He was in Virginia, wasn't he? Who was there around here?"

"Very good question. Why are we talking about Mosby?" Andrew rose to pace around the room.

"Because there weren't any raiders in East Tennessee." Cynthia answered, and then tossed a note over to Jim who hastily put it in his pocket just as Andrew crossed the room in his direction. Andrew nearly laughed. They still reacted as though they thought he'd treat them like grammar school kids. "Is there any other reason?"

"He was a Virginia lawyer, wasn't he?" asked Leona.

"So?" said Larry.

"Well, that meant he was probably a good strategist, don't you think?" said Sylvia, with a frown at Larry.

Andrew nodded. He could safely leave the quelling of Larry up to the class at this point.

"And he wasn't like the other raiders. I mean he didn't dress for camouflage." Susan Haskell's green eyes had been on Andrew the entire class discussion. Her stare was beginning to make him a bit uncomfortable.

"Which meant?" Andrew prompted.

"That he made himself a legend, didn't he? On purpose. That was part of his strategy."

"That's what the other raiders did too," said Cynthia. "Yeah but, he was especially—"

"You mean it wasn't just because he had guts," drawled Larry, looking somehow disappointed.

"So we're back to talking about morale then," said Sylvia.

"That's a very good way to look at it," said Andrew, faintly surprised. "But not necessarily the soldiers' morale, at least the old-line officers."

"They hated the raiders, didn't they?" Gary asked eagerly. "They showed them up."

"Well, whose then?" asked Leona.

"The people's, of course," said Larry with a withering look at Leona.

When the bell rang they all looked disappointed. "We'll pick up here next time;" he sat down at his desk. "Oh, could I see you a minute, Jim?"

Jim paused, looking startled, then bundled his books up awkwardly into his arms and came up the aisle. "What is it, Mr. Jackson?"

Larry Bryge, who had been headed for the front of the room turned around and left with obvious reluctance. Andrew nodded.

"You know, Jim, the presentations are in a week and a half."

"Yes sir."

"It seemed to me your knowledge of Mosby was still a bit thin."

Jim had the grace to look sheepish. "Yeah, I've checked the books out, but—" he shrugged. "You know, you're working us hard, and—"

He looked at the boy without saying anything.

"Don't you worry, Mr. Jackson, I'll have my presentation ready."

"That's exactly what I wanted to hear, Jim."

"Yes sir;" he grinned and inched his way toward the door, then paused. "You know, I think that I'll check out the whole idea of myths and morale with the raiders. I mean school kids today in the South still look up a lot to Mosby, don't they?"

Andrew looked up and smiled. Bingo. "Sounds like a good direction, Jim. See you tomorrow."

Andrew pulled his car carefully into the Cleary's Grocery Store parking lot. When he stepped out of the car, he heard a familiar voice say, "Well, Andrew Jackson, I haven't seen you for a while."

"Jess," he said, turning around smoothly.

"What have you been up to?"

"Grading papers mostly. That honors history class keeps me pretty busy."

"I think you ought to come over for dinner again." Jess put her hands on her hips and nodded her head. "Yes, I think it'd be good for morale. And it looks to me like your morale could use it too." She leaned forward and patted his stomach lightly.

He was uncomfortable. Jess's mouth was smiling, but her eyes looked worried. James must have been talking to her about those fishing trips.

"I don't know, Jess, if I keep feeding my morale at this rate, I'll be the one in the crowd with a basketball in my stomach," he said lightly.

"I don't think there's any danger of that. Come on, I won't take no for an answer now. How about tonight?"

"I've got plans tonight, Jess. How about some night next week?"

"That'll be just fine, Andrew. Put some meat on those bones."

"What?" he asked, startled. A truck wheeled around, exhaust fumes trailing behind it. Both Andrew and Jess backed hastily away.

"Feed you up some, Andrew; you're looking peaked," she cupped her hands and called to him.

"All right, Jess. Thank you." He walked to the car, sure that he'd made a promise he'd never keep. Nothing he said had substance any more.

Fingers trailing across the tops of their heads like the drifting of weeds

The wheels of the car turned in a sucking motion, the air felt heavy and full of lint. The car moved more and more slowly until it lay suspended above the pavement. Andrew watched his hands turn the wheel. Flying gravel crunched under the tires and he was opening the door to the car.

A faded, red cap with the name ANDY *printed in block letters across the bill.*

Feet moving, sensation in the soles only, across the limp, brown grass and through the piles of fall leaves, all crackling with the small voices of things once green.

Another voice reached out to him from the porch. "Welcome home, Andrew," it said.

Broken Echo was seated in a rocking chair on the front porch, its slow creak and corresponding hesitation matching the beat of Andrew's heart. He climbed the steps in the same rhythm, and sat down carefully on the top step.

"I made it." He glanced at Broken Echo's hair; it definitely looked a shade darker. New moon coming, he thought.

"You won the battle then, *Chief Bull Run?*" The Indian's tone was mocking. "You think one day is a revelation?"

He didn't rise to the bait. Instead he waited a moment and then asked, "What now?"

The rocker moved back and forth a little more quickly. Andrew's heart beat faster. At last Broken Echo said, "There is no present. There are only the seven levels."

"In this house?"

Broken Echo nodded his head. A lizard ran down the wall and stared at them both with beadwork black eyes.

"And I must meet them all," he said with heavy finality.

"That's a beginning."

Once Andrew would have asked, "What then?" Now he merely nodded his head and watched the curve of a pale, half moon. He even thought he knew some of the levels: dancing, music. Artforms. But the next moment his intuition made absolutely no sense. He watched the moon spin in the sky.

The door to the cellar creaked open with the reluctance of the unused. A shaft of light from the kitchen lit the dusty staircase. Andrew walked down the stairs as though he were stepping into a cave; the measured tread of his boots beat *drumbeat* slowly on the stairs. At the bottom, with his hand on the rail, stood a young man in his thirties, a bandage over his head like a pirate's scarf.

The man's clothes were wilted and out-of-date: faded brown short trousers and long, thick socks, workboots, a scoop front jacket with tails that brushed the backs of his thighs.

Praeter, Andrew thought.

"Where is Evaline?" The man sounded angry.

Andrew shook his head slowly.

"Madam!" Praeter yelled up the stairs. "Why have you locked an ill man in the cellar? I demand to be let out!" Then he gestured, his movement accompanied by the faint rattle of chains. "Let me out, sir."

"I believe," Andrew said, "that it's much too late for that."

Had it been only a month or so ago that Broken Echo had stood in the same place he now stood? Oh no; he shook his head. Oh no, Praeter, crazy man, slaverunner, you won't take me, Andrew thought, as he backed slowly up the steps. He stopped at the third step from the top, staring at the man, and then, as if by compulsion, twisted the lightbulb from its socket, whirled, and firmly closed the cellar door behind him.

The smell of honeysuckle drifted in the air. Andrew stood looking out over the hills where a wavering light like a candle shone through the window of the Bryge's house. He heard the call of an owl hooting slowly as though it were a clock running down. In the dusk the Bryge's house had changed shape. He squinted at it. He could see smoke rising from an old log cabin chimney. He heard a loud slap and the voice of a child crying. "That'll teach you, Billy Jean," he heard a woman's voice calling. "Stay out of that tub!"

To the side of the house he spotted a small white deer. He stared at it uneasily. It seemed eerily familiar. From overhead came the sound of wings beating the air. Dozens of large, dark shapes were passing overhead, though when he looked up to see them, he could see nothing in the dark. From off in the distance he heard the faint call of a wolf. And from his left the sound of oars quietly dipping into the water.

Someone grabbed him by the hair, jerking him backwards. Whoever it was held him so firmly that he couldn't get loose, no matter how much he punched and kicked. From the man's hands came the sharp, pungent odor of pine.

Other men came through the woods, and, as they circled behind him, Andrew could hear them chanting. He felt a ripping pain at the hairline, a numbness, and then he found himself crawling, blindly, back toward the house. This crawling seemed to go on and on; he could not seem to reach the end of what was surely a tunnel. There were rocks, then gravel, and finally grass underneath him, while in the distance, like the tinny echo of a megaphone, came the sound of an owl, crying faintly now. The movement of his hands against the packed earth, the gravel, the grass, the steps. He collapsed against the steps sobbing. Eventually he crawled to the front door and pulled himself through it.

Opening his eyes as though he were expecting to see tombstones, he coughed at the scorching thickness that poured into his lungs. The room was filled with the scent of burning wool, and a dense, gray smoke. After propping open the front door, he ran toward the kitchen door, waving the smoke in front of him with one hand, covering his eyes with the other. He closed the kitchen door behind him to keep the worst of the smoke out. Soon he would have to get a fan, he thought, to clear out the rest of the air. That thought too was a ritual.

Hearing a cleared throat behind him, he turned without a recognizable start, though his stomach gave a quick hitch.

Andrew squinted. The old Indian looked a bit different somehow. Broken Echo had on the same clothes, the same worn beads, and flat-heeled shoes, the same look about the eyes, only—only he looked—a little older? Andrew stared at him, considering. A little less angry? The kitchen rippled with a haze. Andrew waved his hand in front of his face. The old man stared at him, and then he was gone.

No, this couldn't be right, Andrew thought, it was the new moon, wasn't it? And besides, he had already accepted those tapestries, hadn't he? The night that he and Turkey drank themselves flat on the ground. So why was he burning them again? Or was he? He didn't have any memory of burning the tapestry. And why, now that he'd finally figured out the old man's rhythms, were they changing? Nothing stayed still anymore, he thought, as he went to get the fan.

Much later, after a supper of pot pie and applesauce, he made his way slowly, as though his joints were stiff and sore, to the library. There he lit a fire and searched, as always, for a book to read, finally settling back to his seat by the fire without one.

He heard the rocking chair across the room creaking, and he looked up in surprise. The rocking chair was moving, but there was no one in it. He could hear someone crooning or chanting in rhythm to the rocker. Andrew shook his head. Broken Echo had not been in this room since that one night of the deaths. Why now?

For some time the rocker moved. He watched it. Eventually he began to see better, or Broken Echo became clearer. After a while he could see the old man rocking and crooning, his hair definitely a little whiter, and on his face a slight smile. Andrew looked at him in puzzlement. The old man nodded his head and began to speak softly in Cherokee. Andrew could not understand him, but he listened anyway. It was comforting to hear a voice. Then the old man said in English, "I'm fighting my younger self." He didn't wait for an answer; instead he began another Cherokee croon.

Settling back in his chair, Andrew watched the shadows dance on the walls. They bent and waved until he could scarcely see them.

There was a movement of shadow and light, a stillness in the motion, a quietness of the mind, a comfort in the voice. The body was still, and the mind was drifting. He smelled animals, heard them shifting in the darkness and with them the sound of a cleared throat, a woman's laugh, low in the darkness.

What had come was a circle, the joining of men's hands as they lifted the pipe and passed it on, the rhythm of their thoughts, the faroff neighing of a horse in the background, the call of an owl.

They were comfortable and quiet. He was comfortable and quiet. There was a shifting of the shadows and the sliver of a moon, the moon becoming a circle, the passing of the pipe, the embers of the fire.

An old man, it was Broken Echo, turning toward him slowly, the circle gone, the sliver of moon overhead, the circle of the moon, the broken circle of the moon, the old man sadly handing him a pipe. The old man handing him a pipe with a bowl that was crusted and black as though it had been unused and forgotten. The old man handing him a pipe . . .

"Why, Andrew, you sound quite cheerful." Clara Brown leaned back in her chair and smiled at Andrew. "Much too cheerful for a new teacher just prior to your first six weeks exams."

"Maybe that's because I'm not giving exams." He propped his elbows on the counter and smiled at Clara. "I've given them projects instead."

"They'll take you much longer to grade." Clara's chair creaked as she crossed her legs. Andrew closed his eyes for a moment, then looked at her again.

"True," he shrugged; "but they'll be a bit more interesting. By the time I refine this process for next year I'll—"

She stood up and walked toward Andrew. "Do you really think you'll stay on?" Her voice was casual, but he sensed her interest.

"If Boyles keeps me on staff." As he spoke, he could hear his voice become stiff, almost formal. "Well, I'd better hurry or I'll be late for class." He nodded to her, forced a smile, and then ducked hurriedly through the door. Nothing like making a fool of yourself, Jackson, he thought as he walked down the hall. She knew you had a half an hour until your first class. You could at least have made up something more believable. However, the truth was that Andrew didn't care at all whether she'd found his departure believable or not. With relief he realized that his attraction to Clara must have simply been some momentary thing, a reaching out for comfort, perhaps. The thought of physical contact with her was suddenly almost repugnant.

Besides, he rationalized, even if he were ready, and he was far from ready, it would have been a bad idea to see a woman who worked so closely with him. Definitely better to maintain his distance. Stopping to drink from a water fountain in the hall, Andrew gulped the water down as though he hadn't had anything to drink for some time.

"The Old Praeter house, was built in 1793 by Joseph Praeter on land bordering what was then the Tennessee River," said Larry, "and what is now Ft. Loudoun Lake. It is a huge Southern mansion with interior walls of sixteen-foot heavy oak and exterior walls of adobe brick. Much of the original brick has been replaced because the house has been the target of treasure seekers in the past. Once there were two large apple orchards to either side of the house, and a chestnut tree grove. The land was originally landscaped by two Germans with yellow Persian roses, rare for the time, and night blooming jasmine."

Andrew shifted in his seat and leaned his elbow on the window inset. He felt the urge to grit his teeth, but he resisted it. He gave Larry a nod. Get on with it.

"It has been, at various times, the home of the influential Praeter family, friends of Sam Houston and various state politicians of the late 1700's, a place to transfer slaves and sell them downriver, a guest house for wealthy river travelers, a civil war prison camp, and currently it is rumored to be the home of ghosts."

Several students glanced Andrew's way.

Andrew shifted in his seat a second time. "I hardly think that silly superstitions concern a history class, Larry."

"Just what I was about to say," Larry spoke smoothly.

"What does concern us is the Civil War connection."

A sudden irrational desire to pitch Larry through the nearest window came over Andrew. He could imagine the boy's teeth hitting the metal squares on the window pane, the bulk of his body smashing against the glass. He shivered. Does Larry see any of this when I look at him, he wondered.

Larry continued, his voice containing a kind of rough-edged urbanity which annoyed Andrew further.

"Union troops occupied the Praeter house, initially as troop headquarters for the area, during the Battle of Knoxville. The kitchen, dirt-floor with laid over brick, was used to bury their dead. Probably," he paused and glanced mockingly at Andrew, "the reason for the rumors of ghosts."

Andrew half rose from his seat.

Larry glanced down at his notes. "The walnut rail fence the Union troops dismantled and used for a racetrack. And they did other sorts of damage; for instance they were the first in a long series of treasure hunters to dig holes in the brick looking for family treasure. They didn't know that Will Danforth had left rather hurriedly with all the money and valuables he could carry just two short weeks before. Not because he had had any forewarning of the Union foray, but because he had killed a local bushwhacker. Danforth used what he took with him to good advantage. It purchased him a spot with Mosby's Raiders."

"What does that have to do with anything?" called Cynthia from the back.

Andrew laughed a bitter laugh.

Larry looked at him oddly. "What do you mean, Cynthia?"

"Okay, so we have this house on Ft. Loudoun Lake that's been used for a lot of things, but it doesn't seem to me like a topic for a major report. I mean there are lots of houses like that around here."

"None of them," Larry said slowly, "were troop headquarters at the time of the Battle of Knoxville, and none of them were left relatively intact when the troops left."

"Still—"

"And besides, this house is a local landmark and a part of the county's Civil War history."

"London County wasn't all that important in the Civil War. Knox County was much more important. There wasn't a battle at the Praeter house."

Larry began to look more and more determined.

"That's not exactly true. Mosby's Raiders did come through London County, and there was a skirmish over the possession of the house."

"That's not true, Larry," Andrew said quietly.

"I suppose you should know, President Johnson." Larry sneered.

"That's Jackson, Larry," someone called from behind Andrew. "Johnson was a different President, a boring one."

"Any ex-president will do, won't he?"

"That's enough, Larry." Larry slouched. "Now, Cynthia, while it's true that making this research the grounds for a major project is a bit thin, this is the project that Larry wanted to do, and it would have been better if you'd let him finish before bringing up your doubts. Larry, did you have anything else you wanted to add?"

"Several things, actually. When the Yankee soldiers dug up the old cellar, they found several sets of bones there, some of which they couldn't identify." He paused and cleared his throat. "But they did identify one set of bones, the bones of Joseph Praeter, the first owner of the house. The story is that Praeter had been chained in the cellar by his family, after an

Indian raid on the farm. During the raid Praeter had been scalped by a band of Cherokees, but he lived and crawled back to the house. He was babbling and insane, and he actually tried to do harm to his wife and daughter. So they chained him in the cellar. The soldiers found identifying documents with the body. Oh," he paused and smiled at Andrew, "and they found one more thing. A Cherokee arrow, completely intact, tangled with the bones. Either the family never bothered to take the arrow out after the scalping, or some Indian came along and shot him in the cellar. The soldiers were very amused by the whole thing. They placed bets on which they thought was the likeliest."

Andrew felt a cold spot in the center of his chest. He rubbed it and glared at Larry. "Don't push it, Larry," he said angrily.

"Yes sir, Mr. Johnson, sir," Larry replied, his voice bland. He glanced at his notes again. "The Union soldiers remained in possession of the house for several months, during which time they slaughtered and ate all the surrounding livestock for a fifty mile radius, as well as any other local provisons. When they moved on to Knoxville, they left behind them a starving populace, but they wouldn't have moved on then, except that Will Danforth and Mosby's Raiders returned to drive them out."

"That's not historically correct, Larry." Andrew stood up as though he were readying himself for a fight. He clenched his fists and leaned forward on the desk.

"I've shown you the reports. I found the accounts." Larry shifted his weight to the balls of his feet.

"I read nothing of the sort. This other material is familiar to me but—"

"You had it for weeks! You're calling me a liar, aren't you? Nobody calls me a liar." Larry's voice was incredulous. Larry left the front of the room and circled toward Andrew.

"What do you think you're doing, Larry?" Andrew glared at him.

"Nothing, Mr. Johnson," Larry stopped and looked down at the floor.

"That's enough of that," Andrew said quietly, removing his fists from the desk, and loosening his hands. Cynthia looked at Andrew and then at Larry. Sylvia carefully turned to the left as though she were avoiding some invisible line of fire.

Flinging back his hair, Larry started to talk loudly. "You know who he is, don't you?" He looked around the classroom. "Why did he come in here to teach us history and start with the Civil War? Why didn't he start with Tennessee?" Larry flexed his shoulders.

Andrew thought he could see the cloth tear.

"What if he had?" Gary called out, his face eager.

"President Johnson here," Larry's voice slid through the words, "is a—"

"I said that's enough, Larry," his voice rose. He moved toward the teenager. "My name," his hands gripped the boy's shoulders, "is Andrew Jackson, and yes, I'm a descendent of President Jackson, but that's hardly a topic for discussion for this class. It means as little in the course of current events as does the history of this house you're so fascinated by."

"Anyway, he was a good president, wasn't he?" Cynthia asked. "I mean, he fought in the War of 1812 and he was good for domestic policy, wasn't he?"

Larry stepped away from his hands. He spoke to the class again. "He sent the Cherokees away from their homes on the Trail of Tears, didn't he? Killed half of them doing it, didn't he? Sent them West when they thought crossing the Mississippi meant crossing over to the land of the dead." His voice mocked hers. "Anyone with Cherokee blood, and that's half the state of Tennessee, couldn't forget that, could they?" He glared around the class. "Not that the bastard descendant of Jackson would care about niceties like that. *If* that's what you are." Several members of the class gasped. "You've never bothered to tell people that Jackson only had a few wards and an adopted son, now did you?"

"Larry, come here," he said, moving to his desk, his hands of their own volition opening his drawer and pulling out the paddle he had forgotten he had. The boy's challenge was so extreme that it had to be met with extreme measures, he thought grimly.

He walked toward Larry, who shoved the desk back as though preparing for a fight. He raised the paddle and Larry danced to one side. Ignoring the students' gasps, Andrew swung the paddle at Larry like a bat. Larry evaded the wood and grinned. He was plainly enjoying himself.

"Get the hell out of my classroom, mister, and up to the office."

"I doubt that. You going to tell my cousin on me, Mr. bastard Jackson?"

"Your cousin?" Andrew lowered the paddle and looked at him blankly.

"My cousin. Your boss." Larry's grin widened.

"I said, get the hell out of here and up to the office. I'll march you there, if you don't move now."

"I doubt that. I'll leave, Mr. *Johnson*, but if you think I'm going to the office, you've got it all wrong." Larry strolled out the door.

The bell rang. The class filed out without looking at him.

He knew he should have gotten up and followed the boy out, marched him down the hall to Boyles' office, but somehow he had not been able to move quickly enough and now Larry was out of range.

He shook his head in bewilderment. He had a sudden sense of rising up out of a river, a shaking of the nerves. What, oh my God, have I done? he thought. How had it all happened so quickly?

CHAPTER 11

"Look, Clara," Andrew said, moving in behind her and brushing her back with his fingers. It was late afternoon. The office was deserted, and most of the staff and students had gone. He had caught Clara just as she was putting on her jacket. "Why don't you come out with me for dinner?" he whispered in her ear. Jackson, you can be so wonderfully seductive when you're already facing disaster, he thought wryly.

She turned around and raised one eyebrow. "Surprising offer."

He shrugged. "Not so surprising."

She put her hands on her hips. "Why Andrew Jackson, you hardly would speak to me this morning, and now you want me to go to dinner with you."

"That's right." He laughed. "You coming?" he asked, knowing the answer before he spoke.

"I suppose I'll have to, if for no other reason than to teach you a lesson."

Her wink suddenly looked to him like the exaggerated

motion of a gargoyle, but he ignored the sudden visual distortion. "Pick you up at six?"

She must have made some answer before he left the office, but he could hardly be sure, because in the next moment, it seemed, he was pulling into his driveway, dust foaming up in a cloud for a quarter of a mile down the road.

Would she be waiting for him? he wondered, afraid to open the door. Would she be on the porch looking at him like she could see clear to his childhood, the tips of her breasts erect underneath a navy silk blouse? Would she forgive him for touching someone like Clara? He wanted very much to step around the side of the car and look toward the porch and see her there. Would the small, sturdy, too real shapes of his sons be there beside her? What would she have thought of him today? Weak man, he mocked himself. What happened to your strength?

He quickly stepped out of the car and whirled to slam the door. He watched his feet as he walked toward the house. Left. Right. His feet lurched forward. Left. Right. When he reached the stairs, he held his breath, and looked toward the door.

It was hanging open, the hinges sagging, the door swinging. From inside the house came the piercing whistle of a teakettle.

He ran through the open doorway and into the kitchen; there he slowed to a halt.

Broken Echo stood, his back to Andrew, humming to himself and lifting the kettle from the stove. His hair, dark black and long, hung down his back. He spun around, and his face was young and angry.

"I thought you told me," Andrew's voice was grim, "that this ceremony of yours would work."

"Temporarily."

"Temporarily," Andrew's voice rose. "Temporarily," he yelled. "It didn't even work for two days. Or did you mean for it to?"

"Andrew Jackson," he thought he heard Larry's voice whisper.

"Why don't you sit down," Broken Echo's voice was calm, his hands, as they held the kettle, steady, "and have some tea?" His eyes gleamed with triumph.

"Why don't you," Andrew said, "go to hell?"

He swung on his heel and left.

Clara's home was a small white house with a front porch just large enough for one person to stand. Andrew rang the doorbell and looked around him at the rickety trellis that framed the porch on three sides. He sang in a hoarse voice, "Did you *hear* that lonesome *whis*tle blow?"

The door opened outward. He stepped back off the porch. Clara smiled at him. Her hair, long and falling on her shoulders, was a gleaming brown. Her blue dress had a modest V-neck, but to him it seemed like a plunging neckline. He took her arm, pulling her off the porch.

"How are you, Clara?"

"I'm fine," she said, a bit breathlessly, and stepped back from him. "I thought we might go to the steakhouse," she said, walking quickly ahead of him, her high heels clicking on the broken sidewalk.

"The steakhouse," he rolled the words on his tongue, "sounds just fine."

The steakhouse, one of the few restaurants in Greenback, was on the 411 Highway, and the drive was a short one. He pulled into the parking lot, just barely missing a bright blue "jacked-up" truck. The driver, a dark-haired man in a straw cowboy hat and a plaid, rolled-sleeve shirt, gave Andrew a dirty look when the two vehicles passed, but Andrew just laughed. The truck's tires squealed as they hit the pavement. Clara glanced over with a puzzled, questioning look on her face.

When they entered the doorway, the smell of charcoal grilled steak reached out to meet them. Andrew grinned and patted Clara on the shoulder. Most of the restaurant was full, but the waitress managed to find them seats at a small red Formica table toward the back of the room. As she seated them, Andrew murmured an order for beer. She returned quickly with with two iced glasses and two bottles of Miller beer. "What else would you like?" she asked, pulling an order book out of a crisp white apron pocket.

He looked at Clara, who said, "Ribeye steak, medium well, and tossed salad."

"I'll take the same," he said.

Clara watched the woman walk away. Andrew shifted in his seat.

"Why, Clara, what a nice surprise." A woman's voice with a strong Southern accent.

Clara twisted in her seat. "Hello, Louise," she said, smiling a little. "How are you?"

"Just fine," said the woman, who Andrew now recognized as the Greenback librarian. She looked at Andrew speculatively and then smiled at Clara. "Looks like you're having a night out on the town."

"Seemed like a good idea," he said. He leaned back in his seat. Clara winked at him.

"Oh, I've got those books you requested on Haitian voodoo. Can you tell me why we've got a run on things like that lately?"

"Right;" Andrew hesitated. "Did all of them come in?" he asked dubiously. He hadn't ordered any books, had he? Then he shrugged. "I think some of the students are beginning to be interested in some of the slave background."

"Sounds a little far fetched to me." The librarian winked, and moved on to talk to someone else.

Clara picked up her beer and drank quickly. When she put the glass down half of it was gone. She gasped. "I must have been thirstier than I thought. I better not drink any more until we eat." The she fiddled with her spoon. "Andrew, what's this about voodoo?" Her voice was stiff.

He smiled and clinked his glass against hers. "Really nothing. Most of the slaves in this area of this country were Haitian, you know. Some of the students are looking into their background, that's all. Speaking of backgrounds, how long have you been working at Greenback High, Clara?"

"Oh about five years, I guess," she said, and waved her glass in his direction. "You know, not all the parents are going to take to your background research. Voodoo." She waved her glass again.

"Leave them to me. Say, did you grow up around here?"

"Yes," she said, "but I never thought I'd come back here." Her voice was rueful.

"Why did you?"

"Long story," she said, and sighed.

"I'd like to hear it," he said easily, and drank the rest of his beer, waving the empty glass at the waitress, who nodded.

"I graduated from high school and made it through three years of college before I ran out of money. I worked as a secretary for a while in Knoxville, trying to make enough money to go back to school, and then I met Willie. We got married, but that didn't last. So I came back home to give myself some time to think. My mother got sick;" she shrugged her shoulders. "I'm living in her house now. Anyway, while she was sick I got a job at Greenback High School, and after she died—" She shrugged again.

"Haven't you thought about finishing school?"

"I have. Oh, I probably will but . . ." Her voice said that would never happen. She drained her glass. "Andrew, you ought to be careful with your students. This isn't Atlanta, you know. Having them do this sort of research will upset their parents."

"Leave it, Clara."

The waitress brought the steaks and two more beers. Andrew leaned toward Clara, watching her cut her steak with swift, complete movements. A babble of voices rose around them.

The sloshing of the water along the shore. The movement of two small feet in the water

Andrew shook his head. He couldn't understand those moments when his mind suddenly went blank and there were gaps in what he participated in. Like those moments when you were driving at night, he thought, and you fell asleep on one side of a curve in the road and woke up, heart pounding crazily, at the other side.

"What was that?"

"I can take a hint; I stopped talking about your class. I was just asking you where you grew up, Andrew. It is loud in here, isn't it?" She smiled at him.

"Oh, in Marietta."

The clink of chain against stone, the rubbing of cloth and the moaning that he couldn't get to stop

"That explains why you're different from most of the men around here. They believe in fast cars, fast women, and slow beer."

He laughed and placed his napkin on his plate. "That had the ring of a definite Greenback saying, or is that one of yours?"

"I'd say you're a smart man."

"What would you say to coming by my house for a cup of coffee?"

She looked at him solemnly, and then gave a sudden, decisive nod. "Okay."

the circling movement of a crowd of dancers, faces intent on his, clink of chain against stone

They made the drive together, slowly, without talking, and Andrew watched the roadside lights flash by, lights that created impossibly long shadows from the willow trees that hovered close to the road. Trees, he thought, that had been here as long as the Praeter house. What had they seen?

When they reached the house, the two of them linked arms as though they were teenagers, and Clara laughed uncontrollably when Andrew couldn't find the doorkeys. Eventually he found them in his front shirt pocket, and fumbled until he found the front door key. He turned it in the lock. For a moment nothing happened, and then there was a slight click. The door swung open. He watched the shaft of light from the door move its way across the room, first lighting up the chair by the door and then the empty couch. The door moved back and forth behind them as they entered, making a noise like the quick ticking of a clock.

They stumbled up the stairs together, Clara lurching against him, as her heel caught on one of the rungs. "Andrew, Andrew," she whispered and kissed him on the neck. A shiver rippled its way up to his ear. He pulled her closer to him and then lifted her up in his arms. She seemed heavier and heavier as he carried her up the steps.

Stirring in his arms, she whispered, "What about the couch?"

"No."

She nestled closer in his arms.

"I'm taking *you,*" he swung her up in the air, then pulled her closer to him. She gasped. "to the master bedroom." And she seemed to miss the sound, almost like a groan that came afterwards, the grated name of "Kate."

Was that his voice? Andrew hesitated, the woman almost dead weight in his arms, arms which seemed to stretch impossibly toward the floor. He didn't think so. It sounded as though it came from the cellar. After resting his head on Clara's hair for a moment, he carried her up the stairs. She giggled like a young and annoying girl. His arms tightened around her as if they were closing in on her neck.

———

He trailed his fingers over the fragments of wood, the jagged tips of what remained of the loom.

By now it had reached the proportions of a large, angry sculpture, standing on its own, but resting quite close to the back wall and stretching the length of the room like a staggered set of mountains. Except for the tips of wood which poked their way through the thread at each rise, the wood was completely covered by an overlapping of thick brown wool.

He began to hum to himself as he lifted his sons' small toys and hung them, like ornaments on a Christmas tree, against the surface of the wool.

"Andrew;" he heard an angry feminine voice behind him. "Andrew, you are buck-naked crazy, and I'm going to get even with you. And—" he heard her take a deep breath, "just what the *hell* is this? You left me there for *this?*"

He didn't bother to answer or to turn around.

"Did you hear me, Andrew Jackson?"

After a moment, he shrugged his shoulders, then moved to the right of the structure and hung one of Kate's old slips over one of the sides of the mountain.

She gasped. "Who is that woman? What have you got around here, a harem?"

He looked around him, but he saw no one.

"Why is she holding a lit match?"

To Andrew, the room seemed empty of people. Even Clara had a thin and reedy voice, like the piping of an out-of-tune whistle. He shrugged his shoulders and hung another toy on the woven sculpture that had once been his wife's loom.

"Now you've got me seeing things. I'm going to get even with you. I mean it, Andrew. I'm not some kind of puppy dog. You're worse than the men around here. I should have known when I saw the way you spun into the parking lot with that leer on your face. You and your voodoo. Georgia must grow 'em crazy, but you're not going to take me crazy with you. You just wait and see." He could hear the hiss in the word see. "You just wait and see." Her heels clipped their way across the hardwood floor and down the long series of steps. It seemed to him that he could hear them long after they were gone.

For a moment he stared after her. Then he began to move

his fingers across the wool. When the strands moved against his fingertips, he thought he heard the faint sounds of music, the echo of a finer, softer time. His fingers moved slower against the wool. As though the fabric were a talisman. As though the loom were still whole.

He danced across the patterned rectangle of the reflected moonlight on the floor. With a knife in hand he circled the sculpture of the loom, intent on the woman who stood with a blazing torch at the far end. The light from the torch flickered across her face, shadow, then light, shadow, then light. She had a small, heart-shaped face and long dark hair. The smell of singed wool reached him. He circled closer and more quickly, though she seemed not to see him. The torch smoked like a smudge pot as it touched the wool. She smiled a reflective and entirely self-contained smile. When his knife reached her back, it passed through it and into the wood of the torch, a torch that smashed to the ground in a trail of sparks like the arc of the moon.

In the morning Andrew walked across his side yard and through the trees
the ripping of his hairline, the jerk of a hand against his back
to the Bryges' house. He wore the same clothes he had worn the night before, and he could feel the beard stubble on his neck whisk against his shirt collar.

A redbird sang in a tree just to the side of the path. Andrew nodded to it carefully. With a quick flick of its tail it flew away just as he stepped into the Bryges' yard.

A man with his back to Andrew was filling a watering trough in the front yard. Two swaybacked horses stepped up to drink just as the man turned off the spigot. He turned around, wiping his hands on a towel. He looked at Andrew in surprise.

Andrew cleared his throat. "Are you Mr. Bryge?"

The man nodded, his lips tightening warily. He put the towel down on a fencepost near the trough. He was an older man, but his hair was still black. Andrew stared at him in fascination. Then he said, "I'm you next door neighbor, Andrew Jackson."

"Larry's teacher." The man didn't smile.

"That's right."

"Oh, you wanted to borrow something, maybe. A razor?" The man's face lightened.

Andrew shook his head.

He had dreamed last night of a woman and a torch.

"Some milk then, some coffee?"

He shook his head again. "I wanted to talk to you about Larry."

The man frowned. "Funny time to come calling, isn't it? Aren't you supposed to be at school soon?" He pointedly stared at Andrew's face.

He cleared his throat. "Your son and I had some trouble in the classroom yesterday."

"Yeah, he said so. I didn't think much of it," Larry's father said. His eyes said, but now maybe I'm thinking differently.

"He did a report on the old Praeter house—"

"Yeah," he said. "You know, Mr. Jackson, I wish you wouldn't encourage him about your house."

"Encourage him?" Andrew was taken aback.

"He's always hanging around over there at your place, and I guess the two of you usually get along pretty well, but he's not doing his chores, you know."

"No, I didn't know."

"And I guess he'd behave differently in class, if he wasn't always over there." Larry's father looked Andrew up and down as though he doubted it.

"So you're saying this is my fault?"

"One way or another."

"I see, Mr. Bryge." He straightened his shoulders and jerked at his shirttail. "Well, let me tell you something. I've not invited Larry to visit me except for one night when I first moved to town."

"What do you mean?" The man's voice was flat, but it was obvious he didn't believe Andrew. He looked at him like he was out of his mind.

"Just what I said." Andrew cleared his throat.

The man's faced changed suddenly. He looked wary, and his lips were pressed together in a tight line. Then he said reluctantly, like the words were pulled from him, "We're distant kin to John Sevier, you know."

He stepped back as though the man had struck him. He felt surrounded by the lines of unseen, undying feuds. There was something about a duel between Sevier and Jackson. He frowned. "Look, Mr. Bryge, about Larry—"

"Listen, I don't know, Mr. Jackson, about you, but I've got a breakfast waiting for me in there, and I'm going to eat it. Why don't you come back some time when we can talk this thing over?" And when you—his tone of voice said—are sober. He shook his head and walked into his house, shutting the door firmly.

He stared at the white house, its windows gleaming like shut eyes, and at the closed door. He watched the horses shift their weight, lift their heads, and then lower them again to drink. The smell of dried manure wafted his way, and from behind the house he could hear two dogs barking in the distance. There was no sign of Larry. It seemed to him that he could almost see Larry through that closed door, Larry, seated at the table, his young blond head flung back in defiance against the rungs of a straight-backed kitchen chair.

After a few minutes, Andrew made his way carefully back across the yard and back onto his own land. He climbed the steps to his house, listening to the slow thump-thump of his feet. He reached the top step, and then picked his way over the precarious pile of marble, to the doorway. He swung open the door, and, ignoring the reclining figure of Broken Echo on the couch, he moved toward the kitchen, nodding at the nearly completed tapestry on the wall as he went by. He turned on the eye at the stove, and watched it spiral red. In the act of placing the kettle on the eye, he stood holding it for a moment, and then gently put it down.

As he turned toward the open cellar door, he thought, I don't believe I'll go to school today. Something like relief rippled slowly through him, something like the slipping of a last tie.

"Joseph, do you want me to bring you some biscuits?" a woman's voice called down the stairs.

He heard himself growl something in response.

Evaline came down the stairs, her face pale, a plate of

biscuits in her hands. As she held them out to him from the safety of the stairs, her hands trembled.

He grabbed the biscuits from her hands, dumping most of them on the floor. From somewhere behind him chains rattled. He ignored the sound, cramming a biscuit into his mouth. When he finished, he raised his hand to wipe the crumbs from his mouth and said hoarsely, "I'm not responsible."

"What, Joseph," she asked, her voice horrified.

The form wavered. Broken Echo asked him again. "What Andrew?"

"What are you doing here?"

"You don't think you belong in the cellar alone, do you?"

"I want you out of here."

"You don't trust me."

Andrew couldn't tell whether the voice mocked him or not, or whether it had been Evaline's or Broken Echo's. He could hear the woman softly crying.

"Who are you?" he asked.

"Oh Joseph, I'm so weary of all of this; when will your head heal?"

"I don't think it's my head, oh no; I don't think it's my head that needs healing at all, Evaline," he heard himself say. "How could you have locked me in like a river criminal, like one of my own slaves?"

"Because," she said, rising to go up the stairs, "because, Joseph, you tried to rape me. You tried to rape your own wife. Your daughter is so angry at you for what you've done that she's been found out at midnight twice by the slaves. She's tried to burn down the house with you in it, Joseph." Her dress swished like an out-of-sync whisper with each step. Is that what he had done, he wondered dizzily, tried to rape Clara? No, that didn't make sense. If he had, she'd have been a lot more than *that kind* of angry.

But whoever she was she had left him in the darkness with the sound of chains next to his ears, throbbing, pounding, the rough scrape of the cloth against the rawness of his skin. The top of his head expanded until he saw lights dancing in the corners of the room, like the sweeping spiral of torches across the lawn on a particularly dark night, a yell, he was yelling with the roughness of voice that speaks of days without release. What had he forgotten? It was important. If he just knew what he had forgotten, that would give him the key. "Evaline," he called.

The lights were softer, smoother now, though they still danced in the corners of a room darker than he remembered. Was he in the parlour? "Evaline?" he called, and the roughness of his throat reduced him to coughing. "Evaline? Wife?"

From the top of the stairs came a soft voice, "I cannot bear it any longer, Joseph."

"Where is it that we are? Has Alexander made the whiskey for today? Are the parlour lights not lit yet?"

"Oh Joseph, Alexander has been dead three long years, and the stills are silent. Though the front door stays open, we have no more guests. In truth," her voice broke, "the tale of your screaming goes further than the screams." The door closed with a dull thud.

Moving his arms about fretfully, he felt the weight of the manacles on his wrists; the anger of his flesh against the metal was suddenly more than he could bear. The throbbing of his head against the bandage. A raw scream filled the basement like the rattle of gravel in a closed jar.

Standing in the yard, how had he done that, he was standing in the yard, new growth of green grass around him, the smell of wind in the pines, the movement of the water. Joseph watched proudly as two men carried a live and struggling young lamb. They walked the tops of his walls with the lamb in their arms.

"Sixteen foot thick, the walls are, if they're an inch," called down one of the men. The other hefted the lamb up over his head and ran lightly down a slantwise beam to the ground. "Thick," he said, puffing slightly, "enough for Thomas Jefferson."

The wind waved the tops of the trees, women came up the lawn in silk dresses, their menfolk leading the horses, the tables, loaded with food, had people clustered around them. "Why, Sam Houston, you Indian fighter you," roared someone from just behind Andrew's left ear. One of the men raised his hat in the air, and swept it with a quick and flourishing blow into a sudden, spinning garble of voices.

"We're all," whispered a younger Broken Echo's voice, "bound up in your loss now."

Andrew screamed, "Let me out of here! Get me the hell out of this cellar!"

How had he been chained? Sick and shaken, he had left

the front porch. What had happened then? Staring at the wall, at the ghost of a weaving on the walls, pacing the length of the hallway like a prisoner at the end of a chain.

He could feel the manacles against his wrists. Unyielding. Lifting his arms, he began to pound them on the ground to either side of him. A separate shock travelled up his arms and into his shoulders each time they touched the ground.

"You'll lose your arms," came the trailing, hissing whispers. "Where the fuck are you?"

Whatever cushioned the back of his head was soft. It felt alive. "Evaline?" Andrew asked.

"You have to have that arm taken off before you're eaten alive with maggots." The voice that spoke was gruff and uncompromising. Andrew squinted up at the bearded man hunched over him.

"Please take that leg away. Can't you use that Yank haversack as a pillow, Doc?" Andrew heard himself beg in an unfamiliar voice. Around him came the unceasing cries for water. "That fellow who fought beside me; that's his leg."

The doctor yelled at someone above the rising cries, and the haversack landed at his feet. Lifting Andrew's head and tossing away the leg in one swift motion, the doctor then shoved the sack in as replacement.

"Have you any chloroform?"

The doctor put his thumb into Andrew's leg wound. "No, and I have no time to dillydally with you. Can you lie as still as that man?"

Turning his head, he saw a group of men in gray uniforms huddled over a man in the corner, a man who lay unmoving while they raised the saw to his arm.

The doctor lifted his shirt, and Andrew turned his head at the sight of the small, squirming mass against his arm. The saw touched lightly against his skin with the coolness of an unfevered hand.

The clink of metal against stone wove a raw musical undertone to the Indian's voice. The young Indian's hand rested upon Andrew's arm, the coolness of the hand was the center of his attention. He could see nothing but a faint light from the boarded-up cellar window.

"Is my arm—" he shifted his weight quickly.

The younger Broken Echo ignored Andrew's frantic movement. "I'm winning, you know. The memories of the house are all mixed up inside you, and you can't separate them." His tone was gloating.

Andrew shifted his weight again until he could look at the Indian without blinking. Is this what I have to fight then? At last there's someone tangible to fight, something of substance to resist. For the first time in a long while he had a sense of purpose. "What phase is the moon?" he asked abruptly.

"A little more than a quarter." The younger Broken Echo leaned closer. "You're becoming a real Southern white man, aren't you? That was some night you had with Clara."

He heard the buzz of a saw against bone. I can control these visions, he thought and closed his eyes. When he opened them again, the sound was gone. "Why are you being so accommodating then?"

The other shrugged. "You'd call this accommodating?" he asked softly.

"I can send these phantoms away," Andrew said, and leaned against the man's leg.

"If I'm here, you can perform little tricks, yes. You can call that accommodation if you wish. Any torture has its time of relief. For contrast."

He considered that. Then he said, "I have the upper hand. All I have to do is wait. The moon is changing." He stared upward. "You know these ghosts." His voice was accusing.

"In a manner of speaking." His face loomed closer to Andrew's. "You expect that old man to save you, don't you?"

"What old man?"

"That old man who comes with the full moon. You're waiting for *him*. Well, I wouldn't count on it, white boy. You'll be gone long before then."

"That old man," Andrew said, carefully flexing his arm, "is you."

"So. Does that mean, white boy, that you think we're the same? You should know better by now. Your scalp remembers."

The top of his head tingled. Behind him he felt the shadow of those other times, the grasp of a hand against his throat. No amount of concentration could make that sensation disappear, so he went on the offensive. "You'll be old soon, Broken Echo, how does that feel?"

"My name," the Indian's tone was haughty, "is *not* Broken Echo. The old man and I aren't at all the same. My eyes aren't his."

"How are you different then?" He winced with relief as the hand disappeared from his throat.

"Do you think I would tell you?" He gave Andrew's arm a sharp twist. "That old one, he made a mistake and lost my name for me. Why should I tell it to you? If it weren't for your ancestor I might still have my name."

Pain shot through Andrew like a sharp knife. He moved his arm carefully. Then he shoved the manacle into the other's leg. "I think that you will tell me your name. Sometime."

"It's your *hope* I will eat you alive with, the way you ate us, Old Hickory." The tone was venomous.

"If you were a part of that, why weren't you with them on the Trail of Tears, nameless one? Or why didn't you hide in the mountains with those who stayed?"

He didn't wait to see the other's face, though he heard the surprised catch of breath, and somehow knew he'd landed a strong verbal punch. He had already closed his eyes, and, ignoring the other, begun to probe inwardly. He went down past the layered petals of a dark rose, down past the pinpoint of light that was the deer's eyes, into the darkness still and complete. The manacles slipped from his arms. Broken Echo's voice slipped away. The hand was removed from his arm.

"You caught me by surprise *this* time, white boy. I didn't think you were so strong," he whispered. "My older self may help you for a while. Still, you can't win this fight. Your memories are tangled with the house's memories. They echo each other. You can't change that."

"Andrew," he heard a woman's voice whisper from the cellar door.

Rising, disoriented, he climbed the stairs after the woman who was no longer there. What had he been doing down in the cellar? Wasn't he supposed to have been somewhere? Wasn't he—he stopped, shaking his head in confusion.

There was a knock at the front door.

"Mr. Jackson, Mr. Jackson," someone called.

"Yes, what is it?"

"I brought you something from the school. Mr. Boyles said he couldn't get you on the telephone, and he's been trying for close to three days. He sent me to bring you a note."

Andrew walked to the door. He saw Gary standing outside, looking worried. He had marked Gary, a friend of Larry's, out as a troublemaker that first day, but he'd never fulfilled that promise. Andrew wondered if the boy would today.

"Okay, Gary," he tried to make his voice pleasant. He straightened his clothes. "Here, what is it?"

"I don't know, Mr. Jackson." Gary handed the letter over, his eyes watchful and disappointed. Then he walked away without bothering to say goodbye.

He looked out across the lake, watching the breeze lift the leaves of the trees close to the water's edge. He looked back down to the sealed letter in his hands, took a deep breath, and then opened it.

The letter was in Boyles' handwriting, dark, and sweepingly emphatic.

Mr. Jackson,

I have been trying to reach you ever since you missed our meeting, and then failed to report to school the next day. I had intended to talk with you about the events in your classroom and to issue you a warning, but you now have made that impossible.

Although you are on contract and I could quite easily dismiss you for missing a disciplinary meeting and failing to attend to your class or call in for a substitute, I think that, under the circumstances, it would be cruel of me to do so. On the other hand, I can't allow you to return to the classroom either. Under the circumstances, I've arranged for you to do curriculum research for the remainder of the year. At that point consider your contract expired.

The situation could not continue. I've had complaints from parents, students, several of your neighbors, and the school secretary.

Please stop by to pick up the materials you need for curriculum research.

Underneath his signature, he had written, as though in afterthought, "God help you, Andrew."

Andrew watched the wind carry the fluttering papers to their resting place on the lawn.

CHAPTER 12

Greg's voice sounded to him like a stranger's. Andrew held the receiver closer.

"What did you say, Greg?"

"I'm here in Maryville, Andrew. I should be at your house in a half an hour or so."

Andrew moved the receiver away from his ear and waved it up and down slowly; miniature smoke puffs drifted away from the holes in the receiver.

"Andrew?"

He held the receiver to his ear again. "What's that?"

"I should be at your house in a half an hour or so. Don't you remember? I told you the last time I talked to you I'd be by on my trip to Atlanta."

Andrew didn't remember any phone calls, much less one in which Greg had said he'd stop by, but he didn't say so. "That's right, Greg. I knew you were coming. I just lost track of the days, you know." The smoke sailed across the room like miniature schooners. Andrew amused himself with interpreting the changing shapes: deer to snake, car to wagon, fade to dissolve.

"Schoolteachers. You mark your days off in six week periods." Greg laughed. "Well, I'll see you soon. Hope you've got some coffee. I nearly fell asleep the last fifty miles."

"Be careful, Greg." Was that what had happened to Kate? Had she fallen asleep at the wheel? Andrew mumbled something, and Greg hung up.

He looked around the living room. Clear out the smoke, get rid of the tapestry, and shut the doors to the cellar and the weaving room, he thought. Get dressed. Shave. A lot to do in a half an hour. He climbed the steps to the bathroom, lathered his face, and walked down the hall with his razor. When he locked the door to the weaving room, he carefully didn't look at the "mountain." One trap avoided. He walked back to the bathroom and slowly shaved half his face. Then he walked down the stairs to the cellar and shut the door without looking inside. Second trap. He finished shaving at a mirror in the kitchen and pulled out a coffee can from the cabinet. He filled the Melitta cup with a filter and then with fresh coffee grounds, and placed the tea kettle on to boil.

Then he walked back up the stairs to his bedroom and dressed without looking out the window. Third trap. Each detailed step made it easier for him to ignore certain places in the house. He dressed for the first time in days. How many days? he wondered vaguely, though he didn't really care enough to think about the answer. He had too many other sorts of memories to retrieve to worry about details like time. He had to regain his history.

Maybe he could get Greg to help him remember. Get him talking about the days when they were kids. Those were the memories which were the most vague for Andrew at this point, even more cloudy than memories of his married life. Everyone needed their childhood memories, he knew that, but he couldn't seem to care about them. Maybe taking away your "real" memory dulled your ability to care.

Besides, this way Greg would do most of the talking and maybe he wouldn't notice anything. If it were Margaret, there would have been very little he could have done to fool her. She had always been able to ferret out problems. But Greg had always assumed that Andrew was quiet, reserved. And Greg was too damned practical. If Andrew couldn't fool him, Greg would probably just haul him off to a shrink. Great solution. Andrew laughed bitterly.

He could see the two of them now, Greg dragging him into the psychiatrist's office, past the brown stuffed chairs. The psychiatrist with the pipe in his mouth, leaning back, smoke waving toward the ceiling. No. Revise that thought. Don't think of smoke. The smell of tobacco in the air. "Well, what can I help you with?" a soft voice with a German accent would say. He had always imagined psychiatrists with German accents.

"I've got ghosts in my house, Mr. So-and-So. All sorts of them. There are some in the cellar and some that wander all over the house. I've even got a piano ghost; what do you think of that?"

"Are these ghosts friendly or unfriendly," the psychiatrist would say calmly.

"That depends on what time of the moon it is, Doc. Some of them are always friendly, but most of them do whatever Broken Echo tells them to."

"Broken Echo?" the doctor would ask, raising an eyebrow.

"An old Cherokee ghost."

"And what is it you're doing there?"

"I'm waiting for my family."

The doorbell rang. Andrew froze, and then ran up the stairs to throw on a clean pair of pants and a shirt. He pulled the shirt on hastily, and ripped the bottom button, so he tucked the shirttail in. "Just remember," he cautioned himself. "All you have to do is fool Greg for an hour or so."

And the psychiatrist at the back of his mind said, "Uh hmm, very interesting. Common move on the part of those who've given up—flight from normalcy, we call it."

"Oh, shut up," Andrew muttered, and ran down the stairs. "Hi, Greg," he said, as he pulled open the door.

The man standing on the porch was not Greg, but James. He was not dressed in his usual casual fishing clothes, but in a suit which seemed, by contrast, even more formal than it might have on someone else. Despite the unaccustomed formality, the suit looked like him: tweed jacket with leather patches, black, well-creased pants, and a hat slanted at a slight angle.

"Why, how are you?" said Andrew with an uncomfortable heartiness, a heartiness behind which he tried to hide his sudden delight in unexpectedly seeing James.

"May I come in?" James' tone matched his attire. He held his neck at an unnaturally stiff angle.

Andrew hesitated and then stepped back from the door. "Good, then you can meet my brother."

"No, I don't think I'll be staying that long." James walked beyond Andrew, very nearly pacing the length of the room, then he turned around to face him. "What is it, James?" Andrew asked. He had a feeling of trepidation because this visit suddenly reminded him so much of Jess's first trip to the house. He remembered how kind she had been, so kind that even then he had found himself thinking of how difficult it was for her to tell him about his family. "I'm sorry I haven't called you. I know that Jess invited me for dinner but—" He walked toward the couch, gesturing around him as if the living room were the reason for his silence.

"I'm glad that you haven't called, frankly. It seems to me that under the circumstances you'd do well to stay away from our house, Andrew, and to stay away from Jess." From across the length of the room James glared at him. Andrew watched the curling smoke rise from James' mouth.

"What do you mean?" Andrew turned slowly.

James looked around the living room with a faint look of disgust. Suddenly Andrew saw and smelled the room from what he imagined was James' perspective. A neat living room, but with that disreputable air that comes when someone lives alone and seldom goes out. A closed in, almost mildewed smell, the sort of smell some houses get when inhabited by older, single people. And a room full of chairs that didn't suit Andrew. Dark pink stuffed chairs with formal English curves. Dark furniture lining the wall: bookcases, sideboards, heavily brocaded lamps (had they been there earlier?), and closed, green velvet curtains.

"I mean that I'd prefer it if you didn't come by any more." He walked back toward Andrew.

"What will Jess think about this? If I just drop out of sight."

"I don't think;" James examined the large grandfather clock by the stairs. "I don't think she'll be too surprised."

"If that's it, then why bother about me. I haven't been by for a while."

James rocked back on his boot heels. "I didn't want to take any chances." He stared at Andrew. "Look, I thought on our first fishing trip that you were strange, but small towns attract some odd people sometimes. And I know you haven't done anything to either Jess or me. You've been polite. You've been quiet, for the most part. But you're not comfortable to be around, and that's a fact. And with the latest things that I've heard about I just don't want to take any chances. Jess can be frail at times, and she's always been one to take in visitors. Just how much do you think she can deal with, anyway?" James glared at Andrew. His eyebrows straightened, and he reached his hand up to smooth his forehead.

"What is this?" Andrew asked, suddenly angry. "I've become a leper, a contagious disease, what? Maybe I've come down with that new virus. What is it?" He snapped his fingers as he spoke. "The kill your neighbor virus. Is that it?" He glared at James. "You were one of the people who complained to Boyles, weren't you?"

James didn't respond. He stared at him gravely.

"And what is it I've done that's so awful? I've threatened a high school boy with a paddle in a school where the parents still believe in capital punishment. And only threatened, after all."

"Do you think that what you do around here goes unnoticed, Andrew? We haven't missed the car or the floodlights. Some nights you turn on all the lights and dance around on your lawn like a—" He waved his hands in the air, an out-of-sync conductor.

"Like a madman," Andrew said quietly.

James was silent.

"And so you're worried about my friendship with Jess. You think I'm not good for her. But does Jess believe that?"

"I'm not sure what Jess believes," James said, and pulled a handkerchief out of his pocket.

"You haven't even talked to her because you know it wouldn't make any difference," Andrew said bitterly. "You're trying to warn me off."

"If you thought about what was good for her, you'd—"

"I'll think about it, James." Andrew tried to speak quietly, but he felt a sudden rage, and when he spoke his voice sounded much angrier than he felt. "But I think Jess should speak for herself, don't you?"

The clock began to ring the hour, seven deep notes. A car pulled into the driveway.

Andy had loved to sit in his lap, leaning against his

shoulder, and count the chimes of the clock. That was their nighttime ritual. It was one of the few pieces of furniture they'd had that matched this old place, and so one of the few pieces they'd moved, but he probably would have moved it anyway. Just for the boy.

For the first time James showed visible signs of being angry. His face reddened, and his eyebrows jutted like thick brushes down just above his eyes. "You'll do more than think about it. I'm telling you to stay away from my wife."

"I'm not in the habit of being warned off people." Andrew could feel the blood at his temples pounding.

"You'd better get in the habit, fast." James stalked across the room and out the door. Andrew envied him his passion.

In the driveway a car door slammed.

"Hey, wait, what's wrong?" Andrew heard Greg's voice.

Broken Echo stood behind the front door. "I knew when I saw him coming that he had his wick turned up," he said gleefully.

"I'm not going to stay here. There's no reason in the world for me to stay," Andrew announced. He walked over to the couch and pitched a thick, stiff pink cushion across the room. It sailed into the fireplace with neat precision.

"One does not become so mad at his head that he wears his hat on his buttocks." Broken Echo clapped his hands together. His long black hair streaked with gray bounced gently against his shoulders with each movement.

"Some people," Andrew said through gritted teeth, "only know how to be annoying."

"And to some it comes naturally." Broken Echo bowed.

"Cheap shot. You're getting older, aren't you?"

"Don't count on it. I'm just giddy with my success." Broken Echo stepped back.

"Andrew, Andrew?" Greg peered into the house, but didn't see him. "Andrew, are you home?"

The door banged. "Greg;" Andrew moved toward the door; "hey, Greg, how are you?" He pulled his brother in and gave him a brief hug. Broken Echo strolled toward them. Andrew glared at Broken Echo, and mouthed, "Go away."

"One does not set fire to the roof and then go to bed," Broken Echo whispered.

"Where there is no more land, there remain the holes in the trees," Andrew replied.

"*I* should find a new home?" Broken Echo sighed. "Haven't you satisfied your itch to transplant us yet?"

"What was that?" Greg looked at him, startled.

"Nothing. Just something I'd been reading, and thought was clever."

Greg shrugged. "So, how's everything going, how's your class?"

"My class," Andrew glared at Broken Echo, "is just fine. We're wrapping up six weeks' projects."

"Should be into the second six weeks' by now, shouldn't you?" Greg paced around the room. He looked with some puzzlement at the cushion in the fireplace, and then pulled it out, dusting the ashes from the cover and placing it carefully on a nearby chair.

"I'm still grading," Andrew said hastily.

"Anything good?" Greg paused in the same spot where James had stood a few minutes earlier. He looked suddenly careful.

"Glimmers, here and there," Andrew said carelessly. It wouldn't be long before Greg quit asking. He was always quickly bored by "schooltalk." In fact, he had realized long ago that his brother thought Andrew was unambitious.

"Glimmers," Broken Echo said and then sat down on the sofa, crossing his legs.

the slowly moving spiral of the torches, the widening of the mouths of the dancers, the fireflies in the willow trees, his son sinking into the marshy water

If he keeps this up, he'll send me to the asylum at Eastern State, Andrew thought.

"The world is in a bad way when an egg falls and breaks the bowl," Broken Echo nodded and slowly his feet disappeared from the couch, and then his head, and then his arms, and finally his torso. A finger waved in the air, like a battery-operated baton, and then it was gone as well. Over in a corner of the room, a piano tinkled lightly.

Andrew and Greg sat down in the two chairs flanking the sofa. Greg propped his feet up on the coffee table. "Would you like some coffee?" Andrew asked.

"Maybe later, I've drunk gallons driving here from Virginia." Greg laughed. He leaned back in his chair.

"So what have you been doing with yourself, Greg? Are

things going well?" Andrew cleared his throat. He could feel the back of the chair like a presence behind him.

"We've finished a couple of houses for the university solar projects." He shrugged and then leaned forward, resting his elbows on his knees. "They've cut the funding on the second set."

"Why?" Andrew asked.

Kate dancing in the kitchen with a bowl of salad too full to toss

Greg shrugged. "There are several professors on campus who oppose solar houses. They think they're impractical."

"They're all over the West." Andrew absentmindedly pounded the pillow beside him with his fist.

"And in New England, but that doesn't mean the University of Virginia is ready for them. The last of the old school, that bunch."

"Those houses you've built don't really fit in with those handsome stone buildings on campus." Andrew thumped the pillow again. "That's one of the most beautiful campuses I've ever seen; I really enjoyed my visit there."

The circling of the wolves outside, the sloshing of the water against the reeds, the rhythm of the pounding drum, the echo of his heartbeat

"I didn't think you liked them much." Greg looked at Andrew. "You were the all modern man." He stared at Andrew until Andrew caught himself taking one more swing, and allowed the pillow to slip to the floor.

"Maybe I've begun to appreciate a sense of place," Andrew said uneasily.

"Whatever. Looks like you've been spending a lot of time in this one."

"What do you mean?" Andrew asked, getting up to move casually around the room, his finger trailing over the backs of the chairs.

Billy had loved licorice. He had eaten it without any worry about niceties, the black streaks giving his face the look of a miniature pirate

"You have that cooped up look. Why don't we go for a run later?"

The fabric under his fingers felt stiff and unnatural. Andrew looked down, carefully keeping his tone light. "I thought you were driving on through to Atlanta tonight."

"I was going to, but I'm so tired after that drive I was thinking of staying the night, if it's all right."

"Sure," Andrew said, stifling a grimace. I'm never going to make it, he thought. An entire evening with a stranger. "Instead of going for a run, how about a canoe ride?"

Broken Echo walked casually out of the kitchen. Got to hide him, Andrew thought. He walked over to the stairs, standing in front of the Indian. "Would you like some supper first?"

"He who runs and hides in the bush is not doing it for nothing; if he is not chasing something, we know that something is chasing him." Broken Echo whispered, running his finger like a knife across Andrew's throat.

"An elder cannot see a rat but that it becomes a lizard next time." Andrew muttered without turning around.

"What was that, Andy?" Greg stood and stretched, flexing his shoulder muscles. He looked carefully at his brother.

Broken Echo walked up the stairs.

"I said I've got leftover meatloaf," Andrew said, his eyes following the Indian. He is getting older, he told himself. I've only got to wait a little while and he'll be easier to fight.

"That's fine. Nothing fancy. I'd like to get out and stretch my muscles in that canoe of yours." He followed Andrew into the kitchen and sat down heavily on one of the kitchen chairs.

Andrew pulled the pan of meatloaf from the refrigerator and mechanically pulled the aluminum foil from the pan and placed it in the oven.

From somewhere came the voice of a woman humming, and the movement of the shuttle across the loom

"Hey, you put the foil in the oven and you're getting ready to toss the meatloaf, little brother!" Greg laughed. "Are you sure you don't want to go out to eat?" His voice trembled; he cleared his throat.

"Positive," Andrew said firmly, staring across the room at Greg. "I'm just worn out for some reason. Maybe I'm coming down with the flu. What about if I let you take the canoe ride, Greg, and I turn in early?"

"Are you sure you're all right, Andy?" Greg was clearly startled. He walked up to his brother and placed a hand on his arm.

Andrew resisted the impulse to remove it. "Just tired." He

turned around and put the meatloaf in the oven. He tossed the aluminum foil in the trash.

"You can't mourn forever." *Drumbeat* from the next room.

"It's only been a couple of months."

Greg let him go. A kitchen chair creaked, as Greg settled into it.

Andrew stood with his shoulders hunched and stared at the wall. Had it only been two months? It seemed as though he had been here for years, that he was almost an old man himself, and that he had long ago retired from public office. Retired General Jackson. He restrained an almost overwhelming urge to hunch over the cabinet and weep. The center of his chest ached. He put a fist there for a moment. It was easier when you didn't have to talk to other people. In a moment he slowly turned around, a forced smile on his face.

"Tell me something, Greg. What's your funniest story about when we were kids?" Ignore these feelings and they'll go away. What you have to do is just change the subject, and get a grip on yourself, Jackson.

"What?" Greg leaned back in the chair, nearly tipping it over.

"I was just thinking about some the other day, and I wondered what your favorite was. What about all the times we got into trouble?"

"You mean like the time we tarpapered old man Dennison's yard?" His eyes were still cautious.

"Yeah, that one."

"Or how about the time we got hold of some old sticks of dynamite and took them apart for the gunpowder. And then we made a trail around the Hoyles' yard and set it on fire."

Andrew laughed heartily. He could see the two of them now, dressed in ragged sweatshirts and cutoffs, slipping over the Hoyles' wooden fence after dark. The small yard dog came rushing out from the porch, but it was chained, so the chain pulled it up sharp. He remembered the mixture of moonlight and shadows on the yard, and the trees waving in the wind. The wind, a simple breeze at the level of the yard, had caused the powder to drift slightly, as they poured it. They were careful to put the circle far enough from the house. They didn't intend anything dangerous, just a prank. But we hadn't really known what we were playing with, thought Andrew. The gunpowder'd blazed up like one of those circus hoops at Barnum and Bailey.

He thought he smelled meatloaf burning, and pulled it from the oven, but the meat had just barely browned. He looked at it blankly.

Cutting the top of the meat and tossing it away, it slipped to the floor and he watched it slide on the linoleum, while he ignored the whisper and the laugh of the Indian beside him

"My God, but we were rascals." Andrew laughed as he cut the lukewarm meatloaf. "Still, we never really did anything that hurt anyone. Just scared them a little."

Greg came over and grabbed one of the plates. "I'm really hungry," he said. "Yeah, well, but we weren't as bad as those guys up the street." Not looking at Andrew, he served both plates.

"You mean the ones that stole the cigarette machine and kept it in their attic? And didn't they put the bull in old man Harmon's Auto Shop?"

"That's them. The Baileys." Greg smiled at him. "Reckon they were kin to the circus?" He asked in a mock-mountain dialect.

Andrew looked at his brother with a sudden, wide grin. He'd forgotten how sharp and clear those moments were. For one night he had the armor that he'd needed. And, he realized, he had another way to fight. The younger Broken Echo wanted him isolated, didn't he? Cut off. He'd take a trip tomorrow to the school and pick up those materials. He smiled contentedly. Inside there was the sound of Greg's deep voice as he continued to talk, and outside there was the slow hooting of an owl. It was the old-coat feeling of being home.

Greg just as suddenly relaxed. "What's your favorite memory?" he prompted, as they sat down to dinner. He put a forkful of meatloaf in his mouth and chewed the meat as though it were a mouthful of persimmons. "You can't cook worth shit, older brother!"

Andrew ignored that. "The night we snuck out and took Margaret with us to the neighbor's goatyard. We rode those goats for hours, until we finally fell off them. You know, old man McCarter would have shot us if he'd caught us riding those goats."

"We didn't ride his goats!" Greg put down his fork and

stared at the meatloaf, and then up at Andrew, his face just a little bit too impassive.

Careful, Andrew. He took a deep breath. "Maybe I dreamed it," he said lightly.

"Your memory's never been any too good, now has it?" Greg nodded his head, as though he'd just gotten more proof of an old theory.

"According to all of you, anyway," said Andrew, tracing over the grounds of an old battle.

"Four to—I mean, two to one," said Greg, suddenly looking stricken.

Andrew reached his hand across the table, gripping his brother's hand firmly. "That's right," he said determinedly, "two to one." The drum beat erratically from the stairwell, and from somewhere came the sound of a shrill and out-of-tune whistle.

As he walked into Greenback High School, Andrew was feeling particularly pleased with himself. He had gotten up that morning to see Greg off, and had ignored Broken Echo, walking around the Indian as if he weren't there. And he'd driven into town without having any of those strange lapses of thought, not even an anxiety attack. He was dressed professionally in gray pressed trousers and a crisp white shirt, ready to face a public world. Odd to think of a town the size of Greenback, or a school the size of Greenback High, as the public, but numbers were not the issue after all.

When he came in the door, Clara looked too surprised even to be angry. But she recovered in two seconds and glared at him.

"Hi, Clara;" he leaned on the office countertop; "I came to pick up some curriculum materials Mr. Boyles was to leave me. He wants me to create a new curriculum based on my fall plans."

I know, her expression said, and I damn well don't approve. "They're here," she said and whirled around to pull them from a slot behind her desk. Her face began to flush, but she carried them over to him, laid them down, and then walked back to her desk.

"Clara, I—"

"You what," she asked expressionlessly.

What the hell was it he had done that night? He still couldn't remember—and then he had a flash of a picture. Clara seated in a rocking chair in the bedroom, rocking sensuously back and forth, his fingers brushing and rubbing her legs, her stockings slipping through his fingers. The look on her face wasn't offended. What had he done?

"I'm sorry about the other night, I—" What had she told Boyles, he wondered suddenly. It was unsettling to think that they both knew something about him, while he couldn't remember whatever he'd done at all.

"Bit late," she said, and inserted a piece of paper in her typewriter. She said through gritted teeth, "Will you leave? I'll get Boyles."

"Can we at least talk?" he asked softly.

"What about?" she snapped, "What for?" The tiny, fine wrinkles deepened just enough around her eyes to scare him.

"I wanted to tell you—"

"That you're sorry." She pulled her sweater closer around her, then put her hands down on the typewriter keys. Her fingers clicked over the keys. She slammed the return and yanked out the paper.

"No, no, that I'm not sure what I did." He started to walk around the counter. She turned and stared at him.

"Don't move."

He stopped.

"You what?" she asked belatedly.

the circling wheel of the moon like a pinwheel in the night, the footsteps that followed him when he mounted the stairs, the jagged pieces of tombstone scattered throughout the house

"I've been having some trouble—"

"Right, you could say that," she snapped.

"—with my memory lately. That night we'd been drinking a lot. I—"

"That's the poorest excuse I've heard in a long time." Andrew could hear a group of avidly curious students murmuring behind him. "Bastard," he heard one of them mutter. It sounded like Larry. Why didn't they leave? The bell had rung. Damn small towns anyway. Clara didn't appear to notice. Her angry attention was all on him.

polishing the Volvo, trying to protect it from rust, ignoring the dents and the smashed side of the car. The paint and the

metal which it covered transmitted messages, thousands of
vibrations like tiny drums

A class bell rang assault. Now the bell had rung. He must
have been hearing things. After the bell stopped he said
quietly, "I can't deny that. It may be shabby, but it's the
truth." When she hesitated he added, "Do you think you
could tell me what I did? Don't you think you owe me that?"

She looked at him in disbelief. The crowd of students were
jammed up behind him. He felt someone's hand on his arm,
and, without looking back, pulled loose.

"I don't owe you anything." She turned toward her typewriter and inserted a piece of paper into the platen with so
much force that she ripped the paper. "Look, just get out of
here, alright?"

He stared at her silently. What *had* he done? "Clara, damn
it, I may not even remember this!"

"Look, Mr. Jackson, I think you ought to leave Clara
alone." He turned to face a petite, red-faced girl with averted
eyes.

"I'll leave in a minute," he said quietly, looking back to
Clara for an answer.

"That's ridiculous." She hesitated. "But somehow I think
you believe it."

"Oh yes," he said as she turned back to her typewriter, "oh
yes, I believe it."

He walked past the student who had asked him to leave,
her round, brown eyes watching him. The crowd of students
moved aside with reluctance. He could feel them staring at
him as though he were a museum oddity. If this was contact,
he didn't exactly find it comfortable. Had you expected to? he
asked himself mockingly.

He squinted to dim the glare of the sunlight outside, and
walked toward the car. From behind him he heard a voice,
"Mr. Jackson."

It was Cynthia Dunn. "How are you?" she asked, her face
suddenly open and compassionate.

"Gettin' on," he said at last.

She stared at him.

"Well, I've got to be going."

"Yeah, well, maybe if—maybe you could come back next
year."

"You'll be gone, surely."

"Yes, but my sister won't be;" she brushed back her hair, suddenly looking eager. "Well, you think about it, you hear?"

"All right," he grinned. "I will at that." No need in telling her, he thought. This time next year she'd realize what the situation was.

He should have never taken Clara to that house. He hadn't exactly been himself that night had he? He'd played the macho Southern man, spinning his tires at that neighborhood tough. Not exactly his style. Oh God, what a mess he'd made of things. Whatever he'd done later had made her more angry and embarassed than he'd thought in order for her to join in with whoever had been interested in spiking his job.

As he opened the car door, he felt the touch of a girl's hand on his shoulder. He would have recognized that touch even if he hadn't been expecting it. He had never escaped Greenback a single day without being stopped by Leona Berry, one of those girls who just couldn't let well enough alone. Had he treated Clara like that?

"You know, I'm not going back to classes today. Do you think I could get a ride home?"

What was she doing? Andrew frowned at her. "Alright," he said gruffly, "get in."

Leona sidled into the front seat, looking up at him. He put his hand on the car door, undecided. She smiled a too wide smile. Then she looked up to see Boyles striding down the sidewalk, and she hopped quickly out of the car. Andrew looked at Boyles.

Boyles barked gruffly. "Andrew, I only asked you to stop by for the curriculum materials. I would stay away from Clara; she doesn't need a confused man around." The silent accompanying message read: Stay away from the school altogether and, he looked at Leona pointedly, my students. Leona walked clumsily away.

"I had some unfinished business with Clara."

"I've known Clara for a long time and she's a fine woman. I'd hate to see you unsettle her." Boyles rubbed his chin as though it itched him. "Don't you think you've done enough of that already?"

"Unsettling," Andrew said. "It seems to me that what I've done is settle here."

Boyles gave Andrew a sharp glance, and then a reluctant grin. "Maybe you've settled, but things haven't settled around *you* at all. Look, in spite of everything, I like you, Jackson, or I wouldn't have done what I did. I know what hard times are like, but you've got to stop shoving your grief at people."

Two or three students Andrew didn't recognize walked by staring curiously. Just behind Boyles a student rolled out the classroom window and stared as well.

Andrew almost snapped at Boyles. "You were the one who told me to become a part of the community."

Boyles didn't reply.

"But that was before all this, right?" Andrew nodded unhappily. "Well, you're right, but I didn't want to just leave things the way they were."

Boyles looked relieved and then he nodded. "That makes sense, I guess, if that's all you wanted." He watched Andrew carefully.

"That's all."

Something in his expression must have reassured the principal, because his eyes softened. "Take some time to heal up." The lines around his mouth deepened.

Andrew clenched his fists. Boyles looked at him for a moment, then he deliberately turned his back on Andrew, who stood clenching and unclenching his fists. It seemed like a very long time before Andrew at last climbed silently into his car, and watched the principal walk away, boot heels clicking noisily on the sidewalk in a syncopated rhythm.

Maintain contact in the community, he said to himself. Not only were there a lot of angry people out there, but he couldn't know when he might become "unpredictable." So, you thought it was going to be easy? The younger Broken Echo wants you isolated, remember? He shook his head and laughed rustily. The great romancer, he said to himself. The engine started with a sputter and then roared to life. He pulled out of the parking lot without a backward glance. Chapter closed, he thought wryly, now what?

"Look, I'm tired of dealing with you and your pack of ghosts. I just want you out of here." Andrew paced up and down the living room, just skirting the Indian standing in front of the fireplace each time that he passed. Even when he wasn't looking at the other he felt the strong invasion of the Indian's presence.

"Do you think you're the only one who wants privacy? The only one who feels the rawness of someone's presence?" Broken Echo glared at him. A tiny chipmunk peered over the Indian's shoulder, its black eyes staring intently at Andrew. "At least you can leave if you want to be alone." He folded his arms over his chest.

"You can disappear. You did, anyway." Andrew slapped his fist into the palm of his other hand.

"Temporarily;" the Indian shrugged. He rocked back and forth. "If *you* disappeared, it would be much more effective."

He flung himself onto the couch, bouncing on the hard, pink cushions. "I own this place;" he said, placing his hands behind his head, and bouncing some more.

"And after all the trouble I went to, to convince you that ownership and control are not at all the same thing." The Indian's tone was mocking. A chipmunk scampered down his arm, across to Andrew's legs. Its claws dug through his pants and into Andrew's skin. Andrew shook his leg and threw the animal off onto the carpet. It picked itself up and sat in a lump, ugly as a toad.

"Do you know who you're talking to?" Andrew demanded.

"General Jackson," the Indian drawled. "Joseph Praeter?" He scratched his nose. "Haven't you sorted them out yet?" He stepped quietly back toward the fireplace, where he began to dissolve into a dark, thick smoke. "You must have become awfully cocky to decide to take me on at this point. I'm certain you don't know who you are, much less what you're doing." His mouth wafted into the updraft of the chimney like a small smoke ring.

"Desperate," Andrew muttered, closing his eyes and leaning back against what suddenly seemed to be a hostile couch. It shifted behind him like the back of a bear. He sighed, thinking of the long winter's campaign ahead. "Definitely, Jackson."

CHAPTER 13

The small sparrows skimmed over the surface of the lake, dipping down lightly over the floating skin of the water. From a rocking chair on the porch, Andrew watched them and listened to their calls. It was a peaceful morning. With suddenly sensitive ears he could hear the sounds of animals and birds far down the river. There was a bell-like quality to the air, as though there had been a sound just before he awoke, or as though there would be if only he waited just a while longer. The air against his skin had that quality of unbroken water, and the center of his chest seemed to vibrate with those, as yet, unstruck notes. He remembered suddenly the sound of the hammer dulcimer in his dream, the striking of the hammers on the strings and the vibrancy of the notes themselves.

While the few times in his life when he had felt this way before had been moments of peace and energy, this morning was not one of them. The morning was at peace, but he was restless and waiting, though he knew it would do him no good at all to wait.

After that last conversation with Broken Echo, it seemed

that, temporarily at least, he had driven the old Indian away. In doing so, he had silenced all the movements of the house, all the haunting echoes that had so troubled him. The house had been completely without any illusions, or allusions, he thought wryly, for the past several days.

Like any other individual he had gotten up in the morning to drink large cups of coffee, to plan for the day, to do some of his paperwork, and to putter around the yard, and yet those days had been filled with some sort of waiting and swelling expectancy. As though if he only waited long enough he would be filled. It was the vibration of his waiting that boomed within his chest in huge, hollow notes.

The feeling was so long-forgotten, so foreign to him, that he thought if he looked in the mirror he would see another face; that a strange, vigorous, and somehow lonely face would stare back at him, and behind that face, like a series of shadows, of superimposed photographs, would be another series of faces. A series of faces like Chinese puzzle boxes, he thought, and leaned back into his rocking chair, trying to soothe himself with the slow back-and-forth motion of the chair and the quiet creak of the floorboards underneath.

He missed them, he realized suddenly. All the movements and rhythms of the house, the quick changes of the furniture, the clanking of a completely covered loom, the roaring of an impossibly smashed engine, the gliding boat on the lake, and the odd, endearing jokes of Broken Echo and the strange hostility of the Indian's younger self. He missed them all, even the crazed Praeter and the sensuous lure of those ghosts who had yet to speak in the basement. They had filled his days and nights with unpredictability and mystery, but more than that, they were a part of the house and personalities in their own right. He wanted them back.

He watched the surface of the lake and imagined the edge of the water creeping up the lawn. The birds swept away from the water and into a bare-branched tree at the tip of the land. He didn't have to be lonely; he *could* call them all back: the people, the branches, the wings of the longago birds. He could unlock the door to the cellar and coax Broken Echo out of his hiding place. He could call out the loa, wasn't that what the Indian had called those in the cellar? He kept looking up the term and forgetting what it meant. *The personalities of the loa. Guede, the figure of death and of contradiction, gin*

*drinking mocking man in a tall black hat. Legba, the keeper
of the door between the dream worlds. Didn't Southerners
too pass on their personalities the way someone else might
pass along heirlooms?*

Yet he had no desire to feel the strings of a subtle, and
displacing, manipulation of his reality, and he wasn't really
certain who had been manipulating whom. Had he been
punishing himself somehow by an illusion of the loss of
control? It wouldn't be any more pleasant to think that he had
been willingly cooperating with his own dissolution, than to
think that he had been manipulated by the duality of the
Indian. And it certainly wouldn't be pleasant to think that he
could orchestrate events with the ghosts in his house, because that sort of truth would mean that they were not, after
all, personalities in their own right. He shivered. That was
the most frightening possiblity of all, because if that were
true, then the town, Boyles, Clara, everybody was right; he
was crazy, a fear that he fought hourly.

And what would that do to his visions of his sons? He
couldn't tell through the screen of his own longing whether
he wished those were illusion or reality. A hummingbird flew
nearer, hovering at the edge of the porch and staring at
Andrew, its head cocked to one side. As he looked at the
bird, he smiled with a sudden surge of delight. And, at that
moment, as though making some sort of decision, the bird
flew toward him. Andrew held his breath, while the bird
buzzed up and down his shoulder, just an inch from the skin,
and then down the length of his arm and back up again.
Carefully Andrew turned his head, and the bird perched for a
bare moment at his elbow. When it flew back, hovering on
the air currents, Andrew alternately watched the bird, the
lake, and the few drifting leaves that settled gently to the
ground.

Much later, after the bird had gone, Andrew got up stiffly.
He went into the kitchen and, though he fought the impulse,
he drifted toward the cellar door. For several moments he
stood with his hand gripped tight to the knob. The handle
turned and clicked, and the door began to swing slowly
toward him. Then he slammed and locked it with one quick
motion, leaning his back against it, the wood moving almost
with the sound of tiny drumbeats, his breath coming in gasps

as quick as the beats. If he stayed in the house, he would go down in the cellar. That much was evident.

He caught up his jacket and ran out of the house and toward the car. Moments later, with a squeal of his tires, he pulled into Jess's driveway, only to find both of their cars gone. He walked around the yard and sat on the patio for more than half an hour, staring at the water and getting up to pace the expanse of the yard, then sitting down again. Finally, he left and drove aimlessly around the lakefront.

Later, in the afternoon, when he finally returned home, he had broken the impulse to go down to the cellar. However, he picked up the phone and reluctantly dialed Clara's number. He wasn't sure what day it was, but he thought that she would probably be at home since it was early evening. The phone rang sluggishly, and Andrew counted the rings.

She picked up the receiver on the sixth ring. "Hello," her voice said doubtfully.

"Hello Clara; it's Andrew," he said, and then waited.

There was a silence like the skipped beat of a breath, and then she said, her voice stiff, "Hello."

"Have you thought about what I said to you?"

"I've considered it."

Andrew waited.

"And—" she hesitated, "I've decided that humiliating me once is quite enough, thank you." And before he could say anything else, he heard the definitive click of the receiver.

But, in that moment when he still listened to the clicking of her refusal, he caught a quick flash of something. He had carried Clara from the rocking chair to the bed, and undressed her slowly. He could remember the sensation of his fingers against the softness of her clothes, and the enjoyment that was there between them, as her clothes came off layer by layer. He could remember the catch of his breath as he removed her slip, and the touch of her skin, and the moment at which he trailed his fingers across her arm and traced a series of circles on her stomach, and also the moment at which tiny shivers crossed her skin, and she caught her breath. Finally, the moment in which she closed her eyes and raised her lips toward him, and he turned and walked out the door and down the hall to the loom. Had the loa danced inside him then? Had he been their mouthpiece, an unhealthy one?

She must have remained there for several minutes, he

thought now, thinking at first that he was teasing her with a temporary halt. Then, opening her eyes she would have seen that he was not in the room, and stretched lazily, expecting that he would return from the bathroom. Eventually, though, she would have begun to realize that he was not coming back, and to become first hurt and then angry about the way he had left her. As she dressed she would have felt shaken, but, by the time she was fully clothed, she would have felt like she'd been made a fool of. So she would have gone in search of him, and then, once she'd found him, been both angry and frightened by what she'd seen. Of course, she'd been humiliated. But what could she have told Boyles? Something about the fact that he'd been "no gentleman," he speculated.

She'd been right about the "violence of his loneliness," and she should have stayed away from him. But she'd probably known that all the while she'd been at dinner with him, and certainly as they'd driven out to his house. He'd been aware of what a self-destructive thing both of them were doing, aware of it all the while and completely unable to stop it. It could have been much worse.

Who was he kidding? He put down the phone and rubbed his chin, staring at the empty stairwell. It didn't really matter at this point what could have happened. What mattered was what had happened, and he had no idea how to do anything at all about it. He could send her a card, he supposed, and say something about the fact that he hadn't gotten over his family's death. At least that would be something of an explanation, far too simple, but one that would ease her embarrassment, and perhaps her anger. He had no business using his family's death to ease his own rawness, he thought with sick guilt.

The grandfather clock by the stairwell chimed loudly three times. There was no other sound in the house. Andrew looked around the living room. The couch and the chairs were dark and still. The thick curtains hung stiffly against the windows. The loneliness he felt now was a dry, dusty loneliness, that of something long lived with, rather than the active, welling feeling of the morning. He didn't think that he could face this house alone now, or face all the memories, the voices, it should have had.

It was time for him, he decided as he looked once more around the empty room, to grit his teeth and make do with the afternoon. He'd open the windows to get some air into the house, and do some more work around the place. If he still felt uncomfortable and at loose ends, he'd go out on the lake with his canoe, or go over and try to see Jess again. Despite what James had said, he thought that Jess would see him.

He flung open the windows downstairs in a quick flurry of activity, and then went outside to the front of the house. There he took up where he'd left off the day before, removing the weeds from between the large, octagonal stones on the walkway to the side of the house. It was pleasurable to grip the weeds and dig them up with a quick flip of the small hand shovel, and he quickly fell into a rhythm.

Somehow all too quickly he was done. He walked slowly into the kitchen, fighting the surge of longing, drifting again toward the cellar door. He turned the lock, pulling back the door with one vigorous move. Murmuring voices wafted up the stairway; the scent of moving bodies reached up to him; the sound of a throaty series of laughs. They were back. Like a man to his lover he ran down to join them.

Walking down the stairs with a hollow gourd at the top of his head, a gourd balanced there like some silent mouth waiting to be filled. The gourd whistled, a sound like an old man's snore, with the hollow rush of air. Behind him and in front of him circled bare feet, and feathers brushed his back.

Voices continued to murmur. They were low and throaty, and he still couldn't tell whether they were male or female. Hands brushed his back. Fingers lingered on his arms, holding him lightly in their grasp.

He wore a braided cloak on his shoulders, a cloak which fell away behind him to the floor, and the beads woven into the feathers bounced lightly against his arms. Hands reached for him, and reached again for him. He carried shaker gourds in his own hands and rattled them slowly. Figures with dark black skins ran swiftly on ahead of him. The cellar seemed endless; a cave, or the inside of some huge tunnel.

The end of the tunnel led, he saw, to a small church pew. He sat down on the splintery pew. In front and behind him were many black faces. They had their mouths open and they were singing a spiritual, one that he didn't recognize.

A minister with a white robe stood at the front of the crowd, swaying back and forth from his heels to his toes.

"*And yes, we've got to pray now,*" he said emphatically, waving his hands in a persuasive, hypnotic gesture.

"*Our Father, it is Thy universe!*" he yelled.
It is Thy will.
Let us be at peace:
Let the souls of Thy people be cool:
Thou art our Father;
Remove all evil from our path."

The people around Andrew murmured a quick rush of "yessssss," and Andrew joined them. He could feel the excitement, a quick charge of ecstasy and fear, ecstasy and calm, a rush of air inside the gourd.

The sweep of four black-skinned men in coarse robes down the aisles. The first man's hands cradled a sheaf of grain, the second some sort of cloth, the third a small weaving of an eye, the fourth drummed on a small, skin-covered pot. Four women danced in the aisles to the right. With a rush they met the men at the center aisle and circled with them. They carried objects, tossing them lightly into the air. The wind whistled through the open windows of the church and lifted the women's hair. Andrew shivered violently.

Someone's hands shoved him gently forward, toward the center aisle. He walked slowly to the altar. The minister looked at Andrew over the top of his thick glasses—kind eyes, stern face. Then handed him a large black Bible, open to the Book of Job. The pages rustled in the breeze. He read aloud. His voice was slow and heavy.

When he finished, the minister turned him around by the shoulders three times, and then helped him onto the altar where he lay staring at the ceiling. They placed a jug of water on his forehead. Two, cold drops trickled down into his eyes. Andrew started to speak, but a quick, silencing finger rested against his parched lips. Over his stomach they dipped one of the tapestries. Andrew stared at the eye. It moved. For a moment he thought the eye was the curled form of a snake, and the pupil the curve of its tail.

At his feet stood one of the figures, he couldn't tell whether a woman or a man, he had seen in the aisle earlier. If he squinted down toward his feet, he could see only a blurred form. The wind lifted the form's garments gently. Around him he felt the circling feet, four pairs of heavily moving feet, three pairs of lighter, circling movements. Heavy and light, heavy and light, his eyes grew heavy, and his limbs light. There was the sensation again of a vibration in his chest, the sound of a discordant note. The person at his feet began to speak in a vibrant voice.

"My son, be light of heart and spirit. Do not let the dark winds send you down, for no matter how dark it seems, there is always a stone upon which to stand, always a way for the god of prosperity to send you a small leaf from his pocket. He smiles on all who pacify him." Those who circled Andrew clapped in a syncopated rhythm, the staccato of the fingers against the palms, the movement and the circling of the shadows on the walls, the rhythm of their footsteps . . .

"It is said that you wear around your finger, around your finger, a root called the Wonder of the World tied with a thread of pure linen." The woman's voice came to a sudden halt. Behind her Andrew heard the quick hiss and crack of a whip. Andrew stared at the tapestry in front of him, lifting and falling like a banner desperately held in battle. The eye disappeared; a snake flicked its tongue at him. He heard the crack of a whip.

"Heathens," he heard Praeter's voice yell. "It was not for this that we built you a church!" The wind whistled, or was it the crack of the whip? Andrew shivered again. "Evaline," he called desperately, "at least bring me down some water." There was no answer. He licked his parched lips and prayed for rain.

"Rain. The rain came in torrents the night that they captured me." The black slave with the scar on his face licked his lips. "I could do with some water now," he said hoarsely. I was born in the city of Bournou; my mother was the eldest daughter of a family with only one son. I was the youngest of six children and particularly loved by her and by all of my family, because I was the only boy. It was while I was standing there in the rain that the slave trader came and took me away. When the slave trader came, I went with him willingly, because he said that he would take me many places. I had a hunger to see the world, and to sail on the ship with white wings flying he told me of, and so I went with him." He coughed. "Why are you here in the cellar? What have you *done?" He didn't wait for an answer. "The trader was kind to me. He kept me with him, and I learned the trade of shackling men, until I began to have fits, perhaps from the guilt;" he shrugged, "and so he sold me. Do you have any water?"*

Andrew tried to hand him a glass of water, but as the slave reached for it, Andrew disappeared.

That evening, fingering the root in his pocket, he awaited the return of the older Broken Echo, the one who came when the moon was full. He listened to each noise in the hallway, each movement on the stairs, but the noises he heard were not the noises for which he listened. At last he went out to the yard, where he paced restlessly up and down the newly cleaned cobblestone sidewalk.

He had grown to love that dangerous and contrary old Indian. And, as much as he knew of them, to love his generations of ghosts as well. They weren't simply a puzzle to be solved, or an addictive presence. He'd chased them away because caring about someone, or something, again made him feel too raw. And because they moved him too far from the norm. But he didn't care about that anymore. They'd provide him with enough company to compensate for anything he'd lose. They belonged to the place. He'd realized that this afternoon in the cellar. So he'd call them back; he'd call them all back.

He walked around the house, pacing up and down the stairs. The door to the weaving room stood open, but the room itself was empty. The upstairs study was quiet and the rocker still. When he went back downstairs, even in the cellar there was nothing but the small tapping of a chickadee at the broken crack in the window. Andrew went back outside and waited for the evening. He thought that then he could sustain enough strength or belief to summon up those he waited for.

Dusk thickened, and he watched the spirals of fireflies on the lawn, the spinning spirals of light darting in and around those piles of stone, and the quiet shivering of the trees. There was a great swelling of breeze, and then it was dark, a full moon blazing, and around it a great corona of light. The breeze which whipped past his face made him believe that he might be able to work some magic of his own. He might be able to call back the others, and perhaps even Broken Echo himself. He had sent them away, hadn't he? At any rate, he would try it. He concentrated on the feeling of the breeze.

The lawn stretched on endlessly, the grass tossing as far as the treeline, and in the moonlight there rose up the ghosts of an old slaving cabin, and the tips of teepees. Between them moved the figures of men in blue uniforms, or were they gray? He couldn't tell in the dark. Across the surface of the lake, that gliding surface of the lake, slipped the figures of Indians and manacled slaves. The fog rose between their feet. A village, one he seemed to recognize from an earlier dream, rose up from the dust of the ground all around him; if he stretched out his fingers he could touch the sides of the teepees. These teepees, however, were real; the gleam of their white, birchbark hides was beautiful in the moonlight. He wanted to touch the bark, yet he didn't move, because all around him he heard the wild, ringing sound of the hammer dulcimer in the background, and the sound was paralyzingly lovely.

All of this reminded him of that long ago dream in which he had seen in the moonlight a circle of old men passing a peacepipe, the movement of their hands and the lifting of the pipe which had seemed at last to spiral like the fireflies, so it was that when he turned and saw before him that same circle of old men around the dying coals of a dim and forgotten fire that he did not even start with surprise.

He simply walked up to join them, already stretching out his hand for the pipe that was already coming his way. He could see the pipe, smell the flaming herbs rising from the bowl, and he could feel the stem against his teeth before he took the pipe into his hand and before he actually raised it to his lips. Overhead the circle around the moon blazed all the brighter, as he puffed on the pipe. The old men smiled gently at him, their voices rising in the murmur of an old language. But Broken Echo was not there, and it was not his hand passing the pipe to Andrew. The circle itself was broken, and by the time Andrew had raised the pipe to his lips the fire had died, and he was alone in the moonlight with the sighing of a misty and collapsing village around him. Inviting the ghosts back was not enough, he realized sadly. None of it really worked or lasted without the touch of Broken Echo, and it seemed that the old Indian was not going to be nearly so easy to persuade to show himself as Andrew had hoped.

To lure Broken Echo from wherever he had gone, what would it take? The Indian was the sort of man who was intrigued by actions that he hadn't been able to predict. While Broken Echo might not be evident, he must be watching what Andrew was doing, especially now that Andrew wanted the old Indian around. Bounding up the steps of the house, Andrew darted into the living room and ruffled through the drawers of the sideboard. Triumphantly he came up with a deck of cards. He waved them around in the air, and then ran toward the cellar. After flicking on the light switch, he thundered down the stairs. He seated himself cross-legged on the ground and began to shuffle the cards.

In the corners of the room stood a black man and a black woman in chains. The man was dressed in cotton pants and a cotton shirt, and on his head he wore a calico kerchief. The woman, a slender, muscular mulato, had on a wide-skirted dress and kerchief made from the same calico material. Their faces were grim. A fair-haired Confederate soldier who looked familiar now perched on the steps. He had a rather sheepish grin on his face. "I put my Bible in my pocket," he said to Andrew. "It did save me. What'd she put in the lining? metal? The bullets bounced off it like hail."

For some reason Andrew couldn't quite figure out, he knew what this man meant. He had saved the soldier's life. How? When?

A Yankee soldier appeared next, slapping the Confederate on the back; "I almost got you that time."

Joseph Praeter's appearance brought a sadness into the room, along with the expression of pain in his deep-sunken eyes. His daughter Clarissa came into the room more slowly than the others; her hand appeared first, and only afterward the rest of her. Andrew looked at her with interest. She had long dark hair, and a very pronounced jaw. Her hand, where it rested on the railing of the stairs, was a horsewoman's hand, capable and sure. This is what Sylvia would have been in Clarissa's time, Andrew thought. This is who Clara might have been. Broken Echo walked casually down the steps, jumping over the soldier, and landing with a thump at Andrew's side. He looked up at Clarissa. With tenderness he stretched out his hand; she smiled at him, and then walked down to join him. They loved each other, Andrew thought.

"I'll make you a deal," Broken Echo said; "we play cards. If one of us wins, then among us we choose what happens here in this house and to you. Death and gambling have a lot in common anyway, don't you think?"

"Games of chance. Another sort of moment, eh? An illusion of personal contact," he said bitterly. "And what if I win?"

They all nodded slowly, but only Broken Echo spoke. "Each time you win a hand you can ask one of your burning questions. And if you win the game you choose what happens next."

"*I* really have nothing to lose then. Life isn't my favorite game at the moment anyway. If you take mine, so be it. If I win, you do what I like." He looked around at the group in the cellar. Praeter looked at him for a moment, then rubbed his sunken eyes. The others didn't move at all. They looked so tired. When he realized they would make no response, he asked, "How many hands of cards?" His hands trembled. *Somewhere another man's family* The tears poured down his face, though he kept blinking them away.

"Seven." The black man shifted to lean against the wall; his chains clanked like a dull gourd. *The scent of oranges in the air*

"Seven levels. Very well," Andrew paused; "if I win, I get to do what I want, and—" *They gambled for the ownership of slaves. The slaves gambled, joked, danced to survive. After all his people had done, why should they gamble with him? for revenge?*

"And with each hand you win you can ask us one of your burning personal questions, yes." Broken Echo nodded, rubbing his chin. "But you can't ask about a topic more than once, right?" He looked around at the others. "A fair deal?" His voice rose in question. They all nodded. He released those in chains, and they all settled in an uneasy circle around Andrew.

"Why would you come back?" asked Andrew, looking around the circle at each of the seven in turn.

Praeter's daughter flipped her hair back over her shoulders and replied in a deep, flat voice, "I prefer cards to talk."

"Does it matter why?" asked Praeter. He exchanged a long look with his daughter.

"Yes." Andrew paced up and down the confines of the cellar.

"Then . . . let's say we have a certain responsibility. And maybe we feel responsible for second chances."

"Rewind the tape on who or what a Jackson is?"

"Something like that." The black card dealer smiled and licked his finger. Then he began to shuffle the cards.

"Grief leads to numbness and inattention, is that what you said?" Andrew stopped to ask, his voice tinged with a certain bitterness. *The piano upstairs played a light Bach concerto, which one? It teased at his memory. Where had he heard himself say these words before?*

Broken Echo nodded to the dealer, a tall black man with a scar on his chin. "Begin."

Andrew joined the uneasy circle at the dealer's side. "Wait," he said, holding the dealer's arm. "Don't you think the odds are a mite uneven?" The man nodded, and the scar on the side of his face flashed into view. *Unceasing, tears poured from his eyes. His chest ached. He gasped for air.*

"And when," Broken Echo looked at Andrew with absolute astonishment, "did you expect them to be anything else?"

The dealer lifted the cards high in the air in the traditional card shark's pose, and then shuffled them rapidly. He leaned forward to let Andrew cut the cards and grinned at each member in the circle. "Gentlemen, and lady," he nodded to the black woman on his left side, "and ladies, what game would you like?"

"How about five card stud?" said the Confederate soldier.

"No, we know y'all cheat at five card stud," said the dealer.

"I don't cheat."

"Your mouth is cut cross ways, aint' it, buck? Well, long as you don't see no man wid they mouth cut up and down, you know they'll all lie. And they'll all cheat." The dealer smiled at the soldier.

"Yes, sisters," said the black woman emphatically, and grinned at Clarissa.

"Drop the fake dialect," the soldier rasped. "'You lost that centuries ago." They exchanged glances, and then he relaxed his shoulders.

Broken Echo waved his hand at the dealer. "What about poker?"

"No," Andrew jumped in quickly. "Poker is your game." *The sliding of the car against the railing. The hard thud of the body. He couldn't forget that, couldn't live with it. He was guilty of too much. What he was thinking was familiar, all of it was familiar, but it was out of place wasn't it? Right now he was playing with chance. But wasn't the thought of suicide always a spin on the wheel of chance? No, it's just the place where you're a raw nerve on the edge of absolute weariness. They're not the only ones who are tired.*

"He's got you there, red man," the black woman drawled. "What about pinochle?"

"Fine," said the dealer smiling broadly; "I always liked pinochle." He shuffled the cards and passed them around.

Andrew picked up his hand and looked at it. He could never exactly remember the rules for pinochle. He always got it mixed up with at least two other card games: Spades and Hearts. He had all low cards, except for one king of hearts. He remembered enough to know that he needed suits of court cards. Slowly he counted his cards, hoping for a misdeal, but he was not that lucky. They all bid. The black woman had hearts for trumps. He knew he would lose his king. And he did. In fact, he lost the first hand quickly to her. When he lost, the dealer whooped and hollered and slapped the hands of Praeter and Clarissa. The black woman glared at him as he grabbed the girl's hands. "Now Zora," he said, and winked at her. Andrew watched her slap down her cards and count her points. She had swept the board. The dealer smiled and dealt another round.

"I tell you what," said the dealer after all the cards had been handed out, "why don't we tell stories to pass the time while we play?" A jug of moonshine appeared in his hands, and he began to pass it around the circle. Andrew drank some, sputtered, and passed it on. Their version of moonshine was much stronger than Turkey's. *the sliding on Kate's skin, as she slipped off her navy pinstripe blouse, an argument about a realtor*

"Should we have stopped your younger self? Did we do the right thing?" Andrew asked Broken Echo. "He would have made major changes quickly. Now we'll never know what it would have been like."

Broken Echo looked at him oddly. "Are you prophesying? You're talking about something that hasn't happened yet. I wondered why you weren't worried about him and the results if we won."

"I wouldn't play cards with him, if that's what you mean." Andrew shook his head like a dog with a tick in his ear. What did he remember? Where had this conversation come from?

Broken Echo stared at the wall. "We'll never be certain." He said at last. "But will we do the wrong thing?" He shook his head. "I don't think so. Every war has its casualties, and those that grieve them. Even if you're responsible, you can't force yourself beyond what you can do. The slow, subtle way, where nothing is what it seems, is often best. Even for a fast and shallow age. We have weighed as heavy on our descendents as any other." Then he looked sideways at Andrew. "Did you draw a better hand this time?" But Andrew had drawn exactly the same hand.

He stared at his trembling hands and called for a redeal, but when the cards came around he had the same hand. The tables had turned. "Fine, tell a story," he said patiently. No quarter for the guilty. Still, something that Broken Echo had said, though he didn't understand what either of them had been talking about, had given him some sort of relief. As if it were a conversation they had both had many times, and yet never. What they spoke about was familiar and strange. How could it be both? *Those moments of peace where grief lay for a brief instant forgotten. Wasn't that what these levels were all about? The moments when everything lay poised on the instant of change. Wasn't this game one of those?*

The dealer leaned back, propping himself up by one arm, "And that puts me in the mind of this fellow durin' slavery time who'd climb up in this huge oak tree every Sunday mornin' when he was supposed to be in church, and he'd pray to God and beg him to kill all those white folks. Pretty soon it got to be the talk of the town, what with everybody comin' by on their way to church, especially the young fellows who were courtin', and they wanted to go out of their way to get to church, so they'd drive by. And they'd hear this old fellow hollerin' and prayin' for God to kill them white folks. This one Sunday, when he commenced to prayin' why his master came by, but he beat the old slave up the tree, and when he hollered and carried on, why the master let drop a bunch of rocks all down toward that old slave, and he hollered up there: "Lord, I done asked you to kill all those white folks. Now can't you tell the difference?"

"Now can't you stop these fake stories that you've stolen from somebody else?" the Confederate soldier said and slapped his sides, looking for tobacco and his pipe. He fished them out, and lit the coals, puffing and smiling over the bowl at the others. The dealer watched the glowing coals. "These aren't just stories, man; these are the myths of our lives. They kept us *alive*. We may not remember whose stories they are, but we know what they *mean*."

Andrew had lost another hand. "I think it's my turn to deal," he said and held out his hand for the cards. "Maybe these levels are different levels of history?" Broken Echo smiled and handed Andrew his last hand. The others did the same. He dealt out a round of cards, and then looked at his hand. This time he had a reasonably good deal: no runs, but a jack and a queen set all the way around, and some mixed kings and queens in addition to some tens. He was void in clubs. Smiling, he leaned back and pushed a top hat down lower on his head. Now where had that come from? He wondered.

"A toast." The Confederate stood up and raised his glass. "To the South." Everyone raised their glasses. "The South shall rise again." He winked at Andrew. "Bad joke," said Zora sourly and tipped back her glass to drain the contents.

"I'll drop my dialect if you'll stop those crummy toasts, buck." The dealer waved his cards in the air. The Yankee soldier pulled off his coat and rolled up his sleeves, setting back on his heels as he watched the Confederate soldier gripping his glass. He put the glass gently to the ground beside him, and then smiled a sudden wide smile. "Just for today?" The dealer nodded. "It's a deal." They shook hands with an abrupt solemnity.

Then they played a hand in silence. The top of Andrew's head tingled where the hat rested against it. He felt his face flush unevenly, as though a current of energy rose and subsided there. He felt certain he would win this hand, even though he was low in trumps and lacked several key cards. He played the hand through and triumphantly put down his last card, and quickly swept the last set to his stack of points. He had won by two points.

"Do you know where my family is?" Stupid, stupid, he thought wildly, that's like playing the absolutely wrong card. You asked the wrong question.

"Yes," Broken Echo said simply.

"Where?"

He lifted his hand. "One question."

"That's a child's way out."

"When it comes to death, we are all children." Broken Echo's hand came down in a chopping motion.

At that moment Andrew hated the old Indian. He lunged across the circle, his hands reaching for the old man's neck, only to feel something cold and rigid at his back. Broken Echo reached into his pocket and calmly pulled out a knife. He pointed it at Andrew. "The rules were plain," came the dealer's voice behind him. Without looking at anyone, his hands trembling, Andrew carefully pulled back and straightened his clothing. Tilting his hat back on his head, he shuffled and dealt in silence. Broken Echo had been the wrong person to ask. *You asked the wrong question.*

The second hand he won by one set of cards. Moving more slowly this time, he also thought more deliberately. Then he stared at Clarissa. She looked back at him, her eyes level and her face calm. I can ask her anything, he thought. She knows the answers. But he found himself unable to ask her anything except about herself. "When did you forgive your father?" *For what? Why am I asking her this question?*

She smiled a grim smile. "Long after his death and mine."

Praeter cleared his throat. The circles around his eyes darkened, and he wiped a wisp of thin, oily hair back behind his ear. The light shone on the scars across the top of his head. He shuffled the cards without looking at anyone. Andrew nodded. At least he was getting some kind of answer. There was forgiveness even if it came very late in the game.

The Yankee dealt the next hand. He grinned at Andrew; the circles around his brown eyes were large and puffy. "I'm going to beat you." But Zora took the board, again in a sweep of points.

In a bold move Andrew bid no points in the next round, and he managed to keep from taking a single trick. "Perhaps not." He looked at each face slowly, stopping at the dealer's. "Why are you always thirsty?" *Where am I getting these questions?*

"I was locked by him," jerking a thumb at Praeter, "in the cellar for days without water. Since then, I drink and I drink and I never get enough somehow." The dealer laughed uneasily. And there are some things, thought Andrew, that can't be remedied or answered. They've already happened, and everyone they happened to is dead.

Praeter straightened his back, and looked around the circle. His daughter took his hand in hers, withered and spotted hand resting against smooth and slender fingers.

"That's the way I feel about these answers of yours. They don't satisfy anything, and they make me thirsty for more," Andrew grumbled, as he shuffled and dealt. Each one left his fingers with a certain stickiness. His hands were sweating.

"You white men are always looking for answers for everything," said the dealer. "You ought to leave all that psychology behind. You can't crack the big mysteries like an egg. Death and miracles, they ain't no Sunday mornin' egg."

Praeter's daughter laughed. She flipped through her cards, shuffling them around in a different order. She sang softly, "Life ain't no easy gate, Life ain't no easy gate. It's a river and a road and a fire and a flood. Life ain't no easy gate."

"This is our seventh hand," Zora said, just as she reached across the circle and deftly took Andrew's top hat. This time she went null points, but Andrew smiled grimly. She couldn't possibly make it, because he had all low cards. He watched the cards flash down intently. Did he want to win? Either way, nothing would be as it had been. What he really wanted was his family back, or, short of that, that the ghosts stay and thing go on as they had been. Wasn't that what he wanted? A strange restlessness danced through him like a rough wind. He listened to the wind rattle the windows of the cellar, tested the air as though it would tell him something.

Zora escaped points the first hand, because Broken Echo put down an Ace of Spades, and she followed it with a king. They went through two more rounds of aces in clubs and diamonds before the lead passed to the Yankee, the tip of his tongue sticking out of his mouth as he peered down at his cards. At last he smiled at the black woman, and laid a ten of clubs. But Andrew didn't have any clubs. He only had hearts, and hearts were trumps. He could play another suit, but he needed more points, and he couldn't really afford to lose any of the tricks he'd bid for. Reluctantly he laid down a two of hearts. Broken Echo took the trick with a higher heart, and Zora got rid of yet another high card in diamonds. So, she didn't have any clubs.

Andrew took the next trick, and looked dubiously over his hand. At last he led the Queen of Spades. Did she have spades?

She laughed, and dumped the jack onto the table. "My last high card, Andrew. You should have laid your queen off on the clubs."

"If you'd been watching, you'd have guessed she had high cards left in spades." The Yankee glared at Andrew. Yanks hated to lose, he thought morosely.

She looked at the dealer. "So why are black men always dating white women?"

He raised his hands in mock protest. "Now listen, woman, it wasn't in the deal for us to ask each other these questions. Anyway, you're asking me? I been dead for too long to remember what it's like. And when I died, that wasn't what we were doing."

They all laughed.

"Listen," Zora said abruptly, "I don't like this anyway. We're playing games in the middle of the night." Her ebony hair gleamed as she pulled the scarf from her head. "What right did you have, old man," and she turned to Broken Echo, "letting him into what was ours?" She jabbed her hand in the air. "And just where did you get that root?"

"Yeah." The dealer slapped the woman on the arm, and they both glared at Andrew. Zora half rose from her seat, her eyes intent on Andrew's.

"I went to a church meeting here in the cellar." Andrew pulled out the root.

She settled back into her seat, giving a short, stiff nod.

Broken Echo sighed. "One minute laughing, the next minute howling at the moon."

Andrew shrugged his shoulders. What reason did she have to trust him? He watched as she tugged at the corn-rolled hair at the crown of her head. She watched him watching her without any perceptible change in expression. Whew! Andrew thought. That woman is a powerhouse!

"You've got us playing cards with you because you believe in fate. You've blamed fate for everything that's happened in the South, haven't you? Just as long as what happened was destined *you* don't have to deal with the consequences. And we're the stories that add a little color to the story of your life. You stole our lives and made them into your stories."

"Yeah, that's right," said the Confederate soldier. "You don't know anything about us really, do you?"

"Playing cards is a silly damn way to argue, now isn't it?" The Yankee pitched a pile of cards up into the air and watched them sail across the room to land in a heap by the stairs. "Why the hell are we doing it?"

"You're more than stories to me," Andrew said. "You're family."

Zora stared at him without expression. There was a long silence. Andrew rubbed his eyes. He was disappointed that she hadn't acknowledged what he'd said, but not all that surprised. He walked over to her and handed her the root. She gave him a sudden smile. "The levels have to do with distortions. That's what history *is*. A story the way somebody decided to tell it."

"That's one part of it," the dealer corrected her. "You know there's more."

She shushed him.

"What we decided to do, Andrew, if we won was to test you."

"Test me? Isn't that what you've been doing?"

"No," Praeter said, his voice grating into the air. "What we've been doing is harassing you, teasing you, seducing you. Testing is a rougher set of bonds. You'll not find the loa easy to bear, or even your own dreams. Will you be able to tell the difference?"

"I've carried my own ancestor. I suppose I can bear yours."

And so the card game ended and Andrew, by this time, was almost sorry. He didn't know whether he'd won or lost, but he knew that its ending also meant the ending of something he had grown to cherish and the beginning of something with much higher stakes. It didn't matter. The odds were great enough. And winning might no longer be the issue.

"Very well," he looked around the circle slowly. "To the winner go the choices. Bring on your loa, whatever those are."

But in that moment the cellar was gone, and he was on the front porch in the dark. The night was as quiet as though it had never been disturbed. His body felt as if he had been sitting here for a very long time. Had the game happened? Had he dreamed it?

Sitting down at the top of the stairs, he stared off across the lawn toward the Bryges' house. There was a tiny flicker of light in that direction, like a small flashlight or even a torch, tracking its way through the underbrush between the two houses. Andrew watched its movement with surprise, as it appeared to criss-cross over the wooded area and then to trace a boundary very near where he thought the cemetery lay. Larry, Andrew thought, for some reason Larry was out combing the brush near the cemetery.

Nor did he know why he leaped from the porch and ran through the underbrush, as though to stop the teenager from doing something that both of them would be sorry for. Andrew ran through the brush, his heart pounding, and making a hell of a lot of noise, he thought. Yet when he burst into the clearing where the flashlight played back and forth across the underbrush, he still startled Larry, who turned holding the light in his hand as if it were a handgun.

Do the loa dance between us now?

"Why are you out here this time of night?" Andrew asked evenly, trying not to sound accusatory.

"My sister lost her contact out here this morning," Larry said, shifting the angle of the light so that it shone in Andrew's eyes.

Andrew's shoulder, in a spot just below the lefthand collarbone, unaccountably began to ache and burn. He scratched it irritably. "Put that light down a bit, can't you?"

"Sure, Mr. *Johnson.*"

"Your excuse is deliberately lame, Larry."

"Anything you say, Mr. *Johnson.*" He flashed the light from the ground to Andrew's face and back again.

"So just what *were* you looking for? If you can't tell me right now, I'd like you to get off my land."

Without answering Larry swung the light idly around the clearing and then back to Andrew's face.

"Then get off my land."

"Your land?"

"My land."

"How can you be so sure?"

"What are you talking about, Larry?"

"Just never mind. Just never mind." The flashlight circled around and around.

Andrew jumped at Larry in the dark, and tried to grab hold of him, but all he managed to grasp was some of his hair. He tugged at that. "Get off my land, Larry," he said into what he thought was the teenager's ear.

"Yes, sir, Mr. Johnson, sir," Larry said, and danced back, pulling out of Andrew's grasp. "You've been wantin' to pick a fight with me for a long time, haven't you?" His voice was hoarse. The flashlight rolled down what seemed to be a small hillside.

"I think," Andrew said grimly, trying to find Larry in the dark, "that the feeling has been mutual." His shoulder began to ache more and more in the same spot. He held his arm with the other hand.

There was the sound of something, a brief flare of light and a singed smell filling the air. In the moment of light, Andrew saw Larry staring at him from behind the bore of an old musket. Something hit his shoulder with the force of a baseball.

He held his arm closer to him. "Larry," he called. "Larry?" Someone bent to pick up the flashlight. "Larry?" The light caressed Andrew's face, blinding him, and the afterimage he carried into unconsciousness was the nimbus circling around Broken Echo's face.

CHAPTER 14

Two days later he sat in the waiting room of a doctor's office. The nurse had filled him full of soup and painkillers and left him in the waiting room with instructions not to move. She'd said that he was not the only emergency, but that it wouldn't be long. The soma codeine had left him with a buzz. *I wouldn't be here now,* he thought woozily, *if it weren't for Turkey.*

Turkey had found him wandering around in the underbrush. He had been mouthing insults at John Sevier, and raving for a change in government. If the old man hadn't found him and dropped him off at the doctor's, God knows what would have happened to him. He might have lost an arm. He still might. Though he didn't feel anything much at the moment, except a feverish desire to talk.

At his side a woman cleared her throat. He turned to look at her. She was an attractive older woman with chestnut hair and a slightly weathered face. Her smile was pleasant and her eyes were curious. "You're Andrew Jackson that bought the old Praeter house, aren't you?"

"That's right," Andrew replied, and glanced around the small cinderblock building. The walls were painted light green. There were a few low tables with some magazines on them. He and the woman were the only people talking. A few of the other people waiting glanced at them desultorily, and then went back to their magazines. The covers of the magazines were a blur. He squinted, but all he could make out were the bright colors on the covers.

"I'm Dorothy McKinney; I used to live in there in that old house."

Andrew looked at her again with sharpened interest. Her hazel eyes regarded him shrewdly. "That's a strange place, isn't it?" he asked.

"That's one of the things you might say about it."

"I know your sister," he said heavily. He shifted in his seat and winced at the sudden roaring ache that shot through his nervous system from the shoulder all the way down to his leg. "I know," she said. "You've really hurt that arm, haven't you?"

"Looks that way." He cleared his throat. Got to think about something else. He felt feverish and light headed, but he didn't want to faint in the waiting room. Besides, this might be his only chance to pump this woman for information. He continued in a heavy voice he hardly recognized as his own. "Look, Mrs.—"

"Miss," she corrected.

"Miss McKinney, I'd like to know about some of the things that happened to *you* at the Praeter place."

"I just bet you would," she smiled. "Actually, I miss the old place every once in a while. Not that I'd want to go back for a visit," she added hastily; "but I wouldn't mind reminiscing with somebody who"—she glanced at his arm,—"knows what I'm talking about. Though if I were to guess, I'd say you've got more in the way of experience than *I* ever had."

"Maybe," Andrew smiled.

"So I'll tell you a story or two while we're sitting here. I know that Doc Alec is doing a delivery—"

"A delivery?"

"Of a baby," she said; "so we'll both be waiting a while."

Billy had been only six pounds He closed his eyes and swayed in the chair. He leaned back and tried to steady himself, and to focus on her face.

"How long?" asked Andrew. There had been a "delivery" the night that Jess had come to tell him about Katie.

"Oh, not long," she said; "the nurse came out a while ago and told me they were on the last push."

Kate, her hair wet, and her mouth opened just a little too much in pain. He hadn't seen Andy born, but they had both been determined he would be in on the birth of his second child.

"So I might as well—"

"Okay," Andrew said; "well, tell me a story." He leaned gingerly toward her.

"My sister told me that she mentioned the story about waking up with that Indian in bed with me." Like a radio channel too far out of range, her voice faded in and out. "Well, I saw disappearing pianos and heard rattling chains in the basement. I locked up the cellar just about as soon as I got there, because I heard stories about the ghosts down there, and I can tell *you* I didn't want anything to do with them." She laughed a hearty laugh.

"Why'd you move in then?" His voice quickened. He held his left arm with his right hand and focused on what she was saying. He could hear her much more clearly now.

"For the excitement, I guess. I wasn't all that old, and it seemed like fun to move into a haunted house. It was cheap to rent, and no one else around here would live there." She laughed again. "Anyway, I stayed there for about a year, I guess, before I decided that I didn't really find living in a ghost house all that exciting."

"What do you mean?"

"Well, not much really happened after I cracked that old Indian on the head with a frying pan. It got to be pretty quiet around there, let me tell you." She laughed again. "But you know, it was the darndest thing, when he was gone I kind of missed the old bugger."

Andrew laughed. "I bet you really gave him a crack with that frying pan."

"See what a little storytelling will do for you. You're feeling better already. Just stay here with me, and pretty soon you won't need a doctor."

"Say, did he ever talk to you?"

She looked at him with real surprise. "No," she said slowly. "Does he talk to you?"

"He's said a few things." Andrew nodded. His shoulder throbbed dully, but he ignored it.

"I wouldn't trust him for a minute;" she swung her purse up into her lap as she spoke. Grabbing a Kleenex from the bag, she held it up to her nose just in time to catch a vigorous sneeze. As she lowered the Kleenex to her lap, she said, "He had a shifty look about him."

"What do you mean?" Andrew asked.

"Sometimes he was young and sometimes he was old and sometimes he"—she hesitated—"looked like somebody else entirely."

"I've seen all that," Andrew admitted. He looked around the waiting room. People were idly watching the two of them, but no one seemed to be close enough to overhear the conversation.

"You have? Well then, if I were you I'd move out." She gave a decided nod. "That place is trouble from the word go."

"I know, but it's hard for me to move now."

"Yeah, I heard that you buried your family there," she nodded. "But you can dig 'em up can't you?" She said so with such a hearty, vigorous honesty that it was difficult to take offense.

Andrew looked at her in astonishment. For a moment he was angry, but she merely smiled a tough, old smile. Then he began to laugh. "I suppose I could, but I don't want to."

"Well, you better watch out for that old place, and especially for that Indian. The place and he have done in folks who were a lot better prepared for what might happen than you."

"You mean you?" Andrew asked with a grin.

Her face sobered abruptly. "Me and others. You know that he's the one who married the Praeter girl, I expect?"

Kate had worn a long, opaque veil with handstitched lace flowers

"Yes, but—"

"He finished off her old man with as neat a shot in the ribs with an arrow as I've ever seen. Not that he didn't have reason, what with Praeter foaming at the mouth over his own daughter. Still, that's the sight that made me close up the cellar and board the door shut. Out of pride I stayed on for quite a while before I left. I'm not easy to scare off, I can tell you that."

"I'm sure of it."

Just then a nurse with platinum blonde hair tied neatly back came up to Andrew. She nodded pleasantly to Dorothy McKinney. "We need to take him first, Miss McKinney, if you don't mind. He's hurt his arm pretty badly."

"That's fine," said the older woman, reaching quickly for her Kleenex. "I just have a bad cold. I can wait." She sneezed.

"Thanks, Miss McKinney," he said.

The nurse helped him get to his feet. "Just walk slowly," she said.

Miss McKinney glanced up at him. "You're welcome. I'll tell my sister that you're hurt." She sneezed again. "Listen, ask the old guy why he didn't go West with his people. I don't know why, but that nearly always makes him disappear for days." She looked at him with shrewd eyes. "It must mean something."

Andrew nodded at her. He owed her something for that one. Anything that might take the Indian off-guard could be useful. After the shot he was less certain than ever of Broken Echo.

The nurse led Andrew into a small, square back room. Like the waiting room, it was old-fashioned and sparsely filled. It smelled of medicine. Andrew sat down heavily on the patient's table, which creaked.

She looked at him for a minute, and then said, "The doctor will be along, but you should take your shirt off and let me look at you anyway."

He looked up at her. "Okay," he said, and removed his shirt.

His left shoulder just below the collarbone had a nasty-looking bruise with an irregular hole in the center of the bruise.

"What happened to *you?*" she exclaimed.

"I'm not quite sure."

She brought some cotton and some alcohol over from the stand and swabbed the wound. Andrew winced. It hurt a little, even though his arm still felt numb for the most part.

The doctor slid back the door and came in. "Well, well, so you're the new fellow over across the lake from me," he said in a rough, humorous voice.

"That's me," said Andrew, looking the doctor over with interest. He was a man of medium height with slightly bushy eyebrows and a kind, intelligent look about him. Andrew liked him immediately.

"Got yourself into trouble already, have you?" the doctor asked in a joshing way. "I'd have thought you'd have waited until spring at least."

"Spring came a little early this year, I guess."

"I'd say it did;" the doctor bent over to examine the wound; "yes, I'd certainly say it did."

Andrew looked up into the nurse's eyes, but she seemed troubled so he looked away again.

"This looks," the doctor's voice was grave as he glanced up at Andrew; "like a gunshot wound, but the damndest gunshot wound *I* ever saw." He stepped back a bit and looked at Andrew. "What have you been up to?"

"I saw someone out on my land," Andrew said hoarsely, "so I went out to see who it was and what they were there for. I didn't have a gun. They shot at me," he added, glancing at the doctor's face to see his response.

"Nurse, go call the sheriff's office," Doc Alec said, and moved in again to examine Andrew's arm. "He'd better report this to them."

Andrew shifted uncomfortably.

"Might go all around the lake," the doctor clarified, looking at Andrew with a bright, inquisitive glance.

"Might," Andrew said. He hadn't thought he'd have to lie to the sheriff too. He didn't know if he liked that idea. Why hadn't he told the doctor who it was? He didn't know, but he guessed it was because he thought this thing was between Larry and him.

"You might," said the doctor, "if you have any idea who did it—"

"I don't," said Andrew quickly.

"—tell the sheriff." The doctor bent down again. "I'm going to probe this wound now."

Andrew had an idea that the doctor knew very well that Andrew knew more than he was telling. "Damn."

"It's going to hurt," warned the doctor.

Andrew groaned and lifted his hand to his arm. The nurse came back into the room.

Andy and Billy playing twister in the hall near the staircase. Billy screamed and Andrew came running from the kitchen only to find him laughing and jumping up and down. "Beat you, beat you! I've got muscles!" He raised his small arm up and pointed to his elbow. "Muscles." Andy rolled his eyes.

"Nurse, I think you're going to have to hold that hand;" the doctor grinned. "You could do worse than having her hold your hand," he confided. "It might have been Wednesday."

The nurse blushed, but she moved over to hold Andrew's hand away from the injured arm.

"You have got a huge piece of shot in that arm!" The doctor leaned back, clearly astonished.

"What do you mean?" Andrew asked.

"It looks like one of those old musket balls!" The doctor leaned forward to probe again. Then he said, "Nurse put him down on that table. I think this is going to take a while. And you'd better go get some anesthetic."

The anesthetic was local, so Andrew stayed awake, though he was groggy. And sometimes it seemed to him that the doctor who leaned over him was the military doctor whose face he had glimpsed in the cellar, and sometimes it seemed to him that he talked deliriously about the battle he'd just finished with the Rebs, and how he should have never told his girlfriend that there was "no Rebel bullet marked for him." And sometimes it seemed to him that he was yelling about "that damned Sevier, and the insult to his wife!" And sometimes it was Doc Alec, looking clearly more and more astonished, as he pierced his way into the numbed arm. When he reached the ball and began to move it, Andrew fortunately began to lose consciousness. The room grew blacker and blacker, and in the center of that darkness, Andrew seemed to hear Broken Echo's voice saying, "You just can't leave it alone, can you?" right before he slipped into the quiet, silent center of that voice.

Resting his head against the coolness of the window, Andrew waited for Jess in her car. Apparently Miss McKinney had wasted no time in tracking down her sister. Jess had come to get him, and she'd been bent on driving him to her house to recuperate. As Andrew had expected, James obviously hadn't passed along the fact that he'd warned Andrew to stay away from her, and so he couldn't very well explain why he didn't want to go with her. He'd said something feebly about James not liking him there, and she'd just been astonished, so he let it drop.

She'd gone into the drugstore to fill his prescriptions. The planks of the wooden sidewalk seemed blurred and unnatural. He watched the heat waves rise from them, waves which made him think of the summer. Finally, he closed his eyes.

"Are you all right, Mr. Jackson?" Larry's voice shot at him. He actually sounded concerned.

No thanks to you. "I think so, Larry," he said without opening his eyes. Then he said wearily, "How are you?" Have you been shooting anyone lately?

"I'm fine, well, actually, history is a little boring these days." He laughed a nervous laugh. "What are you doing now?"

"Jess is taking me to her place to rest up for a few days. And for me," he paused, and then said emphatically, "history is anything but boring these days."

"Yeah, well, uh—I can understand that. I mean—listen, I'm sorry about your shoulder. Why didn't you say anything to the sheriff about the fact I was out there?"

"I don't know," Andrew said in a wondering voice. He opened his eyes and looked at Larry.

Larry looked down. He was standing by the car with his hands stuck in his pockets and looking as uncomfortable and guilty as Andrew had ever seen him.

"I honestly don't know," Andrew repeated.

Larry pulled his knife out of his pocket and began to carefully clean his fingernails, working meticulously over each one. Then he folded the pocketknife and put it back into his left pocket.

"Maybe," Andrew said slowly, "we could parley."

Hate flared in Larry's face for a moment, and then he lowered his eyes, veiling his expression. "Sure," he shrugged; "why not?" He covered his pocket with his hand as though to reassure himself of the knife's whereabouts. The moment of discomfort seemed to be gone. He again looked self-assured, shielded.

"What about you coming by Jess's on your way home from school one day?"

"I can't today, but I can come by tomorrow." In spite of himself, he looked suddenly eager. He straightened his shoulders. *The loa did not dance in him completely yet. Perhaps the boy could still become an ally.*

"Fine," Andrew said. Then he rolled up his window so quickly he nearly caught the boy's fingers in it. Watching Jess come out of the drugstore and pause to stare the boy down, he wondered why he had done what he'd done with Larry. Keeping silent about the boy's presence in the woods and this moment just now were as inexplicable as anything he'd done lately.

Yet he'd been alternating for some time between a strange circling certainty and then an uncertainty, like the movements of a dance. Some part of him seemed to feel assured that Larry was not yet an enemy, though he was well on his way to being one. And he wasn't certain yet whether Larry had been responsible for the shot. After all, he sighed, the bullet had not been exactly modern.

Jess climbed into the car and smiled at him. "Why don't you rest a bit on the drive?" she suggested, carefully not saying anything about Larry.

He closed his eyes. Each time he did something positive, he thought as the engine roared to life, he seemed to negate it the next moment. The car creaked and rattled as though in agreement. Andrew opened his eyes and looked out the window. He watched the world flash by in slow motion, enjoying the comfortable quiet that Jess created in the car. The green and gold blur of the changing colors rushed past him, the wind tossed his hair, and he relaxed for the first time in a long while. And with his relaxation, the fever came back full force. His face felt flushed; his temples pounded. Raising one hot hand to his forehead, he strained to see the road ahead of him. Jess spoke to him, but all he could hear was the murmur of her voice. He drifted into a feverish haze. Her voice deepened, became masculine.

He sat on the porch of the old Praeter House, drinking a brandy and smoking a pipe, and speculating on what he and Larry could achieve together. It would help him to know where the boy's enmity came from. Perhaps from his father. Were they really related to the Seviers, he wondered? And what had Larry meant by questioning the title of the land? Or perhaps his anger came from his obvious identification with the Cherokees.

Andrew drew on his pipe. And then there was the question about whether this feud was something Andrew had actually begun, because of his almost immediate response to the boy, or whether Larry had been ready to be antagonistic even before Andrew came to Greenback.

Someone sat down beside him, and Andrew looked around. He expected to see the Indian, but instead it was Joseph Praeter, a scarf decorously wrapped over the top of his head.

"How did you get out?"

Praeter shook his head in silence. Andrew smoked his pipe for a while, watching the puffs rise like tiny clouds from the bowl of the pipe.

"Let me tell you a riddle and see if you can guess it," Andrew said.

Praeter nodded solemnly. His eyes were deepset and sad, perhaps the saddest eyes Andrew had seen, at least since he looked at himself in the mirror in the days just after his family's death. He shivered. Just for a moment there he thought he had heard Kate's voice in the living room.

"There was this guy who went over to Africa to go slave-trading, but his crew got blown off course to this island. Now they had heard about this island;" Andrew lifted his hand theatrically, "before they got there. It had been settled years before by some white men, but even before the white men settled there, there were black men on the island as well. Now the black men always lied and the white men were cannibals."

"You've gotten it wrong," Praeter said gruffly. "The white men always lied and the black men were cannibals."

"No, no, I'm sure that this is right. The white men were cannibals and they always told the truth, and the black men always lied."

"Very well then; it is your joke." Praeter stared ahead of him toward the lake. He was holding his head as though it pained him. His shoulder was bandaged.

"So the slave trader wanted to take the natives with him to sell as slaves, but the trouble was that the natives were light-skinned blacks, and the white men had been there such a long time that it had gotten to be very difficult to tell them apart. The only way that the slave trader could land on the island safely and get away with the black natives was to learn which were which."

"Why didn't he just go on to Africa?" Praeter interrupted. "Or go back to Haiti?"

"You've made the trip, I see."

"Don't toy with me. Your record isn't particularly splendid either." Praeter crouched lower, his head nearly resting on his knees.

"Fair enough. At any rate, he couldn't because he was lost, so he had to land on this island—"

"He could have searched for another island." Praeter stared at him with bloodshot eyes.

"Whose joke is this?" Andrew asked, but he didn't wait for an answer, instead he went on.—"so he had to land on this island. He saw three men standing at the edge of the island and they all looked alike, but he yelled across to them and he said to the man on the left: 'Are you a native or a white man turned brown?' but the answer of the man was covered by the rush of the waves. So he yelled to the second man, 'Are you a native or a tanned white man?'"

"Well, it doesn't make any difference. Why didn't he simply make all of them slaves? No one would have known the difference for months and by that time he'd have been on another trip." Praeter rubbed the top of his head fretfully.

"Do you want to hear the joke or not?" Andrew shook his shoulders.

"It passes the time." Praeter looked out across the lake. His face was pensive. "I don't care, I guess."

"So the second man said 'I'm a white man turned brown, but the man to my right said he was a native' and—"

"Well then, they're all natives, so he might as well have—"

"In the West they would have called you trigger happy." Andrew's tone was wry. He looked over at the other man.

"I only meant that obviously they were all lying."

"Why do you say that?"

"Well, why would any of them tell the truth if a slave trader was landing on the island, so obviously they were all going to lie. And the best lie would be to convince the slave trader that the man next to them was a native."

"Did you find it so when you were trading? What lies did you hear most often?"

Praeter glared at him. "I traded with chiefs who sold away their own villagers. I traded with those who sold their best friends, and sometimes their family members, out of jealousy. In comparison to them my hands were clean."

"Comparisons are a rigged game."

"And what game isn't? Yankee traders bankrolled my trips. British bankers underwrote their loans. Trading in East Tennessee, unlike Virginia and South Carolina, was a minor activity. I repeat, sir, in comparison to them, my hands were clean." Praeter tugged at his kerchief. "What I did took courage, daring, and some amount of common sense, and I did it openly, honestly. I hid my trade from no one."

"That explains the tunnel, no doubt."

"A mere cosmetic convenience so that the neighbors could pretend they knew nothing." Praeter smiled. "Let me tell you something. East Tennessee slaves were better treated than most. Marriages, though unofficial, were recognized, and families were kept together. Slaves could visit from plantation to plantation without any written passes. A slave could buy him or herself free, though that meant leaving the state, of course. Many slaves were able to hire themselves out and keep the money they made, and—"

"Your slaves hardly qualify, since you kept them chained in the basement."

"A matter of a few days." An expression of affronted Southern gentility appeared on the ghost's face.

"It hardly matters whether slaves in Tennessee were better treated than some."

"Your hypocrisy creates a stench." Praeter moved a little further from Andrew and waved a handkerchief in front of his nose.

"Precisely what do you mean?"

"I mean that you are a teacher, and a history teacher at that. You know as well as I do that half the world has been enslaved to the other half in any century you care to pick. The methods are merely different in your day."

"More humane."

"*More* humane? You call mass education humane?" He waved his handkerchief in front of his nose. "I call it a form of narcotics. You must admit that your story is racist."

"Precisely the point."

"Well?" Praeter raised his voice.

"I give up," said Andrew.

"Good," said Praeter. "Does that mean that Evaline will come back to me now?" His voice was plaintive.

"They taught you logic in the 1800's did they?"

"No, I learned that as the centuries have passed," said Praeter, holding his head again.

"This," said Andrew suddenly, "is a dream."

Praeter looked at him for a moment without speaking, and then the scarf disappeared from his head leaving a head of rapidly greying hair. The clothes changed, and finally the face. Broken Echo was dressed as usual.

"I don't think," said Andrew, "that this is very funny. I'm supposed to be at Jess's recooperating."

"What," said Broken Echo, "you don't believe that humor can be dangerous?"

"Oh, I believe that all right. Your jokes are real killers. So you've learned to leave the house, have you?"

"No, but this is the dream world, after all. You are at Jess's." The old man shrugged his shoulders. "And you aren't."

"What level are we on? The seventh?"

"Knee high to a grasshopper," he said in a hoarse voice much older than his normal tones. Then he coughed. "You lost the card game; you can't expect answers."

Andrew ignored that. "I've had two dreams now. Does each level represent a dream? Or do the ghosts represent different levels?" Andrew stared across the lawn. "Is any of this real?" Out on the lake Praeter and his men rowed down the center of the channel. Praeter's black overcoat billowed in the wind. The lake was choppy, and the sky overhead was covered with clouds. To the left of the house he could hear the roar of the green Volvo, despite the fact that the engine had been smashed the night of the accident. Upstairs the loom clanked mechanically, and smoke billowed from the doorway of his house.

"After all this time, you're still worried about reality;" Broken Echo sighed. "Don't you think that's a silly concern at this point?"

"Leave me my little obsessions," replied Andrew. "If the first level corresponded to the first dream, then what was its significance?"

"Still looking for the simple answers, eh?" Broken Echo scratched his arm.

"I'm a simple man." Andrew smiled. "And then the second level would have been"—

—"Or would be"—Broken Echo interjected. He seated himself cross-legged, hovering just above the boards of the porch.

—"Would have *been*," Andrew said firmly, "something about," he snapped his fingers; "something about greed?"

"Tch, tch. How about something about survival?"

"Isn't survival greed?" Andrew rubbed his forehead. The

scene in front of him blurred. *Seven levels: Dreams, survival, existence, ghosts—what else? Perhaps the loa helped you or made you change levels? Like a diver with the bends he was reeling from the pressure. Again his intuitive understanding of what was happening slipped away and everything seemed abstract and pointless.*

"Very interesting, as your friend the mental psychiatrist would say. Survivor's guilt. Do you really feel that way?"

"No, not really." Sighing, he walked around the house toward the Volvo. The car sat silently on the blocks, its two headlights, smashed though they were, shining with a dim light.

"They call that a Freudian slip."

"They call that running away at the mouth where I come from, and I've been doing a lot of it these last few days."

"It's a sign of deteriorating condition, you know," said Broken Echo, suddenly looking exactly like Andrew's image of a psychiatrist, complete down to the white, well trimmed beard. "Talking to yourself, I mean."

"I won't let you do this to me anymore," Andrew announced, looking at the Volvo. He thought, when he looked at first that he had seen Kate behind the wheel, but when he peered more closely he saw that the car was empty.

"Good," said Broken Echo. "That's a nice first step."

"A level, you mean."

"Are you on the level, you mean?" Broken Echo smiled gently, and entirely too innocently, but Andrew didn't bother to reply to that.

Instead he said softly, "I may not be able to close down the dream, but I can take you out of it."

"Remember what happened the last time you did that?"

"You left. But you won't leave this time, will you?"

Behind the Indian the boat continued to row up and down the channel of the lake, while the men's muscles gleamed with sunlight and sweat; however, the loom clanked to a silent halt. Broken Echo looked suddenly interested. "Perhaps," he said, "but you'll still be dreaming. You mount a horse, or the horse rides you;" and his voice trailed off. The grass rippled around Andrew's bare feet, and the Indian left him in delirium.

The drums beat slowly behind him. No, it was the sound of hoofbeats, the increasing gallop of hoofbeats, a sound to which the beat of his heart kept time. To his side a horse snorted and pawed the ground. Who would it be this time? A Rebel soldier? A Yank? "You're in the wrong family," said the light, musical voice behind him.

"That was a damn poor choice of words," he said, turning around slowly.

"Forgive me, I realize that in this house I've forgotten how to talk to polite company." The woman who stood facing him was the woman with the torch the night before.

"You're Clarissa, aren't you?"

"Sometimes. When I remember. But I don't like to remember." Her voice dipped down, taking on a slight monotone. She pulled off a small, wool riding cap. "Forgive me, but I've got to go now." She pulled on her cap again and remounted, gathering her reins.

"Wait."

"No, I can't wait." Her voice was sad and somewhat remote. "The time is such that I have no control over it, at all, at all." The last two phrases came with the lilt of an echo.

The horse galloped faster and faster toward the pasture. They took the fence in one sharp bound and then the horse reared in confusion. She pulled him in and waved reassuringly to Andrew. But in that moment the horse leaped upward and shook her from his back. She fell to the ground in a crumpled heap, and Andrew ran for all his life toward her, only to find himself running toward a receding picture which shrank into a small pinpoint of light. He landed instead in the cellar.

A black slave with a scar on his face whom he recognized as the minister from another dream, crouched, his hands stroking the earthen floor. "She was a slave woman. Her husband was a free man. I took her away from her husband." He pointed a thumb to the black woman seated in the corner of the cellar. "We ran away together." Andrew strained to see her face, but he could see nothing but her form. "That was when Praeter was running a slave trade, and he caught us. Lucky break for him," he coughed. "But then we died on him."

Andrew walked down the steps slowly, his feet beating a rhythmic tattoo. Somewhere a drum banged and an out-of-tune whistle piped thinly.

"Her husband had been a priest, and had never done a day's work in his life, because he'd had twelve wives in his own country. He was a sharecropper just down the road from her plantation. So the two of them would work all day sharecropping in the fields, and then he would walk in the door and sit his keyser down on a chair and order her around. He beat her, and she fought with him. The overseer wouldn't interfere, because it was a family matter.

The only time I ever saw her husband behave well at all was when their child died. He buried that child with every toy and tool in the house, and tied a piece of muslin to a nail at his side. The muslin had many pictures on it which he said would ensure that when the child crossed the sea he would be recognized by his own people. The priest believed that when we died we crossed again to Africa. Some priest." He coughed, and the woman stirred.

"You took me from him," she said gutterally, "and from the grave of my child. Did you think I would be grateful? I only left to get away from him, and then I would have left you also. Men," she spat on the floor; "they are all the same. One priest is the same as another."

"You killed your child." He looked at Andrew. "She threw the boy down a well."

"My husband wouldn't buy him free. No son of mine would be born slave."

Looking at her in sympathy, Andrew lifted his hands. What would I have done? Would I have kept my children alive at any cost?

"What are you looking at, white man? I don't care if all your family was killed; you don't know nothing about what I'm talking about. One game of cards doesn't mean anything. You'll light out and run when the going gets rough."

"Do you still have the root?" The man asked suddenly, ignoring the woman.

Andrew nodded.

"Hold on to it as a favor for me. I don't know if any of us will make it anywhere. Will you die here? Everyone who comes dies here. But if we make it further, you might find that root very useful." He rubbed his head. "Do you have any water?" The shadows lengthened from the corner of the cellar to the man's head, his arms. Dizzily, Andrew watched them come until they swooped toward him like a hawk.

CHAPTER 15

"You've not been too smart lately, Andrew," came the low voice behind him.

Andrew lay on a couch. He could feel the roughened fabric underneath him and the back of the couch to his left. He should have gotten that man water. No matter what it took or the fact that it wouldn't do any good. He should have gotten that man some water. There went a blurred vision to a woman moving away from and toward a large picture window. Am I at Jess's house? he wondered.

The woman turned toward him, her hands on her hips, and said, "I think you should stay here for a while."

"No," he said hoarsely, "I need to finish this thing, Jess."

"You mean *it* needs to finish you."

"I don't think so."

"How did you get hurt?" She walked toward him and as she did, her face came into focus, a face like a cameo.

"What will James think about me being here?" Andrew stirred restlessly on the couch. He knew why James had come to talk to him. This woman was someone special, someone who would take into her home a total stranger who was near the edge. Perhaps even beyond the edge.

"James? Nothing. That's the second time you've said that. Has he . . ." Her hand crept up to a small neat bow tied around her neck. "I don't think he'll say anything. You've been shot after all!"

He couldn't tell her. "I just thought of what an imposition—"

"It's no imposition at all," she replied warmly.

Andrew shifted his weight quickly, but his shoulder had already begun to throb. Jess's face blurred into softness again, and he heard the whisper of her shoes as she crossed the carpet; the whisper seemed to buzz around like a small bee—or was he the one buzzing—until he finally sailed into his frontyard, settling lightly on a stack of timber.

"What are you doing with that lumber?" Broken Echo demanded from his perch on the pile of marble tombstones just to the side of the porch.

Andrew stopped for a moment, several lengths of lumber in his arms. "I'm not sure yet," he said, thinking to himself, something to surprise *you*, witch doctor. "I can see a little gray around the temples." He nodded pleasantly. I have to fight them, he thought. They've left me no choice after all. I may love the idea of them; and it pains me to see them in pain, but that has nothing to do with it at all. This is a matter of survival now.

"Those who count chickens before hatched become turkeys," was the bland reply. He placed a pipe in his mouth and glared at Andrew, who walked around the Indian and toward the back of the house and down the long stretch of grass that led to the end of his land.

Broken Echo followed him. Andrew ignored the Indian and lifted the thin lengths of lumber into a point, spreading the pieces at the bottom into a circle.

"Ha!" Broken Echo crossed his arms. "Do you think that if you make me a teepee, I'll stay in *that*? You're a very foolish man, Old Hickory. Weren't you the one who told your students that history never repeats itself the same way twice?" He cocked his head in a gesture very much like the robin that so often sat on his shoulder.

"We'll see," Andrew said and smiled. "Maybe I have

something else in mind. You're not the only one who can create." He lashed the top together. Then he walked slowly back toward the house to get his box of supplies. When he returned, he found that Broken Echo had picked up the stack of wood and was examining it quizzically. "Cedar," he said, and put the stack down.

Andrew readjusted the spread circle of the wood. Then he took his bundle and laid the fake hickory bark on the frame. He attached it with a staple gun.

"Cheap construction," Broken Echo said, and sniffed as he walked away. Andrew could feel him looking back in puzzlement.

By sunset he had built five more of the fake teepees. He went back inside well pleased with himself.

He fixed dinner, and went up to the study where he ate and worked on some of the curriculum materials. Boyles, it turned out, wanted him to describe the program he would have conducted with his students this year. He had become interested in the project system and the period emphasis program that Andrew had created.

Broken Echo's rocking chair moved. He appeared slowly, his hair a little whiter than before. "Do you plan to move some of my relatives?" he asked gently. "Bring us home to the plantation?" His voice was mocking. "Or perhaps you will move out there and leave me in peace."

"*You* question *me* now?" His mind suddenly felt much less cloudy, in fact his thought processes felt clearer than they had in months. He bent back over his curriculum materials. The Civil War—he thought—is an important period to begin with for southern high-school students because it can provide—

"And do you think that anything will live in that ramshackle thing you call a dwelling—"

"I called it nothing."

"That you construct as a dwelling."

"No," Andrew said thoughtfully, leaning back in his chair and staring at the ceiling, "I don't think that anything will live there. Perhaps I am constructing toys."

Broken Echo rocked back and forth without answering for a while. He drew on his pipe and stared into the empty fireplace. "The conundrums I created for you were real," he said, and the rocking chair quietly slowed until at last Andrew realized the Indian was gone.

Was the old Indian right? he wondered. Maybe he should

just wait for the cycle to come back around, and conduct a defensive war with the young one until then. Then use the time with the old man to fight this thing he was in the middle of. He liked the old man, though he was not at all sure he trusted him. Maybe he even liked the young one. And he was getting used to this notion of the moon. He could almost chart the change now.

No, he decided slowly, it was time he took control, and the only way he could see to do that was by psychological war. He certainly had no other method readily available. Broken Echo was right about some things, but that didn't mean he had the right methods. Maybe the answer was to drive all the ghosts away, and then allow himself to grieve naturally. And, even though he could tell when the changes occurred with the Indian, who was to say how much the young one influenced the other as the cycle fluctuated? No, he would go on the offensive.

Andrew walked down the stairs. Broken Echo was stalking around the living room, picking things up and then putting them down again. Andrew stared at him for a moment and then walked over to the phone, picking up the receiver indecisively. He had thought he would enjoy startling the Indian more, but he realized that the man he wanted to startle wasn't here, and the man he was grieving was the old one he was growing more and more fond of. It left him with a sick but determined feeling.

He hefted the receiver in his hand and stared at the rose colored wallpaper pattern on the wall, thinking of people coming onto the quiet, old property. Sold out, he thought, you've sold out, Andrew, and for what—Do you think these ghosts will level even then? Maybe he'll just scare the hell out of whoever comes.

The quiet around him was tentative and somehow accusing. Broken Echo left the room, slamming the living room door behind him.

Andrew began to dial the number. The dial whispered as it turned. His disappointment in the old man grew as he dialed. Why hadn't Broken Echo stopped him? The dial whispered as it turned. The whisper grew louder. It wasn't, after all, the phone dialing, though he could feel his finger slowly turning in the dial. In another room, he heard two voices whispering loudly, one masculine, one feminine. He tried to rise up to see who was speaking, but the sound buzzed and faded, buzzed and faded, until he closed his eyes.

When he woke again, he had been moved to a bed with freshly ironed sheets. The bed that cradled him was a small four poster with an intricate calico-patterned quilt. There was a window just to his right with a small transparent curtain through which came a soothing amount of light. He felt protected, somehow under a temporary sort of charm. Nothing could go wrong in this place, and no one would be disturbing or odd.

To the left he heard the door opening and turned his head inquiringly. His shoulders locked in pain. He winced.

"How are you feeling?" Jess asked briskly. She carried a tray with a steaming bowl and a plate with fruits and cheese.

"About as well as can be expected." Andrew looked at the tray in her hands.

"You look hungry!"

"I think I can manage a bite."

"How long has it been since you"—she hesitated—"had a homecooked meal?"

"Since the night you had me over for dinner," he said, "unless you count my own cooking as home cooking."

Kate, her hands deftly cutting up carrots, laughing at the boys telling each other dead baby jokes

Andrew tried to sit up, but he couldn't quite manage it. Jess set the tray down and carefully held him while she plumped up the pillow behind his back. She handed him the tray.

"Doc Alec will be over later to have a look at you. He lives next door."

"Is that how you talked him into letting me go?" Andrew dipped his spoon into the vegetable soup.

"Something like that. Andrew, why did Larry Bryge shoot at you?"

He nearly choked on the soup. "Where did you get the idea it was Larry?"

"Did you think the news about you two hadn't gotten around town, especially after you were fired?" Jess's voice was a bit exasperated.

"I was sure that it did, but that doesn't mean that"—

—"That the boy had been stalking you for days?" She

moved over to the window and gently pulled the curtain. "I've known Larry Bryge since he was a little boy. He's always been hotheaded and stubborn, but he's never been like he's been lately. One of you is bad medicine for the other one."

Andy when he was two or three. He held a stuffed dog that had been worn nearly to bits by its flights as a basketball. Once it had had a black muzzle, but now all that was left was a kind of clear plastic. "I want to go outside," he said fretfully. "You can't, Andy." Kate's voice came from somewhere in the other room. "You've got pinkeye, and you have to stay in that dark room. You've got to take your medicine."

Andrew finished off the bowl of soup. "I don't know that it was Larry," he said slowly; "he was out there, but it could have been the Cherokee."

"The sheriff will be out here to ask you the same thing soon, you know. You'd better have an answer for him at least."

"I'll tell him that I don't know who it was. It was dark. I couldn't see because someone blinded me with a flashlight."

Jess sat down on the end of the bed and looked at him steadily. She looked even more like a cameo profile than before. He imagined what it would be like to paint her, to catch that proud lift of the eyes and the gentleness of the mouth. She was a handsome woman. Her hands rested against her legs without any restless movements. Just to watch her calmed him.

"Why would you say that?" she asked softly.

"I don't know," Andrew said, "I don't really know why, except this is a private thing for us to settle, not a public issue."

"Do you mean that you would do something to the boy?" She was clearly startled.

"No, I mean that Larry and I have to work this out together. It has something to do with the Praeter House, and with old family feuds. That's nothing that will make sense to the sheriff." *Larry would be lost if Andrew reported him.*

"Oh, I'm not so sure about that. This wouldn't be the first time this area's seen feuds. Just down the road from you a bit is a place that no one will buy because there's no way to get to the land."

"No road?"

"There's a road, but there's also a family guarding that road. Whoever goes in to look at the property they take in by boat. There were prospective buyers, a couple, who nearly bought that place until they got shot at by the feuders."

"Wait a minute. Is that the place with the white picket fence and the large backyard? No, I don't believe that. Besides, things like that don't happen any more. There aren't any more feuds." Andrew grinned.

He had seen Andy in the water off of that point

"That's the one. And weren't you the fellow just telling me about a feud of your own? This may be the South, but it's still the South, if you know what I mean." She threw back her head and laughed. For that moment she reminded Andrew of her sister.

"Kate and I looked at that house. We very nearly bought it." Andrew began to peel his orange.

"You might have been better off," she said, quickly sobering.

"I don't know, Jess; don't you believe that things happen because they're supposed to?" Andrew leaned back against the pillows and listened to the sound of a slamming car door. Is that James? he wondered. Or the sheriff? He could see that Jess was wondering the same thing.

"So those two innocent buyers who went by road to the property we're talking about, that was supposed to happen to them? Or was it that someone just didn't tell them firmly enough not to try it? They knew about the feud, but they went in anyway." Her hands tightened on her legs.

"You're saying that I'm being foolish? That I'm making myself a challenge?"

"That's about the way it measures up to me." She stood, looking down on him with a touch of pity. "See here, Andrew, since you've been here you've taken all the hard routes. Don't you think it's about time you eased up on yourself, and got a little help."

"You'll help me?"

"Yes, but I'm not enough. Sell that house. Get out of that boy's life. It doesn't really matter how or why this is all happening. What matters is that there's no need to stir up old dust. At least not unless it stirs you up." She put a gentle hand on his shoulder.

"And you don't think I *have* been stirred up?"

"I know *something* has been stirred up." She paused long enough to say, "Think about it," and then she left the room to the tune of a faintly tinkling harpsichord.

The lawn was covered with gaily moving women in hooped dresses and men in long, scooped tailcoats. In a circle near what would later be a huge oak tree, but was now only a newly planted sapling, skipped some half-grown children. There was the sound of a harpsichord, every note falling together with the next so quickly that they created a harmonious babble which lingered in the air.

Against this scene of movement and life Andrew could see, as through a haze, the movement of fat-legged tourists in Bermuda shorts and straw hats, the cynical face of a bored young teenager, the solemn nodding of the two Cherokees he had hired to talk about the Indian Village. The longer he looked the more confused he became until at last he walked up to the back of the crowd to listen to what his guides were saying. The moment he joined the crowd, the blurred overlay faded.

"This is the site of an ancient Cherokee village—"

Andrew looked up in puzzlement at the guide who was speaking. He had his long, black hair done up in braids, and a dyed feather poked from one of the braids. Behind him, just over his shoulder, Andrew could see the top of one of the tents he had made in an afternoon. There were stones piled haphazardly around the bottom of each tent to hide its hasty construction, but the tops actually looked no more convincing.

The people to Andrew's left and right were watching the men with intensity. He could see a woman ahead of him, her straw hat tipped to the very back of her head, nodding as though in affirmation.

"—and this village was the site of some of the Cherokees who ran away from the soldiers of Andrew Jackson—"

Andrew started. The two guides, clearly bored, looked at him. This happened each time they spoke.

"—and remained behind. For a while they hid in the mountains. One of their ancestors was actually the man who scalped one of the former property owners of this house, a man named Joseph Praeter."

A young woman with brown curly hair and the clothes of a college student made a slight sound of surprise. Just to her left Andrew could see the harpsichord player seated on the lawn. He blinked his eyes. The harpsichord disappeared, but the man, still seated cross-legged on the lawn, winked at him. The two guides continued to stare at Andrew as they spoke to the crowd. This prolonged stare, too, had become a part of their spiel. The other one began to speak.

"Yes, the man who killed Joseph Praeter was a well-known Cherokee warrior named by the whites Ray Green Eyes because of his jealousy."

On the other side of the house, he could hear the sounds of the Loudon County Arts Society. They were playing music, making quilts, and selling "made in Japan" souvenirs to the tourists who managed to make their way to the other side of the lawn.

When his brother, Greg, had come to visit, had that been a dream? He didn't remember his brother leaving. What had they said to each other? And how had Andrew carried it off?

Do you always ask questions in threes, he asked himself? Oh God, Andrew, you've bought the farm. He looked around him with distaste at the crowd, the trampled green lawn on which they stood, the rough-hewn platform, the bored faces of his guides. This, he told himself, is either black humor or torture. Perhaps both.

Someone beside Andrew murmured, "I'm part Cherokee, you know," and Andrew shook his head. Then he turned to look into the gently mocking face of Broken Echo. "Isn't that what everybody in East Tennessee claims to be?"

"Later the son of that Indian married Joseph Praeter's daughter," intoned the older guide. Andrew never could remember either of the guides' names.

"They may claim to be Indian, but they don't really want to be. If they were, they'd have to live with cheap Japanese souvenirs. That would leave them again in the arms of the contempt of others. Just another cheap way to play with your stories. This is boring. We know these things. Shall I say a few words about my father and myself?" Broken Echo nodded to Andrew.

"I hardly think that would be wise."

"Have I ever claimed wisdom?" Broken Echo tipped back his hat. A tiny mouse darted around the rim from the back of the hat, peered over the edge, and then poised there for a moment. Broken Echo lowered it gently to the ground.

"What have you claimed?" Andrew suddenly became very interested. He grabbed the Indian's arm, but his hand seemed to slip away of its own accord.

"Good question."

"No, I mean it." Several people in the crowd turned around to glare at Andrew. He looked at Broken Echo and raised an eyebrow, then shrugged as if to say, what can you do.

Broken Echo smiled the first genuine smile Andrew had seen since he began his new project. A faint breeze lifted a few strands of his hair. "I think, oh historical renegade, I have claimed you."

Andrew spread his hands out. "What about these?" he said, with a glance around at the crowd.

"Would you really like to know?"

As if it were the elaborate opening move of a chess game, Andrew stared at the crowd in consideration. The lightly drifting sound of a harpsichord returned. The notes were off-key. He glanced back to Broken Echo, calculating the whiteness of his hair. It was now the color of parchment. "Yes," he said, as though in surprise, "I think I would."

"Then these are nothing more than white smoke."

"They seem," Andrew said wryly, "pretty damn solid to me."

"And so they are, but even the solid dissipates." The old Indian raised his hat in the air.

"How?" Andrew persisted.

"And now you've decided questions are allowed. You'll be difficult to contain."

"Probably," Andrew conceded.

"It's harmless to tell you a thing or two, I suppose." The old man grinned. "But I find it hard to break old habits. Don't worry. They'll leave soon enough."

"You won't hurt them;" Andrew was alarmed and yet intrigued. "Oh no, they're really beyond that sort of thing. You," he smiled, "I can do something with." His pale blue eyes danced.

Larry came around the corner of the house, the old fashioned shirt sleeves pushed up above his elbows. He moved toward Andrew purposefully. Broken Echo rolled his eyes.

"What are you going to do?" Andrew whispered.

"Just leave that to me." The old man slipped by the woman in front of Andrew like an eager young otter.

"There's nobody who has come in for the tour of the house, Andy," Larry said, as he joined Andrew there at the edge of the crowd. His voice was as laconic as ever, but he had a friendlier expression. The antagonism had seemed to slip away when Andrew hired him to run the tours of the house, and of the basement. Andrew had simply known that Larry was at least real. The two of them had to get rid of their slippery, ambiguous antagonism and join forces. Asking Larry to work for him had been a matter of pragmatism. But wasn't this a dream? Were these things real on any level? Then it didn't matter what the two of them said to each other, did it?

"It doesn't look as if they will, Larry."

"Do you think then that I could go home a little early?"

"Oh sure;" Andrew's tone of voice was easy. "In fact, have a couple of days off with pay if you like. The take has been good this week." *Damn you, Andrew. Even on the dream level you can't sustain it, can you? You might have pulled the boy back, but he makes you uneasy.*

Larry clapped Andrew on the shoulder. "Thanks a lot. I know I've only been working for you a few afternoons, but there's a Thanksgiving dance at the Community Center this weekend, and I didn't think I'd get to go, but if you really don't need—"

"That's fine, Larry. Just kiss your girl for me;" Andrew winked at him, and watched him leave with only a slight tinge of guilt. *Why can't you sustain it? Do you want the boy to be taken over by the cellar? Token sacrifice. One Bryge saves one Jackson. Coward.* If Broken Echo was successful, Larry would be out of a job. And Larry hadn't even been momentarily suspicious when Andrew mentioned two days off with pay. It was probably, he reflected, the only job that Larry had ever had.

Andrew watched the two remaining leaves on the nearby tree drift down to settle on the ground.

Larry had been easy enough to persuade to come to work. He had gone over the same afternoon he'd called the chief and Larry had just been coming in from school. Andrew caught him at the gate, and Larry had had time to do no more than give him a sullen look before he had quickly proposed the job.

"You really think you're going to get tourists out here, man?" Larry leaned back on the fence, spreading his arms to either side.

Didn't he and Larry have a feud going? How had they come to be working together?

"I've got the first tour booked in here already. Called the travel agent this afternoon."

"Yeah. How do I know it's a real job? You've been doing some pretty strange things lately. And it's not like I'm your favorite person or anything."

"You've already told your father that you come over to visit me."

Larry didn't even seem surprised.

"And you've really wanted to look the place over, haven't you? What have you got to lose if it's a joke? The afternoon?"

"Maybe a lot if you—"

"If I what?"

"Don't you blame me for your job?" He looked at Andrew steadily. He was unaware that his father had come out onto the porch and was looking at both of them.

"I don't know. Maybe. Maybe I blame a lot of things."

Andrew smiled. The conversation hadn't ended all Larry's doubts, but he had come around, and he'd even helped Andrew furnish the garage, though it hadn't taken much to do that as the place had been furnished rather sparsely.

Suddenly he heard a querulous voice behind him announce, "This is boring. I want to see the house now." Turning around, he saw the angry brown eyes of the woman with the straw hat.

"What do you mean boring?"

"Just look," said several other people crowding up behind her.

Andrew glanced up toward the platform. The two guides were leaning against an old junker Chevrolet. One of them was rapidly downing Budweiser beers one after the other, a look of pained drunkenness on his face. The other was idly talking to him in a low-voiced murmur.

"Boring?" he asked.

"Yeah, we can see this any day," said the woman.

"Why should we pay for this?" asked a man with sharp, angry movements. He shifted from foot to foot restlessly. "We want to see the house."

"The house isn't on the tour."

"Yes it is. I've got it right here on my ticket." He waved a piece of paper in the air.

"I didn't give out tickets," Andrew said. "Give me that."

The man handed the piece of paper to him. On it was printed, like a cheap circus ticket with runny ink, "Tour of house and grounds five dollars."

"Who gave you this?"

The guy shrugged. "I don't know. Some man at the gate."

"Well, they're counterfeit. I don't offer a tour of the house."

"I never," said the first woman. "This is as bad a gyp joint as Ruby Falls. Travel three hundred feet underground to see a little waterfall with a red light on it. I want to see the house, or I want my money back. I shouldn't have to pay for this."

"Yes, why should you." Andrew nodded, his face expressionless. "Here." He threw a few dollar bills in front of him and watched them drift down to the lawn like the leaves. He watched the people bend down to pick up the money, their backs rising into the air. "A man," he commented idly, "shouldn't wear his hat on his buttocks?"

"What?" said the man who had spoken before. He rose with a tight-coiled precision. Andrew looked at him. "Nothing," he said simply. "Just get the hell off my land." He stopped for a moment, and then he stepped toward some of the people who were still bent down, as if he had in mind physically evicting them.

"Look, I'm going to tell anyone I know not to come by here." The woman moved down the lawn a few feet and put her hands on her hips.

"You do that." Andrew began to step closer to the people, moving them before him as if he were shooing a bunch of reluctant geese. "You just do that. Because we're closed to business, darling," he said in his best Southern drawl. "And why don't you," he grabbed one of the tents up from its pile of rocks, "just take this damned thing with you?" He bowed and handed it to her. She gathered it up in her arms, a bulky Christmas tree shape that hid her face. He could only see the top of dark hair and her feet now, but he could still hear her muffled voice. "You," she announced, "are running a cheap operation and I'm going to report you to the Better Business Bureau." By this time, the rest of her group was in the car, and she was the last one facing him.

"You just do that, darling," he said with mock patience, as he watched her walk awkwardly toward the faded blue station wagon that awaited her. "You just do that." He walked around the side lawn to get rid of the even more intrusive arts council, but they had either already taken the hint or Broken Echo had given them the word because they were gone.

He heard the metal gate with the Praeter family crest clang shut and then bounce to a slow silence, and then he walked back up the lawn, looking toward the house, and the small figure of an old, gentle man on the porch. "That's one," he said with satisfaction, "I can live with."

Then he heard a voice behind him, "Mr. Jackson—"

He was already turning when the fist hit him in the nose, and he felt a quick numbness spreading toward his eyes. The punch knocked him backwards. "What the hell—" he asked, hand rising toward his face automatically. He looked up into the faces of his two angry guides. And, as he was still saying "hell, hell, hell—" and the harpsichord was playing behind him, "hell, hell, hell," he could hear their feet moving away from him across the lawn.

Andrew lay on the bed, holding a magazine in outstretched hands, trying desperately to focus on the printed page. He could still feel the force of that blow. Even his dreams were becoming entirely too real. The letters seemed to separate and swim around on the paper, to reform themselves into an alphabet which he couldn't even translate. He moved the article further away, and then brought it up to his eyes. The distance didn't seem to matter. He was looking through the blurred angle of an old and clouded mirror.

James stopped at the doorway of his room. "What are *you* doing here?"

Andrew blinked his eyes, trying to focus on James. "Jess brought me."

"I *told* you—"

"Not to bother her. Yes, you did. But I didn't count on this." Andrew gestured lightly toward his left shoulder. "Didn't she tell you?"

"I came in from the basement; I haven't seen her yet." James frowned and rubbed his forehead.

"If Jess has already settled you in, there's not much that I can do until your shoulder's healed, because I'm not going to turn away a man who's hurt. But I still mean what I say. Until you settle down, I don't want you anywhere near her, you understand?"

"I understand."

James' sharp glance softened. "Maybe being out of that house will do you good."

"As if it could make any difference now. The damn thing's following me around," muttered Andrew.

"What was that?"

Andrew closed his eyes. "Nothing."

"Say, it wasn't just your shoulder was it? You've got a lump on your face as big as a hen's egg." Then he said, "I still don't want you here any longer than necessary, do you hear?"

"I hear." Leaning back against his pillow, the magazine slipped from his fingers to the floor, and he couldn't seem to catch it. It landed in a heap of sprawled paper, he could feel the rise of an unsteady fountain of breath.

There was the hiss of steam, and the smell of something pungent in the air when he woke. He could feel hot stone behind his back, and a hand was reaching toward him, swooping like the wing of a hawk.

"You," said the young Indian, hair still black with only a touch of gray, "have cheap shit medicine dreams."

Reevaluate, Andrew, he told himself silently, I think you've been had. His back was beginning to sting from the heat, but he couldn't begin to focus his eyes. His arms felt weak and limp.

"That was a medicine dream?" He flexed his arm and then lifted himself up to a sitting position. Then he flexed both his arms and rubbed his parboiled skin.

"You thought you were in time again?" the voice was mocking. "You sure are a hell of a talker in your dreams. That was the whole thing. Talk, talk. Cheap-shit talker too." The Indian tossed his hair back over his shoulders. "You throw away people without a second thought, don't you?"

"What's your name?" Andrew asked suddenly.

Silence.

"It wasn't Broken Echo who changed your name. It was you. If you don't like him, you don't like the results, but you were the one who created them. You're as ashamed of what's happened as I am, aren't you? You hate the way that people make a living on the reservation. You hate their loss of pride."

The young Indian turned away without speaking.

"Where did this dream start?" Andrew looked around him.

He was in the garage. At least that much of his dream had some sort of connection. The Indian had lit a fire in the old wood stove that Andrew had dragged out to the garage that long day he had waited for Kate. And there had obviously been large pots of water thrown onto the sides of the stove. Water still dripped down the sides; the steam that rose from the metal dissipated in the few moments that he watched; and because there were empty black kettles stacked up in the garage in piles three deep all around the stove. How long had they been here? Long enough, anyway, for the steam to fill the garage and condense on the walls, and long enough to heat the concrete floor. Who knew where Broken Echo had gotten the kettles? Andrew had given up trying to keep track of even his belongings in the house, because they seemed to change without warning.

"You mean the whole thing, the tourist idea, was a—"

"You got it, as the city folks say." Broken Echo lifted the lid on the stove. The wood embers glowed like large red eyes. "You really don't remember the card game, do you? And that means you don't know why you're here." He laughed. "The bruise you've got on your face, though, that was no dream." He dropped the stove lid with a clang and dusted his hands off on his worn cotton pants.

"You play a—"

"Mean hand of pinochle? Hard game of bridge?" The Indian waved his hand in the air and again the movement reminded Andrew of a hawk's wing.

"Close enough." Andrew got up unsteadily.

"But maybe the old man is right; maybe you've got some stuff in you. Not that last part. That was the same old woolly liberal stuff. We've had enough of that shit, but maybe you—"

"Greg. Was *that* real? What about my shoulder?"

"You want me to tell you everything. You think I'll answer questions now?"

Andrew was suddenly reminded of the old man in his dream. "Maybe." He smiled. "You're on the level, right?"

"Ha! Not bad."

"But which one?"

The Indian replied, "Yeah, that was real."

Now the question had become which question had he answered, Andrew thought wryly. He looked at the young Indian (what do I call him?) who shrugged. *Seven levels:*

dreams, illusions, fragments, echoes, stories, games (or was it songs?), history. Could they peacefully coexist?

Right, Andrew thought. Ask a stupid question and you get two obscure answers. He stamped his feet, feeling the blood race through his body. What happened was that he lost track of the level they were on, he lost that intuitive knowledge that taught him how to operate, and then he didn't know what the hell was happening. One moment he was carrying on a conversation with the Indian that he understood the terms of, and the next moment he had no idea. It had all slipped away from him. How many dream worlds there were. He had never realized before how many. *Ghostways, a voice hissed with a sound like the rising steam.* "You'd better," the Indian strolled casually out the door leaving the fire for Andrew to put out, "take a cold shower."

The water ran in the shower. Andrew tossed and turned, finally flinging off the sheets.

"Look, Jess, I'd just as soon that you hadn't brought Andrew here. I don't think this is one stray you need to pick up. He's a grown man, after all, isn't he?"

"And since when, James, did that stop you from expecting your dinner on time? A man whose entire family has died could use a little coddling, I think." Jess closed the door, and their voices lowered.

Andrew crept out of his bed and down the hall to stand next to their door.

"I don't disagree with that, but I think he ought to go on back home. A man needs to be with his own people when something like this happens. Why he stays around here I'll never know."

"He never should have bought that house," she said. Andrew heard a dull thud, like the sound of a fist striking. He started to open the door, until he belatedly realized she was fluffing up their pillows, as she did for him each night. Same rhythm, same sound.

"He should see it, anyway." James sounded disgruntled.

"That," she said, turning off the light, "would be difficult."

"Why is that house so infernal hard to sell anyway?" he asked.

"It's a place that no local would buy, and few outsiders would want." The bedsprings creaked. "I was never so glad as when Dorothy moved out of there. She like to drove me crazy the months she lived in that house. I mean the stories she used to tell about the furniture shifting around, and the ghosts and the calls in the middle of the night. She even had me spending the night with her a few times, especially after she got locked up in the cellar one time."

"What stories? Ghosts;" he snorted. "What did you mean going over there without telling me about all of this, anyway?"

"You? You wouldn't have a bit more believed any of those stories than—"

"No, I wouldn't have, but I wouldn't have let you go either." His voice was gruff.

"You old pikefish. You're just an out-an-out faker. Don't believe in ghosts." There was a light thump, like a pillow tossed across the room. "Well, I'll tell you something. I saw things that night that would curl the hair you don't have—"

"Since you like it that well, maybe it's time I thought about another investment. It's not a very expensive place." He laughed. "Maybe I'll just buy it from him, so he's free to leave."

"And now who's meddling? You're steaming up the bathroom. Are you going to take a shower, or are you going to jaw?"

He laughed louder. "Now, Jess, don't get all steamed up. Sounds like that place really scared you." The door closed. Then opened again. "All the same. I don't like you taking up with this fellow. And I told him so, too. I went over to his house and told him to stay away from you."

"You did what?" The bedsprings creaked. "James, you didn't."

"I did, and what's more I told him so again. I told him to get well and get out of here. I don't want him bothering you."

"James, I know you're trying to protect me, but you know as well as I do that you can't protect anybody in this world. That car accident shows that. And you can't live their life for them either. After all these years together I thought you were too old for trying to live mine."

"Sometimes you don't know when to take care of yourself."

"And sometimes you don't know when either."

James went striding across the room, and Andrew realized suddenly that he was coming for the door. He crept quickly back down the hall and into bed. The front door slammed. The shower switched off, and then he heard Jess's light steps down the hall. Andrew had just enough time to close his eyes before she opened the door to check on him. He felt her glance like a searchlight, but he kept his breathing light, until the door swung closed, and he heard her steps recede down the hallway.

CHAPTER 16

Andrew reached down to unwrap the sheets from his feet. He moved gingerly over to his left side. Jess leaned against the doorjamb. "You certainly slept long enough." She rubbed her hands, one of the few nervous gestures Andrew had ever seen her make.

"How long?"

"Oh, about twenty-four hours. I told the sheriff you'd be out for at least that long." She looked at him. "That ought to have given you enough time to think up a good lie."

"That's a relief. I thought I'd slept through his visit."

"You should be so lucky." She eyed him suspiciously, still trying, Andrew thought, to see if he had overheard their fight.

He settled back, a pleasant look on his face. "No, but I think I'll spend some time on it now."

"You'd better." The doorbell rang. "That's probably him now."

Andrew grimaced. He wondered if he could quickly slide into a stupor.

In a moment he heard her opening the front door. "Yes?"

she asked, and then he heard a surprised murmur. It couldn't be the sheriff then, Andrew thought. But when Jess returned with Turkey Haines, Andrew was truly surprised. Come to think of it, he wondered, why had it been Haines who'd found him? He couldn't remember much about the car ride to the doctor's office; he'd been delirious for most of it.

"You're a hell-bent-for-leather sort of man and that's for sure, Andrew Jackson." Turkey plopped himself down in a chair in the corner and put his hands behind his head. He eyed the bowl of fruit on the table beside Andrew. Andrew raised his eyebrows and waited to see what Turkey would say next.

"What did Doc Alec say?" He leaned forward and rested a hand on each knee. Andrew tossed him an orange; Turkey caught it in his lap and began to peel the skin. The scent of the orange filled the small room.

They had all been in the weaving room. The scent of oranges filled the air, and Billy ran giggling up to Andrew and shoved some orange peels down the front of his shirt. "All right, small fry," Andy said, and chased the boy around the yarn cabinet.

"He dug an old musket ball out of me, and he said that it would take me more than a few days to recover." Andrew paused for a moment. "How did you find me?"

"I came out to your place to see if you wanted to go to a story-telling next week," Turkey leaned back and smiled. He popped an orange slice in his mouth. "As much as you like those old moldy bits about our county, I thought you might like to hear a bunch of oldtimers telling the stories their grandfathers told to them about the Civil War. When I got there your lights were on; the front door was open. And I could hear something crawling around in your woods. I thought it was an injured animal, maybe a dog or something, so I went out to see what it was. I was sure surprised to find you there, that was for certain, and I knew you were in no shape for a party." He looked at Andrew sharply. "Did the doc sic the sheriff on you?"

"Yeah. I suppose the sheriff'll be out here soon." Andrew leaned back further into his pillows, hoping to quiet the throbbing in his shoulder. He closed his eyes for a moment.

"I can come back, if you want; I just wanted to see how you were." The old man's voice was testy.

"No, no." Andrew opened his eyes and watched the gently waving willow tree outside his window.

"What are you going to tell him?" Turkey popped an orange section into his mouth.

"The truth. That I didn't see who did it." The leaves seemed like large fingers as they dipped and bobbed in the wind. Each leaf was a slightly different color.

"I saw a blond-headed fellow slipping through the trees as I came up. He was laughing. He had been watching you run around with the fever, it looked like to me."

Andrew winced. He put his hand to his shoulder, which suddenly felt twice the size it had before. It throbbed like an abscessed tooth.

"What do you have to say to that?" Turkey put the remainder of the orange down on the small round mahogany table at his elbow.

"That I didn't see who did it, damn it!" He gripped his shoulder with his hand.

"Why would you protect a boy like that?" Turkey was becoming angry. He got up and began to pace around the room. "Look, I'm supposed to be at the courthouse. It's Friday and my son is expecting me, but I came 'round here to see how you were and to tell you about that boy. But I had no idea that you knew already and were just lying low!"

The throbbing in his shoulder eased slightly. "That teenager is no trouble to anyone but me, whatever trouble he is."

"Maybe not, but you don't know that for sure. In a dog pack, they shoot the rabid ones."

Andrew began to laugh helplessly. He patted his shoulder lightly. "Not if they've got a knife." He realized that Turkey wouldn't appreciate black humor at all. "Look, Turkey, I thank you for finding me out there and taking me to the doctor, and I thank you even more for coming by to check up on me and to tell me this. But there's something going on here that I don't understand, something that has to do with that house I'm living in. It's not going to be settled by bringing in the sheriff. It's a feud of some kind—"

"Oh," said Turkey, relief evident in his voice, "well, if you're talking about a feud, then, that's another story. We've been carrying on a feud in my family for well on twenty years or so, and none of us has been killed from it yet."

"What is it all about?" Andrew leaned forward.

"Well, my cousin's cousin stole my uncle's wife about that time, and took her up into the mountains and kept her there. And that was the second thing. The first thing was that when the Democrats in our family came back from World War Two they were voted into power, but the Republicans, those same cousins, wouldn't give up the courthouse. So the Democrats, that was my uncle and his bunch, lay siege to the courthouse, and finally they got in. All the family took sides."

Andrew smiled. "So what's the feud like?"

"We shoot at each other sometimes, but none of us are very good shots. We take each other's jobs sometimes. It's nothing too serious." Turkey sat down and smiled at Andrew.

Andrew looked out the window again and watched the shadows forming on the lawn. "I would say," he said slowly, "that this one is more serious than that."

"But still. A feud's a feud. Ain't nothing can be done about it till it burns itself out, I reckon." Turkey cleared his throat. "Anything I can do? I always enjoyed a good feud. And there's two or three of them against one of you ain't they?"

Andrew smiled at the old man. How had this happened? A supper and a good moonshine drunk and the two of them had become friends. "I'll let you know, but I sure as hell appreciate the offer."

"Anytime," said Turkey, nodding his head and looking proud of himself. "I'm ready, Captain." He saluted.

Then he got up, groaning a bit as he straightened his back. "Well, reckon I'd better get on to work, but you call me if you need me now, you hear?"

"I'll do that." Andrew watched the old man walk to the door. He was quite a character. I wonder how he and Broken Echo would get along. Probably just fine.

"Oh," Turkey came back to say, "if you feel better, do you want to go to that storytelling?"

"Let me see how it goes;" Andrew's shoulders locked again.

"Turkey, you promised me you wouldn't visit too long," came Jess's voice from the hallway.

"Right, right;" the old man ducked out.

Jess walked by and looked in on him. She sat down in the chair by the door, shifting around almost the minute she sat down. "Don't worry," she said suddenly, "about James. You're welcome to stay as long as you like."

"Thanks, Jess." Andrew's voice was weak. He looked out the window at the dusk. The moments when life began again and again and again, he thought. *Was that what the levels were about, those moments? And the loa. What they did was push you into those moments where the doors opened, where the gates of perception yawned wide? Where you were weary with seeing things start again and again and again. Like myths. But there was nothing wrong with myths except the way that people used them.*

They were stalking the white deer together. It was dusk and they were moving through the woods on moccasin soft feet, the occasional stick cracking underneath, and they were stalking the white deer together. Andrew looked over his shoulder to the silent, anticipatory face of Larry? of Broken Echo? of the young Indian? Who was it that he saw? He could never be sure, but, at any rate, the silent, anticipatory face of the one who followed him. And the odd thing, the curious thing, was that Andrew had absolutely no desire to find that deer, that numinous deer with the nettle-sharp feet, the dancing deer of the days when he had never known which memories were his, the days that were the ghosts of the dream world which had pierced his own on so many occasions that he had lost track of time and of memories. The deer which had danced on his back so long ago, in order to keep him in the classroom. A dance that hadn't worked, he reminded himself.

What was the deer? He asked himself that question and recognized at once the danger of allowing the question to take form at all. Like the river, the deer had beauty. Like the river, the deer had charm. And like the river, the deer was entirely dangerous. The symbol hardly mattered. The river. The deer. Broken Echo. Like Broken Echo the deer was a symbol that overlapped more than one way of living. With it one could cross barriers. And Larry had been, Andrew was suddenly certain, intent on killing the deer that night Andrew had surprised him in the woods.

The deer, unlike the men who followed it, was sharply aware, or so Andrew thought. Its ears pricked to alertness. Its soft, fuzzy coat bounced and glowed in the forest. Its feet lifted and fell like the small, graceful movements of an early maturing colt. He imagined holding them in the palm of his hand.

No, he thought, looking back at his follower. And the face of Larry? said silently, yes, and yes again.

A wrongness, the sensation of an absolute wrongness to which the body itself objects, started like a slow flood from the center of his chest and moved outward. They were participating in something so old and so wrong that neither of them would ever recover from it. We'll be locked in the cellar, he wanted to tell Larry. We'll not know what we've done. The sins of the fathers are visited on the sons. Don't you believe in fate? He thought he heard himself yell, but he must have been mistaken. Instead, all that he heard was the soft swish of the deer's legs and the softer following of their deer-stalking feet.

The deer took them to a clearing, and in the clearing, seated in the center of a charred circle, perched Broken Echo, his face at peace. He raised his hands as Andrew entered the clearing, and he nodded to Larry? who stood behind him. There was a momentary pause, a quiet moment like a smile, and then Andrew moved forward uncertainly. The deer stood poised at the edge of the clearing, as though it were ready to run, as though it were a moment of night in a place rapidly sensing the return of morning.

Another medicine dream? he asked the old man silently, and Broken Echo nodded.

"How many dreams have I had without counting them? Are *these* the levels that you've spoken of?" Andrew's voice was hoarse and wrong, he knew this even as he spoke, but he didn't care. He had a burning urgency to be done with mysteries, and that urgency much more intense than any time before, and yet he also knew that he had consented to mystery, consented to the gauze of the truth.

As he stood there he had a brief flash, a fragment of a memory, or was it a dream, a moment with Greg. When had this been, when Greg visited? His face was very puzzled, and worried, he was moving some dishes around on the counter, and saying to Andrew, "Why did you hang up on me when I called you? Were you *that* angry that I made that comment about your lack of emotion over Mom and Dad's death? I know that comment bothered you, but—"

"Hell, yes, I was angry."

"You never respond at the time, do you?" Greg asked. And in that moment Andrew was back in the clearing.

Broken Echo shook his head sadly, and the Indian walked toward the deer. Both of them danced slowly away through the woods, and Andrew woke to the sound of himself panting in the narrow, closed space of a peaceful room. Outside the moonlight sifted its way through the branches of the willow tree and created patterns on the bedquilt.

"You know, the boundaries of these worlds are so fragile. What would you do if we began to play with everyone as we play with you?" He looked at Andrew reflectively. "What do you think of snakes, for instance?"

"I don't think many would put themselves in the state that I have." Andrew paced back and forth in the small clearing. "No one likes snakes." He looked around at Broken Echo. "Why didn't you go West?" he asked abruptly.

"Many Cherokees stayed here."

"Not on a plantation."

He sighed. A squirrel dropped down like a nut from the tree above and landed on his shoulder. "True. My younger self has never quite forgiven myself for that. Do you remember my marriage? I owed her a blood debt. My father scalped hers." He turned away.

"She really had you both by the balls, didn't she?" Andrew said with admiration. "But there was much more to it than that, wasn't there?"

As Broken Echo left, he said, without turning, "And so now you play with my boundaries, do you not?"

A glimmer of thought like the wink of a firefly: were the levels about places where cultures overlap, where time diffuses? He continued to have these moments of entirely wordless and clear insight that lapsed into a deflated silence. A firefly buzzed around the room flying closer and closer to him. It landed with feather light feet on the top of his head and then walked slowly down to his ear. He imagined it stepping inside, light echoing against the canal, and he involuntarily shook it loose to go zipping across the room.

How many days later that Andrew sat in a languorous recuperation on the front patio, feeling the warmth of the sun and watching the gleam of the sunlight against the lightly moving waters of the cove? On this side of the lake, the waters seemed to signify only peace. He saw no visions, dreamed no waking dreams of the movement of men across the waters, saw no long, black boats, did not hear the cries of men who feared leaving with Praeter even more than they feared staying. None of these things haunted him here. Nor did he miss them the way he would have missed them if he had still been at the house. He'd forgotten what true quiet was like.

He felt, like a tiny vibration in the stone, the movement of a footstep at the edge of the patio. "Hello, Turkey," he said, without opening his eyes.

"Are you ready to go, Andrew?" Turkey sounded full of the festival spirit.

"I think so. I've got a picnic lunch that Jess packed us which would probably feed the whole mountain, and a thermos jug full of lemonade."

"Jacket?"

"All set." Andrew stood up and looked at the old man affectionately.

"We're on the road, then!" Turkey slung his jean jacket back over his shoulder and walked toward the car. The house next door to theirs looked green and inviting, a long expanse of lawn and a small, tidy cabin. Andrew looked around him again, sighed, and then got into Turkey's Chevrolet truck. They bounced and slid quickly down the small expanse of unpaved road, and onto the curved country road that Andrew had, by now, memorized.

The sunlit fields flashed by in what seemed to be slow motion, that timeless sense of the day without any urgency, a day set aside for pleasure, and the two of them talked very little on the way to the storytelling. Finally Andrew did ask, "What sort of stories can I expect?"

"Mostly Civil War yarns, and a few other kinds of stories." Turkey turned the steering wheel easily into the schoolyard driveway. Andrew looked at the well-worn hollows of the road, and the small, clapboard schoolhouse and thought that the scene was timeless. Sam Houston must have seen much the same scene during the days when he was going to school: weathered paint on the clapboards, a mixture of grass and worn soil. It wasn't until they walked into the schoolhouse and saw such a large and varied collection of people that the feeling of a disjunction jolted Andrew back to his own time: the crowd was a motley crew of old timers in overalls and white-white hair, what looked to be leftover refugees from the sixties who were in scraggly long hair and torn T-shirts, and a few people in the standard white collar workforce uniform.

Inside the church was a long stretch of pine wood walls, and the smell of pine. The altar at the front of the church was covered with an old red velvet cloth, and the platform of the altar railing, back two or three feet from the actual altar, revealed the traffic of many knees. Andrew imagined the old country revivals that had taken place in this church, the calling of the minister, that old, rolling call of the man used to the strength and the movement of emotion, used to gauging that tide of emotion the way one might gauge the moment when one turned a running herd. These old churches always had an echo of the power of that emotion even when they were empty.

Turkey said to Andrew, "Come on, I want to sing harp."

"I thought we came to hear some stories! What's harp?"

"Singing to shaped notes. You can learn it. Come on. The stories come later." Turkey walked up the center aisle of the church, an aisle carpeted with a rug nearly as worn as the altar cloth, and Andrew followed him to the small choir loft filled with several men about Turkey's age, some of those sixties leftovers, a label he was now less sure of; and several older women who displayed that wry Southern humor he loved.

Turkey sat down in the middle of a bunch of the younger women, women who looked as though they had strong, full voices. He grinned up at Andrew. Andrew shrugged his shoulders and sat down in the empty chair beside the old man.

"We mix up the parts," Turkey said. "Can you sing tenor?"

"My voice is high, but it's not any too—"

"Don't worry about that," Turkey said, and winked at one of the women, who grinned.

"You lead this one, Turkey," someone from the back suggested.

Turkey got to his feet and began rocking back and forth. "Page seventy-nine," he said; "sing the poetry."

Andrew looked at the page. It was full of funny-shaped, geometric notes running across the bar lines like small, old-fashioned footprints. The words were equally strange and old fashioned. "How long," burst out the voices around him, "dear Saviour, oh how long, shall this bright hour delay." Turkey glared at Andrew and Andrew tried to join in, but he didn't know the words or the notes. The voices began a fugal pattern, and circled around him in a thick, full drone with the dirge-like quality of bagpipes. "Fly swift around, ye wheels of time;" and suddenly he began to catch on to the pattern of the song and to the odd, mournful joy of the music. "Oh, what a glorious sight appears, to our believing eyes. The earth and seas are past away." My God, you could kill your throat on this music, he thought, as he sang-yelled the song along with them. "The earth and seas are passed away, and thee, oh rolling skies. And thee, oh rolling skies." They finished the song with a flourish like the last flourish of a harp string. They went through two songs, the second one led by another older man, and then they all stopped abruptly, and turned toward the altar platform.

A man, who looked to be in his seventies and dressed in a faded Civil War uniform, jumped up onto the platform and, without any sort of introduction at all, leaped into a story.

"Why, I remember the days when my grandfather used to tell me stories about the Civil War." The man waved his hands in the flamboyant style of the old country preacher. "We would sit out on the porch, and he would pull out his pecans and commence to crackin' 'em and then the stories would begin. By the time he finished that old bowl of pecans would be full of nothin' but shells, and it would be dark, and then my mother would holler for me to come in and git to bed." He paused for a minute and looked around him at the crowd.

"He joined as a boy too early for anybody to believe he was old enough, but in the final days of the war he was all they had 'round those parts. He would tell me how a boy like him became an army surgeon, just because he had good hands for gentlin' a horse, at places like Bull Run and the kinds of things that he saw there. He was a curious sort of guy. During the middle of a battle, instead of staying where it was safe, he would peer down below onto the battle that was raging, even if he put himself in danger doin' it." The man paused and looked straight at Andrew, then he licked his lips and went on with his story.

"One time he said he heard a sound like a mowing machine and he looked up to see a round shot the size of a melon coming toward him. It struck about three feet away from him and ricocheted beyond sight. So he ran off to help the wounded," the man winked, "and to save himself, and he stopped in front of an abandoned house and rummaged in the closet until he found a half loaf of bread and some apple butter, which he ate until the house tumbled down around him from the force of the explosions outside.

"'Course he wasn't always eatin'. He did a lot of doctorin', but he didn't like to talk to a boy like me of such things, so he mostly told me the stories of gettin' food and the stories of amazement. Like the time when they had found themselves a peacock somewhere and they were determined to eat it, even though there was a battle going on outside. They had marked the hospital with a bright yellow piece of cloth which they tied to the top of a lightning rod on the barn, so they thought maybe they would be safe until some piece of shell passing overhead ripped down the cloth and maybe the lightnin' rod too. And just as he was raising his knife to carve the peacock, and sayin', 'Here goes, boys!' a shell passed over the barn and exploded. So they were compelled to leave that peacock and comfort the wounded, and some hungry soldier slipped in and stole that peacock before they could take a bite of it.

"They thought they were so hungry then, from missing a bite of that peacock, that they were goin' to cross over the river and rest in the shade of the trees."

"What's that?" Andrew whispered to Turkey.

"They thought they were going to die," Turkey whispered.

The man leaned back and tugged at his beard theatrically, and then he roared, "But just then they saw some pretty girls walking down toward the house, and one of the old soldiers ran out and kissed one of the girls on the cheek, and said 'Never mind, my dear, you just tell your beau it was Extra Bill that did it and he'll say it's all right.' And he never minded that those girls and he were on different sides of the fence, just the way that we never mind 'round here, at least today, and this very window in this very church proves that, because it's dedicated to both the Union soldiers and the Rebs. And that's why you'll never hear a one of us say a word if the stories you hear today are about Yankees or Rebs. In this church there's the storytellin' peace on us all for sure."

He paused for a moment and grinned at the crowd and someone whooped a Rebel yell in the back. He brushed off the epaulets on his Yankee uniform ostentatiously. Then he said, "Welcome to the Annual Storytelling Festival here at the Epworth Jubilee Center, where, as Garrison Keel-er says about Lake Woebeegone, 'the men are men, the women are children, and the children are handsome,' or something like that." He leaned back his head and laughed, and the crowd laughed with him.

Andrew grinned with delight. In places like Marietta the attachment to the old Southern storytelling style had long ago disappeared, and he'd certainly never sung anything like this music. Settling back in his chair, he decided he liked it. There was something about the vigor and the rough charm of it that appealed to him.

"The next fellow up on this stage is an old timer for sure. His family has lived around here for more generations than mine has been breathing. Ladies and gentlemen I give you, Turkey Haines."

Turkey winked at Andrew and jumped to his feet. He ran onto the stage and stood there looking at the crowd and tugging on his beard. Andrew laughed.

"My great grandfather," Turkey said slowly, "was a Civil War doctor too, but he stayed around these parts during the war to help out the women and children. A lot of his stories have to do, I reckon, with bringing children into the world. He spanked the bottom of most of your grandparents, and maybe a few of your parents, and he heard them make their first squall at the world. But I don't suppose that would interest any of us here today all that much. I do remember him talking a lot on his sickbed about doctoring at the Civil War prison camp over at the Old Praeter House. He said the sights that were there would turn your eyes, and then your stomach, when you thought about them later."

Andrew straightened his shoulders and looked at Turkey intently.

Turkey glanced around the crowd and looked carefully over Andrew's head.

"The worst one was probably the day he had to amputate a boy's leg, a boy hardly bigger than that boy there." Turkey pointed to a young boy seated to Andrew's left. The boy looked as if he were about fourteen.

"There were sick and wounded men groaning in that dark, old cellar at the Praeter's. Every boy there was wounded and calling for water. He had to operate on most of them that day, and he didn't have a bit of medicine for pain. Once he'd

amputated the leg, he used it as a pillow to prop up the heads
of those he operated on later. Half those boys died anyway
that day, and the rest of them were killed in the Battle of Fort
Sanders in Knoxville the following week after Longstreet's
Patrol released them from prison. For a long time afterwards,
when he delivered your grandparents and mine, he said that
he could hardly bear looking at a baby's face for thinking
about the ones he'd lost all in one week." Turkey paused and
looked out over the crowd. Several men nodded, and Andrew
looked around to see one burly-armed man wiping his eyes
with the corner of his handkerchief.

Wait a minute; I was there in that cellar. I was the boy
whose head he propped up on that severed leg. I wasn't
dreaming. I lived a moment of that boy's life. A shiver ran up
the back of his head. You knew that already, Andrew, he
thought, why are you so surprised now? He glanced up at
Turkey, who stared at him for a moment and then turned back
to look at the crowd.

The master of ceremonies walked quietly up on stage and
waited until Turkey stepped down. Then he said softly, "Now
I'd like to introduce to you a fellow who you all probably
already know. He's been playing music and telling stories in
these parts for the last several years, and he's good at both.
He's a whiz at almost any instrument he picks up, though he's
probably best known for his hammer dulcimer playing. I
guess today he's going to combine the best of all his arts:
music, storytelling, and songwriting. John McCutcheon."

Turkey rustled into the seat beside him. Andrew whispered,
"Good story. I'd like to talk to you about it later."

Turkey nodded.

The man who moved up onto the stage reminded Andrew
of a lumberjack, though he wasn't sure he could say why.
Perhaps because he had that tall, angular, yet solid frame and
that way of moving. He was dressed in jeans, a flannel shirt
open at the neck, and a pair of faded workboots, and he
carried a fiddle in one hand. He stood in front of the mike,
holding the fiddle just behind him, and looking straight at
Andrew.

"This festival is a celebration, not of all the division that
created the Civil War, but of all the ways in which our part of
the country survived that war and what it left us with here.
It's a celebration in the hope that one day we'll all realize the

futility and the 'last resortism' that war is really a sign of. Since I think that's the case, it doesn't really matter what war I sing about today, because many of the same things apply. I wrote this song after hearing about an incident in World War One that reminded me a good deal of stories I'd heard about the Civil War. I'm not the first to write about this incident and I probably won't be the last, but the story I was told created this song. It's called 'Christmas in the Trenches.'"

The man continued to look directly at Andrew in a way that made him vaguely uncomfortable. John McCutcheon's expression was intent. That expression and the sudden quietness of his voice signaled a serious shift in direction, which followed Turkey's lead. He had quieted the crowd so quickly. Andrew looked around him. Every face was turned toward the stage like flowers pointed toward the rain.

My name is Frances Tolliver
I come from Liverpool
Two years ago the war was waiting for me after school
To Belgium and to Flanders
To Germany, to here
I fought for king and country I loved dear

With the first few notes of a rough and mellow voice Andrew warmed to the man. He liked this storytelling more and more all the time. But most of all he liked the feeling that history was happening right here in front of him, that these people *lived* history. Are they the only ones, an inner voice whispered, which he couldn't quite ignore.

I was lying with my messmates
On the cold and rocky ground
When across the lines of battle
Came a most peculiar sound
Says I now listen up me boys
Each soldier strained to hear
As one young German voice sang out so clear

He's singing bloody well you know
My partner says to me
Soon one by one each Germany voice
Joined in in harmony

The canons rested silent
The gas cloud rolled no more
As Christmas brought us respite
From the war

Kate, he thought suddenly, would have liked this, and so
would the boys. The fact that he was thinking of her in the
middle of all this didn't leave him lost and lonely, even
isolated, in a strange crowd the way he had felt that night at
the Greenback Community Center. Instead, he felt sad,
deeply sad. But this time he didn't mind, because the music
and the stories here spoke of sadness too, and of a grief long
held. And it was the kind of grief, like his, that moved from
hilarity to sadness and back so quickly that no one even
noticed the wild swings of their own emotions.

As soon as they were finished
The reverent pause was spent
"God rest you merry gentlemen"
Struck up one lad from Ghent
The next they sang was Stille Nacht
'Tis Silent Night says I
And in two tongues
One song filled up that sky.

There's someone coming towards us
The front line sentry cried
All sights were fixed
On one lone figure
Trudging from their side
His truce flag like a Christmas flag
Shone on that plain so bright
As he bravely strode unarmed
Into the night.

Andrew felt tears coming to his eyes, and he let them roll
down his face unashamedly. All around him there were
people doing much the same.

Then one by one
From either side
Walked into No Man's land

With neither gun nor bayonet
We met there hand to hand

We shared some secret brandy
And wished each other well
And in a flarelit soccer game
We gave 'em hell
We traded chocolates,
Cigarettes, and photographs from home
These sons and fathers far away

From families of their own
Young Sanders played his squeezebox
And they had a violin
This curious and unlikely
Band of men

Soon daylight stole upon us
And France was France once more
With sad farewells
We each began
To settle back to war
But the question haunted every one
That lived that wondrous night
Whose family have I fixed within my sights?

Pausing to look, or so Andrew thought, straight at him
again, the musician then held the violin up to his chin and
began to play an interlude. Andrew closed his eyes. The
music was something that he had no defense against.

It's Christmas in the trenches
Where the frost so bitter hung
The frozen fields of France were warmed
As songs of peace were sung

For the walls they kept between us
To exact the work of war
Had been crumbled and were gone
Forever more

Oh my name is Frances Tolliver
In Liverpool I dwell

Each Christmas come since World War One
I learned its lessons well
That the ones who called the shots
Won't be among the dead and lame
And on each end of the rifle we're the same

John McCutcheon finished the song, and looked once more at Andrew. Then he stood silently for a moment with his fiddle in his hand. After a moment he said, "There are stories like this told about every war, stories in which for a brief moment those on both sides paused to recognize each other's humanity. But those stories about the Civil War have a particular power, because we know that many of those who fought in the war were families, neighbors, who had been drawn to either the Northern or Southern cause. Here in this area the passions of the day were a jumble of hatred, family loyalties, and sorrow. And when the Northern bands played the national anthem and the Southern bands fired back "Dixie" on the picket lines and everyone smiled, the moment was more brief than most, but it was genuine. And yet we never use any of those moments for more than a 'brief respite.' But not everyone is offered that sort of respite, and some had to find it in a desperate struggle to escape. There was a woman who also knew and understood the Civil War better than many. Her name was Harriet Tubman, and she ran an escape route for slaves, a route known as the Underground Railroad. The song I'll sing you now is her song except for a stanza which I added to remind us all that some fights are never over."

One night I dreamed I was in slavery
'Bout 1850 was the time
Sorrow was the only sign
Nothing around to ease my mind
When out of the night
There came a lady
Leading a distant pilgrim band
First mate, she yelled, pointing her hand
Make room on board for this young man

And she said, Come on up
I got a lifeline

Come on up to this train of mine
Come on up I got a lifeline
Come on up to this train of mine
She said her name was Harriet Tubman
And she drove for the Underground Railroad

Hundreds of miles we traveled onwards
Gathering slaves from town to town
Seeking every lost and found
Setting those free who once were bound
Finally my heart was growing weaker
I fell by the wayside
Sinking sand
Firmly did this woman stand
She lifted me up and she took my hand

And she said, Come on up
I got a lifeline
Come on up to this train of mine
Come on up I got a lifeline
Come on up to this train of mine
She said her name was Harriet Tubman
And she drove for the Underground Railroad

Who are these children dressed in red
They must be the ones that Moses led
Who are these children dressed in red
They must be the ones that Sister Moses led

Then I awoke
No more I faltered
Finally strength for the tasks
   were shown
There are sisters and brothers
Leaving their homes
Their history, their people
All they've known
And they are fleeing their homes
In Guatemala, Chile, Brazil, El Salvador
Fleeing from the prisons and war
Through the night and through Mexico
To our Door

Will we sing come on up
I got a lifeline
Come on up to this train of mine
Come on up I got a lifeline
Come on up to this train of mine
She said her name was Harriet Tubman
And she drove for the Underground Railroad

You got to follow
The drinking gourd
Follow
The drinking gourd

And just as quickly as that the song was over. He bowed his head for a moment, and then he left the stage.

Andrew blinked his eyes and looked around him at the warm and silent crowd. Because he was there, and because he laughed, sang, cried, with the crowd, and because he had suddenly received, by proxy, something of the qualities of the music, he suddenly understood much that he hadn't understood before.

The feeling, when he sang those songs, had been the same as the feeling Andrew had had when the frenzy descended upon him in the cellar, a physical understanding of the world, a sense that, despite everything, the heart of what they lived through was the same for all of them. As though he had taken on, like an old coat, the patina of his heritage. He would go back to the old Praeter house, he decided, no matter what the risk. He would go home.

CHAPTER 17

He and Turkey walked silently to the old Chevrolet truck.
The passenger door creaked as Andrew opened it. A cloud of
dust rose from the split upholstery as Andrew settled into the
driver's seat. Kate, Andrew thought. He climbed into the
truck, closing it once and then slamming it again in order to
get it to close. While he had been there in the church he had
been in the center of the crowd, but now he was alone again.

"You miss them, don't you?" asked Turkey softly.

Andrew nodded, looking out the front window and watching
the crowd stream out of the churchyard in their old pickups
and cars, the headlights bouncing along the poorly paved
parking lot and then the driveway that led to the road.
Turkey started the engine and it coughed to life.

"Happens sometimes that kind of sadness after a crowd.
I've been missing my wife for well on fifteen years." Turkey
revved up the engine and then drove out of the parking lot.
Andrew watched the old man's gnarled hands shifting gears,
and the shine of the headlights in front of them like small,
glowing pools. "I missed her again tonight."

"I'm going to move back to the house tomorrow, Turkey," Andrew said abruptly.

"Too soon! You're not healed yet," Turkey snapped.

Andrew rubbed his shoulder. "I feel a lot better. I'm ready to go home."

"Well then, I'll go with you and stay a few days." The gears buzzed as he tried to shift into fourth too soon.

"No, I don't think so. I need some time, Turkey. But I'll call you in a few days to go fishing. How's that?"

"Jess is not going to like this." Turkey shook his head. "She's not going to like this at all."

"I won't tell her until tomorrow. Will you come back and drive me home?"

"If she doesn't stop you, I will." Turkey sounded noncommittal.

They drove along the winding roads in silence for a few minutes. Then Andrew said, "So tell me more about the story you were telling in there. Who was the boy your great grandfather was operating on, and why were so many there dying?"

"I don't know who the boy was," Turkey shrugged. "All of them were part of that prison camp there on the Praeter grounds. And most of them had been pretty badly wounded in a nearby skirmish that got them captured. My father caught wind of it and went over to help out, but by the time he found out and then convinced them to let him in, many of them were already too far gone to save. He wasn't even sure that if he'd gotten there earlier it would have made any difference. He said that the whole time he worked on those boys it seemed like he could hear the rattling of chains all around him and some heavy breathing. He said the thing that annoyed him the most," Turkey stopped a moment and corrected the way he'd taken a curve, "was that there was this captain playing an off-key piano upstairs the whole time he worked. By the time he got done, he wanted to shoot that captain."

"I bet," Andrew muttered.

"What?"

"Nothing. You know, Turkey," Andrew said, and leaned back into the seat, "I dreamed about that boy one night. In fact, I dreamed I *was* that boy."

"What do you mean?" Turkey asked testily.

"I relived that experience with your great grandfather as a

doctor, and my head resting on that severed leg. In my dream, I mean," Andrew added hastily. He watched Turkey's hands turning the steering wheel.

"Sometimes a man has this feeling, you know, like he knows something or has heard it before. I bet you being a history teacher and all, you probably just have remember it from somewhere."

"I don't think so. It was pretty real. And I knew that the boy had a Bible in his front pocket that his girlfriend had reinforced with steel inside the binding, and that that Bible had saved his life."

"I didn't tell you that, but that's what my great-grandfather said the boy had told him." Turkey cleared his throat. "Listen, Andrew, you better be careful with that place. I genuinely, solid four-core leather think you ought not to go back."

"You know something about the place." It was Andrew's turn to be noncommittal.

"Not really, but I can sure see that you do."

"Stories. People tell lots of stories about isolated old houses."

"Sure they do, but the stories about the Praeter House that are run-of-the mill old ghost stories are not the ones that worry me. This one does." They pulled into the long drive-way that led to Jess's house.

"Just a dream," Andrew offered. *Should have kept my mouth shut. That's what I get for having contrary impulses. I want somebody to know what I'm going through, but I don't want them to stop me.*

"Hmmmph."

They pulled into Jess's, and Andrew said, just as Turkey turned the engine off, "Now don't say anything to Jess."

"I won't." Turkey didn't sound convinced.

"Look, if she kicks up too big a fuss, maybe I'll stay a day or so. But promise me that you won't say anything to her about this."

"I won't say anything to her about you moving back over to the house."

"Fine."

They walked toward the house, Andrew's feet clicking on the small, pebbled veranda. Jess opened the kitchen door and the light leaped out and dazzled them. "Well, did you have a good time?"

"It was a fine storytelling," said Turkey.

"Great," said Andrew.

"Can I come in, ma'am, and use your bathroom before I drive on home?" Turkey stood in the doorway, his hands clenched around his old straw hat.

"Certainly. Would you like a piece of pie and a cup of coffee before you drive on back?"

"No, I don't think so." Turkey walked through the kitchen. Jess followed him back to show him the bathroom.

Andrew poured a glass of water and drank it slowly. "Did you have a good time?" came a voice from behind him, the voice of Broken Echo.

"Go away," Andrew said, without turning around.

"What's that?" asked Jess, as she came back through the door.

"I said, as soon as I see Turkey off I think I'll go to bed." Andrew turned around slowly, but saw nothing on Jess's face except a glance at his arm to gauge his pain. Broken Echo had gone.

Jess walked toward the refrigerator, opened it, looked inside, and then closed it again. She laughed at herself, and Andrew chuckled with her. "Sometimes I just plain forget what I'm doing. Anyway, it's probably a good idea for you to go to bed early, don't you think? How's your arm?"

"Hurting some, but I weathered the trip pretty well." Andrew turned back around to rinse his glass at the sink.

She put her hand out to touch him on the shoulder. "Give it a few days, and you can start moving it around some. Maybe you'd like to go down with James on the dock tomorrow and do a little one-handed fishing."

Andrew set the small, flowered glass down carefully. "That might be a good idea," he said, a shade too heartily. He averted his eyes.

"Oh, I almost forgot;" she reached out to hand him a letter, "you got some mail."

Andrew looked at the letterhead. Marietta Realty. Kate's old company. This must be about the condo. He folded the envelope and shoved it in his coat pocket.

Turkey walked back into the room, straightening his old leather vest. "Well, I'd better be getting on down the road."

"Give me a call tomorrow, Turkey," said Andrew.

"I'll do that very thing. Get some rest." Turkey patted him on the back as he went by. "See you, Andrew."

Andrew stumbled twice getting from the kitchen to the bedroom. "You stayed out a bit too long, don't you think?" Jess asked, her voice slightly husky.

"Probably so. Good night."

"Good night. I turned on the air-conditioning for you. The room should be cool."

"Thanks, Jess."

In a moment, as he was pulling off his clothes, he heard her voice outside the door again. "I left you a glass of juice out here to drink," she said softly.

"Fine, I'll get it in a minute." He pulled on his pajamas hastily and opened the door. The orange juice was just outside, but Jess had gone on to bed. He drank it down in one quick gulp and pulled the letter out of his coat pocket. Marietta Realty. He turned the letter over in his hands a moment before he opened it. "Andy: I've got a buyer for your condo, but you've got to come and close the deal before we lose him. Joan." Her signature was scrawled in bold letters across the bottom of the page. Joan had been Kate's favorite person at MR, as she called it, and she had taken over the sale, commission-free, of the condo.

Blast, he needed to get back to the house, but he needed to get money from the sale of the house, especially now that he didn't have much of a job. Who knew if Boyles' charity would really continue? He'd have to go down there and now. It would only take a day's drive there and back, or at the most two, if Margaret insisted he stay over as she probably would. He'd call Joan and work out an appointment for a negotiation for tomorrow. The trouble was, he had this feeling of urgency about the house. It was important for him to get back there. Addition? an inner voice mocked. Who knew whether he had a premonition or a craving. It was a long while before he fell into even a light doze.

Andrew stood back in the shadow of the stairwell and observed.

Praeter grabbed the two men by the jackets and shoved them toward the door. "Manumission Society? Why you've come to the wrong place, by God. You boys are getting thick as thieves in East Tennessee, and it's high time something was done about it. What do you mean coming to me?"

"Would you prefer us to come to you or to the sheriff? We know you're involved in interstate trading, Joseph."

Praeter looked around the yard quickly, and then back to them. The two men, one short and stocky, the other tall and broad-shouldered, stared back at him. "I don't know what you mean."

"Half the county knows, Joseph; you might as well take out more ads in the paper." The shorter man thrust an ad at him from the *Nashville Times*. "Two like wenches, et cetera, et cetera, J. Praeter."

"Send the sheriff after me, by God. He'll have to catch me in the act."

"Look, Joseph, we're not asking you to give up your livelihood, but think about the cover you'd provide yourself by supporting our organization," the taller man said persuasively. The shorter man looked at both of them with distaste. "You know as well as I do that slavery's days are numbered and none of us in Tennessee really want to see the North pitted off against the South. If the South takes in Cuba and Haiti, that's what will happen, and your profits certainly will be damaged."

"That's true, but you know when Andrew Jackson takes office he'll get rid of all your society nonsense anyway. Still, you might have a temporary point." Praeter stroked his chin. "Now let's get this straight. You're blackmailing me to become a member of your society."

"You could put it that way." The shorter man smacked his palm with his fist. "We need the backing of some of the plantation owners."

"Not a person in this county wouldn't know I was a hypocrite."

"That's true," said the shorter man impassively. "But that's nothing new, is it?"

"I suppose not," Praeter said heavily, folding up the ad and placing it in his breast pocket. The two men left and he turned around to face Andrew. "Well, what are you staring at?"

He tried to frame an answer, but the words slipped away from him. He watched them flying around the room, like tiny circling fireflies.

Andrew pushed the accelerator up another five miles an hour, ignoring nausea. He'd been driving for three hours, slumped down in the driver's seat, but he felt like he'd been in the car for half a day. Shadow and then light slid dappled over his arms. The large powerful car moved down the road like a Lincoln Continental over silk, so why did his stomach feel as though he'd been jolted through the bowels of some ramshackle, ten-year-old Datsun with blown shocks? He'd obviously made it across the Georgia state line, though he didn't remember doing so. He could tell by the number of peach stands on either side of the road.

Stretching, he glanced out the window, watching the old women with their flower-basket straw hats picking carefully over the long boxes of peach flats. Then they were gone, and he saw nothing but pastures and Jersey cattle. The pastures gave way to interstate scenery: a road exit; a tall Kentucky Fried Chicken road sign at the exit; and a sign that said, "Y'all need some gas?" and another, bright yellow and red, paint-peeled sign, that read "Crazy Eddy's Firecrackers" written across the chest of a garish Uncle Sam with a jaundiced face. In a moment he had passed that by and come to a sign that read: 25 miles to Chatsworth where carpet is KING.

Roughly another hour and a half to the condo then. Would he make it? He was supposed to meet Joan and her client at five. If he didn't get caught in a speed trap, he should make it with a few minutes to spare.

His estimate was fairly accurate. He did pull into the Condo West's apartment complex just fifteen minutes short of five, but Joan and her client were already standing just inside the door of the condo and chatting. Andrew walked up the steps two a time and shook hands with the client—lawyer, Andrew assessed automatically—before he turned to smile at Joan.

"What happened to you?" she asked, waving a long-fingered hand at him. She was dressed in red, which set off her mahogany brown skin and jet black hair. A hat tilted across one eye.

"Just a sprain," Andrew shot painfully at her and then shrugged and moved quickly toward the client. He hadn't thought it would be this tough to see one of Kate's old friends. In fact, he'd tried not to think about the sale at all. Just do it, he told himself angrily, but none of this showed, he hoped, on his face. He said smoothly to the man, "So, I gather you like the place."

"He's ready to sign, Andy," her voice just slightly unsteady. "But he wants to bargain on the price—"

"What offer are you making?"

"Your agent says that you want ninety thousand for it, but I'd like to offer seventy-five thousand."

Andrew looked at him. The price was entirely too low, and a lawyer could certainly pay more. "Eighty-five thousand."

"I really can't go much more than seventy-five thousand." The man turned to Joan, "maybe we should look at another condo." Then he turned back to Andy.

Joan mouthed, "He'll go for more."

Andrew nodded. "Why don't you look around the place one more time? Let me point out to you some of the improvements we've made."

Joan and her client walked ahead of him through the short foyer and into the living room. Andrew trailed his fingers over the oak paneling. The last thing he had installed. Just a week before they had decided to move, actually. Just a week before he received his notice that he wouldn't be rehired. Kate had refused to have anything but wood throughout the condo. No plaster, no modern, plastic wire shelves. No glass, highly reflecting tables. She had hung the Picasso tapestry, "old two-nose" she'd called it, in the foyer.

"What would become of us," Broken Echo's voice whispered in his ear, "if we were all like Praeter? We would now fall together and twist noses." He chuckled. "Our eyes would not remain in their sockets, for we would twist them out." He leaned forward, his hand resting on Andrew's wounded shoulder. "Who are you now, young man?"

"What difference does it make?" Andrew glanced up to see if the others had heard him, but they were walking around the living room and talking softly. Joan looked as though she was at her most persuasive.

"Everything is now made straight and easy, nor can you contradict what I say. My younger self has won."

"How?" Andrew lowered his voice.

"It will do you no good to know. It was all settled ethihyu hno."

"What?"

"*Tsu li e ni?* Ah. A long time ago. Our people took from

the animals what was theirs. Then your people took what was ours. Then half your people, the cold, blue-eyed ones, took what was yours."

"They gave it back."

"That's what you think. Tell that to your stubborn people of the mountains, and maybe to your coal miners. And so it happens; now we have taken our own again." Andrew turned around and looked at him. He shrugged. "It is a cycle. I would have helped you but"—He shrugged again.—"my younger self is stronger. He split me off."

"He sent you away?"

"Sent who away, Andy?" Joan sounded puzzled; "come on in here, will you?"

Broken Echo had disappeared anyway. Andrew shrugged. He walked into the living room. "I installed oak paneling in the foyer, and that's not simply a thin veneer. The living room has a small greenhouse add-on." He glanced across the room at the miniature greenhouse jutted out like a bay window. Billy had loved to sit there. He'd insisted that he liked it "better'n TV."

"I'm not much of a gardner," the man drawled. He straightened his jacket and smoothed a hand over a dark, curly, designer haircut.

"The kitchen has quite a few improvements too," Andy waved his hand toward the next room. "For instance, we put in some hand-painted French tiles along one wall." The man walked in ahead of him and ran his fingers over the blue and green tilework. "And we added the best dishwasher on the market."

Joan grinned. "Kate never did like housework," she laughed, and then looked guiltily at Andrew.

"No, it's fine, Joan." He walked ahead of them from the room. "I don't know if Joan told you—"

"Yes, she told me. I'm sorry about your loss." The man sounded like he meant it. That made up a bit for the gardener comment, Andrew thought.

He climbed the stairs to the second level. Kate had loved this stairwell. She said that it captured the sunlight. Broken Echo climbed the stairs, moving just ahead of him. It took Andrew a minute to realize he was continuing their previous conversation. "He'll send me away soon. Then it will be too late." His voice was indifferent. "I'm not sure he's wrong. I can't taste coffee anymore. Eh. Eh. So why should I be in charge?" He coughed. "There are new times coming, like the new leaves of spring, but I will miss them."

"There's nothing I can do anyway. I can't very well get from Marietta to the house this afternoon. Even if we sold the condo this minute, I couldn't drive very quickly with this shoulder." He knew his voice didn't sound very convincing. It was hard to think about selling the condo. He couldn't really seem to concentrate on Broken Echo's problems when he was trying to sell the condo and ignore his grief at doing so at the same time. Couldn't the old man give him the time to deal with the condo first? Couldn't he see how hard it was?

Broken Echo pointed a thumb. "What do you need with money anyway? Take whatever he offers; isn't that what you told us, O Man of the People? You personally got half the state of Georgia when you sent the Cherokee off to the West, to the Darkening Land. It's no wonder you're still into real estate, but why quibble over a little piece of property here?"

"You ask a man without a job that?"

"You've got more important things to do. We've got to get you back to Greenback or it will be like the days when you stole land, and told your people it was for the good of the nation. You won't be coming back from or to the same place. Neither one will exist. Isn't that what you Southerners fear most? The loss of a past that never was?"

Andrew closed his eyes. No, I'll go back on my own time and on my own terms. Is that what happened to the Cherokee? His thoughts jeered.

"What was that Andy?" Joan puffed slightly as she climbed the stairs.

"Too many lunch dates, Joan," Andrew turned to face them. "We added a second bathroom upstairs, though that cut down the size of the other bedroom slightly, and there's a half bath downstairs."

"Look, I understand that this place means a lot to you, but I've got to keep my costs within reason. What if I offer you eighty thousand?"

"Take it," Broken Echo whispered from where he floated in a corner of the hall.

Andrew was silent. He looked out the window, and then back again to the old Indian. Sometimes, he thought, it's time for a man to begin to think about his own survival.

"He'll send me to the Darkening Land then. I avoided that once. Do you know what Butler said about it? 'All is as dark as midnight. Oh that my head were waters and mine eyes a fountain of tears that I might weep day and night for the slain of the daughters of my people.' Don't you care about the people of Greenback?"

They certainly cherished me. His thoughts were bitter.

"They did, didn't they?" Where Andrew had been angry, Broken Echo was merely reflective.

He felt ashamed. They had, in their own way, looked after him. No one dealt very well with grief. It went on for far too long, and it reminded them of too much they would prefer to forget. Neighbors dealt better with the smaller difficulties of life. "What is your younger self doing?"

"But what difference does it make? You have decided not to care, have you not?" The old man's hand clapped his hands. "I praise you for your valour. Hold back your gaze from Greenback. And forget all about the family you buried on Praeter land. Their bones merely hold your history."

"Andy? What do you think about the offer?"

Andrew jumped. "Look, I'm sorry. I'm afraid this place brings back a lot of memories."

"If you're not ready to sell it;" the other man sounded disappointed.

"No, it's not that. I'll take your offer." Andrew's voice was quiet and remote. "Why don't you all go down to the living room and work out the details and I'll just look around here?" He waved his hands vaguely. "I'd like a moment to—"

"Sure—fine," they both said quickly and left him there in the hallway.

"I told you to leave my family out of this," Andrew said fiercely.

"I'll tell you what you told someone once. It's a little too late for that." The old man bobbed in the corner.

I'm not going to go running back there and play the town hero. They can take care of themselves, those folks. At least for the afternoon.

"Sure they can." Broken Echo settled back and kicked his foot into the back of Andrew's seat. "They've had as much practice as you have."

"Practice doesn't have a damn thing to do with it." Andrew

sat down on the window seat, and then gasped as a sharp pain shot through his shoulders.

"Right." He whistled a breathy bird call and smiled at Andrew.

"Look, I intended all along to come back to the house. It's as important to me as it is to you. I'm just not going to kill myself to make it back there, so why don't you take off. Go back to the—wherever it is that you go."

Broken Echo gave a sharp cackle of laughter and slapped his knees. "You think those Northerners gave the South back to you." He winked at Andrew and then vanished.

Great, he thought. So now I'm supposed to be responsible for a town that kicked me out, and not just for what happens to the ghosts in that house. Isn't it enough to begin to take responsibility for things? Do I have to take on huge causes at the same time? I was ready to go back and to face the ghosts, but now he wants me to take on the whole fucking town. The old man plays me like a fish. Not this time. He walked around the empty rooms, listening to the kick of his feet across the hardwood floors, a sound as hollow as the center of his chest. At last he went reluctantly down to take the deposit and participate in the signing away of his family. Nothing remained anyway. These condos were too new to retain any sense of memories.

He signed quickly, and the two of them shook on the deal. "Want some coffee, Andy?" Joan asked him, as they watched the man drive away in his cream-colored Volvo.

No, Joan, he thought, that's the last thing I want. But he sighed and said, "I don't think I want coffee, but I sure as hell could use a drink."

"You're on, Captain Eddy's?"

At least she had made a good choice, an old bar fixed up like a sea captain's study. He couldn't have stood anything livelier. "Fine," he forced a smile.

"Listen, Andy, if you don't feel like—"

"Joan, it's okay. I'd like to find out how you're doing."

"Okay, oh, I almost forgot. Margaret wanted you to call her."

"I'd planned to."

"She said she and Jay would be out later, so you might want to call her now. You can use the car phone."

Andrew raised an eyebrow. "The fees must be rising."

"We're having a good season." She flipped her hair back from her face. "I'll just close up here."

He hoped Margaret would understand that he didn't want to stay the night, but he didn't think it was likely. He dialed the number quickly. "Hello, Maggie. Andy."

"Hi, Andy, do you think you're going to be through there in time for supper?"

"I'm not staying, Maggie."

"I made up the guest room."

"It was too hard, selling the condo. I'll come back another time just to see you, but I don't want to stay tonight."

There was a silence on the other end of the line. "Why don't you let your family in this with you?"

"I know that's what you think I need to do, but I've got to do this my way."

Then she sighed. "What is it, Andy, that you think none of us have any idea of? That you've been holed up in that house like someone withstanding a seige or maybe going through a long illness. That you lost your job at the school. That you've worried and scared your neighbors."

"How do you know about that?"

"You've tried to keep a lot from your family, haven't you? Greg was worried to death after he stopped by to see you, so he called me, and I called Jess to give her my number and to ask her to keep an eye on you. She enlisted Turkey, because he was the only visitor you'd had besides a neighbor boy she thinks took a potshot at you."

Her voice was clearly exasperated by now. "If she hadn't, he wouldn't have found you wandering around in the woods, damn it, Andy. She left her sister there to watch you at the doctor's office, because by that time who knew what you'd do next. Maybe we had no right, but if we hadn't done what we did, you'd have probably died out there in the woods before somebody found you. And I'll be damned if I'll lose another member of my family, Andy. I loved them too, God damn it!" Her voice ran down, and she took a deep breath.

He gripped the safety handle in front of him with both hands. "I'm sorry, Margaret," he said slowly and carefully, "I didn't realize that I'd been worrying you so. It's hard to think of someone else when you're—" He stopped and took a deep breath.

"I know, Andy." Her voice was soft and remote. "I understand that, but it's time you started thinking of your friends and your family. There aren't many of us left you know." She sounded suddenly so weary. "You haven't even kept in touch with Kate's parents, and they're going through as much grief as you are. No one expects their children to die. How can you leave the people you love out of your life so completely?"

"I know," he said; "look Margaret, I'll give you a call after Joan and I finish, okay? Maybe I'll stay the night. I'll think about it anyway, okay?"

"Okay, Andy." She didn't sound any less worried, but she sounded resigned. "See you."

"See you." He hung up, and then on an impulse dialed Jess's number. She answered the phone on the first ring.

"Jess?"

"Andrew?"

"Listen, Broken Echo, that old Indian ghost, has showed up here at the condo, and he told me something's happening in Greenback, maybe out at the house, right now. I don't want that on my conscience. Look, don't go out there, but get Turkey to check it out, will you?"

"So far as I know that ghost never left the place, and he never talked to anybody. Andrew, I think you ought to take a few days' vacation while you're there and maybe think about looking for a new job. Go see your sister for a while."

"He's been talking to me, and he's definitely here now." How to convince her of something that sounded damned silly on the face of it.

Broken Echo appeared in the car and waved his hand at Andrew. "Hand over the phone," he mouthed.

Andrew looked at him, and then at the phone dubiously.

"Woman," said Broken Echo, "we haven't got time for this. Don't tell me that no one has heard me speak, because I told you Andrew was in the cellar the day you came to find him. If you don't get a move on, there'll be ghosts overrunning the town of Greenback, and they'll do more than climb in bed with your sister. You won't be able to chase them out with a frying pan."

He handed the phone back to Andrew, who said, "You think that's going to convince her?" Broken Echo shrugged modestly. "I don't have that much left, but I can do persuasion."

"Greenback." She was silent for a long moment. "I'll see what I can round up, but I don't know what Turkey'd do if he found something. All these years and they've never left the house or bothered anyone off the grounds. Why now, Andrew, have you asked yourself that?"

"I've tried not to, Jess, but yes, I've asked myself that. And I don't particularly like the answer. Look, are you going to get Turkey out there or not?"

"I'll send him. Do you think there's anything else I ought to do?"

"He didn't give me any details, just keep your eyes open. See you."

"See you. Wait, are you coming home tonight?"

"I don't know yet, Jess, I'll call you back."

"See you."

Closing his eyes for a moment, he wondered what he thought he'd been doing. Jess and Turkey could not handle what he'd left behind him, and he'd just sent one or both of them into trouble. And he didn't even know what kind. But he couldn't have left it alone, could he? He closed his eyes again as that familiar, disconnected feeling took him down.

Clarissa, Praeter's daughter, ran down the stairs with a tray of food. The planks vibrated lightly beneath her feet. "Here is your dinner, Father," she said breathlessly. She set it down and turned to go.

"Wait a minute, girl. You never stay to talk to your father," Praeter said, without raising his head from his hands.

"We have too many differences."

"We have only one difference and it is insurmountable. How could you marry an Indian?" He spat out the words.

"We've talked of this before. You are a powerless old man." She stood with her hands on her hips. "And we keep you locked up in the basement. You have nothing to say about this matter."

"I have much to say about this matter. You have no right to lock me up here any more." He raised his head and called up the stairs, "Evaline?"

She walked nearer. "She won't let you out."

Praeter grabbed her and wrestled her to the ground. "If an Indian can have you, it's not too late for your father then, is it girl?" He flipped up her skirts. She struck him with the heel of her hand and pushed him back.

"And haven't you tried that too many times already. I told you, you are powerless, old man." She jumped to her feet and walked warily backwards. "Don't try that again." She spat at his feet.

Clarissa disappeared, and Broken Echo sat mournfully looking at Andrew who was lying in the old Praeter bed. "Do you remember when the squirrel slashed your sheets to ribbons? I should have let him bite you. He might have had rabies."

"Why?" Andrew struggled to rise from the bed.

"Because your memories are not just painful for you now."

"I'm sorry." Andrew meant it.

"He succeeded, you know, Old Man Praeter. And I killed him for it. That's why I stayed. I traded the whereabouts of some of my people so that I could remain." He flipped a faded blanket over his shoulder. "I had to stay with her. She was frantic after that. She died from the throw of a horse." He raised his hand, and matter-of-factly watched it tremble. "After all this time," he said softly.

"Do you think she meant to die?" Andrew sat up and peered across the room at him. He seemed to be fuzzy, and out-of-focus.

"I think so, yes." The old man nodded. "When I found her, I picked her up to carry her back to the house. Her horse, the colt she had raised by hand, nearly crazy with the smell of blood, charged me. I died at his hooves."

"You're very revealing these days."

"Do you mean I'm transparent?" Broken Echo chuckled. "That's not too surprising, given everything." He leaned back into the corner. "I'm a very weary man, Andrew. It's been a long century." He paused. "And now, one way or another, it will soon be over. Someone ought to know my story." He shrugged. "It's not all bad, though my younger self will spit on my grave. He remembers what it was like to be Indian. I remember what it was like to be too much in love with the wrong woman. It makes you crazy." He covered his face with his hands. "You know," he said in a muffled voice, "I have never known whether she married me because she loved me, or simply because she hated her father." For the first time, he seemed so vulnerable to Andrew. Did the splitting do this to him, Andrew wondered, and promptly fell back into an uneasy sleep.

Joan hopped into the car cheerfully. "I hope you're sleeping over at Margaret's, Andy, because you don't look in any shape to drive home. Falling asleep at this hour of the day isn't a good sign."

"You know," he said slowly, "I think I should just go on over there now. After talking to Margaret I realize how much I've been neglecting my family, and the settlement of the condo knocked me out more than I realized."

"Are you ready for them? You do look like a man who needs a drink;" she tilted her head. "I did want to talk with you."

"Maybe you're right," he shrugged. "I'll revert to city for the night, then."

"I think it's a hell of an idea. Want me to drive you to Margaret's? You can leave your car here."

"No, I'm not that worn out an old bugger." He forced a laugh, and looked at her more closely. He had always thought she was a beautiful woman, and he'd know that she'd been attracted to him ever since he and Kate had known her. Right now he wanted very much to take her arm and to kiss her in the hollow of her neck.

She smiled at him, as though sensing the change in his mood. "It's okay, Andy, to remember what it's like. Kate wouldn't have wanted you to be a hermit."

His voice was rough. "I'm not ready for anything like that, particularly not with—"

"Your wife's friend, of course not. But somebody. Don't let yourself slam down so long you forget." She slid her finger across his cheek.

His hands trembled. He looked at her for a moment, and then said with an effort, "Listen, thanks Joan, but I'm not near ready for this. The last time I got to thinking this way was much too soon, and it was a disaster. Let's get together when I come back to sign the papers, okay?" He reached for the door handle.

She watched him with concern, as he opened the car door. "Call me if you need anything, you hear?"

He waved to her, then stepped into the car and switched on the ignition.

"I knew you were stupid enough to go for this," said

Broken Echo's voice from the passenger seat. Andrew didn't bother to look at him. "They won't know for a while."

"Why the hell not?"

"Because I've disconnected your sister's phone service at the telephone pole. It'll take a repair man to fix it for them. City folks don't know how to do much." He sniffed.

"Well, maybe you're worth something after all," Andrew said, suddenly and irrationally cheerful.

"Somebody had to make up for the damndest getaway I ever saw." Broken Echo wiped his hand across his mouth.

"At least," said Andrew, "it was a getaway. I couldn't have stayed to talk to Margaret, much less Joan. I almost prefer dealing with your younger self. At least it's territory I've been living with for a while."

"There is that." Broken Echo pulled a bone flute out of his chest pocket and began to play an off-key series of notes. "It can be handy to have a ghost around. Just don't," said Broken Echo with a wink, "get too used to it. We're only good for short distances." Then he sobered abruptly. "I can't, for instance, stop what my younger self is doing in the meantime."

"If your younger self has hurt either of them, I'll show him what it means for a Jackson to be on the warpath." He pressed the accelerator up an extra five miles an hour, and they roared around the corner of the subdivision road and onto the highway where they nearly lost traction.

Broken Echo lifted his mouth from the flute and looked at Andrew impassively. "You have your ancestor's temper. But there are other qualities that will be of more value to you tonight."

"That remains to be seen," said Andrew. He floorboarded the accelerator.

CHAPTER 18

Broken Echo fell asleep the minute they turned onto Highway 411. He had cussed Andrew all the way from the subdivision to the interstate to the highway for being a four-eyed fool of a man who'd get them stopped for speeding before they'd hardly gotten on the road. And then he'd fallen asleep the minute they hit 411.

Asleep he looked just like another old man: slack mouth, wrinkled skin, and the tiredness of a face with the life half gone out of it. Andrew felt pleased that the Indian could be so trusting, so vulnerable.

The road before them was entirely different from the stretch of interstate Andrew had travelled that morning. Huge weeping willows and oak trees shrouded the roadside, and there were few lights. Small, white benches and picnic tables dotted the roadside every few miles, and an occasional car pulled off to the side. Andrew rolled down the window and let the wind sweep through his hair. Whenever they pulled up to a red light in another small town, he realized how cool and moist the air really was, but while the car was moving he was comfortable with the whip of the wind.

He knew this road well and had driven it many times. He knew all the speed traps, and all the areas where the road widened to three lanes or four. He had spent his time as a child going down many of the streams that ran near the highway. Tubing, they called it, when you ran the rapids on a large truck innertube.

They had been on the road an hour, and by that time his first sense of enjoyment, perhaps the secret excitement of the chase combined with his nostalgia, had begun to subside, to be eaten at underneath by a faint unease. He probed it, like a tongue at a sore tooth. What was it? Fear of what they were coming to? No. Worry about Jess and Turkey? No. Because whatever had been happening in Greenback had begun to seem so unreal to him that it was hard to be either afraid or worried. He would ask Broken Echo what they could expect once the Indian awoke.

Another half an hour on the road had gone by before his unease began to rise to the surface. By this time, he'd already begun to try to push it back down. He'd spent that half an hour deliberately remembering childhood tubing trips, backwoods expeditions hunting for arrowheads, and camp fires with whole onions wrapped in aluminum foil sending up a sweet smell to rise with the smoke. He'd always wanted to take the boys camping. And with that thought he could no longer keep anything back.

You have travelled this road many times. You have been here as a boy, and you have been here as a man. You travelled this road on your honeymoon. Flushed face of a red-headed bride in a pair of white shorts and a white T-shirt, arm in the air waving at every car that passed, laughing at the look on your face. You travelled this road when you drove together to look at houses. When she laughed, she threw her head back and laughed with a sound like the call of a French horn. She shook her hair off her shoulders, and turned to look at you with her head cocked. And now you are driving on the road that your wife took the last time she ever drove. The old ache at the center of his chest began to revive. Every mile she saw what you are seeing now. The boys were squirming in the back seat, and every so often she called back to them to "simmer down." You are driving on the road that stopped being yours the day it became so intimately connected with their last ride. You are driving on their road.

"No," said Broken Echo without opening his eyes, "you are

driving on our road. This road was a deer trail, a buffalo trail, long before our feet walked it, long before you poured your black roads. It was the trail that led to the Western Warpath. It was the trail that my people walked to the Darkening Lands with little more than the blankets on their backs, and the salt in their pouches. It was the trail, Andrew Jackson, that your ancestor sent my people on when he became greedy and wanted their Southern lands, not even for his nation but entirely for himself."

He stirred and shifted in his seat, still with his eyes closed. "Ah. But I did not mean to number over old sorrows like those funny rosary beads that some of you white men use to count feelings. The griefs lie over this road like the thousand-hooved feet of many deer. How many lives were lost here we will never know, just as we will never know what goes on in those houses. We see their lights as we pass by." He opened his eyes for a moment and pointed out the window. "But we will never know what it feels like to be a single one of the people in them." He sighed and closed his eyes. "I think that I would have liked your Kate." The old man went quickly back to sleep.

Andrew drove on with a rebellious mix of emotions. Damn you, he thought, glaring every so often over at Broken Echo. Every time I have an honest to God emotion, a moment when I can remember how to *feel*, you lay your goddamned history over it. And yet he admired the Indian for singling out the one unerring connection between the two of them no matter what might be in the way, time after time. Whether he liked it or not. Small wonder that the accuracy of that aim became like a fist in an old wound after a while. Broken Echo, too, must have hated himself for surviving.

The old man woke up and stretched. Andrew looked into his face and saw dark-rimmed eyes with deep pouches under them. The old man said, "Look, this is all very enlightening, but maybe I need to remind you at this point that your sister and her husband can't be too far behind us, two of your friends are in danger because *you* sent them there, I'm getting weaker, and we've got a hell of a long way to go." Broken Echo turned over, his back to Andrew.

"I'm getting damned tired of people telling me what my responsibilities are! I'm as tired as you are, you know; I don't have a lot left either."

"Then," came the old man's voice piping, "you'd better

save your strength as well." And Andrew could get nothing else from him for a very long while.

He pressed the accelerator to the floor and drove at eighty until they came close to the town of Benton, and then he slowed reluctantly to thirty for the crawl down the main street. The small, sleepy town had two industries to support its citizens, a nearby paper plant, which colored the air for miles around and a series of jobs related to a speeding trap. They made it through Benton, then through Etowah, and finally through the only red light in the town of Englewood.

Broken Echo finally stirred. "I'm not sure where it will begin, perhaps not until you reach Greenback, perhaps as far back as Vonore, or even Madisonville, but you must not be surprised at anything that you see. My younger self doesn't think as I do, particularly now, and I don't know what powers he'll have gained while I've been banished."

Andrew pressed the accelerator to the floor just as they passed in rapid succession a fast food restaurant, the Big B, topped by a large sign of a hovering bee just above an ice cream cone. Past an old tire store. Past a bootleg liquor delivery hut which Andrew had stopped at on their last house hunting trip. Only in Englewood, where the police spent most of their time sleeping at the town depot, would the bootlegger sell his wares on the main highway. "Do you have enough strength?"

"I have what I have, just like you."

We'll be there soon, thought Andrew. His hands began to sweat where they rested on the steering wheel. He wiped them, one after the other, on his pants legs. They had probably fifteen minutes before they reached the edge of Madisonville. "What can I expect?"

"Larry has joined them. That should tell you something."

"Something," Andrew said grimly. He continued to drive, watching the small, rolling hills with his peripheral vision. Now that complete dark had settled, it became easy to imagine followers. "So your younger self worked on Larry? That would explain a lot of the ambivalence between us."

"He and the loa."

"The ghosts?"

"The ghosts and the others who are there." He hesitated. "You'll find Larry changed."

"I already have. The question is how much."

The road curved and they were at Madisonville. Speed

limit: forty-four miles an hour, read the sign. The signs had cost the town more than they were worth probably. They'd intended them to warn speeders that speedtraps were precise in Madisonville, but truck drivers and kids stole them as souvenirs.

They turned onto the small bypass and circled around the town. Kate had driven this road too. The boys would have been anxious and tired by this point in the drive, perhaps even asleep. He felt his back begin to curve forward, muscles tense and crooked. I should stop, he thought, and stretch out. No.

"The main thing to remember is that what my younger self is doing will violate all the boundaries. What he has done to you will be mere practice in comparison. History, time, place, family, sex, memory, perceptions and customs of all sorts. Any and all of these things are called into question. If he is successful, he will revise our time, and completely reshape your own reality." He looked at Andrew. "That should please a history teacher least of all. To question these things is good, but to do so with all of them at once can create a violent chaos of the spirit. Any of you might become lost among the ghostways." He sighed. "*Will* you make it?"

"If you make it, then so will I." Andrew nodded twice. They reached the other side of Madisonville; Andrew slowed the car, and in that moment Broken Echo had gone. His heart hammered, then slowed. The ache in his chest increased. The car leaped forward, and he continued to drive, steadily watching the road to either side of him as well as the road ahead. What did it mean? Had the old Indian gone to scout ahead, or had his younger self succeeded in banishing him completely? If so, that would leave Andrew to carry through by himself.

Without Broken Echo it became easier to drift, to remember the feel of the tires against this road which, for some reason, had always seemed to him to have a traction like no other road. It slid past his tires like blacktop that had melted one too many times in the sun. "We'll be there soon," Kate's voice murmured in his ear; "now stop it! You can't trail a string out the window. That's dangerous. Billy cut that string right now! Use the tomato knife! Look what you've done. I told you to cut it." A wail came from the back seat. "Andy, Andy, are you all right? Wait just a minute, son; I'll pull over."

"Mom," came his voice timidly, "a car ran over it. It came back in the window and wrapped around my ear."

"Hold on, Andy, we're pulling over." Andrew slowed the car, and started to pull off the side of the road. He dipped his head toward the steering wheel, and then kept on driving. He drove with one hand, the bandaged arm pressed to his chest. He looked rigidly at the road, and ignored the growing ache in his chest. Vonore, the faded road sign said, unincorporated, and on the other side of town, another sign read, Twelve miles to Greenback.

"Well, son," Kate's voice sounded noticeably brisker, "you're going to be all right. I believe you won't even have a scar."

As they topped a small rise Andrew saw something two dips ahead in the road, though he couldn't make out what it was. He clenched his fist against his chest to still the by now unbearable ache, an ache, he thought, right down to the cellular level. His other hand began to ache as well. Been driving too long. They topped the second rise going eighty.

Kate started to sing. "Don't dump your junk in my backyard, my backyard;" the boys joined her, "my backyard, my backyard. Don't dump your junk in my backyard. My backyard's full."

"I'll do the fish one," called Andy.

"I'll do the pepper," chimed in Billy.

"Fish and chips and vinegar, vinegar, vinegar."

Andrew leaned down toward the windshield and peered ahead of him. It looked like there were people in the road. He slowed down.

"Fish and chips and vinegar, vinegar, vinegar," and then Billy jumped in "pepper, pepper, pepper, pepper, pot."

"No, Billy, that's pepper, pepper, pepper, pop!" said Andy.

"We're almost there now. Come on. Let's sing. Don't dump your junk in my backyard," returned Kate's determinedly cheerful voice, though through it ran an undercurrent of anxiety. "My backyard, my backyard."

There were people in the road, though a haze, maybe a fog, drifted over their shoulders. Andrew slowed down even further. Three black men, their backs glistening in the light, crouched down in the road. Andrew leaned out the window, and waved. "Look out!" he called; "You're in the middle of the road." The men looked up without any sign of recognition. One of them raised his chains in the air as though in resignation. "Look out," cried Andy; "I don't think I can stop."

"My backyard, my backyard." Kate's voice rose, gratingly off-key.

He slammed on the brakes, and the car slid and whirled into the soft blacktop road. Somewhere near him Kate gasped, "Oh my God," and he reached out an automatic hand to steady her and the children, but he couldn't find her anywhere. "The tire, boys, look out!" His bandages ripped, and he bent double in pain, desperately trying to hold the car steady in the turn with his other hand. Then for a strange, uneven moment he found himself pressing against the accelerator. He gritted his teeth and pushed harder. Why, Andy, why? he asked himself over and over. The car smashed against a soft, yielding body which flew ahead of them into the road. "Call," he heard Kate say in a gulping voice, "an ambulance. Someone call an ambulance." Her arm reached out beyond him through the window of the crumpled car, and he felt her palm against his arm just before he smashed into the roadblock.

He was still frantically reaching out for Kate and the boys, when the sirens wound down to a halt. There were police cars, blue lights flashing and sirens blaring, to either side of him. His heart pounded like a sledge hammer, and his eyes were wide and startled as one of the policemen leaped out of the car to his left and demanded, "What the hell were you doing?"

"I f-fell asleep."

"Asleep! Well, I guess you did. How far have you got to go?"

"Just a few miles. I live over on Fort Loudoun Lake."

The policeman's eyes narrowed. "We've been told to detour anyone who's going through. We don't have orders yet about locals, but I don't recognize you."

The other policeman made a move to get out of the car on the right side of him, and then the radio began to crackle and call. "Mac," he called, "we've got a pileup and a fire on the bridge. Let this guy go!" He got back on the radio and yelled at the dispatcher, "Call in the reserves. We're not going to be able to handle this. And you better call in the state."

"Are you going to be all right?" the man demanded.

"I sure as hell don't think I'm going back to sleep." *Don't they realize I must have hit someone?*

"You better not. I don't want to be scraping you up off the highways." He walked away, tipping back his hat as he went.

Andrew leaned over the steering wheel, his chest aching.

Good thing that the man hadn't had time to notice that he had been driving one-handed. "Kate," he said, and pressed his hand up against his aching chest. The hole that had opened the day she died had never closed. He pounded his head against the steering wheel. "Kate, Billy, Andy, Kate—damn it. None of it ever stops." He jumped out of the car, watching the roadcrew reluctantly move the roadblock. He could hear the sound of his shoes slapping the pavement, but curiously all the rest of him seemed numb except for the soles of his feet. He cupped his elbow in his hand and rocked back against the car. "Did I hit someone? Oh damn, if I go back to see—" He peered back toward the bridge. It looked as though the wrecked car had been going the other direction on a four lane. He couldn't have hit them could he? And if he hadn't, and he stopped to see, Jess and Turkey could be—He hadn't felt any smashup. For a moment he stood in indecision.

The roadcrew cleared out the road, and Andrew jumped back into the car, and revved up the motor, quickly pushing up the accelerator as soon as he was out of the range of the roadcrew. His vision had sharpened, adrenalin coursed. Who knew what might be ahead, but he wouldn't have time for anything but instinct.

Off to his left in the distance, he could see irregular flashes of light. To his right, a large area jumped into flame. A fragment of a shell burst through just in front of the car, and he hesitated for an instant, but drove on.

As he rounded the next curve, a heavy fog covered the road. At the center of the curve, barely visible through the mist, sat a small, brick grocery store which Andrew had stopped at many times. The fog lifted for a moment. The door had been struck open, and there were wounded men piled up on the countertops, the floor, and even on the concrete outside. A woman, screaming, was being pushed to the well by two men with muskets. Andrew tried to turn the car into the driveway to help her, but a group of soldiers ran up out of the mist and straight toward him, so he whipped back onto the highway.

The next house was right in the vortex of destruction. Bullets whistled through it in every direction, shattering the glass. Andrew could hear, from the roadside, the sound of wounded begging for water. Along the ridge, just beyond the house, artillery fire, and swarming gray backs shifted busily.

You are now in the midst of history magnified, Andrew told himself grimly.

Just to his left marched by a group of men with green sunbursts at their caps, a sprig of green at the brim, and a half-laughing, half-murderous look in their eyes. They reached within a stone's throw of the battery walls, but no further. Many of them were slaughtered, but the rest lay doggedly, obviously determined to hold the ground they had already taken. As Andrew drove away, he saw them crawling toward the battery wall. He rolled on over bridges covered with straw to muffle the sound, past the fog and out into the fresher night air. At least they hadn't made it into Greenback yet. That was a sign of hope. And he needed those. It didn't matter what level they were on now. It's real enough, damn it. You can't let them take Greenback. The town was a still center of tradition in the middle of a storm, and he needed to know *that* would survive.

The wound throbbed in his shoulder. Andrew looked down to see fresh blood welling from the remains of his bandages. He gritted his teeth and drove on, afraid to find out what would happen if he stopped the car long enough to tend his wound. Would the soldiers be all over him? He imagined bodies crawling against the windshield. Better not risk it. He shifted his weight cautiously and tugged at the bandage, guiding the wheel for a moment with his knee. That nearly ran him off the road, so he gave it up.

Each bend in the road his tension grew. He kept glancing at the roadside, looking back through the rearview mirror, and checking the mile gauge as though it were a clock. Two miles crept by in deceptive silence, and he turned onto the road which led from the highway to Greenback without incident.

A mile from the turn the weather changed without warning. First the wind whipped the trees which hovered above the road, and sent branches scudding in front of the car. He drove over several before it began to seem that instead of branches, he drove over the thin, writhing bodies of blacksnakes. Another bend rounded and standing in the center of the road was a man cracking a large whip over the backs of two small, black girls. Their clothes were wet, and their bodies shivering. He tried to go around the three, but the scene followed the movements of his car, until in desperation he closed his eyes and ran right through them. He waited to feel the bodies against the hood of his car, but the lack of impact scared him even more. How could he know when and how to stop? And the younger Broken Echo, *did he know when to stop?*

He opened his eyes just in time to steer the car through a huge bank of water which lay across the road. The car hit the bank and spun wildly through, spraying water to either side of him. Even so he was able to keep control, because by now a rictus had settled into the hold with which he gripped the wheel. When he reached the other side, he tested the brakes cautiously. They were gone, and though he tried to restore them by repeatedly hitting the pedal and releasing it, they didn't return. A wave of dizziness. He lapped the edges of the blood-soaked bandage on his shoulder laboriously together, and settled back into the seat. Then he pressed the accelerator pedal to the floor. On the way to Greenback he ran over three phantom dogs, a horse, and a small scout band of Indians conducting a larger group of Confederate soldiers directly in the path of the road. None of these made contact with the front of his car, but he was beginning to lose his nerve. At one point he got out to check the car. The right front fender was smashed, but he couldn't be sure when it had happened. On the bridge, or since?

Managing to steer the car around the corner turn from the highway to Main Street, he lost control just afterwards and ran into the front of Lester Cleary's grocery store, shattering the huge paned-glass window. He ducked the glass, and, as the car settled, heard a loud, rolling voice. "Brothers, I had heard in the days of old when the Israelites were in service to the Pharaohs, that they were carried away by the power of an angel, but we have seen nothing like that in these days. Instead what we see is the calling up of old ghosts, and the weakening of old boundaries. We have drawn in all those from the surrounding area, and there are many. Even now, though some of them war, they march to meet with us. Those that are left will be all the more easily converted to our aims. Soon the younger Indians will have called the power to aid them in opening the boundaries."

Carefully raising himself up and looking through his side window, he saw that a muscular black man stood on the steps of the bank, and around him was a mixed crowd of blacks and Indians. On his chest, printed in fluorescent letters was a slogan, Liberty or Death. In his hands and the hands of his followers were curved, beaten down scythe blades with wooden handles, clubs, and long Bowie knives. Down the street came an unsuspecting white family, the children tugging at their father's hands. Over the father's back curled a huge black snake, though none of his family seemed to see it.

Carefully opening the car door furthest from the bank, Andrew crept around the side. He caught the father's eye and tried to wave him frantically toward the shelter of the car. The father looked at him in puzzlement, and the children pointed and laughed. Andrew shrugged his shoulders, and ran from the car to the back of the old train depot. How could you help somebody who couldn't even see the danger? For that matter, how could you take seriously helping them? When he was the only one who seemed to see anything, the danger felt curiously unreal.

As he came around the rear of the building a hand grabbed him. He leaped back. "Ssst," said a Confederate soldier with his hand on a saber. "Oh, you." It was the young boy from the cellar, arm still intact. "Broken Echo sent me to scout for you, but I'd given up hope." His blue eyes were intent on Andrew's face. "We've got a horse for you on the other side of the church. Can you make it that far?"

Andrew nodded.

The soldier glanced at his bandage. "Can you ride?"

"I can ride. What's the situation?"

"Worsening." He glanced around him and stepped back into the shadows of the building. "Broken Echo has been creating diversions, but they won't hold much longer." He pulled his cap off. "The horse, it may not hold all the way to the house."

"What do you mean?"

The soldier's outline started to waver. Andrew called after him, "Don't forget to put your Bible in your pocket." I remember that. So this is how I saved that guy's life. He didn't wait to see the Confederate vanish. He ran around the back of the depot and into the main street of the town. The family had gone, but the mixed band on the steps remained. They were brandishing their scythes at several people in their eighties walking unsteadily down the street.

"You can't," said Andrew breathlessly, "think that with revision you can really change things. Why do you work backwards? Create a world of your own. *After all, you have to leave things to your own descendants.*" He remained where he could quickly make his way around the depot and to the horse.

The black man on the steps slowly turned to look at Andrew, his large eyes calm. "We've already created our own world, and it is tied to this one. If you think that even revision will change that, you're quite mistaken. We've nothing to fear. We *live* where time changes. And there's room for all of us."

Andrew nodded slowly. "So you'll do as Broken Echo did with me. You'll use violence, and then guilt and grief. Old memories. I am a reflective man, and what about these?" He lifted his hand and pointed out the people on the street. "Farmers and their wives. Old couples walking down the street hand in hand." The passersby looked at him in astonishment, and then walked on shaking their heads.

"They will respond as their nature dictates, just as you, though you *are* sensitive."

"Special."

"No, not particularly." The mixed crowd laughed, and hefted their homemade swords. Andrew weighed the risks, looking back over his shoulder toward the depot. Then he shrugged.

"Listen to me;" Andrew walked nearer the edge of the crowd. "Absolute freedom is no better then slavery. It frightens people, makes them callous and brutal."

"You should know."

"I know what it's like to have the parameters continually changing on you. I haven't enjoyed it." He shifted his feet, thinking uneasily of the horse. Weren't they just keeping him here?

"Haven't you? I thought you'd become addicted to it."

Andrew hesitated. "All right, maybe I did, but it doesn't sustain itself. Boundaries are a matter of choice, after all, and choice is a matter of the spirit. Change is important, but we need somewhere to meet, some moment, some edge that touches."

"And that's a matter of opinion." He spat on the sidewalk. "We'll risk it." The crowd laughed at the big man's jeering tone. They had hardly finished before he said softly, "Get him."

Andrew whirled and ran back around the depot and into the woods before the first man rounded the corner after him. The undergrowth sank dry and crackling underneath each footstep. He tried to step more quietly, but nothing stilled the noise, so then he ran ahead with large leaps, intent on getting as much distance as possible between himself and the bank. Something dropped onto his shoulders with a heavy weight, and he whipped the snake from him without a second glance, flinging it as far through the bushes as possible. The horse was tied just to the side of the church. Its flanks were covered with a quick sweat, and it jumped at his touch. "Whoa, boy." He blew into its nostrils.

"I wouldn't count on getting away that quickly," said a deep voice behind him.

Andrew didn't turn around to see who it was. He leaped up onto the horse's back and kicked it in the sides. The horse reared and then jumped across the path of the large black man from the bank, who reached up an effortless hand to grab the horse by the tail. Andrew kicked behind him, connecting his foot with the man's face in a satisfying smash. The horse ran forward and the black man ran after them, keeping pace, and reaching up a hand to pull Andrew from the saddle. The horse reared and jumped sidewise, bringing down its feet upon the feet of the black like a mustang after a rattler. Quick as the man's scream, they ran on ahead and away from him and were soon around the side of the church and running in the grass beside the road that led away from town and toward the Praeter House.

The nervous trot jolted Andrew's shoulder, and he leaned forward into the saddle, until he could kick the horse into a gallop. "Five miles. But I've got a feeling you and me aren't going to make it that far, baby." He looked down to see that what he kicked no longer galloped, and then his mount rose into the air and he slid from its scaled and saddleless back. He blacked out just as the snake plunged its forked tongue directly through the bandage and into his shoulder. The last sound he heard was his own scream.

The snakes looped above his head. Andrew lay on the church bench and watched the men handling the long bodies with careless confidence. One man, seated at the other end of the pew, drank something down in one quick gulp. Suddenly Larry bent over Andrew, a cup in his hand.

"Would you like something to drink?"

Andrew stared at him. The cup smelled vaguely familiar. He lifted his head, and then knocked the cup from Larry's hand. "Poison."

"Right, but if you were a 'true believer' it wouldn't hurt you."

The snake handlers' clothing was modern. The man at the end of the pew tossed his cup into a full paper bag. It rattled around the top of the other cups, and spilled onto the floor. Andrew listened to it roll around on the tile, while he stared at Larry. The boy's eyes were brightly malicious. The others merely seemed interested.

"Don't they know what they're doing?" asked Andrew.

"They do and they don't." Larry sat down beside him, one hand resting on his arm. Andrew shrugged it off.

"It's so hard to see clearly with all this anger and fear in the air. Can't they put those snakes down?"

Outside came the distant sounds of battle, the roar of the canons, the shouts of men, horses' hooves. One of the men opened a stained glass window. Dust from the battle rolled across the empty pews. For a moment the air was clear, and Andrew saw a small, black child playing in the tree limbs, swinging down in an arc.

"Don't," Andrew gasped, just as the man released a knife silently through the air. The scream from the child startled all the men. They looked around in bewilderment. "Don't you *see* that child?" he asked them.

"It's the spirit of the Lord, yes, Lord," said one of them, and threw the snake up in the air above him.

"They're not likely to see it," said Larry. "But they can hear it."

"My God," cried Andrew.

"Yes, Lord," said one of the men; "And the spirit of the Lord said let them enter the house of the Lord and they shall be fed. And not the handling of snakes, nor the drinking of poison shall harm those who fear not for the Lord's sake."

"Don't they know what they're doing?" Andrew got unsteadily to his feet.

"I don't think they see any connection between the handling of snakes and the loosening of traditions," said Larry.

He rose and dusted off his clothing. "Don't you think you ought to come with me? I've got a car, and I'm going out to your house."

"I think not," said Andrew, backing away from Larry. "I think I'll find my own car." Larry started walking slowly toward him. Andrew whirled and broke into a run. His feet thudded across the tile floor to the hardwood foyer and outside. He found an old, white Ford with a rusted shut door on a side street, and he started it up, revving the engine and popping the clutch, just in time to roar slowly away from Larry. The boy would probably beat him on the road, Andrew thought grimly, but at least he had a headstart on him now.

And he had sent Jess and Turkey out to the house in this? It was like sending buck privates into the center of the war zone. They had good spirit and good intentions, but little training. He pressed the accelerator, then smashed it to the floor as though he could push the car's speed beyond its tolerance by mere willpower. He at least had had some experience with what happens when someone deliberately manipulates dreams, illusions, and reality for you with a free hand. The younger Broken Echo might be deadly for them.

Outside the church, the dust rose from the battlefield. A horn sounded, and three Indians went by leading a small handful of Yankee soldiers. One of them brandished a bayonet and stared at Andrew, but he gunned the car and passed them as well.

The white Ford actually turned out to have more horsepower than he would have suspected. He made it halfway to the highway before Larry caught him and roared on by. For a moment, when they ran neck and neck on the road, Andrew thought Larry would ram him, but he merely stared at the older man for a moment, tipped his hat, and then leaped ahead. In a few moments he was gone. He watched Larry disappearing up the road ahead of him, then he gripped the steering wheel as though it would increase his speed, and grimly continued to drive.

CHAPTER 19

After he rounded the final bend, Andrew instinctively, without knowing quite why, slammed on his brakes, the car sliding, sliding, twisting, until at last it crunched across the gravel and settled into a ditch. He could hear the gravel flying wild against the blacktop road, and sense the wheels hovering over the ditch. The rocking back and forth of the car; the wheels hovering over the ditch.

"Snakes," said Broken Echo matter-of-factly from the passenger seat, "don't believe in privacy. They force the issue. They'll crawl into your yard and into your house without a thought for what is natural." The car tipped into the ditch and settled there.

In his backyard and coiled around his house lay a huge snake, its eyes gleaming and its head twisting as it followed the staff of the younger Indian. A huge white light shone from its forehead. Behind it, on the shores of the lake, were piled scores and scores of dead bodies in Northern uniforms; some of them had rolled over and were floating in the lake. As he looked, several men who had seemed dead were rising up from the bodies of their dead comrades. Then they vanished. The snake's hiss reverberated and Andrew started.

"That," said Broken Echo, "is a utkena, and if my younger self succeeds in entertaining it long enough to get that crystal from its forehead, we have only one other hope."

"What hope?" asked Andrew, as he stared at the snake.

It bent down to take Jess's head in its mouth, though neither Jess nor Turkey seemed to notice. She stared at the young Indian. Turkey stared at her. "What are you seeing now?" he kept asking her, and she kept waving him away. The two of them walked calmly down the center of the snake and toward the young Indian. He paid them absolutely no attention. Andrew shivered. The light glowed from the snake's forehead and refracted like that of a many-sided prism across the lawn, flashing and circling. The young Indian waved his staff as though it were a thick and top heavy baton.

"To beat Larry to the capture and the killing of the white deer, and to bargain with my younger self for the possession and use of the utkena crystal. Or you could kill both Larry and my younger self. That would stop this chain. He has ties with all of us here, you see. You'd have to clear the board."

Andrew had had a dream just a few days before. He knew that it had been something important, though all that he could remember lay in a vague sense of dis-ease that had been with him ever since. The tide of wrongness, an ancient wrongness, began to move through him again. The deer. "No!" he cried out.

"Do you have any other suggestions?" came the acid tones of the old Indian. "If he drips deer blood onto the crystal, the events you saw on the way here won't be illusion."

Andrew looked around for the troops that he had seen on the shore, but they were gone. The utkena continued to coil its long body and to circle Jess and Turkey, while the tip of its tail slid across the grass toward Andrew and Broken Echo. Jess and Turkey stopped. The utkena, as if suddenly realizing where they were, began to sink its coils in tight around them. Its eyes were beginning to glaze, and the weaving through the air of its head to slow.

The young Indian began to chant. Andrew could hear him from where he stood.

Now! On the White Pathways I am making my
footprints. One will be able to see
the moving feet of the Utkena going before me.

The Red Lightning will be stretching out in a flashing
sheet in front of me.

Du! Du! Du!
I am an unknown of the Snake clan.

Right here you rest.
You and I are friends.
Make a clash in the very middle of my body!
Ha! Let them be terrified of me!

The snake's head began to dip forward. The younger
Indian's face, white with green and yellow streaks, seemed a
ghostly mask, wholly detached from his body. He reached out
his hand.

Andrew, almost as mesmerized as the snake, shook himself
and leaped forward, futilely intent on beating the other to the
crystal. But before he covered half the ground between them,
the crystal was in the Indian's hand. Broken Echo murmured
in his ear, "He can't do anything more without the blood.
Run, Andrew. I'll try to get the crystal from him."

"You?" Andrew turned to the weary old man beside him, a
man whose body inclined at a half bend, whose eyes were
cloudy.

"Me," said Broken Echo, and straightened his back with an
effort. He walked down the grass toward his younger self with
a spring in his step. He called back over his shoulder, "You're
going to have to kill one of them, either Larry or the deer. I
can't kill my younger self; but you can. And unless you do,
simply killing Larry doesn't solve things. The quickest way
out is to kill the deer."

Andrew shrugged and turned to run into the woods. Behind him he heard the younger Indian call, "Ha, is it you
ts(i)sgoiya? Is it you old conscience worm? Was not the
diidagele:n(v)dhoʔdi-yi, the separation, enough for you?"

"No, young one, it gave me the uhisoʔdi, the chill of
loneliness." Their voices sounded as though they were circling each other.

As Andrew ran, his weariness, the pain of his shoulder, the

other aches and stiffness from the drive, all dropped away, and vigor coursed through him. He felt as though his body had been made for this, as though he had been made for this. And all the while his feet ran lightly through the underbrush, scarcely disturbing the ground beneath him. His new vigor fought with an intuition that prickled at the back of his neck, a voice saying, this is wrong. What you are doing can't be rectified. You think too much, he said to himself, and allowed thought to drop away. The body was all that mattered here.

He paused behind a tree near the clearing of the gravesites, the ones he hadn't been able to bear to visit since he buried them there with the Praeter family. Larry circled the gravestones, his eyes on the luminous white deer that grazed without any sign of fear just above Billy's grave. From the look of Larry the deer had been leading him a chase. His shirt sleeves were torn, and the odd, black top hat he wore looked as though it would fall off at any moment. Larry held onto it with one hand, and had a tight grasp on an old fashioned musket with the other. Just beside him, up against Praeter's gravestone, leaned an old shovel. The deer, on the other hand, seemed perfectly fresh. Ah, the deer, the light, quiet deer, which cropped the grass so contentedly just above his son's head. It moved on casually to Kate's.

Larry put down the musket and picked up the shovel, his eyes still intent on the deer. "What you want is bait?" he said, and then laughed a crude laugh. He jammed the shovel into the earth of Billy's grave and shoved it further with a hard workboot.

Andrew moved quickly out into the clearing. The deer moved toward the opposite edge, its eyes moving back and forth from one of them to the other. "Stop there, Larry. You can't afford, for anyone's sake, most of all your own, to dig any further. Leave my family's bones undisturbed." Oddly enough, he wasn't angry; instead he was curiously calm. This moment was his one chance to save the boy.

Larry stood undecided with the shovel in his hands, his foot still on the top edge of it. The deer's eyes flashed in the moonlight. He stared at Andrew, while across his face flickered a curious mix of emotions: anger, hatred, pain, and something more friendly and more confused. "Why should I?"

"Because you're taking a path that you can't return from and that you'll quickly grow to hate."

"I'm gathering power."

"You're gathering a reflection in the mirror that you'll have to turn away from."

Larry's face twisted. He looked toward the musket, and then back toward Andrew. "Why didn't you report me?" he cried.

"Because you're my next door neighbor and my student. Because everyone deserves the chance to stop just before a choice or to turn away from their own distaste at the wrong one."

"I could have killed you."

"Yes." Andrew waited.

Larry's hands gripped the shovel. The deer drifted a little closer to the trees at the edge of the clearing. He watched the deer with desperate attention.

Andrew continued to wait, a calmness rising up through him from the earth beneath his feet. He waited as though he had been standing there since the night that Larry shot him, since the night that he began to understand a little bit about what the ghosts were doing and who they were. He remembered that this boy, like his own sons, had once run laughing through these woods, had once been equally open and eager. Through the force of his look he tried to remind Larry as well.

Larry pulled the shovel from the ground and raised it over his head, moving toward the edge of the clearing where a series of jars rested unevenly on the ground. They were familiar to Andrew; they were the spirit jars from his sojourn at the church in the cellar.

"I'll smash these then, because I'm sick of being jerked around."

Andrew's voice was still calm, though his breath quickened. "The result will be the same. Your problem is in you, not in these spirits you've answered." He watched the shovel hovering eagerly over the thick, though fragile, pottery jars, and tried to gauge how quickly he could move to save them if the shovel were on the down swing.

The deer moved suddenly, darting off through the woods that lay further beyond the house. With a muffled exclamation, Larry threw down the shovel, grabbed up the musket, and ran off in pursuit. Andrew as quickly followed, that strange vigor and calm coursing still in his blood. He passed

Larry and ran behind the glowing bounce of a tail that beckoned both of them. The moon shone high overhead, and the noise of the fighting seemed far away. Somehow, with a strange, fatalistic certainty, he knew that Jess and Turkey would be all right as long as Broken Echo was there, and as long as the deer remained free. You're risking their lives on an intuition, an inner voice said, but he ignored that as well. Intuition was all that he had left to live for, that, and catching this small, gentle, sharp-footed deer and keeping it safe.

No, he thought, looking back at his follower. And the face of Larry? said silently, yes, and yes again.

A wrongness, the sensation of an absolute wrongness to which the body itself objects, started like a slow flood from the center of his chest and moved outward. They were participating in something so old and so wrong that neither of them would ever recover from it. We'll be locked in the cellar; he wanted to tell Larry. We'll not know what we've done. The sins of the father are visited on the sons. Don't you believe in fate? He thought he heard himself yell, but he must have been mistaken, because the woods were silent. Every insect had stopped. Nothing moved but the soft swish of the deer's legs, the softer following of their deerstalking feet, and the harsh pant of Larry's breath behind him.

The deer took them to a clearing where it stopped in the center, its hide luminous in the moonlight, its eyes steady upon the two of them. Both Andrew and Larry stopped at the edge of the clearing, uncertain, out of breath, and Andrew's energy drained from him like a quickly receding pool of water. He wavered unsteadily on his feet, his shoulder throbbing fiercely. Looking down, he saw that his wound had started to bleed again.

Broken Echo kicked the staff out of his hands. The younger Indian twisted his body out of the old man's reach looking warily at him and then at the utkena. "You fool. Do you want to unleash it on us all."

Larry stepped in front of Andrew, and Andrew stooped to grab a stone. Larry heard him coming and whirled to meet him. He pulled his knife out of his pocket.

The old man darted forward and threw his younger self to the ground.

"You'll have to get beyond me," said Larry. Andrew looked at the deer, again cropping grass.

"What makes you think it'll stay while we fight?" asked Andrew, darting forward toward Larry, and then back out of reach of the swing of the knife. He kicked the boy's hand, and missed. Larry grabbed his foot and twisted it.

"It'll stay," the boy said confidently, throwing Andrew back on the ground, and onto his wounded shoulder.

In the town, James brushed aside three men chasing another with a bayonet. "Jess," he called, "Jess, where are you?" Behind him three Indians beckoned a troop of Confederates down a dusty alley.

Andrew turned to lever himself up with his good arm. He tried to ignore the pain, but a moment's blinding flash debilitated him. He grabbed a large stone the size of two fists.

The old Indian was on top of the younger, the knife at his throat. He pushed his hand back clear to the ground.

Andrew jumped up just as Larry reached for the deer. Andrew smashed him on the back of the head with the stone, just as the deer sidestepped the boy's hands. Larry dropped to the ground. The deer regarded Andrew; he reached out his hand to it, all the while thinking, is this it? Is this the end of it all, that I should take this tender young deer's life? The deer moved toward him as though completely unafraid. Andrew's fingers touched the bright burning of the animal's skin. The deer nosed him, soft velvety snuffle against his palm. It ducked its head confidingly into his side. No, he thought, I'll not do it. He turned away to bend over Larry and put his fingers to the boy's wrist. A strong pulse beat there.

The deer stepped daintily up to the boy, and lipped his clothing. Then it pulled its head back, and darted into bite the boy's chest. Andrew reached its side, his hand on its back, but the deer ignored him. It backed up slowly, pulling and tugging at a black and lacy line which extended from its mouth to the boy's chest. The line snapped in two, and the deer pulled at the second half until it too came loose. Then it flipped the old top hat up with its mouth until the hat landed squarely on Andrew's head. With the hat came a dark kind of setting, a perverse and ironic sense of humor, and a feeling of power. Andrew turned around to leave, and the deer followed him. He waved it back; then looked at Larry again. The boy might come around too quickly and look for the deer. Better that it followed him then. He would chase it away before they reached the house. Then he paused in indecision. The boy could be hurt. He had tried not to hit him hard, but a blow to the head could have given Larry a concussion. The boy had a hefty body and would slow him down, and Broken Echo couldn't hold out much longer. Andrew hefted the boy up over his shoulder and carried him back toward the house. His feet sank into the pine needles, but he managed to make it back to the clearing without stopping once, a feat that filled him with considerable amazement. At the edge of the woods the deer refused to leave him. He grabbed a branch and tried to shoo it away, and the deer shook its head and charged Andrew, its body butting up against him, spilling Larry out onto the grass, and shoving Andrew three feet away and into the yard.

The two Indians were struggling on the ground, each of them holding off the other's knife. Broken Echo was still remarkably intact, though the younger Indian's clothes were ripped in several places.

The older Indian looked up to see Andrew, and said grimly, "I've been holding him for you." He sagged quickly to the ground as though a burden had been removed from him. The utkena settled to the ground as well, its eyes intent on both Andrew and the deer. Jess and Turkey stepped quickly across the tip of its slack tail. They started toward Andrew. "Get the hell up on the porch," he called.

The deer ran past him, butting them both with its forehead. Jess looked up suddenly, as though seeing Andrew for the first time. Turkey turned around. "What the bloody hell—", he called, "Jess look at this." She turned around and promptly fainted. Turkey looked up at Andrew, shook his head. "Women." He carried her in a careful, wide circuit around the snake and the two Indians and up onto the porch.

Neither Indian paid the slightest attention to the two of them. Both stared at Andrew. "Did you kill the boy then?" called Broken Echo. "No, oh I see," he glanced up at the top hat. "You took the loa. I didn't think you'd have the strength."

Andrew shook his head in puzzlement. Later. "Neither I nor anyone else is going to kill this deer," he said, shifting his stance so that his fingers rested in the center of the deer's forehead. The deer nuzzled his ribs, and then rested its head there calmly, staring at the two Indians.

The younger Indian leaped forward, the crystal in his hand raised to stab the deer. Andrew sidestepped him, and the deer moved back to circle around the two of them. Andrew danced left, poised on the balls of his feet. The young Indian moved forward again, and Andrew danced around him. How long can you keep this up, boy? he asked himself.

"Good for you," gasped Broken Echo. Andrew whirled around just in time to sidestep the younger Indian once again. Turkey ran down from the porch to help him.

"Here," Andrew thrust the deer at him, "protect it with your life."

"Aye, aye, captain," said Turkey, scooping up the small deer in one arm. He ran back up to the porch and grabbed a shovel. He held the deer in one arm and lifted the shovel in the other.

Andrew placed himself carefully in front of the porch. The younger Indian darted to the left and to the right trying to get past him. Turkey waved the shovel in the air. "I'm a fightin' for animal rights," he roared; "I thought I'd never see the day."

Andrew threw back his head and laughed, feeling a quick surge of adrenaline. The younger Indian rushed him, and Andrew grabbed him by the arm, yanking him around and, with a strength he never realized he had, tossed him back several feet away from the house.

"Quick," said Broken Echo, "you've got to—" he crawled toward Andrew; "you've got to heal the division, or I'll be"— he coughed, "water under the dam."

What would he do now? He could hear Billy's voice chanting prepositions, "The water went under the dam; the water went over the dam; the water went around the dam; the water went through the dam. Ha, ha, the water flooded the dam and ran away to Texas." No, he groaned under his breath, not now. The younger Indian rushed him, and Andrew threw him to the ground. This time Andrew sat on him, and managed to stay there despite all his struggles.

Broken Echo threw Andrew a knife. "Here," he said, "in order to rejoin us, you have to slit his throat."

Andrew looked down at the younger Indian underneath him. "What's your name?" he asked him.

"Oh no," said the Indian mockingly; "do you think I'd tell *you*, especially now."

"What's your name?"

Silence. His eyes stared up into Andrew's, and in them was a look half-laughing, half-murderous.

"The Ancient One has just come to make the fire rise to its feet." As Andrew spoke, the look died in the Indian's face, to be replaced with what? Fear? Respect? Andrew couldn't tell, because the fleeting expression was as quickly replaced with impassivity.

"Use the knife," said Broken Echo.

The soldier stood poised at the entrance to the alley, his musket pointed at James. "Have you seen Jess?" James called out to an old woman walking by. She looked at the soldier and raised one startled, arthritic hand to her mouth. "Look out," she said in a loud stage whisper.

He looked past the soldier. "What is it?"

Andrew reached quickly down toward the Indian, holding the knife horizontal to the other's throat. "What is your name?" He lowered the knife a shade closer to the younger man's throat.

"My name doesn't matter." He bared his teeth. "You kill easily then."

"No, not easily." He sighed. "Why can't you let your descendants handle this?"

"We are the same."

"Not quite."

"True. We have built a longer shadow of anger."

"Cut his throat," said Broken Echo.

"Yes, why not?" said the younger. "Kill me as you did those on the road." Sweat poured down his face, washing the paint away in streaks, but his eyes were unafraid.

He slammed on the brakes; the car skidded; the slaves looked at him in resignation; a body flew in front of the car. Whose body? Whose body?

"No," said Andrew. He tightened his grip on the knife.

The younger Indian said nothing. He glared at Andrew.

"You see," cried Broken Echo. "He has manipulated you yet again: first by recreating your family's death, and second by using it to cause a second accident on the bridge. What are you waiting for? Kill him." Andrew stared at the knife in his hand, and then reached up to saw a hunk of hair from the younger Indian's head. The tip of the knife grazed the Indian's forehead and drew a thin line of blood. The knife trembled in his fingers. He closed his eyes. Somewhere another man, a woman, a child, would be receiving a message. With the event of the bridge somewhere another grief had begun. A quick welling horror began to rise in him. It couldn't be wrong to kill someone so merciless. How could he manipulate a wreck, and then taunt Andrew with it? He opened his hands and stared at the knife quivering on a trembling palm. He had told Larry that the boy shouldn't do anything he couldn't live with, and this he couldn't live with. Could he? He raised the knife. "No. Him I'll not kill either." He stared at the upraised knife. "His anger is his own and for his own reasons. I'll not add to it."

James whirled at the cock of the trigger, but he still didn't seem to see the soldier. The old woman scuttled away.

"He's dead already, you fool," said Broken Echo. "This is merely ceremonial." He crawled toward the two of them.

"No. If there's one thing I've learned it's that ceremony is real." Andrew stood, his foot on the younger Indian's chest. The younger Indian stared up at him, his chest heaving quickly beneath Andrew's foot. Andrew pitched the knife far into the bushes. His voice, shrill, but under control, began to rise in a chant.

> Very quickly now! You have just come to the middle
>   of his soul!
> Now, in the Seventh Heaven all of you rest,
> All of you fail in nothing.
> May the white smoke rise, lift from me, and take
>   his twined spirit into one
> May the owl cry out in the middle of the night
> And return his brother spirit with his call
> May the world walk backward to see that this is so
> May the Panther and the Red Wolf follow the world's
>   trail
> And see that this self is returned.
> Very quickly now! See that he returns!
>
> Sayii! Damii! Flash of lightning
> See that it is so!

The rustling of the wind, the movement of the waters, the bewilderment of the soldier, who dropped his gun to the ground and watched it creep away like an ancient snake. James looked up and directly into Andrew's eyes. He nodded, as though now he knew what to do, and pulled his jacket firmly around him, zipping the zipper with one smooth move.

Andrew bowed toward the two Indians, first to the ground to his left, and then to the ground to his right. "Let the deer loose," he called to Turkey. The old man gently set the deer to the ground. It walked up to the two Indians, nuzzled each of them, and walked straight through Andrew's legs; just as the two vanished, so did the deer. One very tired looking Broken Echo lay rolling on the ground.

"Whoop, whoop;" Andrew heard his muffled voice; "whoop, whoop.

"What are you laughing about, old man?" Andrew put his hands to his face, then forced himself to lower them. No quarter for the guilty. Regardless of what had been narrowly averted, he had killed someone on the bridge.

"Where did you get all that wisdom from, Andrew Jackson?" He sat up, rubbing his face, and looking vastly amused. "I told you to kill the deer, and you didn't listen. I told you to kill my younger self and you didn't listen. Ah, truly, you have left your humble guide, and you have taken up Ghede, an arrogant healer."

"We're all healers," said Andrew. "Anyway I'm the one who's sick to the bone now. Anger is a poison that sustains. I drew it into me, but it was something I had no right to do. It really was your division, and yours to heal." He stopped slowly, as though he had suddenly realized something. "Maybe it was *my version* of it that I had to heal."

Broken Echo touched him. "It's good that you understand."

"Who or what is Ghede?" asked Turkey.

"The loa Andrew took from Larry." Broken Echo sounded very surprised. "Don't you know yet who the loa is who rides on your back?" He gestured to Andrew's hat. "Ghede. He of the quick and the dead, the laughing drinker of gin, the double-sided face of death, the loa of irony and of whimsy. To Ghede the world of death and departure has a border where raw grief and satire mingle. It is Ghede whose voice informs what we have done here since the beginning."

"Larry," Andrew said, and walked back across the clearing to where Larry lay sprawled at the edge of the woods. He picked Larry up in his arms and carefully carried him over to the porch. When Andrew laid him down, he began to stir and to move his head. He mumbled something and then was still, but his breathing was slow and even.

"Will he be all right?" Andrew asked.

Broken Echo nodded.

"Who or what is a loa?" asked Jess from behind them on the porch. Turkey stared at Broken Echo.

Broken Echo bowed politely to both of them. "I can answer one question for one who has looked in the eyes of the deer. A loa is a compressed ghost, one of power who has been dead a very long time, and who has forgotten self, and taken on the 'self' of the community, or of a group of those who have died. But that combination of ghosts, all taken into one, has a personality. In this case, the personality is that of Ghede. There are other loa who might have been more capricious and less kind. We have been fortunate in the loa's choice."

"What does that have to do with us?" asked Turkey.

Broken Echo bowed in his direction. "And one answer for you as well. Andrew's house has been the home of some of these compressed ghosts." He waved his hands in the air, "They are Haitian, you know," he said to no one in particular. "And they were homeless without some of their own to descend upon."

"They were so long hungry they chose us," Andrew said. "What now?"

"But then, you have touched the skin of the deer, and have no need for either questions or answers, though I'm sure you'll find the habit hard to break," said Broken Echo. "You know what you need to do next."

"Yes, I do. James will be here at any moment, however." He lowered his trembling hands to his waist, holding onto the belt as if for support. "I can't stay here any longer."

Broken Echo gestured. "I'll cut off the head of the utkena and see that it's properly separated and buried. Then I'll join you. Jess and Turkey can talk to James."

"Fine," Jess said quietly. Turkey looked bewildered.

"Will you keep people away from me for a while?" Andrew turned to Jess and Turkey. Turkey nodded dubiously; Jess merely looked from Broken Echo to Andrew. "And look after James?" Jess walked over to the boy and placed a hand on his forehead. "He'll be all right," she said.

Turning for a moment, Andrew looked out across the lake. The fog had lifted, and the sun sparkled on the water. Across the way, two small children paddled soft rafts around the edge of a dock. Further down the lake, a large black barge came puffing slowly in their direction. Somehow morning had arrived.

And so had James. He came walking across the driveway, his jacket collar pulled up around his ears. "Jess," he called, "I've been looking for you all over town. Greenback looks like it got hit by a hurricane. There was a family killed in a wreck on the bridge."

He knew. He had been sure all along that the body on the bridge had been real. Grief begets grief. He had been responsible for creating the same chain for someone else that he had been living through, and that was entirely too much for him to bear. Andrew's voice was numb and toneless. "You see," he said softly to Broken Echo, my resolve is stronger than ever. The poison of grief is too strong. I don't want to live."

James shook his head like a bewildered bulldog. "I was worried about you, Jess." He walked up to her and put his arms around her. She leaned against his shoulder.

"You've walked the ghostways a very long time. If you really want release, you'll find it now." The old man nodded to Andrew, who promptly whirled and ran toward the house like a bridegroom entering a chamber. "Remember," called Broken Echo, "you have the root!"

"Terrific," muttered Andrew, "cryptic to the end." He fumbled frantically in his pocket for the wizened old root, and was surprised to find it still there. "The Root of the World," he said. For the last time he ran into the cellar, bolting the door behind, and then stepping down through the cool and musty air of the stairwell and into the small, dark room.

CHAPTER 20

When he reached the bottom of the steps he found an empty storeroom with rusted chains around the sides of the room, a bolted door behind the stairs, and a few dusty mason jars on the shelves. At the foot of the stairs lay an old tin bucket and a broken broom handle resting on the floor beside it. His smile a rictus, he sat down cross-legged on the floor, raised the tin pail to his lap, and began a syncopated drumbeat.

the ebb and the flow, the rhythm and the blood, the wind blowing past his hair, the sound of the sirens, the body flying wildly down the road ahead of him, the leg beneath his head, the dancers as they bobbed and weaved around the circle. His hand felt weary and light; the pain in his shoulder dropped away. The circle and the pipe the rhythm of the night. He could feel the water lapping against his calves as he sank deeper into the mud. The reckless driving and the whine of the tires against the road. All of these sang throughout the rhythm, all these things were a weaving in the dark; all these things pulled him into the center of the hole that was his chest, into the eye that was the snake, into the eye that was the center of the tapestry. He watched the circling of the *fireflies in the dusk, the crystal at the forehead of the utkena, the coiling and the uncoiling of the tail of the snake, the song of the light, bright deer. All of these things sang a seductive song of seclusion, of isolation, of release, of release, of release from life. The thick, dripping tears came from his eyes like water from a long dry well. He would not go back. The stone of grief had settled, choking, in his throat.*

Wham! Someone kicked the pail from him. As it rattled against the wall Andrew looked up in surprise to see Joseph Praeter. "None of us can escape that easily. You would like, perhaps, to compare a few months to a couple of hundred years?"

"You would like perhaps," said Andrew, standing quickly, "to compare a scalping with the loss of a family. I have, you remember, experienced both. And now I've killed someone on the road, and I've left the scene. Just like whoever killed my family. I have a right to be sick of life. I have a right to go."

"You expected, in the midst of grief, to be continually conscious? The nature of grief is numbness and inattention. I'm not surprised that you hurt someone else." Praeter waved his hand as he added dryly, "You weren't exactly easy on women either. Unfortunately, you can't blame all of that on your grief, any more than you can lay the blame there for what you did to these."

In the corners of the room stood a black man and a black woman in chains. The man was dressed in cotton pants and a cotton shirt. Both of them wore calico kerchiefs. The woman, a slender, muscular mulatto, had on a wide-skirted dress and kerchief made from the calico material. Their faces were grim. The fair-haired Confederate soldier he had seen at the depot now perched on the steps. He had a rather sheepish grin on his face. "I put my Bible in my pocket," he said. "It did save me. What'd she put in the lining? metal? The bullets bounced off it like hail." The Yankee soldier appeared next to him, slapping the Confederate soldier on the back. Where had Andrew seen all of this before? Hadn't it happened earlier? And they'd decided to test him. How?

Joseph Praeter's appearance altered, an expression of pain in his deep-sunken eyes. His daughter Clarissa came into the room more slowly than the others; her hand appeared first, and only afterward the rest of her. Andrew looked at her with interest. She had long dark hair, and a very pronounced jaw. Her hand, where it rested on the railing of the stairs, was a horsewoman's hand, capable and sure. This is what Sylvia would have been in Clarissa's time, Andrew thought. This is who Clara might have been. Broken Echo walked casually down the steps, jumping over the soldier, and landing with a thump at Andrew's side. He looked up at Clarissa, and she walked down to join him. They were repeating a scene that all of them had lived before.

"Don't you understand yet?" asked Broken Echo. "If you choose death, we'll do this all again. You won't be escaping anything. And neither will we. I'll make you a deal. Let's play a game of cards, and if we win, you'll have to do as we choose. You'll experience what we choose."

I've heard this all before, thought Andrew, fate and repeating things.

"And with this game, if you win, you'll decide what happens. Is that fair." His voice rose in a question. They all nodded. Broken Echo released those in chains, and they all settled in an uneasy circle around Andrew.

"Why do you care?" asked Andrew, looking around the circle at each of the seven in turn.

Praeter's daughter flipped her hair back over her shoulders and replied in a deep, flat voice, "I prefer cards to talk."

"Does it matter why?" asked Praeter. He exchanged a long look with his daughter.

"Yes." Andrew paced up and down the confines of the cellar.

"Then . . . let's say we've grown fond of you over the months. And maybe . . . we feel responsible for second chances."

"Grief leads to numbness and inattention, is that what you said?" Andrew stopped to ask, his voice tinged with a certain bitterness. *The piano upstairs played a light Bach concerto, which one? It teased at his memory.*

Broken Echo merely smiled at him and nodded to the dealer, a tall black man with a scar on his chin. "Begin."

"Wait," said Andrew, holding the dealer's arm. "Don't you think the odds are a mite uneven?" The man nodded, and the scar on his face flashed into view. *Unceasing, tears poured from his eyes. His chest ached. He gasped for air.*

"And when," Broken Echo looked at him with absolute astonishment, "did you expect them to be anything else?"

Andrew watched the dealer as he began to shuffle the cards. He lifted them high in the air in the traditional card shark's pose, and then shuffled them rapidly. Then he leaned forward to let Andrew cut the cards, and grinned at each member in the circle. "Gentlemen, what game would you like?"

"How about five card stud?" asked the Confederate.

"You always say that," said the dealer. "We know y'all cheat at five card stud."

"Drop the fake dialect, and deal," the Yankee said. "If you do, I'll buy you a beer with my winnings." They grinned at each other.

"I'll drop my dialect if you'll stop those crummy toasts, buck." The dealer waved his cards in the air. The Yankee pulled off his coat and rolled up his sleeves, setting back on his heels as he watched the Confederate gripping his glass. "Hey Johnny," he said, "it sounds like a good idea." Johnny put his glass gently on the ground beside him, and then smiled a sudden wide smile. "Just for today?" The dealer nodded. "It's a deal." They shook hands with abrupt solemnity.

"What about poker?" asked Broken Echo.

"No;" Andrew jumped in quickly. Wait a minute, hadn't he done all of this before? But something was different.

The sliding of the car against the railing. The hard thud of the body. He couldn't forget that, couldn't live with it. He was guilty of too much. What he was thinking was familiar, all of it familiar, but it was out of place. Suicide was always a spin on the wheel of chance, but hadn't he been nearer the raw edge before? These ghosts aren't the only ones who are tired.

"He's got you there, red man," the black woman drawled. "What about pinochle?"

"Now there's a fine idea, Zora," said the dealer smiling broadly. "I always liked pinochle." He shuffled the cards and passed them around.

"You always say that," said the Confederate, as he fanned out his cards.

Andrew picked up his hand and looked at it. He became more and more convinced that he ought to remember this game, the rules, and the hands. He knew he would lose his king. And he did. In fact, he lost the first hand to Zora. When he lost, the dealer whooped and hollered.

They played cards and told stories. Andrew won the next hand.

"Do you know where my family is?" Stupid, stupid, he thought; you keep asking the same things. You asked the wrong *question*.

"Yes," Broken Echo said simply.

"Where?"

He lifted his hand. "One question."

"When it comes to death, I've only got one question. Can't I get them back?"

"No, but you're learning."

The second hand he won by one set of cards. Moving more slowly this time, he also thought more deliberately. Then he stared at Clarissa. She looked back at him, her eyes level and her face calm. I can ask her anything, he thought. She knows the answers. But he found himself unable to ask her anything except about herself. "When did you forgive your father?"

She smiled a grim smile. "Long after his death and mine."

Praeter cleared his throat. The circles around his eyes darkened, and he wiped a wisp of thin, oily hair back behind his ear. The light shone on the scars across the top of his head. He shuffled the cards without looking at anyone. Andrew nodded. At least he was getting some kind of answer. There was forgiveness even if it came late in the game.

The Yankee dealt the next hand. He grinned at Andrew; the circles around his brown eyes were large and puffy. "I'm going to beat you." But Zora took the board, again in a sweep of points.

In a bold move Andrew bid no points in the next round, and he managed to keep from taking a single trick. "Perhaps not." He looked at each face slowly, stopping at the dealer's. "Why are you always thirsty?"

"I was locked by him," jerking a thumb at Praeter, "in the cellar for days without water. Since then, I drink and I drink and I never get enough." The dealer laughed uneasily. "By the way, my name is Malekiah."

Praeter straightened his back and looked around the circle. His daughter took his hand in hers, withered and spotted hand resting against smooth and slender fingers.

"That's the way I feel about these answers of yours. They don't satisfy anything, and they make me thirsty for more,"

Andrew grumbled, as he shuffled and dealt. Each one left his fingers with a certain stickiness. His hands were sweating.

"You white men are always looking for answers for everything," said Malekiah. "You ought to leave all that psychology behind. You can't crack the big mysteries like an egg. Death and miracles, they ain't no Sunday mornin' egg."

Praeter's daughter laughed. She flipped through her cards, shuffling them around in a different order. She sang softly,

> "Life ain't no easy gate;
> Life ain't no easy gate.
> It's a river, a road, a fire, and a flood.
> Life ain't no easy gate."

"This is our seventh hand," said Zora, just as she reached across the circle and deftly took Andrew's top hat. This time she went null points, but Andrew didn't think she could make it because he held all the low cards. Did he want to win? Either way, nothing would be as it had been. What he really wanted was his family back. That's really why he'd stayed, hoping the house would somehow bring them back to him. Or short of that he wanted the ghosts to stay and things to go on as they had been. Didn't he? A strange restlessness danced through him like a rough wind. He listened to the wind rattle the windows of the cellar, tested the air as though it would tell him something. She beat him on the last trick, and went null points.

"You should have laid off your queen on my clubs," she said.

"Listen," said the Yankee, "if my name isn't Freemain Whittle, but I'm glad you won." He leaned back and patted his stomach.

She looked at the dealer. "So why are black men always dating white women?"

He raised his hands in mock protest. "Now listen, woman, it wasn't in the deal for us to ask questions. Anyway, you're asking me? I been dead too long to remember what it's like. And when I died, that wasn't what we were all doing."

They all laughed.

"Listen," Zora said abruptly, "I don't like this anyway. We're playing games with what we shouldn't be." Her ebony hair gleamed as she pulled the scarf from her head. "What right did you have, old man," she turned to Broken Echo;

"letting him into what's ours?" She jabbed her hand in the air. "And just where did you get that root?"

Andrew pulled it from his pocket. "I went to a church meeting in the cellar."

She sat back with a short, stiff, "hmmph."

Andrew handed the root to her.

Broken Echo sighed. "One minute laughing, the next howling at the moon."

Andrew shrugged. What reason did she have to trust him? He watched her as she tugged at the corn-rolled hair at the crown of her head. She watched him looking at her without any perceptible change in expression. Whew! Andrew thought, That woman is a powerhouse.

"We're just playing cards and telling you stories, but you're still dealing in fate."

"You're right," said Andrew. "There's no point in playing cards over all of this. And you're more than stories to me. You're family."

Zora stared at him with no change of expression. Then she gave him a sudden smile. "The seven levels you've been trying to figure out have to do with distortions. That's what history is."

"That's one part of it," said Malekiah. "There's more."

"What we decided to do, Andrew, if we won, was to test you."

"Test me? Isn't that what you've been doing?"

"And we'll keep on keeping on."

"We've been carrying all our ancestors. It's about time we carried some of yours."

"Did we do the right thing? Should we have stopped your younger self? He would have made changes quickly." Andrew looked at the old Indian.

"We'll never be certain," he said at last. "But did we do the wrong thing?" He shook his head. "I don't think so. Every war has it casualties, and those that grieve them. Even if you're responsible, you can't force yourself beyond what you can do. The slow subtle way, where nothing is what it seems, is often best. Even in a fast and shallow age. We have weighed as heavily on our descendants as we have weighed on yours." He looked sideways at Andrew. "Are you ready to play?"

Those moments of peace where grief lay for a brief instant forgotten. Wasn't that what these levels were all about? The moments when everything lay poised on the instant of change. Wasn't this game one of those?

"No," said Andrew suddenly and decisively. "This is a game we've already played. It doesn't have winners, and winning doesn't matter. I can live with what's happened if you can."

"So to speak," said Broken Echo. "Living isn't our issue. We're simply tired of being fixed in this house, pinned like butterflies to a history full of somebody's stories."

"All of this feels pretty damn lonely to me. I may have lived with all of you, but I don't know anything about you. What good is that?" He shrugged his shoulders. "One thing about the South you can be sure of is that we talk too damn much."

"You read about Joseph, didn't you? He wore a coat of many colors." The dealer flipped the cards into his pocket. "Anyway, you take all this so personally. The old days are gone, white man. Just 'cause we're leaving don't mean our babies are. You will be us. We had to know if you could do that before we were free."

The black woman ignored both of them. She turned to Broken Echo. "Then the outcome could be entirely a matter of opinion now, couldn't it?" Her voice was slow and calm.

"It could be." Broken Echo nodded his head and puffed on his pipe. For some reason Andrew remembered the long, quiet nights in the library with the rocking of the chair and the invisible, but calming, presence of the older man. "But on the other hand, isn't a crazy, patchwork sort of synthesis better than none at all? The South could use some peace. And there are those who'll need what the South has to offer, because at least we haven't forgotten or dumped it all off on someone else."

"And that's only because nobody would let us. Just how many in the South are interested in your fucking synthesis?" The black dealer spoke, his voice resonating in the small cellar like the beat of an angry drum.

"Yes, well, everyone responds according to their natures. Isn't that what you said to our friend on the steps?" He nodded to the dealer. "And there might be enough of us to create one."

"We were doing more than rescuing the town. Those were the stakes?" Andrew straightened his back.

Broken Echo grinned. "Yes. And no. Haven't you learned by now that the deathly serious and the gravely humorous have a great deal in common? You still take these things so seriously. Could we really save a town?" He paused and winked at Andrew. "It is important for you to stay. But if you stay, you'll be dealing with what may be dangerous for our newly born and tenuous peace. Will you speak for the loa?"

He grabbed the older man's hand. "Responsibility is always the hook you catch me on, isn't it old man?" He felt angry and full of a clear, surging sort of power.

"It has its own lure. As does life. Will you stay, then?"

"You owe me something, though."

"Not really."

"All right, but for the sake of what I will do."

"You want to know what the levels are?"

"Yes." Andrew's eyes were steady.

"You expected a straight answer? And you're the man who told the crowd on the steps that reality is a matter of decision. Well, you have all the information you need in order to decipher these things yourself. Part of you knows the answer to all these questions; I mean the deer walked 'through' you, did it not? You carried the root of the world in your pocket, destroyed significant tapestries, took on the mantle, or rather the hat, of Ghede. You'll need to buy a pair of sunglasses, by the way. We can leave you, but he never will." He puffed on his pipe, and then nodded. "You might be able to see something about it from this strange and ill assorted crew. They're rather representative." He waved his hands at the others. Praeter laughed gruffly, and then took his daughter's hand. "And you," he glanced at Andrew, "now you contain many memories."

Andrew looked around the cellar as though he were taking his farewell of it. Even though he would stay, it would never be the same here. He almost hated all of the ghosts in that moment. They'd been here too long. They were quarrelsome and not very easy to be with. They were rich and robust. He was ready to clean house. *the chink and rattle of chain, the sighing of the wind and the children* He handed the root over to Zora, who gave him a broad smile. He squeezed her hand. For the first time she returned his grip. "There are seven stages of grief," she said, gripping his hands.

"Dante's seven levels of hell," said Praeter and laughed until he began to cough.

"So we'll say goodbye to each other."

"Wait," said the dealer in mock surprise. "Did you think it would be so easy? You would just shake our hands, and we, like tiny assed puffs of smoke, would vanish."

"What then?"

"Two ways to get out of this damned cellar. We play cards and start the whole damn thing all over again, or we crawl through the tunnel."

Andrew stared at the door. "I've got claustrophobia."

"And we love tunnels," the Yankee said.

"I get the point. But at least we'll be in there together."

"No, not really." Broken Echo stood, and so did all the others. "These tunnels have a funny way of separating those who are in them. Some people never come out the other side. In case you do, we have some presents for you. You can leave them here. If you return, the cellar will be here, though it'll be quite ordinary."

The Confederate handed him a small version of a weaving with an eye, and then he slowly unbolted the door to the tunnel. While he was crawling inside, the Yankee, dark eyes intent on the opening his fellow soldier was disappearing into, handed Andrew a roughed out carving of a small white deer. The dealer came next.

"You should have set us free at the Battle of New Orleans, Jackson." He tossed a small, curiously shaped white jug at him. Andrew caught it just before it hit the floor. Zora gave him a small, curled snake ring and a quick, sparkling glance. He watched her get down on her hands and knees to enter the tunnel. Praeter, when it came his turn, bit Andrew on the ear, and then left him a small pen-and-ink painting of a river in the mist. In the center of the mist, poised something that might have been the figure of a small boy. Andrew squinted at it. Suddenly unsteady, he sank to the floor just as Clarissa left by the tunnel.

Broken Echo lifted him gently to his feet. Andrew leaned on the old Indian. "You and I," he murmured, "are even."

"Not quite," said Broken Echo, and Andrew braced himself for he scarcely knew what. The startling feel of the old man's lips on the center of his forehead still took him by surprise.

"I'll miss you, old man. This house will be lonely." Andrew's voice grew husky. "In fact, life will be very dull."

"You've gotten used to a diet of sensation, but the simple things will return. And I won't exactly be gone. At least not completely." Broken Echo scratched his head, tilting his hat back. Then he handed it to Andrew.

Andrew smiled. "Are you a candidate for the loa?"

"You've got your memories back, and a new store as well. And—" he hesitated, "wait just a moment."

While Andrew leaned against the doorjamb, Broken Echo walked through him two or three times. "You'll see me around from time to time. I've been"—he laughed,— "compressed. I've become a grandfather after all these years." He sobered. "You're carrying many within you. What will you do now?"

Andrew paused. A flush shifted up and down his face; his chest boomed with the vigor of his heartbeat. He gripped the rim of the door, the stone rough against his fingers. "I don't know exactly."

"Boyles will offer you your old job back, you know."

"Boyles? Why?" Andrew darted a sharp glance at the old Indian.

"I pulled a string or two." Broken Echo handed Andrew a small green lizard, but the lizard promptly disappeared.

"I won't take it. That chapter is over."

"It's more important that he offer it to you than that you take it." He handed him a small bluebird, which perched in Andrew's hands and looked around inquiringly. "The birds always liked you better."

"I'll never work there again, so what difference does it make?"

"It's a part of the smaller changes."

"Affirmative action?" Andrew laughed uneasily.

"You really don't have any idea how much you've changed yet." Broken Echo put his hand on Andrew's shoulder. "How in the world will you live? You and the multitudes inside you."

"I don't know what I'll do. I mean I've just decided—with a little persuasion—to do anything at all. I've got time to consider what I'll do later after you're gone. First, I'll take care of my accident on the bridge." He added fiercely, "I'll

make sure that what's left of that family is taken care of."
Broken Echo nodded sadly. "If there are any survivors."

Andrew hugged the old man, whose skin had already grown transparent and insubstantial, and watched as he backed his way into the tunnel.

"Where does the tunnel go?"

"We didn't say, now did we? Where the head goes, the heart has to follow. This tunnel has two endings, one for you and one for us." The old man cackled. "Don't you believe" —he cackled again,—"in adventure? And this one will make you very angry."

"Will I see you on the other side?"

Broken Echo didn't reply. He backed slowly down the tunnel until even his head was gone. The open black hole yawned in front of Andrew. The open door hung low on its hinges.

Andrew laughed, his ribs sore and aching, until the old man managed to get turned around and down the tunnel. Just like Broken Echo. How he would miss him. Then Andrew took a deep breath and got down on his knees to follow. The mouth of the tunnel contained smooth stones with sharp corners. He could only make it by crawling like the others.

Like a key in a lock, the old man's phrase worked its way through his chest. This tunnel would make him angry. He thought about that the whole time that he crawled there in the dark. The rock against his hands was alternately smooth and broken. The raw edges rasped against his fingers. He rubbed his hand across his face to wipe away the sweat, and left behind a smear of blood. The blood didn't smell like new blood, but like blood from a wound that had festered. He crawled on a bit further. He couldn't really see enough to tell how far it went on or where he was. In just a few feet the sharp edges of the stones had severely bruised his knees. He kept stopping to rest, but stopping hurt worse than moving. Until he moved.

Each time he halted the tunnel seemed smaller and smaller. He kept pressing the sides with his hands, trying to reassure himself that the walls were still the same width as before. He could feel them with his fingers. Large, block letters. Moses and the stone tablets, he thought, and laughed until he coughed.

By the time he had crawled what seemed to be several miles, he had grown good and angry. What had they meant by making him leave by this tunnel or by that damned ridiculous card game? They wouldn't let him die, and they were determined for him not to live either. Perhaps it was just another of Broken Echo's gestures.

Finally he came to a section in the tunnel where he tried to turn back, and found himself stuck like a ship in a bottle. He began to scream. He kept moving as he screamed, because he couldn't bear to be still. Finally, he wrenched himself free and started through the tunnel, back the other way. He couldn't seem to stop screaming. His voice echoed ahead of him. The tunnel went on endlessly. It must, Andrew thought, go underneath the whole yard. By this time his voice had grown so hoarse he could scarcely use it any longer.

At one point he reached a bend and sloshed through water dripping from the ceiling. Raising his head, he tried to drink some of the water; he managed to get some in his mouth. None of it quenched his thirst.

He sat by his wife's bedside, holding her limp hand. "Rachel, would you like a drink of water?" He bent his head and raised her hand to his forehead. "Damn it," he looked around the room at the group of doctors; "do something. Bleed her again."

"We've bled her twice, President Jackson. Once more is more likely to hurt than to help her. I think she's gone, sir."

"She's not gone, young man." He glared around at them, and then lowered his bushy eyebrows. "She's just resting." He raised her hand to his forehead again. "Now turn out the lights." He waved them all out, and sat there in the gathering darkness.

Finally Andrew stopped, and simply sat like a lump in the darkness. The section of the tunnel he had just left had been gradually narrowing, but this one piece of the tunnel, barely a body length long, was wider. Beyond it the tunnel narrowed again. He sat cross-legged in the rounded space, wondering how long he would be able to breathe. Why had they left him here alone in the dark? He stared around him in the blackness. Nothing appealed to him about dying in a goddamned tunnel. He much preferred something quick and inescapable. He pressed his palm to his chest. They hadn't taken the root after all, because here it was. He pressed his palm to his chest.

It seemed as if there were nothing left to do. He stared into the darkness, and then, abruptly, he began to cry in huge, gulping sobs. "Kate, I thought you would come back if I buried you here." The hole in his chest throbbed in and out. It was still there. He pressed the root against it. "I—why didn't they heal me? I can't do this myself." He hugged the root to his chest. He rocked back and forth, his shoulders rubbing painfully against the roof of the tunnel. "I don't want someone else's death on my head. How can I go back to face that? Far easier to stay here."

And far easier to feel sorry for himself than to tap into the blackness of the feelings that he feared. Billy and Andy were lost to him. Kate was lost to him. And all because he was afraid to remember them. They were so young yet. It hadn't been fair that the boys had gone before they'd played their first baseball game, had their first crush on a girl, or driven their first car. There were so many things he hadn't even gotten the chance to show them, or to have them show him. They were so vigorous. He had lost all his moorings. With his parents went a part of his past that he would never regain. With Kate went a partnership he'd never be able to replace; and with his children went his—no, their—future. If he could just have touched them once more, just taken them into his lap and held them where they would be safe.

But there wasn't any sort of safety. He knew that by now. He couldn't shelter them anymore than he could shelter himself. And the only way to avoid fearing the loss of security was to choose not to live your life in fear. He couldn't stay in this tunnel where the world closed in on itself and on him. He would be strong enough to remember them clearly. How far ahead of him were the others? Would they all make it? If they could, he could as well. But they were ghosts, he reminded himself; they didn't have to worry about death.

He pressed his hands, palm out, against the sides of the tunnel. You think you can just choose to feel and it happens like water shooting out of a tube, Jackson. You've decided after all this time to feel, you fucker, and it comes to you just like that. He picked up a rough square of stone and began to pound his left foot with it. He methodically broke every bone in his toes and then turned the stone to pounding on the tunnel wall behind him. It wasn't until he heard the creaking of the walls that he came back to himself, and that was almost too late. He crawled through the bottleneck and on toward the next bend of the tunnel faster than he thought possible, the dust and the rubble from the collapsed wall coming with him. He had rounded two more bends at an agonizingly slow speed before he left the noise and the unsteadiness behind. After that he alternated long periods of crawling through the seemingly endless tunnel with shorter periods of sitting in a kind of mute despair.

Sometime later, long after he had run out of tears and had stopped again, he heard a voice faintly calling, "Andrew? Andrew?" That voice could be Margaret's or Jess's. He continued to sit there. They must have found the other end of the tunnel. If I'm quiet, he thought, they'll go away. If they had found it, he could too, but he wasn't at all certain that was what he wanted. It seemed like a lot of trouble. This is something you're choosing, he thought, how long will you make it go on?

After a while he sighed, and said, "Stop feeling so damned sorry for yourself, Jackson," and began to crawl slowly toward what he hoped was the end of the tunnel. As he kept crawling, he began to feel slightly more cheerful, and then more and more full of a crazy sort of energy. He had made it through the worst of it. Whatever else anyone would have to throw at him, he would throw it right back. Double. His hands were shaking. His knees felt like he had fallen knees first down the side of a mountain; but he was tough, he would make it.

When he finally reached an area where he could see daylight, he realized that the tunnel he had been crawling in, the walls, roof, and floor, were entirely lined with the broken and cracked remains of Praeter's tombstones. And with that, the ironic visitor in the center of his chest laughed hollowly. "Behold and see as ye pass by," he yelled.

"What?" came Jess's voice.

"I said, Behold and see daylight," yelled Andrew, suddenly, crazily full of energy again. What was it that Praeter had said? Anyone in grief created more casualties. No, he'd see to it that the cycle stopped with this new accident. He couldn't be everywhere, but he could see about one family. He lifted the underbrush aside at the mouth of the tunnel and limped through the carved mouth of a boulder and from behind a bush that fronted it. Crawling into the light, he felt that he was the only gray thing in it, the only gray thing on the jutting shore of the peninsula just below his house. He grabbed at the leaves of the bushes, somehow amazed that they were alive and green. Around and across his right foot crawled a series of brown ants. He looked at them and laughed.

"Andrew." He heard Jess's voice, then the quick rush of her feet. She grabbed him from behind, hugging him with what seemed to be an extraordinary amount of force. "We thought you were dead. What happened to your foot?"

He strained to see her face, then patted her hand, and slipped out from under her embrace. "How long was I gone?"

"A week, Andrew," Jess spoke. "They dragged the lake for your body, and searched the woods."

He turned around to face her. "A week?" He ran his hands through his hair, looking around him uncertainly. Jess's eyes were red-rimmed and weary.

"What were you doing?" Turkey's cracked voice called from behind Jess. Andrew looked up to see a picnic table settled on his front lawn. Seated at it were Turkey, Larry, Boyles, James, and Clara. He gave each of them a long look. Larry gave him a slow, boyish grin. Turkey winked at Andrew and slapped Larry on the back.

Clara tucked her hair behind one ear, and turned from a conversation with James. "I think I understand about your memory; at least I'm willing to listen." She moved some of the picnic items to the center of the table where they were surrounded by stacks of paper.

James looked at her in absolute astonishment. "I'm not, but I'm glad you're back. Welcome home, boy."

All their statements were characteristic. He wanted to hold them all in the palms of his hands. How had they become so dear? A third family, he thought; I'm starting over again with a third family. "I—" He ran his hands through his hair and turned back toward the lake.

Jess whispered behind him. "Give him a few minutes."

Andrew heard them move away. He looked out across the lake, and back down toward the shore, watching the breeze ruffle the water. "Yes, and then I've got a phone call to make," he said firmly to Jess, who had stayed. "I've got to find out about that car accident."

"If this cup," she said softly.

"You could take," said Andrew. "Yes, well, that's not the way it works." She slipped her hand into his.

At the peninsula, in the water just beyond the mouth of the tunnel, impatiently holding onto a small post, stood Broken Echo at the front of a boat full of all his friends, the card players. "Glad to see you made it," they yelled as they waved. Broken Echo cupped his hands and called, "You better check on that utkena, man, because if I buried him wrong, he'll make the lake flood. They get angry when you bury them wrong." The boat drifted idly in the current by the shore.

Andrew looked at all of them sadly. At the back of the boat sat three, small still figures: a woman and two children, one of them with a faded baseball cap. Leaving Jess behind, Andrew ran down the shore toward the boat. None of the three looked at him. "Kate?" he said uncertainly.

"Many deaths fed this dream you have had," Broken Echo said. "Would you have rather faced your loss alone?"

"No," said Andrew, taking a step nearer the boat. He waded into the lake and around the side of the boat. The muddy water moved sluggishly in resistance. Praeter turned his head to watch Andrew wade by.

"You can go with us," he said hoarsely, "but they will never know you." Andrew came to the back of the boat and reached out his hand. His fingers passed through Kate's arm. Still she didn't look up.

"What happened," Andrew asked angrily, "to resolution?"

"And whose ending is this anyway?" Broken Echo waved his paddle in the air. "Just whose story do you think this is?"

He heard Jess's voice. "You helped release these ghosts; now let them go." She stood beside him, her hand on his arm, drawing him back toward shore. "As for your family, you've held them here long enough."

Andrew's fingers lingered. He stroked the edges of the boat. *fingers tracing the grooves of wood on Andy's casket* The boat rested buoyant on the water as though eager to be away. He could feel the ghosts' eagerness. All of them had set each other free, had set him free. After all their long years in this house, he understood their eagerness to go.

Yet they were going together, and he would be left alone. Only their love for him now held them at the shore, a love he neither deserved nor understood. After all that had happened to him, where had they summoned up the strength to love him and others like him? He looked at them. Broken Echo with that damnable twinkle in his eye. Praeter whose face had already grown increasingly less hollow and worn, as though the air gave him strength. Clarissa, who he respected, but hardly knew. The soldiers winked at him simultaneously. The Confederate patted his chest pocket. Andrew clasped hands with Malekiah. And Zora, who had been many, who waited calmly, but with a gleam in her eye that he could no longer deny. How could he hold such joy in his hands? No, he'd ruin what was between them that way. He lifted his hands reluctantly.

And what of his family? He stared at the motionless figures as Praeter took the paddle and began to push the boat away from the shore. If only they could have said goodbye. He wanted so much to hear them speak just those words, touch him for a moment. But they had, he realized, they had touched him in a way that he would never forget. Their lives rested in his memory, and he had a great deal to remember. He looked at all those in the boat. At least they won't be alone, he thought, and no amount of goodbyes would ever be enough. Look how long he'd been trying to say goodbye to them all. If people had control of when their loved ones died, they'd all grow to hate each other in the end. The seven nodded at him.

"You're leaving me along again."

"Not alone," said Praeter.

"Never alone," said Broken Echo. "Look back up toward the house."

As he walked back toward Jess, his smile was a moment of relief, and a light joy rose within him like a bubble. He took her hand and glanced up to Turkey, Clara, Larry, and James. He heard the sound of Broken Echo's voice and faced quickly toward the boat.

"You crazy, mad, impossibly stubborn, white man," said Broken Echo, paddling the boat further from shore. "You have turned down the easiest resolution possible. Will you be sorry?" Kate and the children raised their heads just as Andrew nodded to the old Indian. They gave him one blazing look, a look so full of love and of longing that he broke into a sob in that moment before they lowered their heads.

Involuntarily he stepped forward, but stopped without the touch of Jess's hand. That look he had paid dearly for, but he would repeat everything if only he could repeat this one moment of goodbye. Praeter and the dealer moved the paddles forward. Their clothes rippled in the wind. And the two of them rowed slowly, the boat deep in the water as though heavily laden, away.